Pearl

Maker

C.C. Wharton

a novel by

C. C. Wharton

Pearl Maker
by C.C. Wharton

ISBN   0-9778745-4-0

Design & photos by EK Larken

Published by

a division of

PO Box 6034
Louisville, Kentucky 40206-0034

WWW.MOTESBOOKS.COM

This book is for...

my mother,
Evelyn King Connors,
who believed in me

&

my husband, Carl,
who has made it possible.

— CCW 2006

"For truth is precious and divine,
too rich a pearl for carnal swine."

— Samuel Butler

PART ONE

Chapter One

Janet Leigh Ferguson closed her tired eyes, though she knew she wouldn't fall asleep.

The back seat of the new, custom, cream-colored van was too short, even for her small frame, to stretch her full length. There was no pillow on which to lay her head, and her arms were of no use to her tied behind her back. She dreaded the circulation returning when her arm would tingle; she would be unable to rub it.

On the floor on either side of her lay two high school students from the senior English class she taught. Caleb Johnson sat parallel to Jan with his torso behind her head. From the side, he looked older than his seventeen years. His classmate, Murray Simpson, was positioned at her feet, leaning against a small refrigerator under a sink. He showed no signs of sleep either.

Neon light washed through the upper front windshield, the only view the captives could glimpse of the outside. Curtains covered the side and back windows. The van pulled into a gas station and food mart. The driver, a nicely dressed, hatted man, glanced under his lowered bill at the bound figures in the back of the van. Jan and Murray shut their eyes and feigned sleep.

Where were they? One minute Jan was tutoring two students in her classroom, and the next minute the three of them were bound in the back of a strange van traveling toward ... what? Jan felt anger rising from her feet.

Kidnapped. The word crept into her consciousness. But why her? Why Murray and Caleb?

When the driver had started the engine and left their school, miles ago, he'd picked up a cell phone and punched in numbers. "Van driver here." The words echoed in Jan's brain as she tried to remember the exact chain of events that led her into this nightmare. "We have all three. You can make your connections in Georgia now. We'll arrange the connections here." He ended the call.

In the glow from the van's headlights, Jan had been able to see the top of the larger man's head as he peeled back the chain link fence. They had turned to the left onto the dirt road that ran behind the academy to several remote cornfields just beyond the school's grounds. At the end of the dirt road, the van had turned left again.

"Damn, I can't believe this. What the hell just happened?" Caleb muttered. Caleb Johnson was an outstanding athlete, he was amiable, and he was usually just this side of trouble.

Murray and Caleb rearranged themselves so they could look at each other.

"Can we ask what this is all about?" Caleb yelled to the front. Jan worried that his attitude could get him hurt.

"Just keep your mouths shut and you won't be hurt," the driver said calmly. "No harm will come to you if you cooperate." He said nothing more.

The van could have been any recreational vehicle traveling that night. Inside, however, behind the front seats sat a cabinet and panel with all sorts of dials and headphones. That explained the antennae, Jan thought. The van was probably equipped with some sort of listening device, like the vans on those TV detective shows.

In Jan's half-prone position, she could see nothing out of the windows unless the van passed a neon sign. They had kept to the swampy back roads when they first left the school. After a great many turns, the van slowed to a stop. There was no sign of human activity in the vicinity until a man they hadn't seen before opened the door and climbed into the front passenger seat. He too was dressed nicely and wore a hat pulled low over his eyes.

"Everything go okay?" the man asked.

"Fine," the driver replied.

That was all the conversation they would hear. The van driver turned the van around, and Jan was sure that they had backtracked, though she didn't know how far. Within ten minutes they came to what appeared to be a major highway. It had to be Interstate 95, she thought. From the direction the van took, Jan was pretty sure they had headed north.

After a while, the driver pulled into the bright lights of a gas station convenience store. Jan watched the man on the passenger side pump the gas while the driver went into the food mart. She had never been so thirsty. The back of her throat scratched from trying to swallow.

Jan wondered what time it was and whether David was still waiting for her at the Back Door. Wednesday evenings had become teachers' night at the only local bar. Many of the young farmers of the area also came on Wednesdays. Her best buddy, history teacher Lucy Meadows, had promised to come tonight.

How could these men in this van have known that Jan would be tutoring two boys and that no one else would be around the school that evening? She had only made plans that morning. Her home phone must have been tapped. Come to think of it, she had seen this van at the dumpster on the turn to school this week. Still, Jan had told no one about tonight's tutoring session. She hadn't even told David except in the note she had left.

The van driver returned with two hot coffees and two Danish wrapped in plastic. The smell of the microwave-heated sweet rolls and the acidic aroma of the coffee made the captives even hungrier. Caleb stirred and looked around, trying to get his bearings.

The driver glanced in the rearview mirror as he cranked the van. He didn't look back again. Soon the highway offered up its soothing rhythm again. Jan stretched her neck to see Caleb's face. He looked bewildered and dropped his head against the corner of the seat after looking first at Murray and then at Jan. Murray remained solemn. Jan repositioned herself to allow blood to flow in her right arm. She flattened her shoulders and lay on her back, propping her fastened feet on the curtained window above and behind Murray. She concentrated on why this might have happened to her, to them.

Then Jan remembered that she had called her friend Robin to tell her she wouldn't be coming by that afternoon. It was Robin's night for bridge tomorrow and Jan had promised to help her get ready tonight. Jan had called Robin to say she had to grade papers before she went back to school to tutor in the early evening. Maybe that's how these men knew where she was. This obviously wasn't a spur-of-the-moment kidnapping. She doubted now that she would be at Robin's for bridge tomorrow.

What would David think when she didn't show up at the bar? She had left him a note about 6:30 saying she would meet him no later than 8:30.

Jan and David didn't make that much money between them. Private school pay was below that of public school teachers, and David's salary from Production Credit Association was similar to an entry-level banker; there were a few loan opportunities but no high salaries. In their first three years of marriage they were proud to have saved a thousand dollars. So why would anyone want to kidnap her? She certainly wasn't anybody important.

Then she remembered the van driver on the phone, "You can make your connections in Georgia now."

Of course. Jan's parents and grandparents lived in Kingsford, Ga. Her parents were comfortably well-to-do by any standards, and her grandparents on her mother's side were wealthy; but who would know this?

Jan lived a different lifestyle in Riverdale than the one in which she was raised in Kingsford. Jan's grandfather, Ralph Oleander Calhoun, had been the town's major realtor and developer for the past forty years. The Calhoun family at one time owned most of the now more prestigious neighborhoods in Kingsford. Ralph Calhoun – Papa Ralph, as Jan knew him – started out developing his family's land and had since moved on to most major developments within a fifty-mile radius of Kingsford.

Jan's father, Lamar Jameson, was Kingsford's leading contractor, deriving most of his business from his father-in-law. Lamar was a good man and a hard worker, but he did not share his wife's social preoccupations. May Calhoun Jameson had groomed her oldest daughter, Julia Ann, to the social nuances of the South, while Jan had usually been left with the maid as substitute mother during her adolescent years. Still, as second daughter, Jan had been dragged into the social wake of debutante balls and private prep school.

Jan's reverie was interrupted when the van slowed noticeably. "Looks like a truck jack-knifed," the van driver said to his passenger.

If these men knew of her family, then they had reason to kidnap her. Jan was certain now that they were not working independently, but were part of an organized operation. But why Murray and Caleb? Jan turned her gaze to the two boys.

Caleb's father was one of the wealthiest farmers in the state, in spite of the fact that he had only an eighth grade education. Bud Johnson had turned his father's five hundred-acre tobacco farm into the largest and most versatile agricultural operation in South Carolina.

Caleb's parents denied him and his younger brother nothing. Caleb's first vehicle was a brand new 2004 fire-engine-red Ford Ranger pickup. The morning after he totaled it, there was a new black '05 Ranger parked in the driveway.

Murray, on the other hand, came from a family of educators. His father had taught high school and, later, college math until two years ago when he had turned to marketing school supplies. His mother taught English in the public high school. There was no wealth in that family.

Jan sank back into the seat. Perhaps all these men wanted was ransom money. This was no impulsive kidnapping by a deranged individual. These men were too well-dressed, too businesslike.

It must be ten-thirty or eleven by now, she thought. The driver tuned the radio to an easy listening station. Jan felt helpless, yet she perceived no immediate danger. Her fear was of the unknown.

For the first time in her twenty-six years, Jan did not know what tomorrow would bring.

Chapter Two

Hours had passed. The steady lull of the highway nearly put Jan into a trance. She snapped alert when the van left the interstate and headed toward a large bank of lights. First, the glaring neons of businesses glowed only intermittently behind the curtained windows, but soon the van slowed for red lights and stop signs.

The town was little more than a crossroads, and the lights were quickly left behind. Jan felt the van climb and turn. She could see the outline of treed slopes barely visible through the front windshield. Ten minutes, maybe twenty, and the van slowed and pulled onto what sounded like a gravel road. A sky of bright stars told her that they were nowhere near a city, and the full moon, now low on the horizon, lit up the outside as clearly as an early morning sun. The van headed through a thickly wooded area of mountainous terrain. This was very different from the flat sandy land they had left behind.

Her right arm was numb again. It was that time of morning when the air is coolest before dawn. Her back muscles ached and her legs threatened to cramp any minute. Jan jumped when her captors spoke just as the van slowed to turn onto yet another narrow road.

"You sure Punk's okay?" the driver asked the other man. "I don't trust him."

The passenger replied, "He's okay. We've used him several times since that last incident with no problem. He's fine as long as he isn't drinking, and believe me, I checked that cabin thoroughly and took out the little bit of whiskey I found. There's enough food for them for a few days. We should be back late tonight before he has time to get into trouble."

"I see he's already here," the driver said a few minutes later as he pulled to a stop.

"Yeah, well, you had to backtrack to pick me up," the other man said.

Jan could see the top of Caleb's truck cab beside the van. Her car was nowhere in sight.

Caleb and Murray sat up as much as they could, straining to peer out the front windows.

"Okay, let's get them out and move them into the cabin," the driver said.

The men untied their passengers' feet. The driver carefully, even gently, held Jan's elbow as she uncurled her cramped legs. The air felt much nippier than in Riverdale. Dawn's rays were just showing; she watched the brilliant reds and oranges, far different than the pastel sunrises of the low country. They were on top of a hilly plateau with a mountain rising beyond a cabin next to the van.

The men led them into what looked from the outside to be a small hunting lodge. Inside was a great room and kitchen separated by a partial counter lined with stools. A small bathroom was visible behind the kitchen. Two vinyl sofas, a couple of matching chairs framed in heavy wood and a split-log coffee table furnished the room.

The man they called Punk, the rougher man who had driven off in Caleb's truck when they were taken from the school, was inside setting things up.

"Let's fix these kids some breakfast," the van driver ordered.

"We've got a lot of work to do to make sure that everything is pulled off," the other man said. "I'll make sure the back room is comfortable. We can lock them in there so you won't have to worry about them, Punk," he continued as he opened the door opposite the kitchen.

Punk snarled.

"We've got plenty of food for you," the driver continued, ignoring the big man's attitude.

Punk went to the refrigerator while the other two men led Jan, Caleb and Murray to the back room, a bedroom furnished with bunk beds against one wall and a cot against the other. A door next to the cot opened into a bathroom.

"We're going to untie your hands. No funny stuff. You're surrounded by uninhabited mountains. You won't be hurt if you don't make any trouble. When we get what we're after, we'll let you go, unharmed. That man in there will feed you. Here's a deck of cards. Just consider yourselves on loan to us for some money." The driver locked the door behind him.

"What in the hell do those guys want with us? And why me? My parents don't have any dough like Caleb's do. What about you Mrs. Ferguson?" Murray asked.

"I think we should concentrate on getting out of here safely first. We can find out later why we're here," she evaded the question.

The van driver brought in a tray with three plates of over-cooked eggs, buttered toast and three mugs of coffee. He set the food on the card table that he pulled away from the wall. "All we ask is that you be quiet," he said before going out. "Sometimes he," and the man tilted his head toward the other room indicating Punk, "gets irritated with noise," he warned. The man looked at Jan when he said this. His brown eyes were warmer than his voice.

"We're not going to be here today," the van driver continued. "We would like for you to get back to your homes safely, so just lay low and everything will be all right," he repeated as he pulled the door shut and locked it from the other side.

Jan and the boys could hear muffled versions of a conversation taking place on the other side of the door. "I don't think we have enough wood in here, Punk. You were supposed to have all this ready when we arrived," someone snapped.

Punk muttered an unintelligible reply as he stalked out the door. The two men lowered their voices so the captives had to strain to hear the rest of the conversation.

"I had no idea this girl would be so young and attractive. She's a teacher, for Christ's sake. I sure never had any teachers that looked like that."

"Aw, come on. She'll be safe. Punk's only problem is when he's drinking. If all goes as planned, we'll be back by late tonight. I'd worry if we were going to be gone two or three days, but we'll be back."

"Punk's the only one they'll recognize, and he'll be long gone after this job. I don't know about you, but I don't want him around anymore. I thought I'd say something to the boss about it today."

The talking stopped and Caleb and Murray turned back to their breakfast while Jan slowly sipped her coffee. The warmth of the strong brew soothed her, though she lost her appetite after one bite each of eggs and toast. The boys gladly split what she left.

Jan looked slowly around the room. Pretty bare, except the bunk beds and cot, one dresser, the card table and four folding chairs. No curtains. Fabricated paneling made up the walls and a thick, very dirty, wall-to-wall carpet stopped at the bathroom door. Only a bare light bulb swung overhead.

"So, Mrs. Ferguson, does your family have money?" Murray asked a second time.

"Yeah, Mr. Wade says you grew up with a silver spoon in your mouth," Caleb added.

"I've never considered my family to be wealthy. They're just my family. In terms of worldly possessions, perhaps they are affluent," Jan answered as honestly as she could. "What about your families?" Jan turned first to Murray.

"Caleb's folks have tons of money," Murray laughed.

"Oh, we do all right, I guess," Caleb said, embarrassed.

Jan continued to look at Murray. "No, my family doesn't have any money to speak of," Murray said.

"Well, sounds like we won't be here long. Seems they don't mean to hurt us," Caleb said, chewing his last bite.

"Yeah, I don't think we have much to worry about. This'll be over 'fore we know it," Murray added, his voice sounding less confident than the words it spoke.

A stick cracked outside the barred back window. The three looked up to see the unshaven, pock-marked face of the man they knew as Punk. That ugly face was pointed toward Jan. His mouth was open and he drooled slightly. His arms were loaded with wood. When he saw that the three had noticed him, he laughed and walked around the cabin. They heard the door slam.

Jan felt the small knot in her stomach grow, filling her veins with dread, like an incurable cancer suddenly let loose. She knew she was not prepared for what she faced now.

"A penny for your thoughts," Murray said.

Jan looked at him blankly. "I was just thinking about David," she answered. "I'm sure he's worried by now. I'm sure your parents are worried, too. If we do as they said, we'll be home by tomorrow," she added with forced cheer. "I just wish the other two men were going to stay. That Punk fellow makes me nervous," she laughed half-heartedly.

Murray's face turned red as he recognized the threat that she alone faced. "No one will lay a hand on you while we're here, Mrs.

Ferguson, will they Caleb?"

"No way," Caleb echoed emphatically, too young not to believe his words. "Don't you worry, Mrs. Ferguson."

"Maybe we should get some rest," Jan suggested.

"Yeah, that's not a bad idea," Murray agreed. "Let's get our sleep now while the other two are still here and we know we have nothing to worry about."

Before lying down, the boys double-checked all escape possibilities. The two windows were barred from the outside. The small window in the bathroom was made of narrow horizontal glass panels and a crank handle that opened them up and out in vented slits.

Jan was determined to find a way out, but she didn't have the energy to think about it now. She didn't want to think about anything, so she lay face down on the cot and fell instantly asleep.

She slept hard at first. The background whisperings and movements of the two men in the other room gave her subconscious ease; later, however, came the threatening dream.

Jan dreams that she is in downtown Riverdale, shopping at a five-and-dime, much like the one from her childhood in Kingsford. An overly eager white-haired saleswoman is trying to help her find something unnamed that Jan needs right away.

A disagreeable man, so dirty she can't even tell his race, comes shuffling in wearing too-big shoes with the toes cut out and someone else's ill-fitting clothes hanging from angular pieces of bone that should have been shoulders, elbows and knees. He has no hips and his baggy pants hang from a rope tied at the waist. While Jan is talking with the saleswoman, this obnoxious old man shoves his way between them, as if they weren't there or didn't matter. He brushes against Jan roughly, as if to push her aside. He demands toothpicks. He reeks of body odor, a stench surpassed only by the smell of his foul breath, which in her dream Jan sees as evidence of the evil inside him.

Jan is angered that this rude and filthy man has interrupted her. Who is this scumbag stealing the saleswoman's attention? She can pay; she has money!

'Just look at you,' she says to him in the dream, frightened but angry. 'You have nothing, you are nothing. You've been and done nothing your whole life!' She hears herself screaming at him and realizes that this is uncharacteristic of her. But she cannot seem to stop. He only sneers smugly back at her, raising one eyebrow cockily.

The menacing old man follows Jan now, lecherously reaching toward her whenever she pauses. Each time he reaches, she recoils. When Jan is about to yell, he shuffles away, only to return just as she is about to name to the saleswoman what it is that she wants. This happens again and again. Finally, the saleswoman loses interest in Jan, and because she wants that nasty man out of her store, she tries frantically to find his toothpicks instead of helping Jan.

Jan's need is urgent, but the words won't come out. She has no voice.

When she finally finds it, she is sitting straight up on a cot, soundlessly screaming obscenities at an old man and a saleswoman who were most definitely not in a bedroom in a cabin in the middle of an unfamiliar nightmare.

"You all right, Mrs. Ferguson?" Caleb whispered urgently. He and Murray were awake and looking at her.

"I'm fine," she gasped. "Nightmare."

It was mid-afternoon. They had slept a few hours. Jan was glad the time had passed so quickly.

A loud clunk came from the next room.

"I sure hope that's that Punk guy fixing our lunch," Caleb said. "I'm starved."

"Me, too," Murray agreed.

"I guess I could eat something," Jan added.

She had barely uttered the words when they heard the key turn in the lock outside their room. Punk shuffled through the door with a tray of sandwiches and three Cokes. Jan noticed his clothes didn't fit right; they were too small. Punk put the tray of food down on the table and looked at Jan with a disgusting leer. She smelled whiskey.

"Here's y'all's lunch," he said directly to the boys. "I hope I see you later, young lady," he grunted at Jan with tobacco-stained teeth, gapped and filled with dull silver. Her stomach lurched violently. Punk threw his head back in a menacing laugh when he saw her revulsion. She shuddered.

Punk's face was pocked and scarred, which reminded Jan of the old man in her dream. Her captor's belly hung over his belt so far that the buckle was invisible. The middle two buttons of his shirt bulged open, exposing his black, wiry chest and stomach hairs. Jan froze while he was in the room. He slammed the door behind him, locked it and laughed wildly as he walked away.

"Get rid of me, will they? I'll show them," they heard him

mumble.

Caleb and Murray looked at each other. Each was as afraid as Jan, though both knew the worst danger was hers alone.

On the tray were three paper plates, each with a packaged-ham sandwich on white bread, spread with globs of mayonnaise, a handful of potato chips and a mound of applesauce. Three plastic spoons, three paper towels, three Cokes were arranged around the plates. Jan took a bite of applesauce, the least likely food on the plate to have been contaminated.

Murray and Caleb dove into their lunches. Germs were the farthest thought from their minds. Jan was hungry too, but she ate only the chips inside the pile. She ate a hole out of the ham in the middle of each sandwich half.

"You're not hungry?" Caleb asked his teacher.

"No. I'm just nervous," she answered.

"We're not going to let that man hurt you, Mrs. Ferguson. Caleb and I have worked out a plan. If he comes after you, I'll throw Coke in his face and Caleb will tackle him. You can relax now," Murray tried to reassure her.

"Why don't we play a game of cards?" Murray suggested. "I can't stand the suspense of just sitting here. What's your game, Mrs. Ferguson? You play poker?"

"My poker experience is limited. Why don't we play spades or gin rummy instead?" she suggested.

"Okay, spades," Murray decided.

Caleb picked out the best-looking deck of cards from the choices on the dresser. He shuffled while the other two cleared the table.

Murray bid first, then turned to Jan. "Mrs. Ferguson, it's your bid."

"I'm sorry. I guess my mind's not on the game. I'll bid three spades. I mean two," she corrected herself.

"You just told us what was in your hand, Mrs. Ferguson," Caleb said.

"I know. Look, why don't you call me Jan. It will make me feel more comfortable," Jan affected a casual tone. "Three on the table. Let's go."

I've got to find a way out of here. The thought forced its way into every part of her being. She tried to concentrate on the card game, to smile and be the teacher Murray and Caleb knew, but the fear of Punk was overwhelming. Jan anxiously studied the barred windows, the bathroom and the door between her and her threat.

"There's no way out the windows, Mrs. Ferguson, uh, I mean Jan," Murray whispered gently. "Caleb and I checked everything out."

Jan was startled that Murray knew what she was thinking. "Forgive me, boys. I'm just a little nervous. I'll be all right. We'll all be fine," she said quietly.

"Jan, nothing will happen to you as long as we're here," Caleb vowed. He looked directly into her eyes, something he had never done in class.

They heard the crash of a bottle from the next room. "Gawd dammit," Punk garbled drunkenly. "All gone. Now, where'd I put that other'n?"

They heard Punk throwing books off a shelf. He stumbled around, apparently looking through cabinets, knocking things over. Suddenly they heard a tremendous crash. "Well, I'll be damned," Punk shouted gleefully. "Forgot all about these'ns here."

The walls were paper-thin. The captive card players could hear almost every word Punk muttered.

"That's your trick, Jan," Murray said softly, trying to force her attention back to the game.

"I'm sorry. I wasn't paying attention. Look, let's play another game," she said. "I know gin rummy better."

As Jan reached for the cards, her elbow knocked over her Coke can, which hit the floor with a clank. She jumped up and her chair crashed back into the dresser.

"Keep quiet, or I'll have to come in and show you a thing or two!" the man in the next room yelled.

Punk stumbled across the room to the door. "I said *quiet in there!*" he repeated, closer now and fumbling for the lock.

The three froze as the key turned slowly and the door burst open. Murray took up his Coke and took aim. He faced the barrel of a rifle and froze.

The snarling, drunken man who staggered in holding a gun did not look human.

Jan, Caleb and Murray looked at each other and then at him.

"You, girl – you come with me," Punk motioned with a shaking hand.

"Wait just a minute," Murray braved as he and Caleb jumped up at the same time. "You're not taking her anywhere."

"Ha!" the brute bellowed, knocking Caleb to the floor with the butt of the rifle. "You shut up or I'll blow your fuckin' head off," and he aimed the gun between Caleb's eyes.

"You there, the big'n – you tie up that little snot-nose there," Punk motioned Murray toward Caleb.

Murray didn't move.

"I said tie him up!" Punk snarled and threw him the rope he carried in his other hand. "Didn't think I'd have to mess with you little weasels. You can't pull anything over on ole Punk here, no siree. I'll just tell them hot shots when they get back that y'all tried to get away and I had to hog-tie ya, or mebbe shoot ya." He let out his menacing laugh.

"Do what he says," Caleb said. "That thing's prob'ly loaded."

"Damn right, it's loaded ... and I'll use it, too."

Murray lunged and pushed the gun to one side only to have Punk swing the butt up under his chin. Murray sprawled beside Caleb.

Jan glanced into the next room and saw in the late afternoon light a half-full pint of George Dickel on the table and a broken bottle of what looked like the same by the fireplace. Magazine pages were spread all over the room, mostly of naked women in various pornographic poses far more crude than anything she had ever seen.

Murray tied Caleb as he was instructed, but he tied him loosely.

"Now, move over into the bathroom," Punk barked.

Murray inched his way to the bathroom door while Punk checked Caleb's ropes. In a flash Punk kicked Caleb violently in the ribs, knocking him over on his side.

"That ain't tight enough for nothin'. You, there," Punk snarled at Murray while aiming the rifle at Caleb's crotch. "You tie them ropes right this time or I'll ruin your buddy's sex life." Thinking this remark hysterical, Punk laughed heartily, slapping his thigh.

Caleb groaned as Murray helped him back into a sitting position. Murray tied the ropes as tightly as he dared.

"You okay, Caleb?" he whispered.

Caleb moaned but nodded his head *yes*.

"Now, tie his feet!" Murray did as he was told. "Now, you get into that bathroom," Punk snarled.

Murray walked slowly into the bathroom. Punk hit him in the kidneys with the butt of the rifle. "Hurry up!" Punk pushed Murray in and slammed the door behind him, turning the outer knob of the two-lock door, waiting for the click before he let go and turned his lecherous eyes on Jan.

"Now. You, girl, come with me," he leered, pushing Jan in front of him with the barrel of the rifle. He stopped only long enough to slam the bedroom door behind him. Punk held Jan's arm roughly while he locked the door.

Jan had no doubt what would come next. The fact that he was drunk might be to her advantage if she used it. *This will not happen to me*, she told herself. Too afraid to move or speak, she forced calm in order to think. She looked around for deliverance.

"Don't try it, girlie," Punk laughed as if he could read her mind. "I done locked that front door and this here gun's loaded. Now, come here to me."

Jan stayed put. She couldn't have moved unless someone had shoved her from behind.

"Come here to me," he whined pitifully, pointing the gun at her.

"I don't care if you kill me," Jan said finally, more out of fear than courage. "Don't touch me!" she snapped.

"Oh, got me a little live wire, do I? Well, well. Okay then, I'll put the gun down, girlie." He staggered across the room to the table and carefully placed the rifle down.

Jan made a dash for the door. It was locked. She turned around, but he was right behind her. She ducked under his arm and headed for the other side of the room, causing him to fall against the door.

"Don't nobody do that to me," he fumed as he lunged toward her.

He's drunk, Jan kept saying to herself. *He's drunk. If I can just get him to pass out.*

She ran to the corner nearest the bedroom door and then turned and waited for his attack. He lunged again, and again she ducked under his arm. He hit the corner of the sofa and sprawled over its arm and onto the floor. The fall had the opposite effect of what Jan hoped. Instead of being stunned, Punk sobered up.

"You want to play rough, girlie. I can play rough," he rasped, charging her.

She dodged him again, but this time he was ready for her. He sidestepped the same way and grabbed her roughly by the waist. "Aha!"

he yelled triumphantly.

Jan kicked furiously. She screamed without knowing it. Fear tightened its grip in her breast until she could barely breathe. Punk threw her onto the sofa. Nothing separated Jan from what was about to happen except a thin pair of cotton underwear.

Jan had never had sex with anyone except her husband, and she didn't know what to expect. She was surprised her head was so clear and craved befuddlement so that the act would be over before she had time to think. Instead, she found herself in a vacuum with ages of time to think and feel.

Punk pressed an arm against Jan's throat, restricting her breathing. With the other hand, he fumbled with his pants. With amazing dexterity for a man of his size and state of inebriation, he reached under her skirt and ripped her panties. Jan fought blackout; she couldn't breathe even a little. Punk moved his arm, and she jerked straight up with adrenaline strength and shot out from under him.

"No you don't, sugartit!" Drops of drool fell on her forehead as he forced her by her shoulders back onto the sofa. Jan swallowed the vomit that rose in her throat.

Her head hit the back of the sofa arm. Her neck and her head were pushed forward until her chin touched her chest. She could see the huge, hairy belly hanging over her. She saw fat, white thighs, scarred with pockmarks like his face. A wave of nausea overcame her. He pushed her farther down on the sofa so that her head was flattened into the cushion.

When she was a grammar school tomboy, Jan could outrun any boy in her neighborhood. That able-bodied tomboy was lost to her now under the 300 pounds that crushed her hundred-pound frame.

Jan did not expect Punk to kiss her. The act was repulsive. Punk had an odor of week-old sex, sweat and whiskey. His hair smelled greasy.

As the sun disappeared from the horizon and all light left the room, Punk forced his way inside of her. His odious stench made her even more tense. She was not prepared for the excruciating pain.

He thrust once, twice, and the third plunge was so hard and painful that Jan cried out, tears rolling down her cheeks. Punk was finally still. He rolled off of her to the back of the sofa and pushed her onto the floor.

"That'll do me for now," he grunted.

Chapter Three

Jan sobbed. Her legs and arms were like jelly pulled by gravity.

"Come on, girlie. I gotta rest up so's we can do this again," he jeered.

Jan tried to straighten her skirt around her.

"Stop your sniveling. It's not like I kilt ya or nuthin'." He hitched up his pants. "Whooee!" he snorted, wiping his mouth with the back of his hand. "Ain't you some piece of ass!" he whooped.

Before Jan could get to her feet, he pulled her along the floor by one arm and unlocked the bedroom door. Punk threw her through the doorway like a used plaything and slammed the door behind her. The click of the lock was all that separated Jan from her humiliation. She didn't need to look at Caleb to know that he and Murray had heard everything. She lay sobbing in the heap where Punk left her.

"Mrs. Ferguson," Caleb whimpered from his tied position far from her. "There's nothing we could do. I'm so sorry," his voice cracked, and he began to cry.

Jan's anguish turned to embarrassment and then to anger. "My name is Jan, you idiot," Jan cried. She regretted the words as soon as they came out. The hurt on Caleb's face made her cry anew with sorrow for what she had done, sorrow that Caleb and Murray had to go through this, sorrow for every woman through time and history who had suffered this degradation.

"I'm so sorry," she said trying to compose herself. She untied his hands and feet. "I know you couldn't do anything. I wouldn't hurt you for the world, Caleb," she said gently.

Caleb said nothing. As soon as his hands were untied they flew to his eyes. Jan wrapped her skirt tightly around and between her legs and unlocked the bathroom door where Murray waited, his heart pounding.

"I'm so sorry," he called in a loud whisper.

Murray reached out as if to hug her, but Jan shrunk back. She couldn't look him in the eyes. Jan lay on the cot, using a pillow to cover her head in shame and she cried at will.

Caleb and Murray stood in silence, watching in horror as blood steadily oozed onto the cot covering through her thick denim skirt. They felt their inability to prevent her disgrace and they did not know how to comfort her.

"If I could have gotten out of that bathroom .... " Murray lamented as he drove one fist into the palm of his other hand.

Through his tears, Caleb could say nothing. Murray walked over and put his hand on Jan's back as gently as he dared. "Jan," he whispered quietly, "you're bleeding – a lot. Maybe you ought to see if ... if there's something ... wrong ...." he trailed off.

Before the rise of the full moon, night is darkest. The only light in the room was the dim bare bulb overhead that the three had turned on to see better during the late afternoon card game. In the next room Punk was well into his second bottle. He lay on the sofa staring into the evil of his thoughts, emitting the random burp, an occasional maniacal cackle.

Jan calmed down enough to pull herself erect, but she could not bring herself to look into the knowing eyes of the boys. She retreated into the bathroom and shut the door against their concern. She turned the bath water on warm and attempted to wash away her involuntary sin.

The boys could hear the water running in the bathroom. "You think she'll be all right?" Caleb worried. "Seemed like an awful lot of blood."

Murray was up enough on his biology that he didn't think an organ could be ruptured. Neither of them knew enough of the workings of the female body to know just how serious the bleeding was.

Murray turned his attention to Caleb. "You okay?"

"Look, man, I didn't mean to call her Mrs. Ferguson. It was just the first thing that came out. I didn't mean it, man."

Murray hugged Caleb's shoulders awkwardly. "It's okay. She was upset. She knows you didn't mean it. Look, can you imagine what she just went through in there? Who knows what she's going through now? She's hurting, and she's probably embarrassed that we're here. We've got to be strong for her, man. Don't hold that against her."

Caleb's head still hung to his chest. Murray tried again to reassure his friend. "I could tell she feels real bad about what she said to you."

"You think so?" Caleb sounded hopeful.

"Yeah, man. I know she does. Now come on, Caleb, let's figure out what we're going to do next. You heard that bastard say he's coming back for her again. We've got to have some kind of a plan this time."

Murray was not thinking of escape but of stopping the threat in the next room. A *thunk* came from the outer room. By the sound of it, Punk had finally passed out, dropping his bottle on the floor.

"Look under the door," Caleb said. Maybe we can see something."

The space between door and floor was not enough to see anything unless it was within a few feet. The lock was in the doorknob so there was no keyhole. Both boys put their ears against the door and heard Punk's heavy, even breathing.

"I bet he's passed out," Caleb said. "If there's any way to get out of here we better do it now."

"Those other men said that they'd be back tonight, you know," Murray said.

"Hell, we can't trust them," Caleb snapped. "They probably never plan to come back anyway unless it's to kill us. No, man, we got to take our chances now." Caleb was motivated by fear as well as common sense.

Jan was doing a little figuring herself in the bathroom. After carefully washing herself, she could find no damage to her insides other than the shock to her system and what felt like some serious abrasions.

It didn't happen to me, Jan told herself in the small bathroom mirror. *It didn't happen to me, just to my body. He didn't touch the real me. I'll be all right. I'm going to be all right.*

Yet, she felt so dirty, as if she were guilty by being born female or by being too weak to ward him off. For the first time, she felt at one with sin. The image in the mirror blurred. She saw herself as if she were a stranger. The young woman who stared back had large, deep blue eyes that were red and swollen. One side of her face was beginning to turn purple; her eyes puffy, her cheek and jaw bruised.

He's nothing more than the creepy old bum in the store I dreamed about. He's nothing more. He doesn't count.

She washed her face and wondered how God could allow such vermin to exist.

I will get out of here. I will survive, she spoke to the mirror.

She examined the bathroom window to the left of the sink. She could get the screen off from the inside; it was fastened by screws at each corner and in the middle on each side. Then it was only a matter of breaking the individual panes that louvered open.

Jan first tried to unscrew the screen fasteners with her fingernails, but her nails were too short. She looked around the bathroom. Surely there was a nail file, or a comb handle, something she could use. She rummaged through the drawer under the sink and in the medicine cabinet above. In the back of the cabinet she found an old safety razor, one with a handle that turned to open the top. A double-edged razor blade sat conveniently in the top. Her father had had one of these when she was small. He would take the blade out, put shaving cream on her cheeks, and let her "shave" alongside him. Her first leg razor had been like that too, but pink. Her mother had given it to her for her thirteenth birthday.

Jan took the blade out and tried to fit it into the screw head. The razor blade was too thin and flimsy and wouldn't budge the screw. She noticed that the top edge of the opened razor bracket tapered off and was fairly thin. She tried it. It was a tight fit, but when she pushed from the side of the screwhead, the tool slid neatly into place. She held the head of the tool to produce a makeshift screwdriver as she began to unscrew the bottom left screw. Halfway out, the threads got stuck, but after some effort, Jan forced the screw to loosen the rest of the way.

The other screws were fairly easy, though she had to stand on the toilet seat and lean against the wall to reach the middle and top ones. Jan pulled the screen off and laid it in the tub.

The glass panes were connected on the edges with a steel band. If she could get them out, she would have no trouble getting out of the window. Jan tried pushing and pulling but nothing worked. She opened the panes with the rotating handle until they were fully extended, about a forty-five-degree angle from the ground.

There was a knock and Jan jumped.

"Jan, are you all right in there?"

"I'm fine," she whispered.

"Is there anything you need? Anything wrong?"

"No, nothing's wrong, and yes, you can help." Jan opened the door and Murray fell into the bathroom. Caleb was standing directly behind him. Both stared at the window screen in the tub.

"What are you doing?" Murray whispered.

"Do you know if Punk has passed out?" Jan asked.

"I put my ear to the door and heard snoring, so I think he's out cold," Caleb said.

"I got this screen off, and if we can just remove these panes, I think we can get out of here." Jan turned back to the window and pushed on the bottom pane.

"If we break them, we risk waking him up," Murray warned. The look on Jan's face told him she didn't want to gamble.

"I tried to push them; they wouldn't budge," Jan said. "Maybe you can force them out."

"Let me in there," Caleb said pushing his way closer. He was the most mechanically minded of the three. "How'd you unscrew this?"

With a grin Jan held up the razor.

"Maybe we can wedge the steel edges off," Caleb suggested as he tried with his fingers. It didn't work. "Maybe if we break it quickly, he won't wake up. He was pretty drunk, you know, and after two pints of whiskey and … " He didn't finish what everyone was thinking.

"We can put towels around the panes to muffle the sound, maybe, and then just get out as quickly as we can," Jan suggested. The idea was the best they had. They didn't want to be there when the other men returned or when Punk awakened from his drunken stupor, whichever came first.

"We'll need a plan of escape ahead of time," Jan mumbled, thinking aloud as she gathered up the few towels in the small bathroom.

It was about eight o' clock, maybe nine by now – they had no way of telling. The mountain air was much chillier this time of year than the humid air in the flatlands where they lived, and they weren't dressed for it.

"We'll need to take something to keep warm," she said.

The three filed into the bedroom and searched through the drawers of the one chest and the closet. Jan found four thermal underwear shirts in the top drawer, but there were no sweaters or pants. There was nothing in the closet but a summer short-sleeved shirt, so each took a thermal undershirt and layered it over the clothes they'd been wearing since the night before.

"This is better than nothing," she said.

Jan had bloodied the only large towel in the bathroom. She noticed the grimace on Caleb's face when he saw it.

If I'm going to survive, I must forget that and concentrate on the moment, she told herself. Caleb would have to accept blood and sex on his own one day.

"What are we going to break it with?" Murray asked.

A towel rack, the cheap silver metal kind, hung half down inside the tub.

"Try that," she directed.

Caleb was right behind her. Wasting no time, he pried the other end off without making a sound.

"Put your ear to the door and make sure Punk's still out," Jan said to Murray. "Okay, Caleb," Jan instructed, "I'm going to wrap the towel up here and as soon as Murray gets back, you try cracking the pane inside it."

"He's asleep," Murray reported.

The three could hardly fit into the bathroom at one time.

Murray took the towel from Jan. "I don't want you to get cut," he cautioned.

He held the towel around one of the narrow windowpanes making a place in the middle with double toweling. Caleb sharply rapped the padding in the middle of the pane and it easily broke into two pieces. Murray carefully laid the pieces on the screen in the tub. Again Murray held either side of a pane and Caleb hit it. The glass didn't break. He struck again. Another clean break in the middle. Murray laid the glass in the tub with the others.

They paused a moment to listen. There was no sign of stirring from the other room. The rest of the panes came out easily except the top one. The top pane was so high up that the left side fell out of the towel and hit the ground outside with a crash.

"Listen!" Caleb cautioned in a whisper.

"No," Jan said quickly. "We have to get out of here now or we'll not have another chance. If he finds what we've done, he'll kill us … or worse."

"You first," Murray decided. He and Caleb lifted Jan neatly through the window.

The window was chest level from the ground for Jan. She fit through fine, but the boys were somewhat thicker than she. The drop to the ground was not more than four feet and she made it easily, bending her knees to allow a soft and quiet landing. Caleb followed.

"I'm going to run ahead here so we'll know exactly which way to go when Murray gets out," Jan said. He nodded assent and she headed straight through the woods, which were level for a few hundred yards before dropping off. The driveway curved around so that directly below her it was perpendicular to the direction she faced. Caleb's pickup was no longer in the driveway. She guessed that the men took it with them to stash somewhere.

Jan was scanning the direction of the driveway when she heard Punk behind her.

"Think you's getting away with something, don't ya, boys?" he snarled.

Jan turned slowly around, expecting his snake eyes to be on her, but he didn't see her half hidden in the moonlit trees. Punk was pointing that old deer rifle at Murray and looking from one to the other of the boys.

"I been wantin' to do somethin' to you snot-noses, and now's my chance. I cain't help it if I have to shoot ya while yer runnin' away, now can I?" He laughed, baring his ugly teeth.

Jan was surprisingly calm. She glanced on the rocky ground and found next to her right foot a rock that formed a point – a big heavy rock, almost like an arrowhead, and the point made a ridge across one side. She leaned down, picked up the rock and walked forward until she was about ten feet away. If he had turned his head to his right he could have easily seen her, but he was too interested in what he had planned for the boys. Without thinking, Jan drew her arm behind her head and, with the force of her whole arm, threw the rock.

THUD! The rock hit squarely on the side of Punk's head; he reeled backwards, losing the rifle behind him, and fell flat on his back. The rifle landed at Jan's feet as the last dregs of Punk's sickening semen ran down her legs. Punk's head was tilted back and his facial characteristics were even more sinister upside down. His lips were moving. Then, he laughed at her.

In one swift motion, Jan leaned down, picked up the gun, a shell already in its chamber. She aimed between Punk's eyes, and she pulled the trigger: CRACK! She cocked the lever and fired again, this time at his body. CRACK! And again: Cock. CRACK!

The body jerked a little each time she pulled the trigger,

unthinking, unfeeling. And finally: CLICK! Having emptied all three rounds, she stared at the still body, which was bleeding from the head and chest. The eyes were open, staring at the full moon in surprise.

Jan felt nothing more than if she had killed a poisonous snake.

"God!" Murray gasped. "He meant to kill us! We better tie him up."

"He's dead," Jan stated calmly. She knew that she had killed him – that she was rid of him forever.

Chapter Four

Escape was their unifying thought.

"We'll follow the driveway but stay in the woods out of sight," Jan directed as she set a fast pace in front. "We don't want to be seen if the other men return. The driveway will lead us out of here."

"Maybe we ought to take the gun," Caleb suggested.

"No, leave the gun," Jan answered. It lay on the ground at her feet where she had dropped it after spending all three shells. *He loaded one for each of us*, she thought.

In silence, they set up a slow jog entering the protective branches of humanless nature made supernatural by the sheen of the full moon. Jan ran in front, followed by Murray. Caleb brought up the rear. From the bottom of the first ridge they could see the roofline of the cabin that had been their prison. As long as the cabin was in sight, Jan was pushed on by fear. When they reached the bottom, their legs were shaking from the strain of the steep incline.

"I don't care who we see drive by, we stay out of sight," Jan warned when she stopped to catch her breath. "We don't know who we can trust. Is that agreed?"

The boys nodded.

"We'll stick to the woods and parallel the road until we get down to a very public place ... unless either of you has a better idea," she said.

The boys said nothing. They moved steadily ahead.

The land leveled off above and parallel to the road. If anyone were to drive by, the three could see who it was while remaining unseen themselves. Jan resumed a steady jogging pace, driven by the need to be away from that cabin. The road stayed on a plateau for about quarter mile before dropping downhill.

Jan's only thoughts were of maintaining the consistent movement of her legs, breathing steadily, and dodging bushes and rocks. Leaves crunched underfoot and branches snapped loudly. Unseen animals and bugs scurried out of their way.

She stopped for a moment and leaned against a tree. Caleb and Murray stopped abruptly behind her. The full moon created a false sense of daytime. She glanced up; she could no longer see the house of her shame. The past twenty-four hours were like something she had read, but she couldn't remember all of the details. Reality now was focused on finding their way out of the forest. What might happen next never crossed her mind. She existed only for the moment.

"Do you think we could walk awhile?" Murray asked, breathing heavily.

"I thought you were on the soccer team," Jan joked.

The boys were laboring more that she was. While they had bulldozed along, Jan instinctively paced herself. She knew that if they were to keep this up, they would have to rest. Without the cabin in sight, Jan no longer felt quite as threatened.

From their ridge they could see the road, a shimmering blue-black ribbon winding from ridge to ridge. Jan leaned against a tree trunk and slid to the ground. The moon read about ten o' clock – one of those big moons that sat just off the horizon. The night sounds were soothing. The stars were bright, and the moonlight cast shadows as it filtered through the trees. A blanket of leaves and pine needles offered a place to rest.

Jan felt comfortably closed in. She recalled other times in her life when she had been single-minded in purpose. Reality became the people around her, separate from the places and relationships of the past or the future – each different experience its own story with a beginning and an end. She leaned her head against the tree and sighed.

Caleb tilted his head back, but Murray looked at Jan. He caught her eye and gave her a small smile, which Jan returned.

"I sure could use something to eat," Caleb said, pulling his head forward.

"Me, too." Murray grinned at Caleb.

"I guess I could eat something, too, but I don't see a McDonald's around here," Jan said. "It's chillier than we're used to," she said. Jan had nothing but a skirt between her skin and the cold, which was more noticeable now that they were still.

She hugged her shoulders as she watched the boys, their backs to her, surveying the way ahead. They were only seventeen; still children in many ways. She remembered thinking at that age that she knew so much. She could see how little she knew then; she wasn't so sure that she knew much more now.

"Okay, boys, rest period is over."

They began to walk again. There was no longer any reason to run. They had descended about a mile, maybe two. No other roads had emerged from the woods. The virgin forest was clear and a blanket of pine needles cushioned their steps. They walked along in silence for another mile, mostly downhill, when they finally came to the bottom of the road that led to the cabin. It ended at a larger and obviously more frequently traveled road, this one also graveled.

"I suggest we go to the left because it looks like it's downhill," Jan pointed. "Surely there's a town down there."

The moon-silhouetted figures wove through the trees above the road at a fairly fast clip. Soon they found themselves out of breath as the climb took another up-turn. The road leveled somewhat, still winding around the mountain, but not at such a steep decline. They had passed several side roads, but there had been no sign of cars or houses. The forest here had many more hardwoods than the pine thickets of her Georgia home. Rhododendron, mountain laurel and wild dogwood were abundant, particularly when the path neared the stream that they could hear running.

Jan imagined how fish must feel, following their instincts to an unknown destination, tumbling, swirling and twisting as if tossed on the stream herself.

"I vote we take a rest," Caleb spoke up from behind her. They had come to a wooded den with a natural circle of tree elders, under which lay a group of large boulders. The boulders formed an enclosure beneath three majestic hemlocks.

Jan nodded.

Caleb turned into the enclosure first, with Murray and Jan close behind. The boys flopped onto the soft pine cushion, while Jan moved to an indentation in one of the large rocks. Too tired to even talk, they each leaned back and let the night take them in.

It wasn't until Jan awoke at the first peep of sunrise that she knew they had slept.

"How long have you been awake?" Caleb whispered.

"Not long," she said.

Murray stirred and nodded at the other two without speaking.

With daylight came memory of the day before. The boys kept a vision of Punk lying face up on the ground, blood oozing, motionless, dead. If Jan could remember it, this would have been a comforting thought. It was the image of his white, pocked belly and the searing rod piercing her soul that she must fight. This memory was hers and hers alone. She would grapple with it for the rest of her earthly life.

"There's probably a house or something on this road," Murray said.

"We're taking no chances," Jan answered. "A public place is our best shot," she said firmly.

"Let's hope whatever we find serves breakfast," Jan said. "And by the way, boys, the treat's on you," she smiled. "You do have your wallets, don't you?" Jan last remembered seeing her purse and books in the cream-colored van.

The hike down the mountain was long. The cliff on the upper side of the road was no longer level and passable, and the three were forced to travel the road. The first car that pulled slowly up the last hill sent all three diving for the brush on the low side of the road. Jan and Murray grabbed a young tree to keep from sliding, but Caleb clutched a not-so-secure weed which gave way and sent him sliding down the steep incline. The base of an oak tree broke his fall.

Jan scrambled up the bank to catch a fleeting glimpse of the vehicle. If the enemy were near, she wanted to know. She saw only the tail end of an old and rusted station wagon turn the sharp curve up the hill. Children and fishing poles hung out the windows.

At the bottom of the next hill, the road leveled out. They came first to a trout fish farm. Long, concrete ditches simulating the area's natural streams bubbled with schools of fish. A brick office sat at the far end of the fish beds, and behind the operation were three brick homes.

She wondered about the people inside the houses. Were they up yet? What time was it? Probably early morning. Had they eaten breakfast? Had the children gone to school? Bicycles, tricycles, balls and toys littered two of the yards. What day was it? Friday. Could it truly be Friday already? And yet, could it only be Friday, a mere day and a half since she was snatched from her world and all that was familiar?

The boys could think of nothing but their stomachs. Caleb

wondered if the people in the houses were eating bacon or sausage, toast or biscuits. Murray was planning what he would order when they found a restaurant.

The morning was clear and crisp, not too cold. Jan took off her top thermal undershirt. The road flattened out and straightened. Houses – mostly brick ranch, some prefab log homes and a few trailers – were scattered along the road. Two cars and a truck passed them going down the mountain.

They walked abreast in silence. If the boys had thought back on yesterday evening, they would have remembered Jan's inhuman screams and the lustful grunts of her lascivious conqueror, and they would remember the anguish of their impotence. The surprised look on Punk's face as he lay sprawled on the ground with his eyes open would be hard to forget. They would remember most vividly, however, the look on Jan's face when she shot him. Her blue eyes had turned to steel, and her face took on the fearlessness shown by cornered animals in the wild, emboldened by the necessity of their survival.

These were not their thoughts, however. Leaving the forest behind, they found themselves facing a fish camp that stood warm and inviting.

Chapter Five

The Brevard Fish Camp looked busy by mid-morning. Several cars of early lunchers were pulled into the closest parking spaces. Two mothers and their toddlers walked in the front door, followed by a group of Florida tourists. The very ordinariness of it all made the captives' escape anticlimactic somehow.

"I'm going to order me the biggest breakfast ever," Caleb said excitedly as he rushed ahead.

"I think you've missed breakfast, Caleb," Murray said close behind.

The boys were almost to the door before they realized Jan had not moved.

"Jan? You okay? Aren't you hungry?" Murray asked gently as he turned back to her.

"We still don't know who we can trust," Jan insisted.

"Aw, now, you've been watching too much TV," Caleb said.

Murray gave Caleb a warning look. "Why don't we call the sheriff's department as soon as we get inside. There'll be a pay phone," he urged her.

Jan looked doubtful. "Don't you think we should call someone we know first? I mean, what if the sheriff up here is connected somehow?"

Caleb continued to inch toward the door.

"Why don't we call David first, then," Murray suggested. "He can call our parents for us and tell them we're all right."

Jan was satisfied, so Murray took her by the elbow and led her into the fish camp.

"Phone?" Murray asked the first waitress hustling by.

"By the restrooms," she answered, throwing her thumb behind her to the left.

Only a few heads turned as the three threaded their way through tables and booths to the back. The boys looked no different than other campers coming out of the woods, but the back of Jan's skirt was stained with dried blood and her sweatshirt was torn at the shoulder. She tried to cover the bruises on her face with her hair.

Jan's hands shook as she dialed her area code and phone number. "Collect from Jan," she said barely audible.

"Jan, is that you, darling? Are you all right?" David yelled into the phone from the other end.

Jan's knees turned to jelly and her words caught in her throat.

"Jan!! Are you all right? Darling, are you there?" David yelled loud enough for Murray and Caleb to hear from the receiver.

"Yes, yes," she finally answered, choking back tears. "I'm all right. We're all right. We're in Brevard, I think that's in North Carolina, at the Brevard Fish Camp ...." She couldn't finish and handed the phone to Murray.

"Mr. Ferguson, this is Murray Simpson. Jan has has been through a lot." Murray was reluctant to say what. "We've escaped and we're okay now. I think we're in Brevard, North Carolina. Do you know where that is? No. We haven't called the sheriff because Jan, Mrs. Ferguson, is unsure who we can trust."

"There's an FBI agent with me here," David said. "Where's Jan now? Where'd she go?"

"She's just too upset to talk right now. But she's okay. I mean, she'll be okay. FBI agent? Was there a ransom? Could you call mine and Caleb's parents for us?" Murray's thoughts ran ahead of him.

Murray heard someone talking in the background.

"Listen, Murray," David said, "we'll fill you in on the details later. I'm putting Ken Thompson on the phone. He's an FBI agent from Columbia. He'll tell you what to do next."

"The FBI is there," Murray whispered to Caleb and Jan.

Jan went into the ladies room while Murray talked with the FBI agent.

"Son, tell me where you are," Thompson said authoritatively.

"This is Murray Simpson and we've been kidnapped, and, well, I just don't know where to start," he began.

"I know. I know all that," Thompson said. "Just tell me where you are and we'll have someone there to get you as soon as possible. Are you safe? Any of you hurt?" he continued.

"We're fine now. We're at a restaurant, fish camp, in Brevard, in North Carolina. We just got here and we're hungry mostly. We have no car and hardly any money," Murray answered impatiently.

"All right, son, we'll have the local sheriff's department take you into protective custody right now. Our closest agent is in Asheville, so it will take some time for him to get to you. Go on and get something to eat and just do what the sheriff says when he gets there," Thompson advised.

Murray gave Thompson the pay phone number after being assured that his and Caleb's parents would be contacted.

Meanwhile, in the bathroom, Jan looked at herself in the mirror. Her face looked tired and drawn. The bruises covered the upper side of her face near her eye. Her hair was dirty and unkempt and her mouth still had caked blood where she had bitten her lip. She rolled up the sleeves to her sweatshirt to see the bruises she felt on her forearms. Her thighs ached as if they had been beaten with a meat tenderizer. Her sides hurt; her vagina throbbed; and though she had not bled since last night, urinating was painful.

The boys waited patiently outside the bathroom door after using the restroom.

"Jan? Are you all right?" Murray whispered as he rapped lightly on the door.

"I'm fine," she answered. *Yes, I'm fine*, she repeated to her reflection in the mirror. She dried her face and hands.

The fish camp was more crowded now. There were more mothers with young children, working men in dirty dungarees and three-piece-suit businessmen, secretaries and old people, sitting at the tables, eating and drinking and talking as if this were a day like any other. Jan had to remind herself it was a normal day for them. She forced a smile and motioned for the boys to move forward and find a table.

"They're sending an FBI agent from Asheville for us," Murray informed them. "A sheriff is supposed to come look after us here. David wanted to talk to you again, Jan. I promised we'd take care of you if he will just get us home," he said patting her hand tentatively.

"You're right. I am fine. We're all fine," she emphasized. "Let's order," she said as a waitress approached their table.

The boys ordered trout, and Jan ordered a hamburger.

"Hamburger," the waitress explained. "Girl, this is a fish camp. What you talking about wanting a hamburger? 'Course we *have* hamburgers; we carry anything anybody could *want*, but seems like to me you'd want some of that fresh *trout* we brought in this morning."

"I just want a hamburger," Jan insisted. Her stomach turned at the thought of picking through flaky fish flesh that had struggled in vain to escape the unrelenting rod only to be hooked and tossed aside.

"It's your lunch," the waitress answered saucily. "Fries? Onion rings?"

"A hamburger and iced tea," Jan ordered, handing the menu back without looking up. The waitress just shrugged and headed to the kitchen.

"How's this sheriff or deputy or whatever supposed to know who we are?" Caleb asked, munching on his fifth pack of crackers.

"I told the FBI man at Mr. Ferguson's what we look like and what we're wearing," Murray answered.

"But if our phone is tapped, the kidnappers will know we're here. They could send someone over dressed like a sheriff's deputy. It could be a trick. How will we know?" Panic rose in Jan's voice.

"We've just got to trust them," Murray said reassuringly. "There're too many people here to try anything. I think those men are long gone by now. Just don't think about it. We're safe here." Murray's voice was warm but firm.

Twenty minutes passed before a uniformed officer came through the door. He glanced their way, but didn't approach, going instead to a stool at the counter.

"I'll handle this," Murray said after wiping his mouth with his napkin.

The man was asking the waitress about the three of them when Murray tapped him on the shoulder. The other two watched Murray point in their direction and saw the sheriff nod, not looking overly concerned. Then Murray turned his back to them while glancing occasionally in Jan's direction.

Jan looked away, and when she returned her gaze, the sheriff looked at her with the compassion of a father. The tall, sturdy man walked over to their table. "I'm Sheriff Melvin Lander. You're safe now."

The sheriff let them finish lunch while he paid the bill. The other diners stared.

"What you got there, Sheriff?" their waitress asked Lander at the register.

"Well, now, Maureen, I can't rightly tell you, now. But I'm sure you'll find out soon enough," he answered with a wink.

Jan sat in the front seat of the sheriff's car while the two boys climbed in the back. The day was cloudy, with a fall nip the air. Jan watched the houses, the streets, trailers, and businesses as they traveled the outskirts of Brevard going toward downtown. She floated along watching the day like scenery on the riverbank.

Sheriff Lander called his deputies over the dispatch radio and directed them to check the area around the cabin. He knew exactly where it was, in one of the most remote areas of Pisgah National Forest. "Wrap up what you find there and bring it in," he instructed. He was careful not to mention the body in front of Jan.

Murray had told the sheriff that the shooting was clearly self-defense, and that he and Caleb owed their lives to their teacher. He also told him that Jan had not mentioned the shooting, and to his knowledge, she was not aware of it.

"We have a real nice little hospital here in Brevard," Sheriff Lander said to his passengers. "You'll need to be checked for exposure," he said, not mentioning that all rape cases required immediate medical attention to find evidence against the rapist. "The FBI agent who called me from Riverdale, I believe your husband was with him, Mrs. Ferguson, assured me that y'all's families are making travel arrangements to meet you here in Brevard. I'll tell you as soon as I hear what those plans are," he rambled on.

Jan gazed silently out the window. There was no indication that she heard what the sheriff said, though the boys answered politely from the back seat.

Jan could have cut her finger for all the attention she received in the doctor's office waiting room. At least no one was asking her questions, or staring, she thought as she thumbed through the worn magazines in the waiting room. After talking with the receptionist, Sheriff Lander sat next to Jan on the waiting room couch, twirling his hat between his open knees.

"Jan Ferguson, come this way please," a nurse called. "We'll see to you boys as soon as the next room is available," she addressed Caleb and Murray.

"Now, honey, you just take off your things and lay them on

the chair over there and slip on this little paper gown I have here. The doctor'll be in soon," a tall, striking nurse directed.

Jan did as she was told and climbed on the examining table to wait, her bare legs swinging slightly. She wished she had brought the magazine from the waiting room to pass the time. She was unaware that Sheriff Lander was speaking with the doctor, telling him that she was raped. The same nurse returned to take her blood pressure and her temperature. She left.

Dr. Sam Morris was an older man of the school of doctoring that considers a pat on the hand and a little sympathy as good as any medicine. He was startled at first by her youthful appearance. He had expected an older woman when the sheriff said she was a teacher. Why, she looked as young as her two students out there.

"Mrs. Ferguson? Hello, there. I'm Dr. Morris. Sheriff Lander tells me you've been through quite an ordeal; spent the night in the forest, I understand. Well, now don't you worry about a thing. This will be a simple examination," he talked as he peered into her eyes with a small flashlight, checked her glands, her throat, listened to her chest. Jan flinched when the doctor touched her right side. "That hurt?"

She nodded.

He pressed again, moving his fingers up and down her rib cage on both sides, squeezed and examined her arms. "Umm," was all he said.

"You certainly have taken a lick on your right side there," Dr. Morris said as he covered her up. "You could possibly have a severely bruised or even cracked rib, but since both would be treated the same, I'm not going to take x-rays. We'll bind it for you and the soreness should go away in a couple of weeks. You also have severe contusions – that's a fancy name for bruises –" he smiled down at her – "on both arms. And the obvious ones on your face here," he touched her gently, "but they, too, will go away with time."

"Now, Mrs. Ferguson, Jan, I'm going to have to examine you a bit farther to check for internal damage," the doctor continued in a fatherly tone. "I'm sure you have had a PAP smear. Just lie back; that's it. Now, put your feet in these stirrups while I warm this instrument under the hot water faucet."

Jan lay back and braced herself, every muscle in her body involuntarily snapped taut. She had always hated going to the gynecologist.

Dr. Morris continued talking as he crossed the room. "Are you married?" he asked.

"Yes."

"Is it a good marriage?"

"I've never really thought about it. We haven't been married that long. Yes, I guess it is," she hesitated. "Why?"

He turned to look her in the eye. "Because a great many women that this happens to have no one. A loving husband can make you see that what has happened to you is something that one terrible person has done. There is no way I can feel a fraction of what you are feeling, but I want you to know that what has happened to you is a one-time thing. There's no reason for you to distrust men in general," he counseled.

Dr. Morris patted Jan's hand before disappearing between her legs. *If I ever got hold of this man, I'd cut his nuts out,* he fumed in thought.

"You don't have to worry," Jan said unexpectedly. "I killed him."

Dr. Morris, trying not to react to her confession, allowed his face to look no more shocked by what she had said than hers did.

"I shot him," she repeated, propping herself up on her elbows. "I killed him."

"Are you sure?" Dr. Morris asked. "Does the sheriff know?"

"I don't know. This is the first I've thought of it. He hasn't asked me anything about it," Jan replied.

"You shouldn't tell me something like that in confidence, young lady." The doctor's voice turned harsh. He seemed to want to protect himself from something Jan didn't recognize. "I'm only a medical doctor," Dr. Morris said. Just that, and nothing more.

Jan lay back for the final examination and closed her eyes, letting the tears drop slowly into her ears.

"You're going to have to relax, dear. Slide on down the table a bit," the doctor coaxed.

She closed her eyes and scrolled through memories to find one that would help her relax. She thought of the gently swaying wheat outside her classroom window.

"You've got some mighty bad bruises here," the doctor reported, lightly fingering her inner thighs. "Umm," he said as he examined farther and collected whatever samples he could, considering the passage of time since the attack.

There was no tear in the vaginal wall, though there were several serious abrasions and contusions. Dr. Morris gave Jan a salve to ease the discomfort. There was little more he could do, so he left Jan in silence and sent the nurse in with a clean set of clothes and instructions to shower in the doctor's private bathroom.

Afterward, the sheriff took the three to his office to meet the FBI agent from Asheville for questioning.

"Why don't you start from the beginning, when you were first kidnapped?" FBI agent Harry Leamon directed.

So, Jan began.

She told him that she taught eighth, ninth and twelfth grade English and a vocabulary course for tenth graders at Riverdale Academy, a small private school located five miles outside of the rural, agriculturally-dependent town of the same name in the northeastern corner of South Carolina. Built during the 1960s on donated farm land, the school consisted of paired, one story, brick buildings. One building housed grades K-6, and the other served grades 7-12. A gymnasium sat on a knoll between the schools and the soccer field. Students came from both North and South Carolina, and most were the children of farm families.

She told how she had agreed, a bit resentfully, to review Murray and Caleb for a big test on Friday because they had to miss class on Thursday. The board of directors was treating the soccer team to a special lunch at the same time she had scheduled the review for the whole class. The soccer team had a chance at the finals in the regional private league, but declining grades threatened to bench the team's co-captains.

Jan relived the opening and shutting of the school's front door that evening; she replayed the echoes of the footsteps approaching her classroom. She definitely remembered having locked the front door behind her. The heavy, determined steps had been their only warning. They came fast.

"We heard those heavy footsteps in the hall. I thought it was Coach, checking to make sure we came for review," Murray said first. "Two men burst into the classroom. One was well over six foot, and the other was medium height and build. The smaller guy was dressed real nice, and the big man wore jeans and a plaid shirt."

"The big man turned out to be Punk," Caleb added. "They both wore hats. The short, well-dressed man had on a beaver fur hat and Punk had on a farm cap. Both pulled their hats low over their eyes so we couldn't see anything but their chins."

"The well-dressed man addressed us by our names when they came in," Jan said.

Jan remembered the ball of fear that had knotted and plopped at the pit of her stomach.

"The small man told us to come with them. He didn't sound threatening at the time," Murray said.

Jan couldn't remember what happened next. She had had been too stunned to speak or to move. She remembered the guns.

"We made a move for the door, but the short man pulled out a handgun. I was more afraid of Punk than that gun," Murray related.

"They told us to get all our stuff so there wouldn't be any signs we were there. They wanted my keys! I said, *You're crazy, man. You're not taking my truck*," Caleb said. The Ranger was Caleb's pride.

Jan could still hear the sharp metal snap of the pistol safety. Caleb had reluctantly reached into his pocket and pulled out his keys. He threw them to the larger man standing menacingly at the door.

"They took our cell phones, too. My car was gone when we walked out of the school," Jan remembered. "Oh, and Punk had a handgun, not the rifle I shot him with. They led us behind the upper school building where a cream-colored van was parked on the other side of the fence behind the open-air basketball court. I recognized the van because every day this week it was parked beside the dumpster on the edge of town, just before the turn to the school. The van was brand new and loaded with all sorts of antennae," she said, adding, "I think our house phone was bugged, too."

"Our agents found the textbooks," Leamon said.

"There was a hole in the fence," Jan continued. "That morning Coach Howell had reported that a hole had been cut in the back fence beyond the lower school's playground. The vines were heavy along this stretch, and Coach had moved them to retrieve a ball during P.E. Somebody said it was supposed to be fixed the next day."

"The shorter man opened the back door to the van and told Punk to tie us up," Caleb said. "He smelled like old beer and body stink. It was gross."

"Punk tied our hands and feet. He shoved us on the van floor. We couldn't move much or see anything. We stayed there until we got to the cabin," Murray said.

"Okay. Now let's skip ahead to the shooting," Leamon said.

Jan turned pale.

"I think Mrs. Ferguson has had enough for now. I'm going to let her lie down in the back of my office on the cot," Sheriff Lander said when he saw Jan's face. "You boys stay with Agent Leamon and finish giving your statements."

Chapter Six

While Jan slept on the sheriff's cot, her parents and grandparents in Georgia and her husband in South Carolina were relieved and grateful beyond words. Jan's parents had contacted the FBI on Wednesday night when they received a ransom note. The kidnappers had not contacted Jan's husband; but her parents and grandparents both were given notes. The boys' parents also had been contacted.

An agent from Atlanta went to Jan's Georgia family and an agent from Columbia visited her husband and the boy's parents. The ransom note asked for a midnight rendezvous from the Riverdale parties and an eleven o'clock meeting for the Georgia parties on Thursday night in remote locations of each town. The hour difference accommodated the time zone change between the two sites.

But when the time for drop-off came, no one picked up the pay off. At this point, Jan's and the boys' families knew no more than they had known when they first received the payment demands. Jan's father and Caleb's father waited for several hours in their designated spots with FBI agents hidden on the deserted streets of the pick-up points. By four in the morning the fathers gave up and went home, leaving a lone agent concealed nearby.

When the FBI realized that no one was going to pick up the ransom money, the agents retrieved the suitcases full of cash and returned them to the banks. The Kingsford FBI agents turned in their reports and left the rest of the wrap-up to Ken Thompson in Riverdale and Harry Leamon in Brevard.

May Jameson and Meemaw cried when they heard Jan was safe. Their tears turned bitter when they learned she had been raped.

"No one must ever know of this. If no one knows, she can

forget about it, as if it never happened," May said to anyone who would listen. May lived her life ignoring the unpleasant. *If you don't think about it, it can't bother you*, was her motto.

Meemaw went one step farther. *If you refuse to acknowledge it, then it just didn't happen*, she always said.

Lamar and Papa Ralph sent the women off to bed after two sleepless nights. May first had to call her eldest daughter, Julia Ann. "She has a right to know about her sister," she said. "I think I'll call Peterson, too. I certainly don't want him hearing this from someone else."

Jan's family had a unified reaction to the shooting. "I wish I could've killed that son-of-a-bitch myself," Papa Ralph spoke for them all. "At least it's over and we can go on from here."

"The first thing we need to do is get our little girl home," Lamar said as he made his way to the phone. "She'll probably want to see David, so I'll fly him to go get her and fly them both back here."

"I don't think she'll be coming home today, sir," the FBI agent said politely. "There will have to be a preliminary hearing. Just routine. The earliest they can get that together will be tomorrow."

This last bit of information did not sit well with Jan's family. Hadn't their daughter been through enough? Whose side was the law on anyway? Couldn't they let her rest a few days before facing a hearing? The facts were obvious. Why did she have to stay there at all?

The family's discontent didn't change what had to be done. "I best get John Larsen over here," Papa Ralph said.

John Larsen was Papa Ralph's attorney. Papa Ralph put John through college and law school, and at one time he had been the company attorney. After three years he returned to law school to specialize in criminal law. He still handled all the family business as well as complicated company legal matters, but he had his own practice now.

When Papa Ralph first called John and presented the situation, John asked him if he wouldn't prefer to consult a more prestigious criminal law firm out of Atlanta or even Washington, D.C. Papa Ralph would hear nothing of this. This was his granddaughter they were talking about. She needed all the family around she could get. And, after all, John was family.

John cared for the Jameson children as much as he did for his own nieces and nephews. During his college summers when he worked for Papa Ralph, he had enjoyed driving the Jameson children to their lessons and activities.

Of the three Jameson children, John knew Jan the least. She was painfully shy as a child. Jan was a serious honor student in high school and college. Julia Ann was considered the beauty of the family because of her classic good looks, her dress and her social graces. Their brother, Peterson, was the potential politician, both in his looks and in his social know-how. They both had May's craving for social approval and applause; whereas, Jan, who was more in temperament like her father, had steered clear of the limelight.

Lamar wanted to leave for Brevard immediately, but Papa Ralph convinced him that they should take an afternoon flight to Asheville and rent a car.

When David called the Johnson's house with the news of their son's escape, the Simpsons were there, too. Agent Harold Lee had returned from retrieving the money from a dumpster. The Simpsons had only been able to come up with $50,000, and the rest came from the Johnsons. The Riverdale families had taken the local South Carolina National Bank president into their confidences at six on Thursday morning.

The Simpsons and the Johnsons couldn't understand why their boys had to stay in Brevard. Couldn't they just tape their testimony and come home? No? Well, then, if the boys weren't coming home, they would have to go to them. Both families decided to drive rather than fly. The Johnsons offered to have the Simpsons ride with them in their deluxe travel van, but the Simpsons said they'd rather take the family sedan.

David flew with Ken Thompson in a government Cessna, and a car was waiting for them at the private airstrip on the outskirts of Brevard. Before they left, Thompson had pieced together the sequence of events, the rape, the shooting and the escape, over the phone with Sheriff Lander. He passed the information on to David and the boys' families.

Raped. David couldn't get past the word to the feeling. *Killed.* His wife had been raped and she had killed her rapist. An organized kidnapping ring had kidnapped his wife; her captor had raped her; and she had killed him to escape. David had been in a dream since Wednesday night. Each new turn of events was as unexpected as the last.

David was not able to digest this new information until he and Thompson were underway to Brevard. His gut reaction was not compassion for Jan, or even outrage at her violator, but an overwhelming sense of helplessness. Had he not vowed on their wedding day to protect her for life? Yet, he had been unable to prevent her dishonor. Her captors did not include him in the ransom.

"What does this preliminary hearing mean?" David asked Thompson halfway through the two-hour flight. "Surely, Jan won't be charged with the shooting?"

"Well, these things are unsure. Who would have ever thought that heiress, Patty Hearst, would have been convicted?" Thompson answered. "We're probably looking at self-defense. From what I can understand, he would have killed her ... the boys, too."

"According to the law, a shooting of any kind requires a hearing. A judge will decide whether the killing happened in self-defense. If he says it's not self-defense, then the case will go to the grand jury for a preliminary hearing. The grand jury will then decide if a crime was committed, but that jury meets only twice a year."

David nodded, taking this all in.

"My contact in the area is Harry Leamon out of Asheville," Thompson continued. "He says the district attorney for Brevard's judicial district is a stickler for detail. Leamon said that since this man was lying down and was unarmed when he was shot, the DA is pushing for an inquest."

Thompson purposefully didn't mention to David that public opinion would have a bearing on the case also. He knew that justice would not be done if David's young wife were charged with murder; he also knew that he could not predict what would happen.

"I don't want Jan to have to relive this," David said, fishing for reassurance.

Thompson had none to give. "You never can be sure," he said. "When it comes to the judicial system and the courts, we just have to wait and see. Right now your wife's emotional welfare is important. She's been through a lot. In our experience, the horror of a kidnapping, not knowing what has happened or why, the disorientation of not knowing where you are, is enough to cause mental anguish. With rape on top of that ... well, I hope she gets psychiatric counseling immediately."

"This is all too absurd!" said David, outraged. "As if she hasn't been through enough!"

"I know, son," Thompson said sympathetically.

David wasn't prepared to handle the overwhelming responsibility suddenly placed on his shoulders. He listened, but he did not fully understand. He just wanted to hold Jan and see for himself how she was. He wanted to make up for not being able to protect her. For all he knew, she might feel hostile toward him just because he was male. He knew from his experience of the past day and half that he couldn't predict what would happen next.

Jan woke to a musty smell that reminded her of camp. There was little light in the room; there were no windows. Her husband was standing over her, his hands in the pockets of his belted khakis, collar open on his heavily starched white shirt, ash blond hair neatly combed, smelling of Royal Copenhagen. Cologne? Was this a dream? She shut her eyes for a moment.

No, not a dream, she saw when she reopened them. David Riley Ferguson stood over her, his pleasing, though non-descript facial features the same as always. Only there was something unsettling in his grey-blue eyes, a distinct furrow in his sandy eyebrows. Yet, he was smiling down at her.

Calm was a good word for David, Jan thought. She looked up at him and smiled; then she looked beyond him to get her bearings. She saw a bookshelf with law enforcement manuals and a locked cabinet of guns. Guns ... yes, now she remembered.

"You okay, sweetie?" David asked gently as he bent to kiss her forehead.

"Fine," she said evenly. "You must have been worried sick."

"Don't worry about me. I'm here to take care of you," he said as he sat next to her on the cot and took her hand. Jan noticed as if for the first time that his hands were quite small; the fingers were short – *like banker's hands*, she thought. "The doctor says that you're fine physically except for some nasty bruises and cuts and a cracked rib. They'll heal with time," he said lamely.

Good old David. Jan smiled. Then she saw in his face that he knew. A lump of shame rose in her throat. "I killed him, so it doesn't matter now," she said, trying to hold back the tears.

"Shh. Don't talk, honey. You need to rest," David said, not wanting to hear more.

"No, I need to talk," Jan insisted. "I know that it shouldn't have happened, but it did and I'm not even sorry I killed him."

"It's okay, Jan. Let's not talk about it right now," David persisted.

Jan was unable to explain what she was feeling. She couldn't tell if David truly wanted her to rest or if he didn't want to share in the horror. She looked him in the eyes and realized the latter. He had been the one person she thought would understand; but this was too much. She began to cry for the loneliness she felt.

Thompson knocked gently on the door. "May I come in? Hello, Mrs. Ferguson, I'm Ken Thompson with the FBI. Do you think you're up to answering a few questions?"

Jan nodded. He pulled up the only chair in the room to ask her about certain points of the testimony the boys had given earlier that afternoon. He was more than understanding and intended to be much more pointed with his questions than the sheriff had wanted to be.

"I'm going down the hall and look for the sheriff to see just what is going on here," David said, and he hurried out the door.

"Murray and Caleb said that you saved their lives," Thompson began when he was settled. "That was a very brave thing to do after what you went through. I imagine that you really wanted to run away. You could have, they told me."

"No, I couldn't leave them stranded there. And I didn't save them – not consciously anyway," Jan answered truthfully.

It was only the two of them in the room now. Jan was relieved that someone wanted to know the details. She needed to say it out loud to define for herself what happened.

"I shot that man because he had no right to live," Jan looked right at Thompson when she said this.

"You realize, Jan, that what you say in here can be used against you in a court of law. Maybe you ought to have a lawyer present." Thompson had been unprepared for her answer. She should have had a lawyer, but they had all felt from the boys' testimony that the case was cut-and-dried self-defense. Thompson wished now he had waited until Jan's family attorney was there. He was due to arrive some time early that evening with Jan's parents and grandparents.

"No, I want it on the record from the start. I don't know if I saved Caleb and Murray. I don't know if that man would have killed us if I hadn't killed him. All I know is that the gun was at my feet; I picked it up and shot."

Ken Thompson shook his head. In his own mind he was sure that the shooting was self-defense. But this young lady could complicate matters if she insisted on taking full responsibility for killing her attacker. All too often he had seen victims suffer because the courts persisted in protecting the rights of the criminal. Thompson didn't want to hear anything incriminating from Jan that he might have to repeat in court later. If she were to testify at the inquest and had to reveal the gory details of her degradation, Thompson was not sure Jan would be able to keep her vengeance from showing.

Thompson could hear David pacing in the next room. He decided it best to keep David and the boys busy, so he sent them to arrange hotel accommodations.

"David," he said opening the door. "Those boys out there need some direction. You know, something to do before their families arrive. Why don't you take them with you and arrange hotel rooms. You'll need at least six rooms, I think."

"I'd rather stay with Jan," David protested.

"It's all right, David. I'm fine," Jan called from the little cot.

David reluctantly went to find the boys. Though the area of Western North Carolina was known for its quaint bed-and-breakfast inns, David thought it more appropriate to stay at the Holiday Inn right off the highway. He dreaded having May and Meemaw come, knowing that they would try their best to turn this into a social event.

Six rooms. They might as well be part of a wedding party. Hopefully, one night would be all that was needed and they would be headed home tomorrow.

Chapter Seven

The Johnsons, Simpsons, Jamesons, Blounts and John Larsen arrived early evening within an hour of each other.

Jan's family arrived in full array. David and Jan just had come to the hotel from the sheriff's office when May bounded out of the back of their rented Lexus, hair coiffed and purse dangling daintily from her arm.

"My baby," she exclaimed with outstretched arms. "It's all right now, darling. We'll take care of everything," she said in Jan's ear. Jan felt comfortable in the embrace of her mother's familiar perfume.

"Just look at you," May said holding Jan by the shoulders at arms' length.

Jan had on the borrowed pair of brown, corduroy pants two sizes too big and a gold sweatshirt that proclaimed *Brevard High School*.

"Surely there will be stores open here until nine. It's only seven now. We can buy you a few necessities before dinner," May said taking charge.

"For God's sake, May, this is no time to think about shopping. Can't you see that the child is exhausted? And you want to go dragging her around some mall," Lamar continued irritably while he started unloading suitcases.

"It's all right, mother. David packed me a few things. I just haven't had time to change into them," Jan said.

"We'll have plenty of time tomorrow to shop, dear. David, did you bring Jan's gown?"

"Gown? No, I forgot," David said.

"Just what did you expect her to sleep in?" May gently admonished her son-in-law. David had been in the family long enough to know she didn't mean what her tone of voice conveyed; that was just May's way. "Well, no matter now. You can borrow one of mine, dear, and we'll buy you plenty of gowns tomorrow. You can never have too many gowns."

Jan was self-conscious over the difference in the families. The Johnsons and Simpsons had unpacked the few clothes they brought and were now watching the news in their respective hotel rooms while their boys slept peacefully in the room between them. They had filled their ice buckets and found the drink and snack machines.

May and Meemaw set up a bar area while their men unloaded the car. As always, they had brought their own pillows, coffee pots, snacks and liquor. Then they went around to the dining room and arranged to have a table for all the families together, so that they could "get to know one another," May explained.

Lamar hugged his daughter and told her he loved her, not knowing what else to say. Papa Ralph patted her shoulder in his gruff way and told her to remember that she "came from good stock" and that "Calhouns can overcome anything." Then he winked and called her a sweet girl.

The Johnsons and Simpsons came out of their rooms to tell Mrs. Ferguson they would be indebted to her forever for saving their sons' lives. They declined an invitation from May to come in for drinks, saying they preferred to wake their boys and meet everyone downstairs at eight.

Jan allowed her family their solicitations, knowing that this was all they knew to do. She almost felt she was no older than Murray and Caleb. Poor David. He also wanted to take care of her, but he was outdone by Jan's family, and she knew it left him feeling as helpless as she did.

That evening's dinner was a social disaster. Alice Johnson tried her best to keep up with May and Meemaw in social graces and conversation. Bud Johnson caught Caleb up on farming business. Marge, Jim and Murray Simpson ate in silence, responding to the social chatter with an occasional nod. Papa Ralph tried unsuccessfully to prove to whomever would listen that land development was much like farming. Lamar patted his daughter's hand every once in a while and asked if she needed anything. John Larsen and David discussed the legal aspects of farm foreclosures.

Jan said nothing.

After dinner, the boys and their families retired to their rooms. May herded the rest into the Jameson's room for an after dinner drink and a family discussion of the matters at hand. Jan smiled politely while her parents, her grandparents, her husband and her attorney planned what would happen to her next.

"Now, Jan, I know that in the past I've spoken disdainfully of psychiatrists and the like, but even I think you should get some counseling when we get back home," Lamar told his daughter. "I've already lined up a good man in Atlanta. My college buddy, Bill Smythe, recommended him. You remember Dr. Smythe from Birmingham? Well, this is a doctor he knows in Atlanta – just a minute, honey, I know I had his name .... Here it is: Dr. Charles Oliver Carey IV, psychiatrist and clinical psychologist specializing in post traumatic stress."

Jan nodded, uninterested.

"Now, Bill tells me that this is the best man in the business. Those two titles just mean that he can treat you psychologically to get over this, and he can prescribe drugs, if that's what he feels you need. Honey, are you listening? Lamar asked. "This is all right with you, isn't it?"

"Sure, Daddy," Jan said. She had no feeling about it one way or the other. She was just waiting – waiting to feel something.

Jan knew that she could not go back to her life in Riverdale. She was no longer the young wife and teacher that had been kidnapped just a couple of days before. She didn't recognize who or what she was anymore.

Lamar continued. "He gave you a tentative appointment for Monday. Smythe seems to think the quicker you start dealing with this sort of thing, the better off you'll be. I told him I wouldn't push you and that if you weren't ready for this come Monday, we'd postpone," he said anxiously.

"Monday's fine, Daddy."

"All right, then. Now, this good lawyer here needs to talk with you. Honey, try to be as honest as you can with John. He's trying to help you, so you need to cooperate with him," Lamar advised.

John Larsen, taking Lamar's seat beside her on the bed, told Jan that the district attorney had arranged the preliminary hearing for Saturday at ten in the morning. "Jan? We need to talk about what is going to happen tomorrow morning," he said. "Why don't we go to my room? You can ask David to come along, if you like."

David was sitting across the room on the other bed, listening absentmindedly while Papa Ralph filled him with business advice. Occasionally he glanced her way. Jan wondered how he felt. The Bible said a man had every right to leave his wife if she committed adultery with another man. It didn't say anything about rape. Jan remembered a poem from *Spoon River Anthology*. It told of a woman who was kicked out by her husband because he found out that she had been raped when she was eight years old. The townspeople of Spoon River praised the husband – for, after all, she wasn't the package he had thought.

Jan knew David didn't believe that. Still, she decided to spare him the details and went alone to John's room. If she had seen the hurt on David's face when she left the room, she might have chosen differently.

John explained the purpose of the preliminary hearing and told her what to expect. "Now, as your attorney, I need to know everything."

"I'll tell you anything you need to know, only I want to spare David, my whole family, as much of the detail as possible," Jan said tiredly.

"Why don't you start from the beginning?" John said gently.

"Wednesday night, I went to school about seven to tutor Caleb and Murray. A little after eight, we heard someone come into the school. I *know* I had locked the door when we'd come in. We heard the footsteps down the hall. Two men – the man Punk and the man we later referred to as Van Driver – walked in, asked if I was Jan Ferguson, pulled out guns and told us to get into the van. They tied us up. Punk took Caleb's keys and drove in his truck. My car was already gone. About an hour, I don't really know how long, maybe more, the van driver stopped and picked up another man. About sunrise the van pulled up the road to the cabin."

Jan recounted the events of the past two days with little emotion. "Caleb's pickup was already there in the driveway and so was Punk. The men untied us and took us to the back bedroom. They were actually very polite, making sure we were comfortable and ordering Punk to keep us fed and warm. They told us we would be fine as long we lay low. They said that they hoped to be back sometime that night to get us home safely by Friday. When Punk went outside to get more wood, we heard the men talking about him, saying stuff, you know."

"What stuff?" John asked pointedly.

"Just stuff." Jan crossed and uncrossed her legs. How could she tell him that she had foreseen her downfall in that conversation; her fate had been laid out clearly for her before it even came to be, leaving her to wait in dread for it to come.

"Jan, I know this is difficult for you. But, more than likely, you will have to tell this again tomorrow in front of the judge, the district attorney, the sheriff, the coroner, me and whoever else happens to be there," John said. "You are also going to have to tell this over to the FBI agents who want to catch this ring. Wouldn't you rather say it first out loud to me in this room than waiting to tell it in front of everyone else tomorrow?"

Jan fidgeted. She looked around the room. Finally she stood up and walked nervously about. "I have this image, this terrible recurring image, but to put it into words ...." she trailed off. "You're right, of course. Stuff, yes. They were talking about how Punk had a thing for young women and how they'd had trouble with him before. They said he was okay as long as he didn't drink. They said they didn't think he would be around anymore after this job."

"You must have been scared," John said sympathetically. "So, what did you do?"

"They brought us a deck of cards so that we wouldn't be bored. They were very nice." She paused. Every muscle in her body ached, and she was tired, so very, very tired.

"And then the men left?" John said trying to urge her on.

"Yes, they left. We slept. Then he brought us some sandwiches."

"Who? Who brought you the sandwiches?" John pushed.

"Punk. He leered at me," she hesitated.

"Is that when?" John ventured.

"No, no, I had plenty of time to feel the anticipation of what was to come. He'd been drinking; I could smell it on him. We ate lunch and played cards. Caleb and Murray tried their best to keep my mind off of him, but they knew, too."

Jan was crying, but she continued with her story. "If only I'd been more cautious; if only I hadn't knocked over that Coke."

"Jan, you weren't alone. The boys were there, too." John tried to steer Jan away from the self-imposed guilt she had developed. He'd had enough basic psychology from law school to know that it's normal for a woman to feel that the attack might have been her own fault somehow.

He'd covered many rape cases before, but this girl he knew personally.

He walked across the room and put his arms around Jan as best he could. "You're just tired, honey. You had nothing whatsoever to do with this, and I won't hear of you saying that again. You need some rest. My God, who wouldn't after all you've been through? Just tell your story tomorrow and you'll prove self-defense. Just tell how this man came after you again. After all, he was holding a gun on the boys, was he not?"

Jan gained her composure. "No," she said moving out of John's embrace, "he did not come after me again. I shot him before he had the chance; I shot him while he was down because I couldn't bear the thought of him getting back up again."

Chapter Eight

Frank Woods was young to be district attorney. Thirty-three was hardly wet behind the ears according to those fifty-and-older working-class men connected to the Transylvania County Courthouse in Brevard. Ed Brown, the bailiff for the past thirty-five years, said before he even came that Frank Woods would be trouble. Frank had written a letter to all the employees of the courthouse and directed the retiring district attorney, Paul Laughter, to read it aloud at his going-away celebration.

"I believe in the laws of our nation and our states, for without them, personal freedom would give way to chaos and autocracy. Therefore, I aim to use the letter of the law against those who break the law rather than against their victims. I expect all court employees of my district to follow strict courtroom behavior, as I run a tight ship," Paul Laughter read from Woods' letter.

"I hate to run off and leave you with this guy," (polite laughter) "but, well, you know how it is. I understand that his uncle is the state senator who is chairman of the nominating subcommittee of the North Carolina Senate Judiciary Committee," Paul had said apologetically.

Paul had served only one year of his eighth four-year term, but his wife was diagnosed with terminal cancer, and he was taking early retirement. Frank Woods was appointed to finish Paul's term. Frank could impress anyone with his resume at the age of thirty-three, but in person he was an intolerable nitpicker for rules and what he considered solemn decorum and courtroom manners.

Ed Brown had Frank Woods pegged the minute he heard the letter. "I bet a week's wages this new DA is a little feller. Little fellers are always trying to act bigger than their britches." Ed paused while Sheriff

Lander snickered behind his right hand, which was almost always twirling and pulling at his bushy moustache. "He's probably Baptist. They're always legalistic about everything under the sun." Ed was enjoying himself. "Prob'ly got real limp, greasy sorta hair – or maybe one of them *poofahnts*."

Willa Lander, Sheriff Melvin Lander's thirty-two-year-old daughter, had compassion for the new DA before she even met him. Willa had privileged information about Frank Wood's background, and she made sure that all her cronies knew it. Willa was friends at the University of North Carolina at Asheville with a first cousin of Frank's on his father's side. She thought his story was wrought with class-based drama and irony.

"Frank's parents were just made for a D.H. Lawrence novel, don't you think?" Willa would interrupt her own story. "You see ...." and she would go on.

Frank's mother was the dainty, reserved, shy daughter of wealthy parents. But she was painfully introverted. She met Frank Sr. in the theater department of Appalachian State University. He came from several generations of Woods who grew burley tobacco in the Boone, North Carolina, area. He dropped out of high school in the ninth grade to work as a car mechanic. For extra money, he hired on at the university theater department.

It was love at first sight for Frank Sr., and no man had ever paid attention to Grace before. Grace's parents objected, but Grace was stubborn and eloped with Frank Sr. anyway. When Frank Jr. reached puberty, his grandfather offered to send him to private school if he would live with Grace's parents. When Grandfather later sent him to law school, Frank Jr. vowed to make the Woods name proud beyond his mountain clan.

Within her friend's bantering tales about her persnickety cousin, Willa recognized a kindred soul. She could see clearly that this poor man had been unappreciated. She, too, had grown up among simple people who did not recognize her obvious talents. She had been taunted and teased as a child for being large.

By the time District Attorney Frank Woods arrived, the courthouse staff and other business regulars had formed their own opinions of him. As it was to turn out, these attitudes were tame compared to the ones formed six months *after* his arrival. But the week before he was due to take office, Frank wrote to all courthouse employees and requested a meeting.

"The judicial system is dependent on such men and women as yourselves who take care of the daily details of a courthouse and the business carried on within," he began arrogantly.

Willa was awed. Nobody before had taken her job as seriously as she did.

"In a show of community spirit," Frank continued, "each of you can be the best he can be by following these simple rules."

Frank went on to say that all employees were required to tend to daily grooming habits. He further directed the employees to brush their teeth, wash their face and comb their hair before arriving to work. Daily baths or showers, deodorant and manicured nails were required for all. Men were to wear a coat and tie at all times, and no boots allowed. Women were to wear dresses or skirts, below the knees, closed-toe shoes and proper underclothing.

"After all, we want to inspire the confidence of the public in our judicial system," Frank ended.

"I only own one suit, and that's for weddings and funerals," Ed Brown said.

"Well sir, Mr. Bailiff, if you can't follow the specifications for your job, perhaps you are working in the wrong place. Now I know this is a big change for some of you older employees, but look on this as a whole new job and a boost in your career."

Willa smiled smugly as she looked around at the loose and unprofessional attire of her colleagues. She was one of few who already met Mr. Woods' high standards.

In addition to rules on dress, manners and decorum, Frank had devised an elaborate list of rules which, when broken, earned demerits that equaled docked pay. The money was put into an account that accumulated until the end of the year. This money was reward for top employees, to be judged by Frank. Tardiness, absences, excessive breaks and even excessive talking were covered under the demerit system.

No doubt about it, Frank Woods planned on making the Transylvania County Courthouse a model in his judicial district. He wanted to prove to Uncle Ernest, his mother's brother, that he more than deserved this appointment.

When Willa called Frank that Friday afternoon with the news of the man shot up in Pisgah by a girl he raped, Frank's heart leapt with the possibilities of such a case. He forced himself to wait until after dinner that evening when Willa could share details of the kidnapping she had learned at the family supper table.

"Daddy says she's a teacher and the two boys are her students. But she sure didn't look like any teacher I ever had; she looked just as much like a student as those boys did. She's a little thing, too." Willa had befriended Frank from the beginning by filling him in on unreported breaches of the rules of his new system. She had also taken a few hundred dollars from her nest egg and spent it on more flattering clothes. Ed Brown, one of the courthouse regulars, swore she was wearing makeup now.

"But the most amazing thing, Mr. Woods, is that even though she was kidnapped and raped by this man she killed, she told Daddy that she killed him and he wasn't even coming after her. Daddy says that she doesn't know what she's saying because of all she's been through."

Frank snapped to attention with this latest bit of detail. He had hope for a case, after all. He patted Willa's arm. "Thank you for sharing this. But let's keep what you tell me *our little secret*," he said.

Sheriff Lander would be mortified if he knew his eldest daughter had repeated confidential information shared around the family dinner table. He had never had reason to suspect she would do such a thing before. The sheriff had, however, noticed many things about Willa that had changed since the new DA arrived, and he didn't like what he saw.

Chapter Nine

By the time the preliminary hearing began at ten a.m. the next morning, news of the kidnapping, shooting and escape had somehow reached not only the local newspaper, the *Transylvania Gazette*, but also the larger regional paper in Asheville, the *Asheville Citizen-Times*.

Jan, her family, the boys, their parents and John Larsen were already at the courthouse when the press arrived. Sheriff Lander couldn't figure out how they found out so quickly. The local reporter only came to check the arrest sheet and report on Mondays and Wednesdays, and the Asheville press rarely personally checked his reports. Then he glanced over at his daughter leaning against the water fountain with a self-righteous expression.

Damn it, Sheriff Lander thought. *That girl's meddling has gone too far this time, even if she is my own flesh and blood.*

"Sheriff Lander!" Finley Holbert, the young, local reporter, yelled as he ran up to the sheriff. "I understand there has been a kidnapping, rape and a shooting." The boy was so excited he could hardly stand it. This was his territory and the veteran Asheville reporter, Virgil Noland, had to follow his cue. "Could you give us the details, please?"

"Now, boys, we haven't even had the hearing yet. You just get on out of here, and I'll get you what you need in plenty of time. Don't you be getting in the way of the judicial process now, you hear?" Sheriff Lander said sternly.

But the Asheville reporter had already spotted Jan, the only person to fit the description Willa gave over the phone, and he was on her like a cat on tuna.

"Excuse me, Mrs. Ferguson?" he said as his photographer

started snapping pictures. "I'm Virgil Noland with the *Asheville Citizen.* Could I talk with you a moment?"

Jan was horrified. Was there no end to the news of her shame?

"Get on out of here, boy," Papa Ralph said gruffly. "There's nothing you need to know here."

John came to the rescue. "Excuse me, but Mrs. Ferguson has no comment. You can get your information from the sheriff's report in due time."

"Information, hell!" Papa Ralph shouted. "There'll be no information because it's none of your damn business! Don't you think she's been through enough without you plastering what you know nothing about all over the papers?"

"Now, Ralph," Lamar said. "These young men are just trying to do their jobs. I know they wouldn't do anything to jeopardize justice, now would you, boys?"

Frank Woods appeared and summoned Jan, Caleb, Murray and John into the courtroom.

"Why, gentlemen of the press, if you will just wait until after this hearing, I'll be glad to answer all of your questions. You can wait in the courthouse lobby," Frank said taking full advantage of the situation. "We must let justice take its due course, after all," he added as he followed the others into the courtroom and the bailiff shut the door behind him.

"You young men might as well go on home, because there will be no public information concerning my daughter!" May flew at the reporters and photographer with a vengeance.

Lamar grabbed May by the arm. "Come on, May." He turned to Papa Ralph, Meemaw and David. "We might as well go around the corner for a cup of coffee. We're not doing anyone any good here."

The Simpsons and Johnsons were relieved to follow Lamar.

Inside the courtroom, Jan and the boys were ushered to an area below the judge's bench where six jurors sat. The four men and two women could have been people from any small Southern town. The jurors were middle-aged to older. Jan couldn't remember what it was they had to decide. She had already told anyone who would listen that she shot the beast.

Frank was in his element. He explained to the jurors and to Jan and the boys that this hearing was just a formality to determine if, in fact, a crime was committed. "These fine citizens have come here on a

Saturday to take all the evidence presented by the sheriff, the coroner and the witnesses present at the time. They are here to see justice done, as are the rest of the court. I'll be doing the questioning. Please swear in the witnesses."

Sheriff Lander was planning to keep mum about Jan's confession because her lawyer was not present at the time. Coroner Buddy Lee had no recourse but to state the condition of the body at the cabin. He could not get around the fact that the man had been shot while lying on his back and that he had been unarmed. He also could not hide the fact that there were three bullet wounds at close range.

Buddy Lee read from the coroner's report which stated that the man had been in a prone position already when shot, that he had a contusion to the right side of his head, that the contusion had caused him to fall and that the shots were fired after he fell.

"Now, let's see, you are Mrs. Ferguson?" the D.A. asked. "And which of you men is Mr. Simpson?"

Murray raised his hand.

"And you must be Mr. Johnson." Frank nodded toward Caleb.

Caleb barely returned the nod; his hands were folded nervously in front of him.

"Now, Mr. Johnson and Mr. Simpson, I have before me here statements made by both of you that you believe that if Mrs. Ferguson had not shot and killed Mr. McQuirk, then Mr. McQuirk would have killed the two of you. Is that correct?"

Caleb nodded and Murray spoke out, "Yes, sir."

"Was Mr. McQuirk in a lying position when he was shot by Mrs. Ferguson?"

Again Caleb nodded and Murray spoke up, "Yes, sir."

"I see. Can you tell me how a man flat on his back with no weapon could have killed you?"

"He had already come after us with the gun and he would have killed us then if Mrs. Ferguson hadn't hit him with that rock," Caleb practically shouted.

"I see. Then how did Mrs. Ferguson come to have the gun, and how did Mr. McQuirk come to be lying down on his back?" Frank asked.

"You see, sir," Murray said, "we had just escaped from the bathroom window. Jan, Mrs. Ferguson, ran ahead, while we, Caleb and I, were still climbing out of the window. Punk came around the side of the cabin with the gun. He was laughing about how he could shoot us because we were escaping. But he didn't see Jan through the trees. She was trying to save us, and she threw a rock that hit him in the side of the head, and he fell down. He lost his rifle when he fell, and it landed at Mrs. Ferguson's feet." Murray looked expectantly at the D.A.

"Mrs. Ferguson," the D.A. turned his attention to Jan. "Did it ever occur to you that since you had the gun in your hands at the time that Mr. McQuirk was lying prone and, I might add, facing away from you, that you had the upper hand in the situation without having to resort to killing him? And even if you had meant only to wound the man, why did you pull the trigger a second and even a third time?"

Feeling the D.A.'s accusation, Jan said nothing.

"He would've come after us. He would've killed us!" Caleb yelled. "She saved our lives."

"Mr. Woods, I don't believe ..." John Larsen began.

"Counselor, there is nothing for you to believe or not to believe. I want only the facts in this case." Frank turned again to Jan. "Young woman, I realize that you have been through a terrible ordeal, but you still have your life. Mr. McQuirk was entitled to as fair a trial for what he did to you as you are for what you did to him."

Frank then turned to the jurors. "Ladies and gentlemen of the jury, I would like to remind you that you are not to consider what happened before the shooting, or what could have happened moments later, but the exact moment only of the shooting and the subsequent death. You must not be swayed by sympathy for Mrs. Ferguson to determine if this case should go before a grand jury for indictment. It is my and your duty to uphold the letter of the law. After all, what is our great system of judicial democracy and freedom all about without the law?"

The preliminary hearing went quickly. The jurors felt they had no choice but to turn the matter over to the grand jury. The ruling was simply that Artemis Delmer McQuirk had died due to three gunshot wounds to the head and upper torso, at the hand of Janet Jameson Ferguson.

"Janet Jameson Ferguson," Woods looked directly at her. "I have no choice under the laws of our state but to charge you with the second-degree murder of Artemis Delmer McQuirk. Whether or not you are indicted for murder in the death of Mr. McQuirk will be up to the grand jury. In the meantime, I will set a bond of $50,000 and release you into the custody of your family. The grand jury meets the second Monday after the New Year, and twelve jurors will be the ones to decide whether or not to put this case before a jury of the citizens of this fair county."

John Larsen did not protest. He did not even look worried. "Jan, this means nothing. I don't see how a grand jury would indict you. We can go home now and face the rest after the New Year." He put his arm around Jan and walked her out of the courtroom.

Frank Woods ran ahead and opened the door. "Perhaps I can escort you to the magistrate's office where you will post bond," Frank said smugly.

"We can handle it ourselves, thank you," John replied without even looking his way.

Sheriff Lander, the coroner and the boys were waiting in the hall. The forlorn group watched in silent hatred as Frank rounded the corner.

"You call that justice?" Caleb fumed helplessly.

"The bastard," Sheriff Lander muttered. "I'm so sorry, Mrs. Ferguson, but I have no choice but to take you to the magistrate's office to post bond. And it being Saturday and all, I'm going to have to round him up first. But you and the boys and Mr. Larsen can wait in my office. Don't you worry, honey," he said patting her shoulder. "I'm not about to put you in jail. I'll send a deputy to bring your husband and family over."

Ken Thompson, as special agent in charge of the kidnapping aspect of the case, was waiting for them when they returned to Sheriff Lander's office. Jan and the boys were his only concrete link to the interstate kidnapping ring. He and Sheriff Lander had tried to talk Woods out of seeking prosecution for Jan.

"This is just a formality," John assured the family members gathered in the sheriff's office. "Jan will need to talk with Ken Thompson here for a minute, but after we post bond, we're all free to go."

Lamar wrote out a check for five thousand dollars, ten percent of the bond as required. The magistrate informed Jan that she would be expected to appear before the grand jury of Transylvania County on January 10, 2006. If the grand jury returned a true bill, Jan's case would then go to superior court in Brevard, probably in early spring, the magistrate said.

The sheriff stepped forward. "I just want you folks to know that we aren't proud about this in our county. That Woods is just a young upstart who is trying to make something of himself. If I have anything to do with it, this will be the end of his public career," the sheriff apologized. "If I had the chance, I would've killed that son-of-a-bitch up there myself. The way I see it, you did us a favor, though I know you didn't mean to. It's times like these that make me not want to run for sheriff come next election," he said to Lamar and Papa Ralph.

"We're much obliged," Papa Ralph said, patting the sheriff on the back before turning to his family. "Now, what say let's grab us a bite to eat at a nice mountain spot before we head back to Atlanta?"

"Are you up for lunch?" Lamar asked his daughter, kissing her on the head.

"Sure, Dad. I know David's about to starve because he didn't eat much breakfast," she said.

"John?"

"I have some business to attend to first. I'll meet you back at the plane," he answered.

John had called a law school friend, Leonard Snelling, to get some background on Frank Woods.

"I want you to know that I'm not at all surprised to see that you are taking this case," Leonard said as they sat down to a window table at a local restaurant.

"She's like family. I've worked for her grandfather since I was in high school," John said. "He put me through school, you know. She's innocent. There's no way any law can punish someone who defends herself and then is morally compelled to feel responsible for the death of her attacker."

"But you really want to know about Frank Woods, right?" Leonard grinned.

"I don't understand how anyone can possibly see Jan as guilty, not after what she went through," John said.

"In all fairness to Woods, John, your client has continually said that she shot the man by choice, that it was not self defense," Leonard pointed out. "Also, the man she killed didn't plot to kidnap her. Other men hired him to be driver, guard and lookout."

"That's supposed to be confidential information," John said displeased.

"It's not common knowledge in the community, but this

72

kind of case can't be kept secret from local law circles; you know that," Leonard said. "And the letter of the law does support Woods' prosecution – you're going to have to face that," he said.

"There's not a jury in the world who would convict her; not after they realize that the man would have killed them all if she hadn't shot him. This confession of hers is some weird way she has of abolishing herself of the guilt she feels for the whole ordeal. At least she's allowing me to plead not guilty for her," John said. "But that's my problem. I need to know what I'm up against with Woods."

"Woods has been out of law school maybe six years," Leonard began. "He graduated from Cumberland Law School in Birmingham, Alabama, and then he joined the D.A.'s office over in Hickory. Within six months, he was second assistant to the solicitor there, and when he heard from his uncle, the senator, that there was going to be an opening here in Brevard, he applied for the job even before our last D.A. announced his resignation," Leonard explained.

"How can that happen? It takes years to groom for such a job," John asked.

"His uncle on his mother's side is a state senator. This Woods has been looking for a controversial case to prove himself," Leonard offered.

"So, when he found out about Jan's confession to the sheriff, he jumped right on the case to prosecute her?" John added.

"Right. Lander's upset that the information was leaked. He feels bad about this, like it's his fault or something that she's been charged with murder. I keep telling him he wouldn't have been doing his job if he'd not let Woods hear the tapes when asked. You have a situation where doing one's job and telling the truth is incriminating. It happens," Leonard said.

"Sheriff Lander's been great. I just hate to see such a weasel as Woods further his career at Jan's expense. Guys like him give us all a bad name," John said. "If he really thought that he was right, that Jan deserved punishment, it would be different. But he's such a damned wimp, he couldn't look me in the eye. He looked Jan in the eye, though; tried to intimidate her from the beginning. But Jan's one tough cookie. He won't get to her very easily," John rambled in rage.

"Will she take the psychiatric help?" Leonard asked. "Surely a doctor can claim temporary insanity from fear and stress," he suggested.

"That's what I'm hoping for. It's my only real defense, other than depending on the sympathy of the jury," John said. "But I suppose Transylvania County is like any rural community; a lot of white laborers who keep their women in their place and have little sympathy for the sexual dangers a young woman may fall into."

"Now wait a minute. I'd like to take up for my community. My wife and I are happy here," Leonard said. "You may be partly right. Not many locals would see a killing as equal to a rape. But try to look past the stereotypes; give us some credit."

"Point taken," John said.

"Look, John, you can use my office and my staff any time you need to when you're here. If I can help in any way, you let me know. Meantime, I'll keep my ear out for all the legal gossip and let you know if Woods is planning any surprises," Leonard said earnestly.

"Thanks. I guess that's all we can do right now," John said as he shook Leonard's hand and stood to go.

David agreed with Jan's parents that the best thing now was for Jan to return to Georgia with her family. He arranged to take several more days off work to go with her. He also arranged through the academy headmaster for Jan to take an open-ended leave of absence.

While Jan and her family were posting bond, Caleb and Murray and their families had returned to the hotel to pack. They wanted to get on back to Riverdale. They waited to leave, however, so that the boys could say goodbye to Mrs. Ferguson. It was a tearful farewell.

"I've done some research on the prosecutor," John Larsen was telling Papa Ralph and Lamar over the roar of the plane engine as they took off for Atlanta. "He only has a few years of practice under his belt, and he has a crusader's drive to do everything by the book."

"Where'd you get your information?" Papa Ralph asked.

"I looked up a law school friend in Brevard. He said Frank Woods has been giving them all headaches since he stepped into the position eight months ago. Woods sees Jan's case as a way to be recognized as one of America's up-and-coming young prosecutors."

"Damn shame we're going to have to rub his nose in his own shit," Papa Ralph growled.

"Now, Ralph, the main thing is to get this guy to see that he has no case against Jan," Lamar warned his father-in-law. "Don't go and rile the guy by trying to show him up. If you make him mad, he might just fight harder. Flies are best caught with sugar. You know that."

"I'm not going to do anything to jeopardize my granddaughter's safety, Lamar. I'm just saying that the little upstart ought to learn who the real criminals are in this world instead of picking on someone like Jan," he said.

David put a comforting arm around Jan, who found this irritating, and she rearranged her seating.

"The most important thing for you to remember, Jan – all of you – is to let me do all the talking from here on out to Woods, the press, everyone," John said. "And, Jan, I don't want to hear any nonsense like you've been talking these past two days."

"Now, you listen to John," Papa Ralph directed Jan. "You just keep your mouth shut and let us worry about how everything is done."

"We're just trying to protect you," Lamar said, gently patting Jan's knee. "I know you're worried and don't want to lie to anyone, but honey, you have to let us handle this."

Jan had heard all she could take. "How can any of you handle this? When not one of you was there! This Frank Woods won't be asking *you* the questions, he'll be asking *me*. I was there. I can't lie about what took place; I have to tell it the way it happened!"

Jan's outburst startled them all. She had been so quiet, so accepting. The general consensus was that she was still in shock.

"We don't want you to lie," John said, trying not to upset her. "We just want you to structure what you say to your advantage. You don't want to end up in jail, do you?"

All four men were looking at her. She ignored the question and turned toward the window to watch the passing of the quilted patches of farmland that spread out below them.

Chapter Ten

"Everything is going to be all right now, darling," May said hugging Jan to her in the car on the way home from Atlanta. "We're going home." She ran her fingers through Jan's hair as she had done when Jan was a child.

Jan looked around at her family. They fell eagerly into unrelated conversations, trying to block out this *unpleasantness*, as May referred to the events of the past few days. She was beginning to appreciate the cocoon of protection they wove around her.

"Don't you think so, Jan, darling?" Jan heard her mother ask. "Jan, are you all right? Did you hear me ask you if going to the psychiatrist on Monday is too soon?"

Jan turned back from the window. "Monday is fine, Mother," she answered.

The silence on the remainder of the ride home did not prepare the weary group for the welcoming they received at 21 Calhoun Street. Three vans and a car were parked at the front of the house and at least ten people were milling around on the front lawn.

Not even John could have guessed that the press would be so far reaching. He figured by Monday the news would begin to be known, but not today. He knew Woods was responsible. The local TV station and one from Atlanta, plus the *Kingsford Times* and the *Atlanta Constitution* were represented.

It was close to 10 p.m. when Lamar pulled down his drive with John right behind him. The crowd in the yard jumped into action. Lights appeared and flashes went off everywhere. Lamar slowly unfolded from the car. "There's no story here and no comments, so y'all just go on home," he fumed.

But the horde edged themselves on with their competitive force. "Mr. Jameson!" several reporters called at once. "Sir, is it true that your daughter has been charged with killing her abductor and rapist?"

"Mr. Jameson, can you tell us something about this kidnapping ring?"

John pushed his way through the swarm. "Gentlemen, ladies, please," he said. "Lamar, get in the car. Let me handle this," he shouted over to Lamar.

"Please, people of the press, I am Mrs. Ferguson's attorney."

The crowd finally heard him and turned, quieting. "We have just returned from a difficult trip," he said without shouting, "and Mrs. Ferguson, all of us, are exhausted. I cannot give you any details without jeopardizing the case. I suggest you leave and give this woman and her family some peace."

"Your name, sir," someone from the back yelled.

"John Larsen, L-a-r-s-e-n, Kingsford attorney," he replied. "I'm sorry I can't be of more help at this time. Now, if you'll excuse us."

The media mass began breaking up, talking over the scant details with each other, shooting distant, useless images as the family made a dash for the house.

Jan's safe cocoon fell away. All these people knew what she had endured, and they were going to tell the rest of the world.

"Why, Jan, honey, you're shaking like a leaf," May said. "Are you cold, dear?" She put her arm around her daughter and rubbed her shoulders. "Don't pay any attention to those uncouth reporters, darling. Come take a nice, long bath while I fix us a hot toddy," May whispered soothingly.

On Monday, May insisted on driving Jan to Atlanta for her 4:30 doctor's appointment. David desperately wanted to go along, but May insisted that Jan would be more comfortable with "just the girls." He felt useless and anxious in Kingsford, and he was eager to return to work in Riverdale. Jan showed no desire to return with him.

Jan had numbly agreed to go shopping with May before the appointment. Though David had brought a few of her clothes, nothing appealed to her. Nothing interested her in the stores either. May brought her suits, dresses and tailored pants to try on.

"Mom," Jan said, "I'd rather pick my clothes out."

"All right, dear, just tell me what style you have in mind, and I'll ask the salesgirl to help us," May said.

"I don't want the woman to help me, I don't want *anyone* to help me." Jan was getting frustrated. She didn't care how she looked; she just wanted to be comfortable.

After choosing several cotton skirts, a cardigan and a turtleneck, Jan headed for the jeans section.

"Don't forget something dressy, dear," May pushed. "You must show those people in court that you are someone. Try some silks, dear. You may have anything you want."

Two linen dresses, a silk skirt and several pairs of shoes later, the mother and daughter went for coffee before Jan's appointment. The cafe was directly across the street from the office complex where she was to meet Dr. Chad Carey at 4:30.

At 4:15 Jan stood up and told her mother that she would meet her back there after she was finished. May said nothing.

Dr. Charles Oliver Carey IV leaned back in his desk chair, removed his glasses and rubbed his eyes. For him, psychiatry had become not the treatment of mental disorders, but the treatment of people who were too weak and too shallow to take control of their own lives. Any hocus-pocus television evangelist could probably be as likely to help these people. After fifteen years of practice, Dr. Carey had treated manic-depressives, schizophrenics, trauma victims and other disorders. But too many of his patients had merely personality quirks or severe insecurity.

His last patient was a disaster. When Mrs. Matthews went into her usual tirade over her husband, who had left her two years prior, Dr. Carey had jumped out of his chair and, attempting shock value, had yelled, "So what? So damn what, Mrs. Matthews? It's over and done with. It was over the minute he walked out. Are you going to live through this the rest of your life, or are you going to do something about your future? Your life today is far better than when you were married to the jerk. You ought to thank him for doing you a favor and handing you back control over your own life."

Dr. Carey turned quite a few patients away with this attitude. Money or not, he could not bring himself to humor someone who refused to face a very manageable problem and then do something about it.

In his present state of mind, the psychiatrist did not see how he could professionally deal with his last patient of the day. He had agreed to take her on as an emergency at the request of a fellow psychiatrist he knew mostly through meetings and conventions. Bill Smythe lived in the small town of Kingsford, about an hour from Atlanta. The patient's father had called Carey Saturday at home to make today's appointment.

This woman had been through a real trauma. The story was all over the newspapers and the television, but Dr. Carey had not had a chance to catch all the details. He dropped his head into his hands just as the door opened and he looked up into the eyes of a petite and attractive young woman. She was dressed in a full skirt, a loose fitting blouse, and lace-up boots.

When Jan looked at Dr. Carey she was taken aback. He was nothing like the stereotypical psychiatrist she had envisioned after knowing her father's friend, Dr. Smythe. She was coming to this psychiatrist to ease the minds of her family. In her mind, she knew exactly what had happened to her and how to deal with it. She felt no aftermath other than not being able to dismiss certain involuntary scenes that flashed through her mind. What had happened to her was between her and God.

Jan had always been a churchgoer, a believer in a simple faith. Now looking back on her years in church, she decided that she hadn't been soulfully involved. She knew that whatever transgression was implied in those horrid couple of days, she wanted the expert on sin, not man.

"Please, have a seat. Call me Chad," Dr. Carey said rising. He sensed her defiance as he motioned her to the chair just to the side of his desk rather than the formidable couch against the opposite wall. "Did you fill out a medical chart? Just preliminary, you know, so I can check your physical well being." He smiled as he took the form.

Jan relaxed in Dr. Carey's office. There was no flourescent lighting; only beautiful lamps of varied sizes and shapes gently illuminated the office. Yes, this office probably suits this man, she thought as she stole a glance his way. She had noticed the dirty buck oxfords he wore when he pulled his legs off his desk. He must be in his forties, she guessed. He had blue eyes and an open-collared shirt under his loosened tie. He wasn't athletically built, but he was lean, tall and he looked emotionally human about the eyes. Behind the doctor's desk were only a few medical histories, some Freud and Jung, but most of the books were literature and philosophy: Proust, Plato, Aristotle, the Greek plays, Beowulf, C.S. Lewis, Tolkein, Vonnegut. Several translations of the Bible were scattered in between.

"Let's see, Jan," Dr. Carey hesitated, and Jan realized he didn't quite know what to do with her. She felt comforted knowing that he knew as little about her as she knew about him.

Dr. Carey scanned the notes he had taken from Lamar. "Well, you're not at all what I had pictured as ...." Dr. Carey stopped himself.

"Someone who killed a man after he raped her?" Jan suggested. It was easy to state the reality.

"Well, yes," Dr. Carey smiled warmly. "Is it hard for you to say those words aloud? 'Rape' and 'killed'?" he asked.

"Not really. I can talk about the facts; it all seems so long ago. Far away." She sat expectantly, smiling slightly, waiting for him to continue.

He leaned across the edge of the desk and, folding his hands before him, looked at Jan and decided that the best way to handle her case was by following what he felt naturally.

"Why don't you tell me a little bit about yourself, Jan?" Only in severe personality disorders had this question failed to work, because most people have a natural love of talking about themselves.

"There's not much to tell," Jan smiled. "I live in Riverdale, South Carolina, where I teach high school English. I'm married to an officer at the savings and loan. My parents sent me to you because I've gone through what, I guess, should be called a trauma."

"You said, 'should be called a trauma.' Do you not feel your experience was a trauma?" Dr. Carey asked.

"Well, I suppose at the time it was a trauma, as I was certainly frightened, but I have no overlapping fears or anger. I catch visions of different parts sometimes. It's over; there is no threat of that man coming after me again. He's dead. I don't mistrust all men; this man certainly wasn't representative of most men. I've learned something about human nature and myself in general." Almost without a pause, she steered the conversation in his direction. "I see you like to read."

"Yes," he answered. Jan was telling him all the points he would eventually persuade her to see after several probing sessions of admitting to anger, hurt and fear. Now what?

Jan laughed. "You look so serious. You don't have to treat me with kid gloves; I won't break."

"So, what do you like to read?" Dr. Cary asked, pulling his folded hands across the desk and leaning back in his chair.

"Mostly fiction. Many of the authors you have on your shelf," she said. "I've discovered a new love for poetry since I've been teaching," she said.

"And how long have you been teaching?" he asked.

"This is my second year," she answered.

"Do you plan to continue teaching? Go back to your life in Riverdale?"

Jan's hands were on the arms of her chair; she gently rubbed the worn wooden curves.

Dr. Carey saw that Jan couldn't get past now to the future. He knew that she was using all of her might to hold herself together to reason and think her way through the feelings he was sure she was having. He sat patiently and waited.

"I may take an extended leave of absence. I may take the rest of the year off. I don't know right now," she said guardedly. "Do ask me another one," she leaned forward with that reassuring smile. Or was she covering up?

"I understand that there were two students kidnapped with you," Dr. Cary probed carefully.

Jan nodded.

"Did they witness you being raped?"

"No," Jan said quietly, looking down at her hands. She began to shake uncontrollably. "No," she repeated, swallowing hard. "But they heard."

"And you don't want to go back to your job because you don't want to face them, is that it?" he asked.

Jan looked up. "We went through a lot together. We have a bond. It's the other students I don't want to see. I just don't want to teach anymore. I don't know what I want to do, but I don't want to teach. Teaching is such a limited and, many times, humiliating job. It has nothing to do with English, with words, of which I'm so fond. Because of this court case hanging over my head, I'll have a lot of waiting to do," she said.

"How do you feel about your charges and the legal battle ahead?" the doctor asked.

"How does anyone feel about facing a murder trial? If you were the district attorney you would have said, *How do you feel about having to face a trial for killing the man who raped you?*" Jan wasn't hostile, but she was no longer smiling.

"I'm sorry. I didn't mean to be so insensitive. You have probably answered so many questions already and have had to tell the story over and over again. You don't have to talk about it if you don't want to, but you can also tell me things you can't tell others. I'm not family, and I'm not out to get you," Dr. Carey said.

His kindness overwhelmed Jan. She fought the lump in her throat.

"It's not that I mind talking about it, about what happened. It's just that nobody wants to hear the part I want to talk about. They want the goriness, the tale, the facts. Nobody will talk to me about what really counts, about the big picture. Am I an adulteress? Why do I feel no guilt for killing that man? Would he have been treated as awfully as I have if he had been charged with my rape? But then I would have to see him again, have to know that he was out there somewhere and that he would be back; he would find me and do that again. Now, I know he won't be back." Jan surprised herself; she wept.

Dr. Carey rose from his desk and hugged her shoulders.

"I'm sorry. I didn't know I was going to do that," Jan whimpered, trying to pull herself together after a minute.

"I'm glad. Crying is cleansing. May I get you a Coke or a cup of coffee?" Dr. Carey asked. He walked back to his desk. "Here. I have a clean coffee cup. I'll split my Coke with you."

"Thank you. That would be nice." Jan gave a half smile. "You know, when I think back on the whole story now, it plays like a detective novel. It keeps playing back in slow motion." She paused and looked Dr. Carey in the eye. "I am a totally different person today than I was a week ago. You know what I mean?" She sipped her Coke.

"Yes. I do." He took a sip, waiting for her to go on. But she sat quietly.

"Of course you are a changed person. You have confronted pure evil; and you conquered it," he led into the subject he wanted.

"Yes, I did, didn't I?" Jan smiled. "On that level it is so simple. Do you believe in good and evil?" she asked.

"Most definitely. We are all capable of both. That is part of the human dilemma. But you didn't willingly choose evil. It was thrust upon you."

"Oh, but I did choose evil. I chose to kill that man, and I don't feel guilty about it. I feel guilty about being raped. Do you think God can separate the act from the people in the act?"

"Whoa. You've raised some heavy theological questions. Your

guilt for being raped stems from your memory of being part of it. Your guilt is really shame and the hopelessness you felt in not being able to prevent the act." Dr. Carey recognized her spiritual struggle and he didn't want to be too secular in his approach.

"Yes, I see that. But it doesn't change the way I feel." Jan waited for him to continue.

"No, of course not," he said gently. "You're still working through this. As you've said, there are so many levels to face, and your family and those connected with your possible trial are only allowing you to deal with the surface level. That's what I'm for. You can tell me anything on any level with no fear of judgment or personal feelings on my part. I am your sounding board," he nodded. "As for the spiritual questions you raise of guilt and sin, only your God can answer those questions. You have to turn within yourself to listen for God's answer."

He paused.

"That can be difficult, but I believe you have already begun the process on your own. I'd like to help you with the rest of it," he offered.

Jan waited.

"Jan, I know I have just met you, but I cannot see anything evil about you at all," Dr. Carey said.

His secretary buzzed and Dr. Carey picked up the phone. "Uh-huh, um, well, send her in," he said.

"It's probably my mother," Jan said wearily. "She wants to talk with you."

Dr. Carey nodded at Jan as May stepped through the door.

"Hello, Dr. Carey. I'm May Jameson, Jan's mother. She extended a manicured hand. "So, how is my girl?" she asked.

"She is just fine, Mrs. Jameson. I would like to see her every other day for a couple of weeks. Is that okay with you, Jan?" He looked directly at her when he asked.

"Yes," she nodded.

"I'm free before ten every morning, or, if you prefer afternoons, I'm free after 4:30 or 5," he said looking up from his appointment book.

"Mornings," Jan said.

"But dear, you would have to leave the house by 7:30 in the morning for the long drive," May fretted.

"That's fine. I like mornings best," Jan insisted.

Jan rose from her seat and extended her hand. "Thank you, Dr.

Carey. I'll see you Wednesday."

"I want to thank you again for taking us on such short notice, Dr. Carey," May said. "I've written our mailing address and phone number in case you need to get in touch with us and for billing purposes. Jan's father and I will be paying for her treatment."

May handed him a folded piece of paper she pulled from her purse.

After they left, Dr. Carey opened the paper to find a long note. May was concerned about what she considered *bizarre behavior* on the part of her daughter. May noted that Jan's taste in clothes had *changed drastically* and *she keeps saying she has to have loose clothing; she can't be confined.* May also mentioned that Jan slept *alone in her old bedroom rather than sleep with her husband in the guest room.* May's noted ended with a few words on her daughter's mood, saying that Jan was consistently *self-absorbed and irritable.*

Dr. Carey smiled, remembering that note as he started his car later that afternoon. This information was helpful, but he saw behind it a mother who had always taken control for her daughter. He knew that the result of this kind of relationship is usually an adult who cannot make her own decisions. Sometimes trauma will shake the rebel, causing the undefined woman to give herself clarity. The doctor was also aware that there existed other cases in which trauma pushed the person to self-destruction, or even schizophrenia, giving herself varied definitive characters but no whole.

In this particular case, it all remained to be seen.

Jan's key to her new definition of self was that she had not given in to the trauma but had faced it and conquered it by killing the man who raped her.

Dr. Carey wanted to buy all the area newspapers and read as much about the case now as he could find.

PART TWO

Chapter One

Jan opened her eyes leisurely and found herself in her childhood room. She had always felt secure in this room. For a brief moment, that security returned and she forgot herself in time, until she sat up and caught herself in the mirror. The innocence was gone. She looked tired and sad.

Late that evening, David would be coming from Riverdale for Thanksgiving.

"We haven't had the whole family together in years," May said at least once an hour. "Let's see, how long has it been, Jan? Three years? With all your family here and having such a lovely time, you'll forget all this mess in no time. That's all you need, a good dose of family support," Jan's mother told her last night when she kissed her goodnight.

Jan knew May was wrong, but she appreciated her well-meaning solicitations. She was looking forward to Thanksgiving. Papa Ralph had a weekend farmhouse fifteen miles outside Kingsford where the yearly Thanksgiving feast was held.

Jan could not think beyond Thanksgiving. She couldn't see herself going back to Riverdale. She thought about their little brick, one-story house in a neighborhood with few trees. They had a formal living room she only used for bridge. The yard, which once seemed so spacious, she now remembered as its true small size. The street was too close to the house; the neighbors were too near. She couldn't think of a single person she would miss there.

Her old radio clock said 5:30 a.m. No one else was up. She pulled on her jeans and a sweatshirt and headed to the car. She found herself in one of the older neighborhoods at her family's church, St.

Peter's Episcopal. A round stained glass window of St. Peter in his fishing boat adorned the front entrance. The original church was now a small, intimate chapel attached to the left of the main newer building.

For lack of anything else to do with herself, Jan visited the little chapel. This would be a quiet place to think, she reasoned.

The old, hand-hewn pews were lined four on the left facing the altar and five on the right. A brass railing separated the congregation from the altar. Jan walked to the front pew on the right, bowed before the majestic, hand-carved, oak cross against the altar's back wall, and knelt on the worn velvet kneeling bench.

"Dear God, I don't know what to say, or even how to feel. I know to kill a man is wrong, but that you forgive a repentant heart. I feel no remorse. I just feel dirty. I feel ...." Jan found her head in her hands and her body wracked with sobs. "I'm so sorry, so sorry, God. I feel the sickening thrust; I can't stop feeling him. I want to kill him again."

She cried for a full five minutes before she finally relaxed and sat back on the pew. She wiped her eyes and asked aloud, "What now?"

"Well, praying is a start, even if you don't know what you're praying for."

Startled, Jan turned around, mortified that someone had witnessed her emotion.

"I didn't mean to scare you. I don't want to intrude either. I come here most mornings to pray too, and sometimes I don't know what to pray for or about."

Jan found herself looking at a youngish man, early to mid-thirties. He was wearing jeans and a sweatshirt. He had blue eyes and short, black, wavy hair.

"I, I didn't know anyone was here. Forgive my emotion. I'll, I'm leaving now anyway," she stammered.

"Don't leave on my account. It's I who am sorry. I started not to come in, but I thought maybe you might just need someone to talk to."

"No, no, thank you. I have to be going now." Jan all but ran from the chapel and drove away.

The rest of the family would be rising now and she didn't want to cause alarm. She hoped she never saw that man again.

When she walked in the kitchen door, Lamar was on the phone to her grandparents.

"Never mind. She just walked in. Everything's okay." He

hung up. "Where have you been, sweetheart? I was worried. I couldn't imagine where you had gone this early."

"You don't have to worry about me, Dad. I just went for a drive since I was up."

Lamar could see she'd been crying. "Still, you could leave us a note or something when you go out. We worry, you know." He hugged her. "How about some of my famous pancakes?"

"Sure. I'll fix some coffee."

"So, have you decided when you're going back to Riverdale?" Lamar asked cautiously.

"Oh, I don't know. With this trial coming up, I'll miss so much work. It doesn't seem fair to the school or to my students to keep leaving them for long periods of time with a substitute. Maybe I ought to resign now," she said, starting the ancient coffee pot.

"I understand your concern, but after this ugly mess is over, won't you want your job back? You shouldn't give your job up completely, do you think?"

"Daddy, none of us knows the outcome of this trial," she argued.

"No jury in their right minds would convict you for killing that scum," he interrupted. "Jan, this will end. You'll go right back to your life, and time will take care of everything, believe me."

"That's just it, Dad, no matter what the outcome, I can't go back to my life like it was, because I am not who I was. I don't care how much you or Mom or David or even I don't want this to change my life, it has changed it. I can't ever go back. I don't mean I don't want to go back to David; I just don't want to go back to my life the way it was," she tried to explain.

Lamar continued flipping pancakes. "I'd do anything to take this all away, honey, and you know I would. But you're probably right. You can stay here as long or as short as you need. There will always be a place for you here, but we won't hold you down, either."

Jan came up behind her father and gave him a squeeze. "I know, Dad, and I appreciate you. I wish I had some answer for you right now. Hell, I wish I had some answers for me."

"You two are up mighty early." May swept into the kitchen, white silk robe flowing, hair combed and face fixed. "Are those pancakes I smell? Why, Lamar, it's been years since you've made those. What a great way to start off our Thanksgiving week. By the time this holiday's over, you'll be feeling quite yourself again, dear. You'll see."

Jan didn't answer directly. "Coffee, mother?"

"Yes, dear. Now, there's only one thing we must do today, darling girl. You are my darling girl, you know." May reached over and smoothed Jan's hair off her forehead. "By the way ..." Jan could tell by the tone that something was to follow, something her mother had set up to 'help.'

"I've asked the new minister at our church, Rev. Tyler, to stop by the club for lunch."

"Mother, I wish you hadn't. Let me choose who I want to talk to," Jan said exasperated.

"I didn't say I asked him because of you, dear. You don't have to talk with anyone you don't want to," May said cagily.

"May, we said we wouldn't meddle," Lamar protested.

"Now hear me out, you two. It's not like this is some planned confession. He's new and it's about time we did something for him," May hurried on before either one could interrupt. "Now I have a hair appointment so I won't be able to stay for lunch, but we can have a toddy together before I go. Rev. Tyler is not like our beloved Rev. McDonald, but he has quite a background in counseling. He's a bit of a crusader, takes on causes, you know, but that's all right."

"Mother, really, I don't want to meet this man. Can't you wait until I attend a service or something?" Jan argued.

"Dear, I've already asked him. Besides, he's always getting people involved in projects, none which I care for personally, but if you're going to stay here a while, it's best for you to get involved, get your mind off things. I'm only trying to do what's best for you," May said, starting on her pancakes.

"May, I won't have you pushing this girl. Not now," Lamar started.

"Oh, look at the time. I must get my clothes on and go to the florist before our luncheon. I'm not meddling, dear. It's just lunch, for goodness sake." May headed out of the kitchen with her coffee cup in hand. "Now, Jan, I'll pick you up after I go to the florist, unless you want to come along."

"Mother, wait. Let me just drive there myself. How will I get home if you're going off to your hair appointment?" Jan yelled after her.

"I'm sure Rev. Tyler won't mind bringing you home," May said. She hurried up the stairs out of earshot.

Jan continued eating her pancakes in silence.

"I know your mother can be infuriating sometimes, but she means well. She may be right," Lamar said cautiously. "Taking on a project outside of yourself is best. Any head doctor would tell you that. Maybe once you get to know this minister .... I don't know, it's just that you never mention what happened, not even the trial. I can understand why it would be harder to share this with your family," he continued.

"*It! This!* What is '*it*' and '*this*,' Dad?" Jan burst out. Her anger and emotion startled Lamar. "You say I won't talk about *it*, meaning being kidnapped, raped and killing a man, when none of you will talk about the subjects by their names. You tiptoe around the words; you refer vaguely to the upcoming trial, for God's sake, and you say *I* won't talk about it? Mother acts as if *it* never even happened!"

"I know, honey, but it's hard to deal with something like this when it has happened to someone you love so much, your own child. We're all having to deal with what happened to you, as I'm sure David is. We don't want to be responsible for saying or doing the wrong thing, so all we can do is tell you how much we love you and be there for you. To tell the truth, we'd probably all benefit from talking to someone objective," Lamar tried to calm Jan.

She regretted her words. She knew she was trying to protect them, also; protect them from the ugly details of something that frightened and horrified them even in vagueness.

"Look, Dad, isn't there some kind of paperwork I can do for you?" she asked, changing the subject.

"I guess that means you've decided not to return to Riverdale with David on Monday? Is it because you are afraid of seeing those two students? You know you can always go home without going back to work," Lamar said.

"I wouldn't mind seeing Caleb and Murray," Jan said. "We became close through that experience. I just would like to stay here a while, if that's okay?" she asked with a smile.

"You know we love having you any time. My goodness, this big old house has plenty of room. But I worry about you and David being separated for so long right now. Maybe he's who you really need the most," Lamar said.

"It has nothing to do with David," Jan tried to explain. "It's the town, the area, that house, my life there. I don't think that's me any more," she said.

"Whatever the reasons," Lamar said, "you stay here as long as you need to, and your mother and I will be the happier for it. As for work, my office is in the process of switching all of our records to computer. I feel like an illiterate around that thing, so I'm sure there's plenty you can do. I've been thinking about getting a computer for the house anyway, to make myself learn how to use it. Would you like that?"

"Sure," Jan said. "But I'll have to come work with your staff first to learn your business, won't I?" she asked.

"That's fine. You could start as soon as next Tuesday. After a holiday, Betty Jean and Sue always need a day to get the office back in top working order."

The phone rang. Nobody bothered answering the phone when May was home.

"Jan!" May called down the stairs. "Sweetheart, it's John Larsen."

"Hello," Jan said. "Don't you even take Thanksgiving week off?" she joked.

"I wish we all could, Jan, but the Brevard district attorney just called and said that the grand jury will meet the first week of the New Year after the Christmas holidays, probably that Monday or Tuesday, and he wants you there to walk through the scene with them." John paused for Jan to respond. "Jan?"

"Yes," she answered.

"I wanted you to know in advance so you could prepare," he said.

"Sure. Thanks," she answered.

"They'll probably want you to revisit the cabin and that area," he added.

Jan had never expected to have to physically walk into that place again. It was one thing to relive it in her mind every time she had to retell the story, but to have to actually be there, to see and touch and feel, as if it were happening all over, the details making it that much more real in her mind. Even now she could feel Punk's heaviness on her, smell his breath, feel the pain.

Then she would see him on the ground, head turned back and around, those gross, red-rimmed dark eyes, the greasy hair, the stubble, the filth, the sneer, and she was glad all over again that she had killed him, had done it herself so that there was no mistaking that he could ever come back.

"Mom will probably want to go along," Jan finally said. "Why don't you let me find out?"

"I'm here, Jan," May said, having not ever hung up the phone. "We'll all want to go, John. I'll make travel and lodging arrangements," she said with that forced cheerfulness that Jan hated.

"'Bye, John," Jan said. She hung up rather than listen to the rest of May's conversation.

Lamar left for work, and Jan sat alone in the kitchen sipping her coffee. She decided that she definitely could not go back to her life in Riverdale, her married life, until this trial was behind her. For all she knew, she could be going to jail.

Jan's sheltered view of the world was fast changing. Evil existed and not just in Punk. Injustice and hatred had never been able to touch her before. Now she was thrown on the other side where very little was left that supported life as she had known it.

"Don't forget, I'll pick you up at eleven fifty-five sharp," May said as she came into the kitchen trailing her strong perfumed scent. "Why don't you take a nice, long, hot bath, wash your hair, fix yourself up, you know, make yourself feel better," she said as she headed out the back door.

Jan knew her mother was right. She had not rolled her hair, had not put on the least bit of makeup, since she left Riverdale. She went upstairs and took a leisurely, hot shower.

May honked out front promptly at five minutes before noon. Jan already had her hand on the front door knob before the horn blew, and she hurried to the car.

"You look so nice," her mother said pleasantly as she got in.

As they pulled into the country club parking lot, May turned to Jan. "Now, dear, I'm dreadfully sorry I must leave you for lunch. Maybe it's best. Sometimes I feel that you don't open up when I'm around." Jan saw her mother's brief look of regret. "Well," May continued, "at least I can have a Bloody Mary with you."

"Mother, this is a minister. We can't drink at lunch," Jan said.

"Oh, no, it's perfectly all right, dear. Remember, Father Tyler is Episcopalian – and as you know, we 'whiskeypalians' dearly love our midday Bloody Marys."

There weren't many people at the club for lunch because

Thanksgiving was the following day. May and Jan walked into the large cocktail room and found Father Tyler seated and thumbing through a magazine.

"Father Tyler? I'd like you to meet my daughter, Janet. Jan, dear, this is Father Tyler of whom I've spoken."

Jan was instantly embarrassed to look into the deep blue eyes of the man who had been in the pew behind her in the chapel this morning.

"Why, it's nice to meet you, Janet. Or do you prefer Jan?" Father Tyler asked politely with no mention of their earlier chance meeting other than the twinkle in his eyes.

Jan shook his hand and nodded.

"Now, I regret that I won't be able to stay for lunch with the two of you, but perhaps it's best that way, as I've already said to Jan. Give you two a chance to talk. Come along; I will have a pre-luncheon Bloody Mary with you," May said, and she looped one arm through Father Tyler's arm and one through Jan's.

"I shouldn't, but it is Thanksgiving Eve, and I do love a Bloody Mary," Father Tyler said jovially.

May lifted her eyebrows smugly at Jan and led the way to a table by the window on what was called the dining porch. It overlooked the ninth hole of the club's golf course. A putting tee was located just below.

"Oh, there's Myrt playing golf with Maude. I'm so glad to see her out. She's been sick and depressed for months now. This is a good sign. See, dear," May said as she turned back to Jan. "I have this intuition that a lot more is getting better already."

After the drinks arrived, May turned to the minister. "Father Tyler, how are things at the parish? We haven't been in a while."

Father Tyler smiled knowingly.

"I guess you have noticed, but under the circumstances, we thought it best to stay out of the public eye," May explained. "Why I wouldn't be surprised if those pushy reporters didn't follow us to church."

"One did show up, I believe," Father Tyler chuckled. "He sat in the back. He had a camera and notebook, and he kept looking toward the door. He stayed for my sermon, though," the minister smiled and turned to Jan.

"It seems to me we need freedom *from* the press instead of

freedom *of* the press," May said haughtily. "Really, they have no respect. I saw an interview on television the other day with the wife of a man being buried ... at the graveside! Now, that's going too far. Anyway, Father, Martha Ann tells me that you're branching out in the community and taking on the city's youth single-handedly."

"Jan, your mother is referring to a pilot program for which our church has volunteered to provide our facilities as an after-school hangout for junior high and high school students. There are an abundance of programs for grades kindergarten through six, but no program for the older children. With both parents working in most families, this age can get into some serious trouble. We're building a gym, but for now we use the Sunday School playground. We have tutors, all volunteer members of the church and some who aren't members but who just like the program. Different people have donated a pool table, two ping pong tables, cards, checkers, board games, puzzles ... but we'll have no television."

Father Tyler didn't hide his enthusiasm for his program. "We depend a great deal on volunteers. If you're going to be here for a while, Jan, perhaps you would like to come by and check out our program. There's always something to do to help out."

"Well, I don't know," Jan stammered.

"Why, dear, that is just perfect! Volunteering would be much better than hanging around the house all day," May said. She looked at her watch. "Oh, my, I'm late. You dears order anything you like and just sign my name and number, Jan. Love you, sweetie," she said as she blew Jan a kiss.

"You look much better," Father Tyler said. "I hope I didn't intrude on your quiet time this morning."

"Oh, no. I guess I'm just a little embarrassed," Jan said sheepishly. "I had no idea you were Father Tyler."

"Call me Grant, please. My friends do. Your mother does sometimes, but most of the time she likes to call me by my title. I'm serious about your coming to check out the program," Grant said warmly.

"Oh, so you think I need charity work? Mother has been pushing me to talk to you. Is that because of your program?" Jan's resentment showed.

"No, Jan. I thought maybe you'd like to come and volunteer is all. I don't even know you. How would I know what you need? Besides, you're a young woman, not a teenage girl," he replied gently.

"I'm sorry for jumping to conclusions," Jan said. "It's just that I assume that everyone who meets me must be thinking of what happened, of why I'm back here right now," Jan said. She was surprised to hear herself open up to this man.

"I understand," he said, smiling. "Your mother is really a delight," Grant laughed to lighten the moment.

"Yes, but I seem to appreciate her more now that I don't live here," Jan said.

"Oh, so your stay here is temporary?" he asked.

"Yes, but I don't know how temporary. I just don't know much about the future right now," she said.

"Of course you don't. You've only had a short while to process all of this, haven't you? Any shock needs time. I think counselors, and I say this with respect, are needed when one doesn't take time to deal with a major shaking up of one's existence as she has known it. I have found that these times can be exciting, a learning period where you can see the world as if for the first time again. Not that it lasts, because then your new self, or real self as the case may be, becomes the norm."

He stopped short, shook his head, and held both hands up in a gesture of surrender and apology.

"Here I go rambling. That's a bad habit of mine, not knowing when to stop," Grant apologized.

Jan stared at him in disbelief. It was as if this man had read her thoughts of this morning. Maybe he overheard her in church. Maybe he had experienced his own suffering. "Actually, I have had those thoughts myself, but what do I know?" she said.

"Probably a lot more than you think," Grant said seriously. "Everyone knows a lot more than she thinks. The trick is to trust what you know and what you think. That's when God is strongest in your life. I hope you don't think I'm preaching or anything," Grant said.

They were interrupted by the arrival of lunch. Jan felt oddly comfortable with Grant Tyler. The minister and the young woman in transition exchanged the surface details of their lives.

"How come you never married?" Jan asked.

"I guess because I never found a lady with whom I could converse as easily as I can with you," he said simply. "I know you have a legitimate reason to need to have someone with whom you can talk, but I'd like to talk with you more even if you don't need to talk to me.

So, how about a nice Thanksgiving Day walk tomorrow afternoon after the big feast?" he asked.

"But we won't know what time each other will be through with lunch, and my whole family will be here, and David, my husband, flies in tonight, and well, we're pretty unpredictable," Jan stammered.

Grant laughed. "I happen to know for a fact that we will be eating Thanksgiving dinner at the exact same time." He paused and smiled. "Your mother invited me to have Thanksgiving with your family tomorrow. I hope that's okay with you?" he asked.

"Of course. How nice. Yes, we'd love to have you, and I'll look forward to that walk," she said.

Chapter Two

The big city presses had gone on to more recent news and the local paper, owned by dear friends of the Calhouns, respectfully stayed away. Thanksgiving promised to be quiet at the family farm.

David didn't arrive until late Wednesday evening. He drove, hoping that Jan would go back to Riverdale with him after the weekend. He knew as soon as he saw her that she wouldn't.

Julia Ann and her husband James arrived about eleven on Thanksgiving morning. They planned to spend only one night, as Julia Ann was hosting the Junior League tea on Saturday afternoon.

"I was so hoping we could spend some sisterly time together," Julia Ann said. "I would have talked with you when I called, but Mother said it was best to leave you alone for right now. James and I have thought of nothing but you since this horrible nightmare. How would you like to spend a few days with us in Birmingham? I do have a luncheon next week and a few meetings, but you could come along, of course," Julia Ann babbled on. She was truly her mother's daughter.

Jan could think of no worse place to spend her seclusion. "No, thank you, Julia Ann. I really have no plans right now. I'm taking each day one at a time."

"That's best, you know. Mother has kept me up on everything. I wish there were something I could do." Julia Ann looked around anxiously. "Where's James when I need him? He could at least help me unload."

Julia Ann went looking for James and Jan grabbed a load off the front seat. Jan had seen her sister only once since last Christmas. She and her mother had spent a night at her house while Jan was visiting in the summer. She had missed her brother, Peterson, however, because he'd spent the summer sailing with college friends. But today, Peterson was expected any moment with his roommate from Washington and Lee.

The men went out to the farmhouse early to watch the ball games while the women stayed behind to get the rest of the meal together. The Jameson's maid, Retha, had cooked most of the meal the day before. Jan doubted that May had ever cooked an entire meal.

This year May's politician brother, Uncle Ralph, showed up with Meemaw and Papa Ralph. He had served Georgia as state senator for eight years, but now he was running for a U.S. Senate seat. He hugged Jan before joining the men in front of the television. "I've been thinking about you, honey. I'm afraid I've just been too busy to let you know."

Jan knew that Uncle Ralph was wary of her pending murder charges and the effect this could have on his campaign. John warned Jan that the press and public would not separate her from her family members, even those she was not close to.

Rev. Tyler arrived after the women, bringing along a pumpkin pie he had made and a bottle of Port. "It makes me feel a part of the family if I contribute," he told May.

Peterson was the last to arrive. His friend dropped him off at the house just after the women left, so he rummaged around and found the spare keys to Lamar's car, just as he had done in high school. When he drove up, Jan was alone outside unloading the last of the food that May had brought from her kitchen in town. "Sweet sister of mine," he said turning the car off. "I would've called or written, but Mom said it best to leave you alone right now," he said with a tinge of neglectful guilt. He gave her that schoolboy grin. "You know, I've been taking quite a few psychology courses – if you'd like to talk with me later."

Jan didn't have a chance to refuse before May came out. "Peterson, darling – why, look at your hair. You couldn't have your hair cut before you came home? Well, never mind, we're glad you're here before we've eaten. Couldn't you have worn a nicer pair of trousers, dear?" May continued admonishing her youngest child and only son.

"Always the mother hen," Peterson joked as he picked up May and swung her around.

"Peterson, put me down this instant!" she squealed. But she was smiling with surprised delight.

The meal wasn't served until 2:30 that afternoon, though the spread included plenty of hors d'oeuvres with the pre-dinner cocktails. The meal was like many others across the South that day. The women basked in the spread, the men ate too much, and everyone talked at once. Jan sat between David and Father Tyler, who hit it off while pulling for the same teams. She carried on bits of conversations with different groups, asking Julia Ann and James details of their lives, complementing her mother on the dishes, asking Peterson about his courses. Silver clinked against china; the crystal wine and water goblets were filled often.

During desert, Jan slipped off unnoticed to the bathroom. Behind the shut door, she turned on the water and leaned against the back of the toilet, resting her eyes, listening to the happy sounds of her family in the next room. At least no one had asked her to tell *her story* as the facts had come to be known. Jan was tired of facts; she tired of trying to find meaning in everything, to reject guilt, as Dr. Carey tried to encourage her to do, or to accept it, as the courts would surely try to do. She just wanted to *be*.

"We wondered where you were," Julia Ann said when Jan returned to the dining room. "Why don't you go on in with the men, and I'll clean up with Mother and Meemaw?"

"Anyone for a walk?" Father Tyler asked as she walked into the den. "We already know the outcome of this less-than-exciting football game," he joked with the men.

"I'll go," David said, looking at Jan.

"Might as well walk off some of this spread," Lamar said rising. Peterson followed him.

Papa Ralph and Uncle Ralph stayed behind to discuss politics and business and James went off in search of a nap.

The five set out across the cow pasture toward the wooded hill. The late afternoon was crisp and clear. When Jan lagged behind, lost in her own thoughts, David slowed to catch up with her.

"Have you decided to come back to Riverdale ... and me?" he asked. "I mean, I haven't noticed signs of packing. I'm not trying to rush you or anything, darling, it's just that, well, I mean how long is this going to be? It seems to me that you're letting this thing take over your life. You can find a comparable psychiatrist in our area, can't you? The grand jury doesn't meet until January. Surely you're not talking about staying with your parents until the hearing is over, are you?" David didn't hide his anxiety.

"I don't know," she hesitated. "I mean, I like Dr. Carey; I feel comfortable with him. If I switch, I'd just have to start all over again, and I don't want to do that." She looked away so as not to be influenced by his hurt look.

"Then just come for a week and then come back here a week. You don't have to go back to school. They found a sub who wants the job full time. Shouldn't we be going through this thing together? I mean, I know I'm not the one who all this happened to; but dammit, Jan, this affects me too. My whole life has been uprooted, too. I don't even feel adequate as your husband. I know you want to avoid the stares, the whispering behind your back, because, God knows, I've tried to avoid it, but I can't. I have to go on about my life like nothing happened. At work, at restaurants, there's always small talk, some people come right out and ask how you are and how I feel about everything. Can you imagine? Others avoid me for fear of saying the wrong thing."

"Oh, honey, that must be awful for you," Jan interrupted.

"No, it's *you* we need to think about. Only, I need you, and I'd think you'd need me, too – especially now," he ended pitifully.

"I don't know, David," Jan started.

The gap had closed between the couple and the rest of the group, so the conversation dropped.

"What a beautiful day," Father Tyler exclaimed. "This would be a great outing for my after-school kids. Do you think Mr. Calhoun would let me bring them here sometime?" he asked Lamar. Then, turning to Jan he said, "You know the offer still stands. We'd love to have you help out, even if just on the public relations side and some office work."

Jan wondered if Father Tyler had overheard the conversation between her and David and was offering her a reason to stay in Kingsford.

When the walkers returned, Julia Ann put her arm around Jan. "You must have put in quite a bit of time making your delicious dishes, Sis. You know, I'm not going to say I can fully empathize with what you've been through, but I do have a good ear for listening if you need someone to talk to," she said in sisterly earnest.

"I see Mom has been working on you, too," Jan said.

"She's worried about you, honey. We all are. I would have said that even if Mother hadn't said a word," she answered. "Well, then, maybe I can confide in you. I'm pregnant," Julia Ann said with a glowing smile.

"Oh, Julia Ann, I'm so happy for you. This is great," Jan said.

"I didn't upset you did I? I've been so afraid to say anything to anyone what with your situation and all."

Jan winced at the word *situation*. "You mean you haven't told Mother yet?" she asked, quickly changing the subject.

"No. I thought I'd see how you reacted first to make sure my news won't get in the way."

"Oh, Julia Ann this is just the thing to get Mother's mind off me. Go tell her right this minute. And tell Daddy, too," she said as she pushed her sister out the kitchen door.

David came into the kitchen as Julia Ann was leaving it. "I'm glad to catch you alone," he said.

"We were alone on the walk this afternoon some," Jan said.

"Not really. I feel like Rev. Tyler keeps his ears open around you," David said pointedly.

"And you're glad he's a man of the cloth so that you'll have nothing to worry about?" Jan laughed.

"No," David said defensively. "I know that I'm not qualified to help you, to be for you what you need right now. I don't like Riverdale that much, particularly without you there. I hate my job; I hate selling farmers these great loans and then turning around and closing them down when they run up on bum luck. I swear, Jan, it's so depressing. Did you know that two farmers over in Dillon County committed suicide in the past two weeks?"

"Oh, David, why didn't you tell me? You poor thing," Jan exclaimed.

"One of them was a grain elevator owner who had hedged against market futures using other farmers' grain as collateral. When they opened the grain bin after he died, it was empty. Five of my major customers have been affected. Ob McKnight cried in my office," he complained. "I hate to sound so down. I've thought of quitting, but that would be running out on these farmers. Dad says it would also look bad on my resume."

"Of course. I understand," Jan said. "My future is so uncertain, maybe it's best we both relearn independence right now," she suggested.

"Jan, please don't even say that. I couldn't bear it for you or for me. Surely there isn't a jury in the nation that would convict you of murdering that man, not after what he did to you," he said heatedly.

"Oh no? Did you read about the seventeen-year-old boy in Cumberland County who was sentenced to twelve years in prison for killing his father, even though his father had first tried to kill him with a gun? Whose father for twenty-five years had also beat and terrorized the boy, his older brother and sister, and their mother? The prosecutor said that the murder was *unusually gruesome.* But what happened was that after the father had been shot, the boy walked by him and he grabbed the boy and tried to choke him. So, the boy grabbed a knife and slashed his father's throat. Then, he and his mother buried the body under the house, but the hole wasn't big enough, so the boy had to break his father's legs. That judge also wouldn't allow the jury to hear that family testify about the abuse they had suffered all those years. I tell you, David, sometimes I feel that there's no hope for justice."

"Honey, you have got to quit reading the newspaper," David said. "News is depressing."

For the rest of the weekend, Jan and David were left alone. On Friday they rode around, and Jan told David about all the people in the different houses – folks she knew or had known. They went to lunch at the local bar and grill and then sat through two movies at the Plaza Cinema out near the factories road. Afterwards, they stopped at a new downtown bar before returning to the Jamesons' for dinner. They had little to say to each other.

"How long do you plan to stay with us, David?" May asked as she cleared the table.

"I was thinking of leaving Sunday and taking Jan with me. I have some business to complete before I go into work on Monday," David answered.

Lamar puffed on his pipe. He had said little to David in the few days his son-in-law had been there. Lamar was annoyed that David had not been more supportive of Jan. He decided to let them work things out for themselves and not interfere.

Jan did not actively decide to return to Riverdale with David on Sunday; she just couldn't think of a reason not to go. Her family had rallied around, pushing her toward what she knew she ought to do.

"This will be best, you'll see. Home is where your husband is," Julia Ann had said before she and James left.

Peterson's ride back to school picked him up mid-day Saturday. He hugged Jan hard and promised to keep in touch better.

David's parents drove over from Atlanta for Saturday lunch to see Jan and David.

"I believe this has been as hard on our David as it has been on your Jan," Mrs. Ferguson told May over their cocktails. She had cancelled an evening at the Atlanta Ballet to come over. "I just don't know how our young people have been able to bear up under the strain," she said. "Have you heard any more about the trial? I can't imagine someone thinking Jan would kill anyone on purpose. Of course, she had every right to," Mrs. Ferguson rambled on.

Jan could tell that Mrs. Ferguson grated on her mother's nerves as much as she did on Jan's. Mrs. Ferguson seemed thrilled that Jan would finally be going home with her husband "where she belonged."

Jan made it clear that though she was going to Riverdale for a visit with her husband, she would not give up her sessions with Dr. Carey. When the doctor had called on Friday to check on Jan, they talked for over thirty minutes. He agreed that going back to Riverdale would be good, but added, "Remember, you're not the same person you were when you left." He was glad her stay would be short.

Dr. Carey had come to enjoy his sessions with Jan, but he was worried about her court case. He knew that John Larsen planned to use self-defense as her defense. Yet Jan continued to maintain that she had had a choice. Perhaps a break from the three-day-a-week schedule would allow Dr. Carey time to decide what approach to take next.

"Just don't stay away more than one or two weeks," Dr. Carey said. "I'm getting used to you, you know."

Rev. Tyler came by on Saturday night to wish her well. "I can see why you wouldn't want to go back to teaching," he said, as if reading her mind. All were gathered in the family room where most of them told her to go back to her job and try to make life as close to normal as possible.

The Reverend said, "You could visit the school, if if feels right. I'll bet your students would be glad to see you. But just take things one day at a time and search your heart for what you really want." Then he shook hands with David, Lamar and Mr. Ferguson, and he was gone.

May scowled after him. Such comments, and in front of everyone else no less, she thought. "That's our new minister," she said apologetically to the Fergusons. "A bit wet behind the ears, I'm afraid."

As she packed, Jan thought of Rev. Tyler's words, "Search your heart for what you really want." How could she search her heart when she couldn't open it? She felt as if her heart were an oyster that she couldn't pry open. Her wounds had healed, her anger had disappeared, and public embarrassment had dulled, but, she couldn't feel.

On Sunday, David was beside himself with excitement on the trip back to Riverdale. "Your headmaster and Lucy called every few days to see when you were coming back. They said not to worry about your classes; the substitute has an English degree. The school is going to hold your place for a while." David squeezed Jan's hand. "I've told everyone not to call us, we'll call them, so you can get back into the swing of things on your own time. Jan? Honey? I'm not bothering you with all this talk, am I?"

Jan smiled, but said nothing.

David continued. "All the guys at work are really glad you're coming back. They know I've been lost without you. I've even cleaned the house."

Jan wasn't listening to his words. They were just words, and she knew David was nervous about having her back, nervous about their sleeping arrangements, nervous that he would say or do the wrong thing. She watched his face. It was a strong face: handsome, amber green eyes; large intelligent forehead; short straight hair. He had never been much of an outdoorsman, but he loved puttering in the yard. David kept their little yard immaculate.

What had first attracted her to him? David was the first man to take a serious interest in her. Other boys found her to be too serious. David also took his studies seriously, and their courtship had begun in the library. He had the nicest manners. David had been raised the same way she had.

Jan's family took to David right away. "Such a nice boy, and from such a nice family," May had said. The phrase *all-American* came to mind. He loved football and basketball, joined the right fraternity and took his father's advice. Even in lovemaking, David was nice.

"Jan? Did you hear me?" David interrupted her thoughts. "Dr. McGuire said he wanted to pay you a visit, but I told him to wait until you were ready. We're lucky to have him as our minister, you know. What do you want to do once we get home?" David tried to pull Jan out of her silence.

"Oh, I don't know. Tomorrow I'll call the headmaster and tell him I'm resigning so he can hire a permanent replacement. I don't really feel like going to the school," she thought out loud.

"Caleb and Murray want to see you. I hope it's okay that I told them they could," David ventured.

"Sure. But if it's okay, try to keep everyone else away," she answered.

"Even Lucy? She's really missed you. And James Wade? They have been a big help to me through this," he said.

Jan frowned. "I'm just not ready."

"Okay," David said, and he quit trying to fill the quiet.

On the last leg of the trip from Florence to Riverdale, Jan saw the countryside as if for the first time. Even in the bareness of the fall, the swamps and ponds on either side of the road oozed a soft mist touched by swags of moss hanging from the water oaks. Most of the cotton had been picked, but dots of cotton lint left behind gave an interesting contrast in color. Jan had lived here amidst this earthen beauty, yet she had never touched it.

Jan and David had barely unpacked the car before their nosey, elderly neighbor Lilly Adams was ringing the doorbell with a chicken casserole in hand.

"Jan, hon, I've saved all the newspaper reports for you. It must have been just awful. I can't even imagine. We're so glad you're back," Mrs. Adams began. The 'we' included herself and two cats who had become her entire life since her husband had died ten years before.

Jan tried to be gracious, though she knew the casserole was made with Miracle Whip and Minute Rice.

"I'll just come in and set this on the counter and maybe help out a bit," she continued with one step in the door. Usually, Jan was careful to be polite, and Mrs. Adams would come in and snoop around on the pretense of "helping out," sometimes settling in to watch whatever was on television.

"Thank you so much, Mrs. Adams, but if you don't mind, David and I need some time alone. I hope you understand," Jan said without moving from the doorway.

"Well, of course I understand. You know when my Lenny was alive, we used to cherish our alone time, too, what with his work, and church, there just never seemed to be enough time. And sometimes ...."

Jan cut her off. "Yes, well, thank you for understanding." She shut the door while Mrs. Adams was still talking.

The phone rang before Mrs. Adams was back in her own identical brick ranch house.

"It's for you, sweetheart," David said with his hand over the mouthpiece.

"Please, no," she pleaded. But it was David's immediate boss's wife and he didn't want to be rude.

"Jan? I'm so glad you're finally back. Your ordeal must have been just horrible. We really missed you at bridge last week, and you're all we could talk about."

Jan could just imagine.

"Are you here to stay? We all just cannot believe the newspaper reports. They don't really think they can try you for murder do they? It is just too awful," Loraine Meekins went on without waiting for Jan to answer.

Because Melvin and David were good friends, the two couples went out socially together. Loraine's children attended the academy, and Loraine was always pumping Jan for information about students, parents and other teachers at the school. She was not Jan's favorite person.

"Why don't we get together for lunch tomorrow? I know David will have to work even though you're home. We can go to Florence shopping so you won't have to run into anyone. You must be dying for someone to talk to, stuck away over there in Georgia with your parents," Loraine continued.

Jan forced herself to be polite. "Thank you, Loraine, but I have some important business to take care of while I'm here. I won't be here long, you know."

"How about you and David coming for dinner tomorrow night, or the next?" she pushed.

"Thanks, but no thanks," Jan said more firmly this time. "Look, I'm expecting a phone call so I have to go. Say hello to Melvin and the children for me," she said, and she hung up.

"I thought you were really coming home," David said after she hung up.

"Honey, you know I'm going to have to have sessions with Dr. Carey, and John Larsen needs me nearby to help with my defense ...." she trailed off, trying to sound as if she couldn't help not staying.

Jan knew that before Loraine could get another dial tone, she would be calling Sue and Nancy, the other bankers' wives, to embellish their conversations, and after that the phones in Riverdale just would not stop ringing. She unplugged the kitchen phone. David, without being asked, unplugged the phone in their bedroom.

Jan was up before David the next morning. She felt it important to at least make an effort for him. She fixed eggs and cinnamon toast. The cupboards and refrigerator were almost bare. She made a mental note of the things she would need and planned to drive to Florence to the grocery.

"What's on your agenda today?" David asked.

"Grocery shopping first," she said.

"I didn't eat many meals here," he explained. "I ate at the cafe up town a few times, and there has been no end to the invitations for dinner. It's been easier to be around people than to come back here alone," he confessed.

Jan nodded. They ate in silence.

"I wish I could stay home with you, but I have this job to go to." David tried to sound jovial, but Jan could see the confusion in his face. "Anything you want to do tonight? Maybe go to a movie? You don't have to see Caleb and Murray right away, you know. Why don't you give yourself a few days to settle in first?" he asked hopefully.

"Sure, you're probably right," she said.

David kissed Jan on the top of her head and left.

Jan poured herself another cup of coffee. She hadn't slept well, and she wanted to ward off the temptation of a nap. The day was overcast and cool. She saw a school bus go by at 7:45. A few neighborhood mothers drove by with children. Everyone who passed by stared at her house. The house was just as Jan had left it three weeks ago, but it seemed unfamiliar. Would she ever feel at home here again?

She looked around at the furnishings. She couldn't find anything she had picked out herself. All were wedding presents or family furniture from both sides. Her mother and David had picked out a china pattern. The one Jan wanted "wasn't formal enough," according to May. Had she really been that uninvolved in her life? Had she really been that complacent and bendable? Her surroundings answered *yes*.

There were few things that Jan cherished: the print of a tricycle done by a college friend; her books neatly and categorically arranged on various shelves; a series of black-and-white photographs she had shot in college during a visual arts course. She had married David right out of college and had never lived alone.

What now? She couldn't stay here, not even for the week she

had promised David. What was she to do with herself? There was no one she wanted to see except Caleb and Murray.

And David? Jan didn't know how she felt about him anymore. She couldn't live with her parents. She couldn't stay here.

Her grandfather's farmhouse drifted to mind. No one went out there any more except on Thanksgiving. She'd be a quarter hour from her parents' house; she could stay out of their social whirl.

And far enough from David ….

Jan couldn't help David right now. She had to help herself.

Chapter Three

Talking her parents and grandparents into letting her live in the farmhouse had been easy. They were so relieved that she would at least be close, and she could continue with Dr. Carey. May did express concern about Jan's marriage, but suggested that David could come visit.

David had been none too pleased with Jan's decision. Yet, after her third day in Riverdale, he too could see that Jan no longer fit into their life as it had been. He wondered if he did. David was sure that Jan's reunion with Caleb and Murray would throw her back to her old self, but Jan did not put on her teacher personality when they came. Their bond opened them up to be who they were. David had never seen two teenage boys mature so quickly. For the first time, Caleb was considering college.

"I want to be a lawyer," he told Jan. "I want to keep the law from hurting people like you," he said with youthful ambition.

Jan smiled and hugged him. "You'll make a great lawyer, Caleb."

"I wish I was already a lawyer so I could represent you now," he said.

"What about you?" she asked Murray.

"Law. Caleb and I have discussed opening a practice together. Who knows?" He shrugged and he and Caleb exchanged glances.

"And school?" she asked.

"Shoot, I wish I'd listened to you sooner and started caring about my grades," Caleb said.

"You can make up for it in college. I meant how is it being back at school?" she asked.

"We stayed out the first couple of days after we got back," Caleb said. "But now everything's back to normal, or almost."

"We stick to sports and studying. That's a change for you, huh, Caleb?" Murray laughed.

"Maybe a little," Caleb chuckled. "We're spending a lot of time with our own lawyer trying to help you. You know Bryson McNeil? He's letting us do research for him ... to get experience."

"Is this really you, Caleb? What about all those girls and partying?" Jan teased.

Caleb grinned, embarrassed. "Oh, I've changed. That stuff doesn't interest me any more."

"Not even girls?" she kidded.

"Well …. "

David had little to say during the visit. He sensed the connection between the three and resented not being part of it. His resentment was growing more noticeable. When Jan told him after the boys had left that she planned to return to Kingsford on Friday, he figured the sooner the better; he needed to be alone to decide what direction his own life would take.

Jan tried to stay upbeat during the rest of her visit. Sometimes David responded, but as Friday came closer, he became more withdrawn.

"I know this is hard on you, even unfair," she tried cautiously on the last night. "Perhaps this won't last long. Maybe I just need isolation for a while," she suggested.

"It's all right. I only want what's best for you," he said, but he turned over to hide his anger.

Jan was unable to move into the farmhouse until December 9, as May and Meemaw insisted on hiring crews of people to clean and paint and generally shape up the place. New curtains and bed linens had to be purchased – bath towels, supplies. May and Meemaw threw themselves into the project. Jan let them.

Jan joked with Dr. Carey about her mother and grandmother's decorating spree.

"Anyone who loves you will feel better about doing something, anything, to help, even if it isn't exactly what you want. Perhaps David could be enlisted in some special project having to do with your new home when he comes for Christmas," he suggested.

"I don't know," Jan said. "He's pretty resentful right now that I've chosen to do this instead of picking up life where I left off. I don't blame him, though. Sometimes I think I'm being irresponsible, taking all this time and effort for myself. I couldn't do it if I had children. Hell, I couldn't do it without my family's money."

"Jan," Dr. Carey said with one of those looks that meant he was going to say something personal, "I honestly think that eventually you would have needed this time even if you hadn't been kidnapped, even without facing a trial and all the other trappings that are dragging this ordeal out. I don't believe you went into your marriage as a complete person. The best hope now is to first become whole, and then work on your marriage."

Jan was silent. She wasn't comfortable discussing David or her marriage. This, too, was becoming a source of guilt.

All doubts receded the first night alone in the farmhouse. Jan insisted she was tired and couldn't dine with her parents. May and Lamar showed up anyway. Her mother brought a fried chicken dinner from the grocery deli. Lamar stayed in the car.

"Well?" May hesitated at the door after handing over the meal.

"Thank you for driving out here to bring my dinner, Mom. I really appreciate it. I'll be fine," she said, "and I'll see you at church in the morning."

"All right, if you think you'll be okay. But you call if you get scared, or come on into town anytime you want," May said before leaving.

Jan waved at her father before shutting the door. She looked around at her little house. There was only one bedroom with a connecting bath. She and the other grandchildren had orchestrated slumber parties here until they were through their teens.

"My own place," she said to herself. She felt contented.

Jan began working at her father's office as soon as she returned from Riverdale. She had known his office staff, Betty Jean and Sue, for years. They were grateful for her help.

Rev. Tyler came by to see Jan at her parents' house several times. He was interested and concerned. On the second visit, he asked if she would be a tutor for his afternoon youth program.

"I find working with young people, particularly in groups, demands total giving and opening of oneself," Jan said slowly. "And, right now, I'm not comfortable opening myself like that. Maybe because I no longer know what's inside? Anyway, it wouldn't be fair to the kids," she tried to explain.

Rev. Tyler was understanding and patient, though he knew that the best healing was in helping others. That's why he had chosen this profession; that's how he healed from his own suffering. *She wants to avoid exposure,* he guessed. *She's carrying around a guilt she can't shake and she's seeking forgiveness,* he thought to himself.

Rev. Tyler had seen Jan slipping into the chapel early every morning since her return to Kingsford. He had changed his own quiet time in the chapel so that she could be alone. Once or twice he quietly checked on her, trying to find a clue of how best to help her. She mostly sat on her knees and looked at the altar, or sat back on the pew and flipped through the prayer book, never resting on any certain page or text.

The Reverend had dreamed about Jan many nights since he first met her. As a minister, he felt he was being called upon by God to help this young woman. As a man, he was attracted to Jan as strongly as he had ever been attracted to only one other woman before.

The Rev. Grant Tyler touched something deep in Jan. He wasn't pushy or preachy; on the contrary, he listened to her as no one else did. Dr. Carey listened, but then he was always analyzing what she said. Rev. Tyler seemed to listen to her soul with no judgment. He didn't try to talk her out of her guilt; he accepted it.

Jan was truly grateful for her parents supporting her at this time. To make up for it, she reluctantly agreed to go to church and Sunday lunch the following morning. The sermon topic was listed in the bulletin: *Heart vs. Reason.*

"Reason is our gift from God. It separates us from the animals. But it is through our hearts that God speaks to us. God can change our souls through our hearts," Rev. Tyler began.

Jan felt as if the minister were speaking directly to her.

"It is reason which allow us to justify our sins and, therefore, not become responsible for them," he preached.

Jan's face turned red. She glanced to see if her parents noticed, but they sat expressionless.

"Do you feel settled in your new home?" Rev. Tyler asked her when she shook his hand on the way out of the sanctuary.

"Why, yes. Thank you." Jan looked closely to see if he had directed his sermon at her. His face was merely kind.

"I ask because I would like to bring you a house-warming present this afternoon," he said.

"How nice, Rev. Tyler," May butted in. "Why don't you join us for lunch at the country club? We've persuaded Jan to come," she insisted.

"Thank you, but I have a previous engagement. I promised a sick friend that I'd eat half his lunch at the hospital today if he would eat the other half. He hasn't been eating lately." He turned back to Jan. "I'll come by about 2:30, if that's all right with you?"

"Yes. That will be fine," she said.

Sunday lunch was the family's first public outing since Jan came to Kingsford from Brevard. The reason she was in Kingsford was old news now, so people were less curious and more polite. John joined them for lunch. Jan's attorney tried to spend non-client time with her. He needed to know what made her tick in order to defend her.

It was two o'clock when Jan pulled up at the gate to the farm. This gate was kept locked; it was part of a fence that marked the boundary line between the highway and the front pastures of the two-hundred-acre farm. The farmhouse, her house, was set down a lane beyond the second set of pastures in a wooded grove of pines interspersed with dogwoods and a few ancient oaks. Beyond the small yard flowed a stream. Another fence surrounded the house area. She knew she was supposed to lock both gates behind her when she was home, but today she left them open.

Jan changed into jeans and a sweatshirt. She felt as nervous as a schoolgirl for some reason. She straightened pillows and washed the morning's dishes. She was sweeping when Rev. Tyler arrived, not hearing his approach until he slammed his car door. He walked up carrying a brown paper bag.

"My, this place certainly has improved," he said, noting the changes made since his visit at Thanksgiving. "You've done wonders," he added.

"Not me. Mom and Meemaw," Jan laughed.

"Well, they have good taste," he said. "I've brought something for your house-warming – or should I say *yard-warming*?"

Jan opened the brown paper bag and, to her delight, found flower bulbs. She had mentioned to Rev. Tyler that she would like to have a garden to tend. "What a thoughtful and personal gift," she said.

"That's not all of it. I've been busy and only had time to gather these. The rest will come tomorrow on my day off. We have so much work to do to get a garden going for spring planting. I'm afraid bulbs and trees are about all you can plant this time of year. Are you free tomorrow?" he asked.

"I have an appointment with Dr. Carey in the morning, but I should be back just after lunch," she said.

"Why don't we meet at my house tomorrow and go together to get what we need? Then, if you're up to it, we'll come back here and begin the muscle work," he said.

"Oh, I couldn't let you do that. Just tell me what to do. Your time is so valuable," Jan protested.

"But I want to. In return, I get half of the vegetables this summer," he said.

"I can think of nothing better," she said as excited as a child. "May I fix you a glass of tea? Water? Beer?" she asked.

"No, thanks. Show me around, and then we can go pick a garden spot. I won't be able to stay long. I have to go to the funeral home this evening and then to the home of one of our parishioners who died last night."

It was a perfect Sunday afternoon. The air was crisp and clear. Even in the grays and browns of late fall, the earthy beauty was prevalent. They walked the entire fenced area surrounding the house, three acres in all. The fence had been recently mended and strengthened. An overgrown putting green took up a full quarter of the grassy area. At the other end of the yard, just before the tree line, lay a sunny spot with dying grass.

"Perfect," Rev. Tyler commented. "Tomorrow we'll dig up the grass and weeds and begin a bed. It'll be dirty work," he said.

"I don't mind. I'm looking forward to it," Jan said.

The reverend visited for two hours. They walked the front side of the farm, ending on the trail they had taken at Thanksgiving.

"It's so beautiful and peaceful here," the minister commented. "Thank you for sharing it with me."

Jan smiled.

"I'll be off. See you tomorrow then?" he asked. They walked back to the house in silence.

"What about your after-school program?" Jan asked as he opened his car door. "Do you take a day off from that, as well?"

"The Y.M.C.A. provides free swim on Mondays, so the kids go there instead. The older ones are trained as lifeguards; they take duty and teach swimming. Most of these kids have never had the opportunity to swim," he said. "I work hard, but I'm no martyr," he added. "I take time for myself and my friends." He started the car. "See you tomorrow."

Jan waved goodbye. "Thank you again, Father Tyler."

"Grant. After all, we've established that we're friends. I'll lock the gate on the way out."

During their session the next morning, Dr. Carey encouraged Jan's gardening plans. "There's nothing healthier than digging in the dirt," he said. "My wife and I are both avid gardeners," he added.

Jan talked of nothing but the gardening project, asking Dr. Carey questions about soil, fertilizing, watering.

"I don't think I've ever seen you this excited. You haven't even told me about moving into your own house," he laughed.

So Jan spent a long while telling Dr. Carey about the farmhouse and the new experience of living alone.

"I wish I had done this before I married David," she said.

"Many people don't – particularly women," Dr. Carey said. "You have to depend totally on yourself to recognize and trust your natural intuition. Women are often ridiculed for their strong intuitions, when all they're doing is listening to that inner voice."

He paused, folded his hands under his chin and regarded Jan for a long moment. "But even independent women can experience guilt connected to being raped," he said cautiously. "Part of that feeling is shame and embarrassment; part of it is the feeling that your soul has been defiled; part is disgust at yourself for not being able to have more control, for the irrational feeling of somehow not having resisted enough," he said.

Jan listened, saying nothing.

"True guilt, however, implies responsibility for the act. You are not responsible for the act of rape," he stated.

"But I am responsible for killing a man," Jan said quietly.

Dr. Carey shook his head. "Self-survival instinct. The reason you feel no guilt for shooting that man is that you listened to your instinct and you knew, as you know now, that Punk would have raped you again and killed all three of you," he argued.

For the first time since he had been seeing her, Jan did not argue back. "Perhaps," she said simply.

Dr. Carey leaned back in his chair and smiled. Two nights on her own with plans for a garden and she was softening.

"Jan, would you like an easier schedule with me during the Christmas holidays? I think we can lengthen the time between visits." He pulled out his schedule book. "We can start this week with only two visits; say, come back on Thursday?"

Jan nodded.

"Okay, nine o' clock, Thursday, Dec. 14. And then only two days the week before Christmas; say, Monday and Thursday again? And only one visit between Christmas and the New Year," Dr. Carey wrote as Jan nodded approval.

"You and your wife don't get away for Christmas?" she asked.

"No, I find that Christmas is the most difficult time of the year for many of my patients. I like to be available. My parents have been coming to visit us for Christmas since we've been married. We take vacation in the late spring," he said. "So, go plant your garden." He stood. "And I'll see you on Thursday. Give this schedule to my secretary on the way out, if you don't mind."

Jan did not shop in Atlanta this day or visit any museums, but drove straight back to her farm outside of Kingsford in anticipation of the afternoon of gardening ahead. Dropping even one visit a week to Dr. Carey gave Jan more time to work for Lamar and more time to settle into her home.

Having something concrete to do made a difference in Jan's outlook on life. Her future still did not move much past a few days at a time, but each day her tomorrow had stability and purpose. For weeks she had not been able to foresee into the next few hours. She knew that after the New Year the interruptions to her life would return, but for now she felt full.

"You must have had a good visit with Dr. Carey," Grant said as he leaned on his hoe to rest.

"Why, yes, I did," Jan smiled.

"You know, I have a minor in psychology," Grant said. "But it seems to me that only the rich receive the mental help they need, while many others don't have the funds for counseling. And insurance companies can be slow to approve psychological treatment."

"Is that why you chose the ministry?" Jan asked as she pulled at a stubborn clump of grass.

"My counseling training has come in handy, but I see that work in spiritual terms. I believe that some mental disorders can be traced to spiritual weaknesses. I have a theory that as a person leaves the spiritual realm behind and replaces God with himself, or puts too much emphasis on temporal concerns of job and material possessions, he becomes off balance. Of course, there are millions of people out there with natural chemical imbalances that can be hereditary or brought on by trauma," he said.

Jan sat back on her heels. Was Grant trying to direct a point her way? His back was to her now, once again absorbed in hoeing.

"Very few of the kids who come to my after-school program have any spiritual teaching," he said leaning on his hoe again. "If nothing else, I hope to offer them a knowledge of spiritual existence and spiritual truths." Grant wiped his brow and continued hoeing. "Anyway, your Dr. Carey seems to have helped you."

Jan paused before answering. "Yes, I suppose." Another pause. "But you know, I think living here on my own and working this garden have been of equal help." Jan did not like the direction the conversation was headed. Grant was her friend because he wasn't overly concerned about her recent life-changing experience.

"Bet you're right." Grant sat back on his heels and smiled as if he knew something she didn't. "Let's take a break."

The next week Grant came by every evening, except Wednesday, with new types of nutrients and nitrogen to build up the garden soil. He stayed for dinner Tuesday and took her out to dinner Friday at the local Greek restaurant.

So much had happened this first week of independence. There were only one and a half weeks until Christmas, and Jan still had so much to do. On the morning of December 16, Jan poured a second cup of coffee and finished the morning paper to celebrate her one week of independence. She was leaving to shop when the phone rang.

"Jan? So, how are you?" David asked with reserved concern. This move had not set well with him and he had been avoiding her phone calls. He called Wednesday night, only to complain about how much work he had. He cut the conversation short after hearing about Jan's garden and Grant's help.

"So, what are you up to today, Ms. Independent?" David asked.

"I'm getting ready to go Christmas shopping. Anything I can buy for you? Do you want me to buy something for your parents?" Jan resented having to offer to do his family shopping.

Dr. Carey told her that self-respect included not allowing even mates or parents to take advantage of her. He said her guilt over the rape, her inability to stop it, was much like her self-reproach over letting others dump on her. Jan thought this idea a little far-fetched, but she did find herself more openly resentful of David.

"That would be a big help. You know, we've been swamped trying to get these farmers in financial line before the end of the year. It's just as well you're not here, because you'd never see me. Look, the reason I'm calling is that Mother and Dad want to know our Christmas plans. I thought maybe I'd come there Christmas Eve, so we can spend one night there, and then we can go on to Atlanta on Christmas Day for a few days," David said.

Jan did not want to go to David's parents' house with him. And she did not want David to sleep in her new home.

She liked her in-laws okay, but they tended to be self-absorbed and tactless, particularly in situations concerning Jan. David's older sister, her husband the insurance agent, and their two overweight and spoiled daughters lived in Atlanta, also. She didn't relish facing their comments and prying questions.

"I'm so glad we'll at least spend a few days together. Everyone here would love to see you, too. I may not spend more than one night with you at your parents' because I also have work to do for Daddy and more meetings with John," she said gently.

Silence.

"David? Are you there?" she asked.

"Yes. Fine. Whatever you want. Just don't forget to get my parents something. And what about Sally and her kids?" he said dumping the whole family on her.

"Perhaps it would mean more to your family if you also personally chose something for each person," Jan suggested.

Silence.

"I mean, I'll, of course, get something from the two of us," she added.

"Well, I can't sit here talking on the phone all day," David said brusquely. "I have work to do. I'll call before Christmas, and we can finalize plans. Goodbye. Take care."

Her mother had always said that you don't just marry the man ... you marry his entire family.

Chapter Four

A Jameson-Calhoun Christmas in Kingsford was one steeped with tradition and a string of family gatherings. First, there was Christmas Eve dinner at Meemaw and Papa Ralph's. In attendance were May and Lamar and whoever of their children made it; Uncle Ralph and whatever blonde he had in tow and whichever children were on the outs with his ex-wife; Cousin Lady, a distant cousin of Meemaw's who had no living family; Papa Ralph's brother, Uncle Percy, and his wife, Leila, who had no children.

Eugene and Belle were there to do the cooking, serving and cleaning, but they were also included in the Bible story and family prayer. This year May persuaded Julia Ann and James and Peterson to make a special effort to be home to support 'Janet' as she had taken to calling Jan. Jan figured the formality meant either her mother was trying to give her dignity in the face of such ongoing exposure, or she was trying to change Jan into someone else.

Grant and John had been invited this year for Christmas Eve. John said he preferred to be with his parents. He knew that his presence would change the family focus to the trial. Grant had already invited to his house his divorced mother, Tommie Tyler, of Birmingham, as well as several parishioners who had no family and no invitations.

Jan was disappointed, but Grant knew that she and David needed time together. Though their friendship was evident, Grant was also ministering to Jan, and he had practically felt the hair go up on David's neck when they met for lunch earlier that day. Grant's mother came along. She was a petite woman with pretty silver hair. Jan was struck by her natural appearance, her simple beauty. Jan liked her right away. David tried to talk farming and finances for a while and ended up in a sullen silence.

Uncle Ralph came Christmas Eve without a blonde. He brought his oldest son, Ralph Oleander Calhoun III (known as "Cal"), who was a carbon copy of his father. His other children spent most holidays with their mother.

The evening began at five-thirty with cocktails. Everyone dressed in the finest Christmas apparel. At six sharp, Belle and Eugene were invited in from the kitchen to hear the Bible reading of Luke, Chapter Two. When they were younger, the grandchildren took turns reading the Christmas passage each year. Peterson was given the honor this year because he was the youngest present. Afterward, Papa Ralph asked all gathered to bow in prayer, and he thanked the good Lord for all the blessings of those who gathered. Drinks were replenished, and gifts to and from those present were distributed and opened.

Meemaw had the last present to unwrap, a bottle of bath oil from Uncle Ralph.

"I know that's your favorite, Mother," he said from across the room.

"Why, thank you, darling. Of course it is," Meemaw replied with a warm smile.

Jan knew that the bottle of bath oil would be stashed under the bathroom sink with the other six bottles already there. She had never known her grandmother to use the stuff, and she always wondered why Uncle Ralph continued to give it. Maybe someone should tell him.

David had little to say. His gift pile was larger this year. Meemaw and May felt so sorry for him, what with Jan living in Kingsford now and the turmoil he was going through. They gave him not only his yearly dress-white Brooks Brothers shirt, but also a shaving kit, tie and a clock radio.

The family members moved into the dining room where a card table had been added in the enclave of the French doors to make room for the expansion of family. Fine table linens, silver flatware, family china and candlelight all sparkled as Jan remembered from earlier days. She was no longer filled with the awe this glitter used to bring. The meal was excellent, as always, and the conversation remained bland. No one tip-toed around sensitive subjects, for family meals were marked by safe, surface conversation.

"Everything looks so nice."

"I've never seen so much food."

"You've really outdone yourself, Meemaw."

These were the introductory statements carried over from decades of family gatherings. The dialogue later moved to exclamations over new clothes, new hairstyles, glasses ... anything noncommittal and pleasant. Silences were filled by clinking silverware and the squeak of the swinging door as Belle and Eugene came back and forth to bring seconds and refill glasses.

David didn't even attempt to join in, though in the past he had said that Jan's family knew what a real Christmas was all about, while his family always ate out at one of the finer restaurants in Atlanta. Whether separated by the pity of the others or embroiled in his own self-turmoil over the direction of his life, David might as well have been a blind date Jan had brought along.

"I think I'll turn in," David said as soon as they were back at the Jameson's.

"You aren't going to the eleven o' clock Christmas Eve service?" she asked

"I'm awfully tired, Jan. Besides the drive over, I have worked fifteen-hour days since you left," he said irritably.

"I know, dear. It's all right. I'll see you in the morning," Jan said calmly, and she kissed him on the cheek.

May suggested another round of drinks before the service, which all agreed to. They were almost late and had to sit shoulder-to-shoulder on one of the back pews. Grant winked at Jan as he walked down the aisle for the procession.

"If I didn't know better, I'd say that preacher is sweet on you," Julia Ann leaned over to whisper.

May poked Julia Ann in the ribs with her elbow. "Shush. The good reverend has been counseling Jan. Kindly say nothing more," she said in a whisper Jan could overhear.

Christmas Eve dinner loomed surreal in comparison to the Christmas Eve candlelight service. Jan was thrown into the reality of Christ's Mass; she felt at one with the scorned Mary who, though a virgin, was pregnant before her marriage to Joseph. Stripped of the gifts, the traditions, the family gathering, Christmas became simply the Mother and Child, supported by Joseph, surrounded by farm animals, hay, shepherds and all the angels of heaven.

In years before, Jan had scoffed at many of the Christmas Eve parishioners for she knew that this was the only service they attended the whole year. But this Christmas Eve, Jan truly knew the meaning of being a sinner. She was one with her fellow parishioners, a communion of sinful souls in search of forgiveness.

Jan and David left Kingsford before the family brunch. At first, May had been upset that they were going to miss the Christmas Day gathering.

"Everyone is dying to see you, honey," her mother whined.

If Jan were to stay, she would be the center of attention and that would not be fair to Peterson, who was home from college, or Julia Ann, showing with her first pregnancy. Secretly, May was relieved that the family would not have to concentrate on tiptoeing around certain subjects to protect Jan. Now she could discuss Jan's unfortunate situation with whomever would listen.

Somehow there had not been enough time for David to see the farmhouse and the changes she had made there. She didn't offer and he didn't ask. Jan figured that he was relieved not to have to face her newly-found independence.

David's parents had never been the warmest people, but on this Christmas Day they were barely civil. David's father made an effort, his mother faked concern, but his sister was outwardly hostile. The Christmas dinner was held in the evening at the family's country club in their immediate suburb. The meal was a disaster. David's two nieces whined the entire meal and one spilt her milk, on purpose from Jan's point of view, across the table and into her father's lap. The father jumped up from the table yelling obscenities, the little girl burst into tears, and the mother turned on Jan.

"This is all your fault," she screamed. "We have all been so upset over what you've done to poor David. It would have been better if you hadn't come at all." She snatched the little girl from her high chair and stomped off to the ladies room to clean her up.

At this point, the older girl started crying because she was missing the *Charlie Brown Christmas Special.*

David did not defend Jan; he was enjoying the extra sympathy thrown his way, but at least he didn't join in the abuse. It was Jan's turn to head straight to bed, after thanking the Fergusons for the meal and the nice gown, a flannel "granny gown" like the ones she had received every Christmas since she and David had been married.

"David, I'm sorry to have upset your family. I'd no intention of doing so," she said to the other twin bed. Though David's sister's room had a double bed, Jan and David had been put in his old bedroom every time they visited. For once, Jan was thankful for the sleeping arrangements, although in their early married days they had sneaked from bed to bed, and once they'd even pushed the beds together.

Silence.

"David?"

"Of course, I know there was no intent on your part, only you cannot blame my family for not understanding, just as I don't understand, why you've allowed this incident to change your life, to change my life, dammit. Do you ever plan to come back home? Just what am I supposed to think? That maybe you wanted this all along, but now you have an *excuse* to leave? How can I be supportive when you're five hundred miles away?"

She knew he had things he needed to say, so she let him talk.

"I just bet a lot of these crazy ideas of yours have come from that kooky doctor. I can't believe that man thinks it's right to allow a one-time tragedy in your life to get the better of you. You're merely giving into it instead of conquering it. Couldn't we prepare for your trial just as well from Riverdale? Hell, it's closer to Brevard than Kingsford is. And why take on this new responsibility in your father's company? You have a perfectly good job waiting for you at home."

He paused. She remained silent.

"No, you can't blame my family at all, Janet, because I myself will never understand."

He turned his back to her and pulled the covers tightly around his neck. David only called her *Janet* when he was angry beyond reason.

"David, I understand your resentment – and your family's, if that's any consolation. I just don't know how to explain any better than I already have why I must do this," Jan said.

"If you don't mind, I'm very tired. I forgot to tell you that I have to leave first thing in the morning to be back in the office. Bobby Lane killed himself last night."

"Oh, David, I'm so sorry. What happened? Why didn't you tell me?" Jan exclaimed.

"He filed bankruptcy three days ago after I told him he couldn't have any more loans. His car ran off the road on a tight curve. A neighbor who lives on that road said he must've been going at least ninety miles an hour," David sighed.

"Oh, David. It's not your fault, honey. I'm so sorry," Jan tried to comfort him.

"I haven't exactly had a lone moment with you," David snapped. "I'd rather you not continue trying to *explain* things to me. Actions speak louder than words, and your actions are telling me I have to rethink my own life, rethink our relationship," he said pitifully.

"Could we have breakfast together before you leave? We could go to the breakfast bar at Shoney's. And we don't even have to talk; we'll just eat. David?"

He didn't answer, and Jan didn't force the issue.

The next morning, they left quietly.

"Is it me? Am I hard-hearted, or are my observations about David's family on the money?" Jan asked Dr. Carey. For the fourth time in the last thirty minutes, Jan bounded from her chair to walk the office floor.

Dr. Carey smiled and let her continue talking it out; he knew she needed to.

"It's as if, all of a sudden, I cannot tolerate shallowness and conceit, pigheadedness and pettiness. I don't know." She paused by the now familiar book case, running her fingers along the most-loved titles. "All of a sudden life seems so short, and I feel compelled to separate myself from anyone or anything that has no true importance in the big picture. You know what I mean?" Jan finally spent her pent-up energy and sat again in front of her confidant. "So, do you think I would have come to this point in my life anyway? Or has my downfall become my saving grace?"

"My, aren't we philosophical today?" Dr. Carey laughed.

"I'm serious, Dr. Carey. These are the things I think about all the time, and I really want to know," she said earnestly.

Dr. Carey sobered his humor. "I believe you have a natural depth that would have led you to these conclusions eventually, if more gradually. Many women come to these same deductions after having a first child. Children can also put life into perspective. Even during pregnancy, these feelings can develop."

The doctor was beaming, and not at Jan. "I didn't think you had any children," Jan said.

"My wife just found out she's pregnant," Dr. Carey said excitedly.

"Congratulations. That's great," Jan said sincerely.

"Jan," he said, back in his doctor mode, "recognizing people for what they are is healthy, but you also have to learn to be tolerant. The fact that these people are your in-laws makes them harder to ignore than if they were acquaintances or neighbors."

She waited for him to continue.

"What about David? How do you see him in all of this? Do you see him differently?" he asked.

Jan thought for a moment. "I don't know. I can't blame him for the way he's acting right now. I haven't exactly been fair to him. Right now, I feel like a sister toward him. Surely he senses that. Do you think I'll ever feel the way I used to about David?" she asked Dr. Carey directly.

"I can't answer that for you, Jan. I can only guide you to be honest with your feelings," he answered.

"You said I have a natural depth. How can you tell? Does David?" Jan asked.

Dr. Carey smiled. "Now, this is not a scientific theory, young lady, it is merely my observation of humans. I perceive a sense about each patient during my first consultation. Some give an aura of openness or depth of personality, even when experiencing mental anguish. Others seem, I don't know, spiritless. You don't look into their eyes; you look at them. Of this group, there are two subgroups: one has possibilities of what I call 'opening the window to one's soul,' so to speak, while the other either was born without the ability to do this, or has locked the window so securely that opening it is now impossible.

"These are very unscientific terms. People with schizophrenia, chemical imbalance, trauma-related personality disorders, cannot help their condition. Many times there are physical causes, a certain gene they were born with, a trauma that triggers a chemical imbalance, whatever. But the person beyond the disorder still comes through."

"You sound like a preacher," Jan joked. "My time is up and I'm starved. I could only find coffee and a piece of toast at the Ferguson's this morning." Jan stood and extended her hand as she always did. "I'll see you a week from today, then."

"Let's make it Wednesday. I usually save the day after New Year's for severe depression cases, and you, young lady, are not depressed. But this hearing is fast approaching – January 9th isn't it? – so, I want to see you twice a week, including the Friday before you leave," Dr. Carey said in his professional tone.

The week between Christmas and New Year, Lamar's

construction company office staff were crazy with year-end wrap up work. Jan was glad for the work, and the staff was especially grateful for the extra help. She typed and transferred fourth quarter and year-end records into the computer. This week there was no going out to lunch, but Lamar brought them various delicious meals every day.

"I can't tell you what an asset you've been to Betty Jean and Sue," Lamar said on Thursday evening. It was about 6 p.m. and they were still at the office. "Why don't you knock off for the day and come home for dinner with me? I know you're a totally independent woman and all, but your mother and I both miss you. It would mean a great deal to her, you know." Lamar gave his daughter that look she couldn't refuse. "Plus, an inside source told me that Retha fixed her famous turkey hash and beaten biscuits."

Jan laughed. "All right. I'd love to come."

"So, dear, will David be coming here for the New Year?" May asked during dinner.

"I don't know. I've tried to call him for the past three days, but he's never home. He's been working hard," Jan answered.

"Maybe you can go there, dear," Her mother said hopefully. Jan had fallen easily into the single life and May was worried about her daughter's marriage. Other than Uncle Ralph, there had never been a divorce in the Calhoun or Jameson families.

"I have to meet with John to prepare for the Grand Jury hearing, so I'll probably stay here," she said casually.

"We'll be going to the club; you're welcome to come with us," May said.

"I've never liked New Year's Eve. All that forced partying, you know; but thanks for the invite," Jan smiled. "Tell Retha tomorrow that this is a great dinner. I'm glad I came."

Jan did have to meet with John. He was more nervous about this case than any other. John knew too well the blunt meanness a district attorney could use, particularly in a rape case. Jan's apparent unending strength worried John even more, for it could be a front that would crumble in the first five minutes of grilling. He had talked several times a week with Caleb and Murray's attorney in Riverdale. He wanted to make sure that every base was covered. Surely the Grand Jury hearing would be the end of all this.

David finally called Jan Friday morning while she was at Lamar's office.

"David. I've been trying to call you for days," she began.

"I've done nothing but work my ass off," he cut in rudely.

"Yes, dear. I was just going to say you must be working long hours, poor thing," Jan said.

"Are you coming for New Year's or not?" he asked abruptly. "I have to work the day before and the day after. Lucy Meadows is going in with a bunch of the farm wives and renting the country club for a big party. I thought you might want to go," he said.

"I'm sorry, David. I have to meet with John every day. The hearing is January 9th, you know," she said.

"Yes, I know. And I doubt I can get away then. I mean, I either work, or I quit my job to follow you around. It can't be both ways."

Jan knew that David was too angry; it would be best not to start an argument. "Of course, I understand. I hadn't even expected you to go. Mom and Dad are going. And John, of course. Besides, this whole mess should be over by then, John says. You just do what you need to do there," Jan said nicely.

A pause. "You never even asked me to go with you," David said, clearly hurt.

No. I didn't ask you to go with me because you act like this, Jan thought to herself. Then to David she said, "David, honey, I didn't want to put undue pressure on you when your job has been so demanding. I'm trying to burden you with this as little as possible."

Her heart went out to him. She knew that David needed her to need him through this. She just couldn't go that far right now. She needed distance from all those who needed her. To act like she needed him now would be to ignore her own desires, and Dr. Carey warned her of the consequences of that.

Secretly, Jan was pleased to have no New Year's Eve plans. Like other Sunday evenings, she planned to don her pajamas and watch a movie, perhaps an old Alfred Hitchcock, and retire early. To celebrate, she would pop some popcorn and maybe even drink a beer. She could start writing in the journal that Dr. Carey had given her. He'd suggested that writing her feelings would help her see herself more clearly.

Routine and solitude gave Jan a chance to think. Her life had rushed forward for years now without her taking time to reflect. She had rushed to work, rushed through preparations and plans for six classes a day, rushed to the store, rushed home to clean and cook and rushed from one social gathering to another. What would life be like at a reasonable pace?

Jan was successful at avoiding well-meaning people she knew in Kingsford. After running into a few of May's friends at the grocery store, Jan changed to early morning shopping before work. From there, she would visit the chapel, to find the direction she needed for that day.

Some days she woke up full of angst. Anybody else might be worried about the upcoming hearing, but Jan woke up those days worried over her soul. If God said that killing another human is a sin, why did she feel no guilt? Why did she feel culpable for being raped? She felt dirty, for she could not shake this *sin*. The remorse she felt the strongest, however, concerned her relationship with David. None of this was his fault. He knew as well as she that her love for him had changed.

These days, Jan paced the chapel, talking out loud to a cross that wouldn't answer back and a sculpture of the Virgin Mary who gave Jan that same sweet smile no matter what she said. Other days, Jan sat in the chapel and thought of nothing. She just sat and listened. On these days she was filled with calm, not needing to know the answers. Now she must concentrate on learning to live a life that was hers, not the fulfillment of others.

Her battle with guilt she had not been able to share with Dr. Carey. He talked of guilt almost every session, trying to make sure she was not feeling needless responsibility for her rape. John tried to get her to see her shooting Punk as self-defense. Jan did try, but every time, the angst returned because she could not change the picture in her head of that night.

She had not thought whether or not Punk was a threat to her life; she had not thought whether or not Punk was a threat to the lives of Murray and Caleb. She only saw those ugly eyes, the sneer, the greasy hair and pocked, oily face, the drool she could still taste. She killed that man because she hated him for what he had done to her ... and for what she knew he could do again. Killing him took away her fear, but the act could not free her of feeling dirty.

Only Grant witnessed Jan's anguish, and only Grant knew her struggle with herself and God. But he knew that now was not the time to merely heal. Jan had to struggle to be reborn.

Jan could not remember a New Year's Day when she did not nurse a dreadful hangover while trying to be sociable at football bowl parties. She was looking forward to being alone to welcome in the New Year. A storm was forecast for late afternoon. The cold rain started about three-thirty, and the temperature dropped quickly. She turned up the heat and changed into sweats. The TV broadcast severe thunderstorm warnings followed by a cold front.

By six, the winds had picked up and howled around the house. Branches fell and knocked against the windows and the spurts of blinding lightning revealed the bending trees. At six-thirty, the power went out. Even the phone was dead. Jan groped around for the flashlight her father gave her. She made her way to the dining room buffet where she knew there would be a supply of candles and matches.

Once the house was lit by candlelight, Jan felt more at ease. She had just finished a good book and she couldn't find another in the house she wanted to read, so she curled up in the den with the journal. She wrote the date and the weather, but she couldn't do more. The past was still too close to see objectively, and her future was on hold.

A fierce bolt of lightning struck nearby, followed closely by a loud clap of thunder. *Bang! Bang!* She froze. Could a tree have fallen and hit the door? The banging continued. Someone was at the door. She hadn't heard a car drive up. She had locked both gates so a car couldn't get through. *Bang! Bang!*

"Silly, get a hold of yourself," she said aloud. It was probably her father checking on her. Boldly she made her way to the kitchen and shone her flashlight out the door window. There stood Grant underneath layers of coat and raincoat, holding his hood close around his neck.

Jan quickly unlocked the door and ushered him in. "Why? ... What? ... " Jan stammered.

"Sorry to barge in like this, but I thought you might want some company. I tried to call ahead, but your line is out. I see your electricity is out, too," he said, removing his dripping outerwear. "I hope you don't mind I've come?" he asked.

"No, not a bit. But you must have walked from the highway. I locked both the gates," she said with concern.

Grant grinned and pulled a key from his pocket. "Your father slipped me this key after church today. He said that he liked me checking up on you, so he made a duplicate."

Jan shook her head and smiled, helping Grant out of his coat. "What's that?" she asked, referring to the bulk under his arm.

"Just a little New Year's celebration," Grant said, and he pulled out of a plastic grocery bag a bottle of champagne and a Scrabble game.

"How do you always know my mood?" Jan smiled.

By midnight the storm had cleared, leaving crisp, cold air in its wake. The champagne bottle was empty and Jan and Grant had played two games of Scrabble. He won the first game, but Jan pulled ahead in the last thirty minutes of the second game. The lights came back on about eleven, but Jan rushed around giddily turning them all off.

"I don't know when I've had a better New Year's Eve," Grant said as he put away the game.

"And I don't know when I've drunk an entire bottle of champagne," Jan laughed.

There was nothing more to say, and Jan watched Grant's face as he finished replacing the game's box top. She wasn't prepared for him to meet her stare. They held the gaze until Jan began to blush. Had she never noticed how deep blue Grant's eyes were? David's eyes were also blue, but a light blue, not such a deep, sad blue.

He grinned at her flushed cheeks.

"I must be off. Happy New Year, Jan Ferguson," and he kissed her lightly on the forehead. "By the way," he said as he walked to the door, "your dad tells me that you are headed to Brevard next Sunday or Monday."

"That's right. It has to do with the hearing, you know. I have to appear before the grand jury to determine my guilt or my innocence," Jan tried to sound lighthearted.

"Surely, no jury, grand or not, would ever .... " Grant began.

"Don't," Jan interrupted. "Everyone says that, but I have to be prepared for either outcome," she added seriously.

"I brought this up because it just so happens that I have business with the Western North Carolina diocese in Asheville and will be heading that way myself on Monday. I suggested to your father that I look after you and your mother until Lamar can meet you there in the middle of the week. My business shouldn't take more than a day and I can be free to be of assistance to you and your mother. I was planning to stay a few extra days to do some hiking," Grant said. "David will be meeting you there, too, won't he?" he asked.

"He can't get away right now," Jan said. She paused. Jan wanted as few people involved in her case as possible. It was going to be bad enough walking through that cabin with the boys, John Larsen, law enforcement, and twelve new strangers.

"Jan?" Grant ventured. "I mean, I can't be much help to you Monday and Tuesday, but I can be there after that," he said.

"Oh," Jan said relieved. "Tuesday is the day you'll be tied up? Well, sure, I don't see why not."

Chapter Five

Jan had little time to herself between New Year's and January 7, when she, May and Meemaw were to leave for Brevard. The three women were going to make the trip in two days, leaving Saturday afternoon and stopping in Greenville, South Carolina. Jan wanted to drive the whole way on Monday, but as usual, she had little say.

John Larsen had detectives finishing up reports on Punk's character, family, upbringing, anything that could prove his violent nature. He questioned and re-questioned the sheriff's deputies and the FBI agents involved in details concerning the placement of the body and the layout of the cabin. He flew to South Carolina to meet with Caleb and Murray and their lawyer. Bryson McNeil was a local Riverside boy whose father had been an attorney and South Carolina state representative for twelve years. He met every day with Jan.

Jan saw Dr. Carey the Wednesday and Friday before she left.

"Jan, I want us to discuss guilt. Some guilt is healthy, for it tells us that we did wrong. Societal guilt, produced by what society thinks is right for everybody, is an unnecessary acceptance of someone else's judgment," Dr. Carey said Wednesday morning. Dr. Carey allotted two hours for this week's sessions because, like John, he wanted her mentally prepared for the consequences of claiming guilt in front of the grand jury.

"We've already discussed this, Dr. Carey," Jan said.

"You've told me that you feel guilty for being raped by one Artemis Delmer McQuirk and that you do not feel remorse for killing him," he replied seriously, not taking his eyes from hers. "Don't you see, Jan, that your guilt over this rape has to do with your own feelings, not with your participation in the act, and not because you somehow caused it or could have avoided it?"

"I do see, Dr. Carey. Objectively I see that. I'm intelligent, college educated; I've had psychology 101. But that doesn't erase the memory of those feelings every time that scene comes to mind. No matter how I try to push it away, no matter how I try not to think on it, the rape replays itself over and over, not in sequence, but in bits and pieces of smell, touch, taste, and surrealistic sights and sounds," Jan desperately tried to explain.

"Tell me what you see, what you hear, what you taste and smell and feel," Dr. Carey said leaning forward earnestly.

"I'd rather not."

"What do you smell, Jan?" Dr. Carey persisted.

Jan shut her eyes. "I ... I smell stale whiskey on rotten breath. I smell sweat, a foul stench – a smell of evil, of fear. I remember trying not to vomit, but thinking that vomit would smell better."

"What do you see?"

"I see drool at the edges of his mouth. I see that sneer of his lips, his black, empty eyes. He's so gross, with his hairy belly, all pocked – white, like molded wood chips – his thighs too. His hair is greasy. I don't want it to touch me. His nose seems big and marked with dirt. His teeth smell rotten; they're crooked, half of them missing and stained."

Jan looked up at Dr. Carey. "I hate seeing these bits and pieces of him. If I could see him whole, I wouldn't be afraid. I could conquer one whole image. It's the fragments I can't erase."

"What do you hear, Jan?" Dr. Carey pushed on.

She shut her eyes again. "I hear his breathing. It's raspy, congested. I hear his foul words, his grunting. I hear the silence when I can't hear him, expecting sound, straining for a warning. I hear screaming. *That's my voice.* I hear whimpering. Caleb. I hear abandoned sobbing." Jan looked at her hands, her face contorted.

Dr. Carey forced her on. "What else do you hear?"

"I hear his maniacal laugh. It sends shivers down my spine. Then, silence. The windowpane crashes, and I know he'll come after us. I hear the curdling laugh behind me. He won't stop laughing, even when I knock him to the ground with a rock." Jan looked up.

"The gunshots. Did you hear the gunshots?" he asked.

"No. I don't remember hearing gunshots. Just silence. Just seeing his wicked blood spurting and splattering on the leaves." Jan looked calm.

"Jan, what do you feel? With your touch, your skin, what do you feel?"

"I don't know. I don't want to talk about it," she stammered.

"Jan what did you feel, on your skin?"

"He hurt me." Jan started to cry silently. "He hurt my arm when he pulled me. His hands were so rough and scaly. I could feel his belt buckle digging into my flesh; his zipper pinched my thigh when he pulled it down. It hurt so. My neck ached; he pulled my hair." Jan stopped. She wiped the tears with the back of her hand.

"What did you feel, Jan?" Dr. Carey persisted.

"I felt weighted down. He was so heavy. Then my head was pressed into my chest. I could hardly breathe, could only swallow so as not to vomit. The vomit felt hot and burned in the back of my throat. I was trying to move my head to breathe. I wasn't ready for it. Wasn't ready for the pain, the mean thrust. I thought I was going to be split in two. It didn't stop. It happened and happened again, and then it was as if the foulest being had puked into my soul. My soul! I could feel his oozing evil spread through me, into my bowels, my veins, my very heart." Jan was crying, with her head down, her forehead leaned against her hands.

Dr. Carey let her cry. Never before had he felt such empathy for a patient. He felt ravished, as if he had been raped. He had pulled the fragments from her so she could put her memories into perspective. He wanted her to see the picture as a whole before she faced a jury.

The doctor quietly slipped out the back door of his office and ran upstairs for two Cokes. When he returned, Jan had calmed. She didn't seem to notice that he had left.

"I'm sorry I had to do that, Jan," Dr. Carey said as he patted her shoulder. "Would you like some Coke?"

She accepted the cold drink gratefully, and Dr. Carey moved to the chair behind his desk.

"You're right, you know," Jan said.

"How's that?" the doctor asked.

"I mean, if any of us saw ourselves making love to our own mates and enjoying it, our faces would portray something different than a pleasing feeling," she suggested.

"It's true, many artists portray a pained or sadistic facial expression during the throes of orgasm," he answered.

"Perhaps some of the guilt is David's reaction and my family's. If I had been beaten to a pulp instead of being raped, the reaction would be different. Rape changes the picture somehow. Whether the guilt is mine or not, they can't forget. Rape brings out feelings of inadequacy in the men. It's as if they should have been able to protect me from it."

"You should be in my profession. You describe these feelings and reactions just fine. They are normal. Most of all, I want you to see that they are typical for the situation," he said.

"Did you know that fear has a taste?" Jan asked.

"How so?"

"The fear I felt when we were first kidnapped was an unknown and unpleasant taste, but not unbearable. The fear of what was to come, of what Punk would do to me, and did do, was bitter tasting, awful. I guess it's all in the senses, our bodies' reaction to certain given situations." Jan sipped on her Coke.

"And what do your senses tell you now?" Dr. Carey asked.

"Now, I think I can see the whole, though not the whole of the experience. There are really four parts to that: the kidnapping, the rape, the shooting and, finally, our escape."

"Ah, but you mentioned the rape as a whole," Dr. Carey said hopefully.

"I believe it is a whole now. I believe I can accept my body's human frailties. Perhaps I thought before I had none," she said.

"But you do, Jan. We all do. It is part of our human condition. So is self-survival, which we'll discuss Friday." He smiled as she rose, threw her can into the nearby trashcan, and walked toward the door.

"Maybe accepting my humanity is part of growing up," she said as she reached the door. "But growing up means leaving childhood behind ... and sometimes the people in it," she said and shut the door behind her.

Dr. Carey opened his top drawer and switched off the tape recorder. He never let his patients know they were being taped, but the tapes helped him review cases. Once the patient left for whatever reason, the tapes were destroyed. Only the factual information was retained in files.

John Larsen had called the doctor yesterday and wanted to know if Dr. Carey would tape these important sessions with Jan to help with her defense. The psychiatrist was a man of unquestionable integrity and professionalism. He knew that to turn this or any other tapes over to the attorney, or anyone else, would be a breach of trust with his patient. Dr. Carey would have to come up with another way to help Jan's case.

The grand jury hearing was in less than a week, and surely by her own testimony, the jurors would see she was innocent, Dr. Carey thought to himself. If Jan responded as he hoped she would during Friday's session, then Jan herself would have to admit to self-defense. He would call Larsen back on Friday and let him know how the session had gone. He ejected the tape and placed it in the wall safe behind his desk.

When Jan returned to Dr. Carey's office on Friday, she thought that his job was almost done. She had successfully put the rape scene into a whole that she could acknowledge because she knew the outcome. She did not know that Dr. Carey was far from through with her therapy, for he felt as responsible for having her cleared in court as John Larsen.

"You're not planning to go to this hearing alone, are you, Jan?" Dr. Carey began.

"Why, Dr. Carey, you've become an expert on *in media res*," Jan laughed. "What happened to 'good morning, Jan,' and 'how are you today'?"

"Sorry. I've had you on my mind quite a bit and I want to make sure that you're ready to face this," he said solemnly.

"Now, Doc, the other day you praised me on my strength and clear thinking about the situation," Jan smiled.

"I know. I just want to make sure I've prepared you sufficiently for all you'll face," he replied.

"I thought that was John Larsen's job," Jan answered.

"He can only arm you with legalistic facts. I want to arm you emotionally," he said.

"All right. To answer your question, no I'm not going alone. My mother and grandmother will accompany me. John Larsen will be there, and Caleb and Murray, and their lawyer," she said.

"What about David? I'd think he'd want to be there," Dr. Carey asked, puzzled.

"He's under a great deal of pressure at work." She hesitated. "Besides, I'd rather him not go. I don't want to have to relive this in front of him."

"You need someone close; a friend," Dr. Carey suggested.

"My minister will be there Tuesday night after the hearing."

"Your minister? Oh, yes, the friend who started you gardening. Are you close?" Dr. Carey made a mental connection as he asked the question.

"I can talk to Grant about anything. He listens and he doesn't judge. He doesn't know me from my past. He accepts me for who I am right now," she answered.

"You can talk to me about anything and I like who you are," Dr. Carey said, feigning hurt but smiling all the while.

"My dad pays you to talk to me," she joked back. "Yes, I can talk to you about anything, only you're not going to share yourself in return; so, even though I like you, you are more of a sounding board than a friend."

"You're right. That's as it should be," he said kindly. "How does David feel about your new friendship with this young bachelor minister?"

"He likes him okay. He acts a bit jealous, but David is jealous of everything about my new life right now. He can't understand why I won't come back to Riverdale and pick right back up where we left off. I don't blame him. That's just the way it is," Jan said.

"Perhaps he would like to be given a chance to find a new self with you. He may also want a fresh start," Dr. Carey suggested.

"I don't think so. David is only comfortable with status quo," she said.

"So were you at one time," he said.

"I know." Jan paused and looked at the waiting face on the other side of the desk. "I don't want David around right now. I want to be independent, to live alone and make decisions based on only what I want at the present. I know that sounds selfish, but if David were here, I would have to consider him in every move I made, every decision. Eventually I would be catering to him as I always have. I have to establish myself as whole first."

"I understand perfectly. As your psychiatrist I will point out that your attitude is the most mentally healthy you could have. But what about after all this court business is over and you are able to resume a normal life? What then?" he asked.

"First of all, who's to say I won't be in jail?" Jan frowned. "If not, I honestly don't think David will like me as I am now," she said.

"I think you should let him be the judge of that. Maybe you're underestimating him," Dr. Carey replied.

"Maybe." Jan said nothing more.

"Enough of David," Dr. Carey said and leaned back in his chair with his elbows on the chairs arms and fingertips pressed together. "Have you ever been hunting?" he asked.

"Hunting?"

"Yes. Have you ever shot an animal or bird with a rifle or shotgun? You said you were a good shot with a rifle in high school."

"I first took riflery at summer camp and I loved it. I had a high school friend, a boy, and we used to ride horses together. One summer he lent me one of his .22-caliber rifles and we started target shooting. The Christmas break after I started college he took me and a small-gauge shotgun duck hunting at his uncle's pond. At the time I didn't know it was a baited pond – you know where they plant corn so the ducks and geese will come?

"It was late December and an unusually cold, dreary day. We came to the pond before dawn and waded into the thickest of this wooded swamp. It was dark and foggy and so quiet. I had never heard such quiet. We reached a log sticking out of the water and stopped, barely breathing, and we just listened. A rush of movement filled the air, and I saw it was a flock of ducks flying onto the pond. The first one I could see clearly landed right in front of me. He was so beautiful, such vivid greens and a mark of purple on the side of his neck. I forgot why we were there and just stared at this duck in his habitat.

"Then my friend started whispering for me to shoot. I was confused. Shoot? But he was so pretty and he hadn't moved. Danny was frantic and whispered that we had practiced for this day, take the chance. I raised the gun to my shoulder. Still the duck sat unaware. I aimed, but I couldn't pull the trigger. Danny yelled *shoot*, and I guess I just reacted. I shot the duck and he looked at me dazed before falling over in the water.

"Danny sent his dog in after the duck and was slapping me on the back and congratulating me, but all I could see was that duck's eyes staring at me like he trusted me. I cried all the way home. I wanted to cook and eat the duck so the killing wouldn't be a waste, but Danny had him stuffed for me. Every time I looked at that duck, I remembered why I don't like to hunt." Jan stopped. "Do you hunt?"

"No," he answered. He leaned forward in his counseling mode.

"Jan, if you feel guilty over having shot and killed a duck on a hunting trip, I don't see how you could ever kill a human being unless it was for self-defense."

"Oh, so that's where this was leading," Jan said. "But I didn't kill a human being. I killed a snake. And I didn't wait for that snake to bite me again before I killed it," she said adamantly.

"Exactly. You had no choice because you knew that man would have killed you and those boys, just like a poisonous snake loose in your yard might harm you," he said.

"You don't understand," Jan tried again. "It was my choice to kill him that saved me. I did not wait to react, as I have waited my whole life to do. I took charge and attacked first," she said.

"What if the rock you first threw had killed him. Wouldn't that be you saving the boys, for he was going to shoot them?" Dr. Carey tried.

"But it didn't. He was down but he wasn't dead, and I wasn't about to let him get up. He looked at me with those leering eyes; he laughed – laughed as if he thought I had no more control over killing him than over what he did to me. I showed him I had control. I shot him right between those ugly, evil eyes. Don't you see? I was released from my fear of him and from my own inhibition to act."

"Jan. Oh, Jan." Dr. Carey put his head in his hands and shook it back and forth. "As your psychiatrist, I see – yes, I see. But as your friend and someone who cares whether or not you go to jail, I must warn you not to speak this way to the court or to the jury. Simply answer yes or no. It is up to them to prove your guilt. It is very possible – yes, even probable – that your recent rape and the pressing fear of escaping made you momentarily insane. You know that should this come to trial I will be asked to testify as to your mental state. I want you to know that if I have to, I will describe a patient experiencing temporary insanity," he said not taking his eyes from hers.

"Please, please don't, Dr. Carey. That would give me an excuse, a reactionary reason to have shot him. I need to know that I took action. I will take whatever consequences for my choice," she pleaded.

"Let's just hope your grand jury members have more sense than that district attorney," he said.

"You've been talking to John Larsen, haven't you? I thought our sessions were confidential between patient and doctor," she accused.

"Now, wait a minute. Of course I've talked with John. He has to know how best to defend you and I can easily be called as a witness. That's fact. I have not, and won't, discuss the details of our meetings here. I merely give a professional diagnosis of the situation based on our sessions, but without revealing the specific contents of those sessions," he defended.

"I'm sorry, Dr. Carey. Of course you wouldn't. I trust you. I'm only asking as your patient, and your friend, please don't tell anyone I was temporarily insane. Don't you see that would make everything I am now as false as I was before this happened?" she begged.

The red light on Dr. Carey's phone began blinking. "Yes," he said into the receiver, irritated. "Tell her she's early and she'll just have to wait a few minutes."

"Your next client?" Jan asked.

"Yes." He leaned over the desk and looked into her eyes. "Jan, I promise that I will try not to make such a professional call, but if it comes between that and you going to jail, well, I can't make any more promise than that."

He rose from his seat and walked around to her, took her hand and placed an arm around her shoulder. "Good luck on Tuesday. Remember, you can save yourself from the courts without compromising who you are or the truths and strengths you have recovered. Now, if you don't mind, I'm going to usher you out the back door here so that I can make a quick phone call before admitting the next patient."

The doctor sat quietly in his chair. He was tired, but he needed to think. He knew that, by the textbook, Jan possibly did suffer temporary insanity after going through the rape and the fear caused by the kidnapping. He also knew that because she was a moral person, her mind was trying to put the blame on the shooting, not on the instinct of self-defense. She was sane enough at the time however, to realize that for one split second she had had a choice. She could have chosen not to shoot Punk but to take her chances and run.

Dr. Carey had to convince Jan that she had not consciously chosen to kill, but had acted in self-defense. He reached for the phone.

"John Larsen, please. John, this Chad Carey. We need to talk before you go to Brevard."

Chapter Six

The crisp day highlighted the majestic Appalachian mountain chain as it rose from the plains beyond Spartanburg, South Carolina, and just into North Carolina on interstate highway 26. The sudden height was imposing in its contrast to the flat, expansive plains below.

"What a gorgeous day," May exclaimed from the driver's seat.

"Yes, aren't we lucky to have such beautiful weather," Meemaw said. "But it's a bit chilly. May, did you pack enough warm clothes for you and Jan?"

The three generations of women traveled comfortably in their relationships with each other. Life to come, life ongoing and life just keeping up ran through the conversation.

"We'll have some time before dinner when we arrive," May said in the rearview mirror. "Is there anything you would like to do or see after we unpack?"

"Not particularly," Jan said.

"Why don't we poke around in some of the local antique shops?" Meemaw suggested. "You know that old farmhouse could use some new furnishings," she said to her granddaughter.

"That would be fine," Jan answered. She knew that the alternative was sitting in the hotel room watching television.

May had taken a three-room suite for them at a recently renovated inn. The old section of the inn had quaint rooms decorated from the twenties, but a newer section provided elegantly furnished suites and adjoining rooms.

John had warned that the press would try to find where they were staying and so May registered in Meemaw's maiden name, Julia May Thomas. John did not add that the press would have a heyday if they knew that Jan and her family were staying in such luxury. She was already characterized as a 'society princess.' Frank Woods used the phrase to his advantage. He vowed to prove that the rich and spoiled would be prosecuted to the full extent of the law.

The press accentuated Jan's family's social and economic standing in Georgia. A few of the big-city papers disclosed her modest lifestyle with David in Riverdale. Some reporters made note that Jan had chosen to return to her family's pampered life.

In contrast, the papers played up Punk's backwoods, mountain rearing in a poverty-stricken home of ten kids, with a drunkard father and a mother who claimed she 'did what she could.' Jan never saw these articles. She had quit reading the paper and watching the news. She read only fiction and watched old movies and sitcoms.

John warned May not to be too concerned with Jan's dress during the hearing. The press was expecting a socialite. If she wore simple clothes, the jurors would see her straightforwardness and honesty, he advised. It might help if May and Meemaw dressed down a bit too, he said. John knew not to give any of this advice to Jan, for she thought that image playing was dishonest. Jan wondered why her mother never suggested what she should wear for the trip. She didn't even protest when Jan wore jeans and a sweater for the drive to Brevard.

The three women had a press-free day. After browsing in the shops, they enjoyed a delicious meal in the elegant but empty dining room of the inn. Jan had never traveled entirely alone with her mother and grandmother. Tonight she saw a different side of her maternal family. Her grandmother told of growing up an only child and traveling with her parents. Her mother revealed naughty things she did as a teenager in boarding school. Jan had no idea how delightful these women could be.

Jan woke early to a cloudy and much colder day. Her mother and grandmother were still asleep. She threw on her jeans and headed downstairs for breakfast.

"Two eggs over easy, grits, biscuit, coffee and orange juice," she ordered without consulting the menu. She opened her new *Atlantic Monthly* and turned to the table of contents.

"Mind if I join you, beautiful?" a familiar voice asked

Jan was glad to see John. "Aren't you a bit early?" she asked.

"I spent the night in Asheville and got up early." He sat down. "So, are you nervous?" he asked.

"No. Should I be?"

"I don't know, honey, but facing yet another group of strangers might unnerve you at first," he suggested. "I know you're glad your mother and grandmother are here," he added.

Jan didn't respond.

"You are glad May and Meemaw are here, aren't you?" John asked.

"Will we definitely have to walk through the cabin?" she asked.

"Only if the jurors feel it is necessary to help them understand exactly what happened. It is a possibility, but not a sure thing," he answered.

"If we do, I don't want Mother and Meemaw to go," Jan said.

"I understand. They probably wouldn't be allowed, anyway," he assured her. "Only the jurors, law officers, lawyers, you and the boys would go."

"Have you seen the boys yet?" she asked.

"Caleb, Murray and Bryson McNeil stayed at my hotel. They were eating breakfast when I left. They'll meet us at the courthouse at 9:45," he said.

"Their parents didn't come?" she asked.

"No. The boys wanted to do this on their own."

"I wish I were here alone," Jan said. "I really enjoyed Mom and Meemaw last night, but I don't want them around today. I'm just glad David and Daddy and Papa Ralph aren't here."

"Jan, I can ask them not to come to the courthouse," John suggested. "I know you'd feel more comfortable without them there."

"Oh, it's not for me. It's for them," Jan said. "I just don't think they'll be able to stand the details. I'm used to them now, but they haven't heard the whole story."

"I see your point, but maybe you're not giving them enough credit. Maybe they want to be part of this with you, to hear it so they can better understand. Why don't you give them a choice, at least?" John said.

At 9:45, Jan, John, May and Meemaw walked into the lobby of the Transylvania County courthouse. Caleb and Murray were already there with Bryson McNeil, talking with Sheriff Lander and Coroner Buddy Lee. Leonard Snelling, John's local attorney friend, was there as Jan's local legal representation.

"Well, if it isn't my two sidekicks," Jan greeted the boys. They hugged together.

John made the proper introductions.

"Mrs. Ferguson, you're looking mighty fine," Sheriff Lander said in his gentle way. "Good morning, ladies," he greeted the other two women.

Coroner Lee nodded at each of the three ladies in turn. He didn't feel part of the official welcoming committee.

"Now, let me explain what's going to be happening in there," Sheriff Lander began, motioning toward the closed courtroom doors. "The grand jury met with the district attorney – you all prob'ly recall Mr. Frank Woods – well, he met with them yesterday to hear charges brought against several persons, such as yourself here, who have been charged with federal crimes in this county. Beginning today, the jury will hear testimony concerning these cases. By Friday they will decide which cases will receive a true bill. Your case is the first on the docket and, therefore, the first to be heard today.

"Mr. Woods will act as prosecutor, but he will not question any witnesses. He has already given his reasons for finding you guilty and will only be present as the prosecution. The grand jury may also question him," the sheriff explained formally.

"I will be in the courtroom with you," Sheriff Lander spoke directly to Jan. "If you need anything – water, the ladies room, anything – you let me know. Ladies," he turned to May and Meemaw. "You may sit in the observation pews, but you are not to say a word, or I will have to ask you to leave," he said. "Mrs. Ferguson, you, Murray, Caleb and your lawyers will sit at the defendants' table, and I will sit right behind you all. Now, are there any questions?"

The sheriff paused. "I wish you the best of luck. I'm awfully sorry to have to drag you back up here again, but I'm sure these twelve grand jurors will do right by you." Sheriff Lander patted Jan clumsily on the shoulder.

The bailiff opened the majestic courtroom doors and led the way for the somber group. John entered first wearing his dark blue, pinstriped suit, followed by Jan in a simple linen skirt and sweater. Next was Bryson McNeil in a brown tweed suit, and the boys in their Sunday best. May and Meemaw brought up the rear. They had dressed down for the occasion in simple day suits and little jewelry.

They barely had time to settle before the bailiff opened the juror's door beside the judge's bench, and in walked Frank Woods in a black suit carrying an expensive leather brief case. He nodded smugly to John, but did not look at Jan. Behind him came the court recorder, the clerk of court and the twelve grand jurors.

John had been given a rundown on the jury members from Leonard. Five white men sat on the jury: the owner of a hardware store, an agricultural extension agent, a bank officer, an insurance company owner, and a funeral parlor owner. Only three blacks, all male, sat in the jurors box: a Zion Baptist Church minister, a retired high school principal and a handyman who ran a crew to service the rich and elderly. The four women on the jury were white: a wealthy widow of a former judge, a middle-aged housewife, a real estate agent, and a retired teacher. John and Leonard expected sympathy from this jury for a young, ravished wife and high school teacher. They also knew that all but possibly the handyman would be ultra conservative where the law was concerned. The defenders expected Frank Woods to harp on the legal points and to warn against sympathy for the accused at the expense of the strict letter of the law.

The twelve grand jurors had already studied the facts of Jan's case: the FBI reports, the sheriff's reports, Dr. Sam Morris' examination and the coroner's report. They now wanted to question Jan and the boys.

After all formalities were dismissed, the foreman, who was the insurance agency owner, rose from his seat and asked Coroner Lee to draw a diagram of the murder on a portable blackboard. Specifically they wanted to know the position of McQuirk's body at the time of death and the position of the defendant.

Lee drew an outline of a body on its back with the feet facing the side of the cabin, the head pointing toward a stick figure of Jan in the trees. He then drew two stick figures of the boys standing just to the side of the body's feet.

"Did the body fall in this position after being shot the first time?" the foreman asked.

"No sir. The body fell due to a blow on the head by a rock thrown from about fifteen feet. The body was already in this position when shot," Lee said.

"Then how did the body receive a bullet wound between the eyes if he wasn't standing and facing the defendant?" the foreman asked.

"At the time of the first shot, the head was turned to look at the defendant," Lee replied.

The jurors put their heads together and whispered, and the foreman referred to a notebook he had on his lap. "May we ask the defendant some questions?" he asked John Larsen.

"Certainly. Mrs. Ferguson, will you please take the stand and let the clerk of court swear you in," he said loudly. Then he leaned to whisper in her ear. "Just relax and tell the course of events as they happened."

Jan nodded and walked to the witness chair and turned to be sworn in.

"Mrs. Ferguson, we regret the horrible ordeal you have endured, but could you tell us exactly how you came to shoot Mr. McQuirk?" the foreman asked.

Jan remained calm. "We had just taken the window panes out of the bathroom window to escape. We had thought we'd heard the man pass out in the next room. He'd been drinking. I was first to go out the window, so I ran ahead toward the woods to see which way we ought to head when the boys followed. Caleb and Murray got out the window, but before they could run to the woods, Punk – that's the name those other men had called him – came around the side of the house with a gun. He couldn't see me because the trees hid me.

"He said he was glad to have an excuse to shoot the boys. He asked where his 'girlie' was. There was a rock at my feet and I leaned down and picked it up and threw it as hard as I could at his head. It hit him on the side of the head and he turned and fell backwards and the rifle flew out of his hands and landed at my feet. I picked it up and shot him."

"Did Mr. McQuirk say anything threatening to you while he was on the ground? Was he unconscious? Where were the boys at this time?" the foreman asked all at once.

"The boys were on the other side of him. I don't know if he said anything threatening, but he was conscious because I could see his evil eyes," she stated.

The widowed judge's wife leaned over and whispered to the foreman. "Did you consider tying or locking the man up since you had the rifle and you were now in control of the situation?" the foreman asked.

"No. I wanted him dead," Jan answered.

Meemaw put her head in her hands; May wiped silent tears.

"Could you not have kept the rifle with you for protection and just run away?" the foreman persisted.

"Then he would have come after me and he would always be coming after me. I would never be free," she answered.

John jumped from his seat. "Mr. Foreman, you must realize that my client was under undue stress and not thinking clearly. It all happened very fast. Perhaps you should ask the boys who were with her to clarify the scene," he insisted.

"Thank you. We plan to do that. Now, Mrs. Ferguson, let me ask you one more time. Did you, at the time that you held the gun on Mr. McQuirk while he was lying on the ground, feel threatened for your own or your students' lives?" the foreman continued questioning Jan.

"I just didn't want him to get up again," Jan stated unemotionally.

The jurors put their heads together and whispered some more. "Thank you, Mrs. Ferguson. That will be all. Could we question Murray Simpson now?" the foreman asked.

Murray took the stand and was sworn in.

"Mr. Simpson, did you feel that your life was threatened by Mr. McQuirk while he had the rifle on you and Mr. Johnson?" he asked.

"Yes, sir. He said he was going to shoot us," Murray answered.

"Did you feel equally threatened after he had thrown the rifle from his hands and Mrs. Ferguson picked it up and held it on him?" he asked.

"He kept his eyes on Mrs. Ferguson, but he did threaten her. He said when he threw her into the room the first time that he would come and get her and do it to her again," Murray said.

"Do what to her again, young man?" the foreman asked.

"You know ... rape her," Murray said. He didn't look at Jan.

"But did he say anything threatening to her when she held the gun?" he asked.

"I don't know, sir. I thought I saw his lips move," Murray testified.

"But did you hear anything?" the foreman persisted.

"No, sir."

"That's all, son. Thank you." The foreman dismissed Murray and asked for Caleb to take the stand.

"Mr. Johnson, did you feel that your life was threatened while Mr. McQuirk held a gun on you?" he asked.

"Yes, sir. He said he was glad he had an excuse to shoot us, because we had escaped and all," Caleb answered.

"Once Mr. McQuirk had fallen to the ground and Mrs. Ferguson had the rifle, did you still feel threatened?" the foreman asked.

"Like Murray, I knew that if that man ever got up, we'd be dead," Caleb said.

"But he didn't have the gun. Mrs. Ferguson had the gun. Could you not suggest to Mrs. Ferguson to tie the man up somewhere?" the foreman asked.

"There was no time. She shot him before we had time to think. And if she hadn't of, I'd of shot that bastard myself for what he did to her," Caleb said emotionally. "She saved our lives. That man was going to kill us, and she saved our lives!" Caleb showed his frustration.

"Thank you, young man. That will be all," the foreman said.

"Now, wait a minute. Just what were we supposed to tie him up with, or where were we supposed to lock him up? You weren't there. You don't know what it was like! He was a big man, bigger than me and Murray, and strong. What would you have done?" Caleb yelled.

"I understand, son. But that will be all," the foreman said kindly as Bryson came to the stand to lead Caleb away.

The jurors put their heads together and whispered again. Then they called Frank Woods over. "Maybe if we saw the scene, we would see more of a threatening situation. Is it possible for us to go to this cabin?" the foreman asked.

Frank looked over at John Leonard and Bryson McNeil who nodded agreement. "Yes. We'll meet back here after lunch and take you up there," he said to the jurors. "Is that all right with you, Sheriff Lander? Mr. Lee? All right, then – we'll meet in front of the courthouse at two p.m."

Lunch was a blur to Jan. Sheriff Lander had reserved a private room at the Western Steer on the edge of town for the visitors. May kept asking John what all this meant. "Why are these people making Jan go to that horrid cabin and relive this nightmare over again?"

"May, I think the jurors are doing everything they can not to indict Jan, but by her testimony alone they would have to. The trip to the cabin could help them find concrete evidence of self-defense," John explained.

"What more do they want? They all said that man would have killed them. Jan, honey, can't you just tell these people it was self-defense?" May was becoming hysterical.

"Look, May, you and Meemaw won't be able to go to the cabin with us. Why don't you ladies go back to the inn for lunch and rest until we're finished? Jan will be fine," John said.

"Jan, honey?" May looked at her daughter.

"John's right, Mom. You and Meemaw have heard enough already. Your being here would make it worse," Jan said honestly.

"Well, if you think it best, dear. Meemaw? I guess we best be going. Now, you call us the minute you get back," May said.

"I'll bring her back to the inn when this is over," John assured them as he walked the ladies to the door.

"John," May could not hide the concern in her voice. "When will the Grand Jury give us a decision?"

"Not until they've decided on all the cases before them. They could decide as early as Thursday if the other cases are easy. Leonard Snelling thinks they are, but if there are anymore lengthy hearings required, it may be as late as Friday afternoon," he said. "Look, you ladies go on back to the inn; call Lamar and Papa Ralph to let them know what's going on. That'll make you feel better. They may even want to come up and wait with you," John tried to calm them.

"You sound as if you think they're going to send her to trial. That's what you think, isn't it, John?" May whined.

"May, I just don't know. Please, you and Meemaw go on back to the inn now."

Meemaw took May by the arm and led her through the parking lot to the car.

The gathering in front of the courthouse at two o'clock could have been a comedy. The jurors were trying to decide who would ride with whom, the sheriff wanted Jan, John and Leonard with him and the coroner, and nobody would ride with Frank Woods. Two photographers snapped pictures of anyone looking their way, and two reporters yelled at Frank and the sheriff for statements.

"Gentlemen, please. This is not a public hearing. As I said before," Frank emphasized for show, "I can let you know nothing until the true bills are returned."

"I don't know how they knew we were going up there today," Frank said innocently to Sheriff Lander.

"Yeah, I bet you don't," Lander said accusingly. He was not fully aware of the alliance between Frank and his daughter, Willa, but he suspected. Willa had moved out of the house just before Christmas, a move she had never wanted to make before, and found an apartment in town.

Jan said nothing during the ride to the cabin. She wished with all her might that Dr. Carey were there. He could help her put this into perspective. Nausea churned in her stomach.

"Why don't you start at the beginning and show us through the cabin, just as when you first were brought here." The foreman spoke to Jan and the boys in general.

Jan stared at the cabin. She didn't think she could go inside.

Murray answered. "We were brought here in a van by two other men who left soon after they brought us. Punk was already here, but we had first seen him at the school. I think he drove Caleb's truck up here."

The jurors crowded around to hear and looked at the gravel drive, trying to imagine just where Caleb's pickup had been parked and where the van had pulled up.

"Then they took us inside where Punk was," Murray continued. The jurors and the rest of the entourage followed him into the cabin. Jan stayed at the back with John and Leonard, while the sheriff rushed ahead to hold the door open for everyone.

"Punk was just kind of standing over there by that bar, looking at us. He was looking mostly at Jan ... Mrs. Ferguson," Murray said.

Jan heard no more of what Murray was saying when she saw the sofa. She stopped, not wanting to go further, not wanting to remember the fear. But she remembered Dr. Carey's asking her about the rape, and she could see it as a film in her head about someone else. She was afraid to breathe; afraid she would smell something of Punk, something of her shame. She only smelled cabin smells of winter wood; closed-up musty smells, as any cabin would have.

Murray led the group into the bedroom and told, with interjections by Caleb, how Punk had brought their breakfast while the men were still there, how they had slept and how they played cards as a distraction to pass the time before lunch. He looked at Jan before continuing.

Saying it herself, seeing it in her head, was one thing, but Jan did not want to hear Murray and Caleb describe her rape. The little lunch she had eaten threatened to come up. "John, I'm going to be sick," she whispered.

"Sure, come on outside for some fresh air. You don't need to hear this, honey. Leonard, take notes, okay? I'm going to step outside with Jan." John led her to a large rock near the driveway.

Jan started to sit, but she bolted for the nearest tree and retched violently. John came to pat her back.

"Go away. I'm so embarrassed. I'm okay. It must have been something I ate," she said between retches.

"It's all right, honey. I understand. Don't be embarrassed," John said. He had worried that this would be too much. When she finished he offered her his handkerchief and led her back to the rock.

"I'm going to step inside and see if there's anything to drink in that refrigerator. Will you be okay out here a few minutes?" he asked.

"Sure." Jan looked back at the cabin as John went in. It could have been any mountain cabin. It wasn't as big or as dark as she remembered it. It was just a cabin. Punk was dead; the cabin no longer held her fear. Jan was glad she had killed Punk. She couldn't see beyond that to care or even imagine the outcome of this hearing. She had faced the scene of her shame, had vomited out the residue of its effects, and now she could continue through life unafraid.

"Jan?" It was John. "Look, I found a Coke. This will make you feel better. When you're up to it, the jurors are going to need you on the other side of the cabin to walk through the shooting. Do you think you can do that?" John was concerned.

"Thanks." Jan took a long swallow before answering. "Yes. That's no problem. I'm fine now," she said.

"Jan, please, can't you say it was self-defense? Can't you say you were afraid he was going to kill you – to kill Murray and Caleb?" John pleaded.

"I can only say what happened," Jan answered.

The grand jurors did not ask Jan to hold a rifle or throw a rock; they asked her and the boys to stand in the positions they were in when the shooting occurred. Murray continued to be the spokesman. When asked if that was how she remembered it, Jan nodded yes.

"It seems this man was far enough away from all of them that he couldn't grab them at the moment," a juror commented.

Nothing else was said, and the group piled in their vehicles and headed down the mountain. There was noting left to do except wait for the decision at the end of the week.

Chapter Seven

The press had found where they were staying; cameramen and reporters were camped on the inn lawn near the front door.

The innkeepers, who had thrown several people out of the building for harassing their guests, threatened to call the police. The owner finally had called the sheriff's department to report the disturbance and warned the other guests. Sheriff Lander sent Jan and John the back way in John's car, while he took Leonard with him to the inn entrance. He told reporters that because of them, Jan would be forced to take lodgings elsewhere. He asked them "as ladies and gentlemen" to vacate the premises.

May and Meemaw had felt like prisoners in their suite all afternoon. They were tired of gin rummy, so they began an early cocktail hour when Jan and John finally arrived.

"Jan, darling, how did it go? Are you all right? You look washed out. Let me fix you a drink, darling. John, what will you have?" May rushed to the makeshift bar before either could answer.

Jan kissed her grandmother and sat next to her on the sofa. Meemaw patted her knee, as she had when Jan was small.

"Not for me, May. As soon as the coast is clear from the press, I'm going to meet Leonard in his office. He's found some old records on this McQuirk fellow," John said.

"John, can you tell us how you think the grand jury will rule?" Meemaw asked in her quiet mAnnr.

"No, Meemaw, I wish I could, but I have no idea which way they'll go," John said as he looked at Jan.

Jan met his gaze.

Dr. Carey had talked with John at length on Friday afternoon, explaining that Jan had made progress, adding that until she considered Punk a fellow human being, she could not feel liable for his death and its circumstances. "Let's just hope she reaches the point of accountability before she has to face a jury trial. I can't do this for her. It must come from within," the doctor explained to the attorney.

John walked to Jan and squatted in front of her. "I'm going to get you out of this, Jan, in spite of yourself," he said. "We have at least until Thursday before we know anything, so take this time to relax and enjoy the mountains. I'll be out of pocket tomorrow. I have a few leads to chase, but I'll be staying with the Snellings if you need me." John paused, not taking his eyes from Jan's. "Please, kid, consider your future; consider your family."

Jan nodded, but there was no way John could tell from her face if what he said had registered. He rose slowly and leaned to kiss her on the forehead before leaving.

"Jan, darling, don't you think you should call David and let him know how things went today? I know he's been worried," May said handing Jan a bourbon and water.

"I tried to call him all weekend and he was never home. I even tried his office." Jan didn't care to speak with David now, but she knew she should.

Her mother was already dialing David's office. "David Ferguson, please. This is his mother-in-law, May Jameson. Hello, David, dear? How are you? Did you take a little time off this weekend? That's nice. Jan said she tried to call and couldn't get up with you. Well, I thought you might want to talk to her about how the hearing went today. No, we won't know anything until Thursday at the earliest. Here, let Jan tell you," May said and she handed the phone to Jan.

Jan first took a long drink of the bourbon. "Hello, David. Yes, I'm fine. I don't know how it went. They asked me and Murray and Caleb questions, and we answered them; that's all I can tell you. Yes, we had to go to the cabin with the jury members. It was okay. How are you? What did you do this weekend? Good. You needed some time off. Well, there's nothing more to tell you until we hear the grand jury's decision, so I guess I'll let you get back to work. Sure. Talk to you later." Jan hung up.

Her mother and grandmother had been staring at her intently as they listened to her end of the conversation. Both of them wanted to mention that Jan had failed to tell her husband that she loved him; but they refrained.

Jan wished she were back in Kingsford. At least there she could keep busy. Here there was nothing to keep her hands and her mind occupied. Here there was no escape from the lingering angst. There was something she wasn't seeing. She needed her chapel at St. Peter's. She needed her farmhouse tucked in the woods. She needed …

A loud knock disturbed her thoughts. "Rev. Tyler, you're a bit early!" May exclaimed as she opened the door. "I haven't even had a chance to tell Jan you called and are joining us for dinner. Jan, dear, look who's here."

Jan looked at her answer to prayer.

"Mrs. Calhoun," Grant nodded at Meemaw. "Well, Jan, have you survived the hearing?" he asked with concern.

"I'm just fine," she answered.

May gave the minister a meaningful look.

"Your mother tells me the press has been quite a bother. But I know of a great little mountain restaurant about five miles from town. How about you ladies get your coats and we'll leave now and do a little car touring first," Grant said, infusing life back into the somber room.

Grant always knew just what to say and do. He insisted on driving, so Meemaw sat in front and May and Jan sat in the back seat of his Jeep Cherokee. Jan found herself watching the set of his head when he turned to talk, the way his black hair waved on either side of the nape of his neck, the touch of gray at his temples.

"Your car is not one I would expect a minister to drive," May said making conversation. "Somehow I expected something a bit more … conservative."

Grant laughed, never offended by May's offhanded remarks. "I didn't know cars were political. I needed something with four-wheel drive and roomy enough to take the young people and their luggage on weekend camping trips and retreats. I admit, I did consider my image with the youth when I picked this out. I really wanted a restored classic Wagoneer, but I couldn't afford it," he said.

His laugh was deep and musical, not brash and high pitched like David's, Jan noticed. His hands were not at all what she would expect for a preacher. He had large, manly hands, with sturdy, long fingers.

Dinner was just what the doctor ordered – a quaint mountain restaurant serving fresh trout, homemade yeast bread, fresh winter squash and carrots. The conversation was light and fun. May and Meemaw showed interest in Grant's youth projects and offered financial support. The day, the future, was easy to forget.

"Ladies, I happen to know an absolutely beautiful hiking spot that's only forty-five minutes from here. Anyone interested in a day hike and picnic tomorrow?" Grant looked equally at the three.

"Heavens, no. I'm much too old for hiking," Meemaw laughed.

"We had in mind to visit the Biltmore House in Asheville tomorrow. Isn't that something you would like to do, Jan?" May asked pointedly.

May liked the ministering that Rev. Tyler did for Jan, but she was wary of them spending so much time together without David around. Jan was a married woman, after all, and Rev. Tyler was a man of the cloth. What would people say?

"I would like to go on that hike. A little exercise will do me good," Jan said. "Why don't you and Meemaw go to the Biltmore House, and we'll hike and meet you back for dinner," Jan suggested.

"Well," May pursed her lips.

"I think that's a marvelous idea, darling," Meemaw said enthusiastically.

The next day could not have been more beautiful. The bare limbs of winter stood stark against a brilliant sea-blue sky. There was not a cloud in sight and the detail of undergrowth and rock shone clearly.

Jan liked it when Grant wore jeans and his old boots. When he wore his collar, she thought of him as her pastor. When he was dressed in his casual attire, she felt he was her friend.

They talked little while traveling the Blue Ridge Parkway. Mostly they enjoyed the beauty of the day and the comfortable silence afforded by each other's company. Grant took the Sylva exit and turned onto a little-traveled road before reaching the town limits. He parked his Cherokee just off the road on a flat area above a rushing stream. Before locking the car, he pulled two backpacks from the back and handed one to Jan.

"What's this?" she asked.

"I told you I was bringing a picnic lunch. I added a blanket for a table. I also brought first aid supplies and other necessities. Once we start hiking, we'll want to take off our jackets, and now we have a way to carry them. "You're not a true hiker if you don't have a backpack."

Jan smiled and stood still while Grant slipped the smaller of the backpacks and a canteen of water over her shoulders and strapped the hip strap. He put on the other backpack and led the way.

They didn't talk at first. Jan was watching her feet so she wouldn't trip and fall following the rocky stream. "I guess you bring lots of girls out here to hike," Jan joked.

"No, just you," Grant replied. "I've always come alone on this trail. It's not an easy trail, for one thing – and for another, it's my secret refuge from the world. And," he paused and looked at her, "I haven't wanted to share it with anyone before."

Jan's heart jumped involuntarily. Was she excited or was she afraid?

Some parts of the trail were barely more than ruts up a sharp incline; other parts were bordered on one side by sheer rock and on the other by a sharp drop to the stream below. Fallen trees provided easy stream crossing, but much of the way was climb-and-jump. Jan found it easy to step out of her life and travel into the trail. The emotional severity of yesterday's hearing, the worry of the outcome ... everything fell away.

An hour and a half later, the trail had become rockier, the trees were stubby and sparse, and the air was thinner. Jan rested after each difficult incline. In the midst of a gully, she looked up and saw sheer rock ahead. Then Grant led her through stunted, wooded underbrush to a clearing of dried winter grasses. The meadow was perhaps fifteen by twenty-five feet. Large rocks dotted the landscape that was bordered by a sheer rock cliff on one side and a long, sharp drop on the other. The contrast of the brown grass, the gray rock and the sparse evergreen against the brilliant winter blue sky took her breath away.

They sat and rested for a few minutes before setting up for lunch. "How did you ever find such a place? Did someone bring you here?" Jan asked.

"No." He smiled. "I'm sure I'm not the only one who has ever been here, but I found this myself, and I've never met another human up here," he answered.

"What were you doing here to have found this place?" Jan asked.

"Oh, running away from life, as I'm sure you would like to do now," he said, fastening his blue eyes on hers.

"What would you have to run away from?" she asked.

"Everyone has something to run from at some time. Hurt, fear, guilt and grief are universal. I've always found nature to be the great consoler," he said simply. "Let's unpack our picnic and enjoy the view – and perhaps I will tell you of my own turmoil and crossroads in life," he said.

Jan began to unpack her backpack. "Why, you've brought a gourmet feast!" she exclaimed.

There was wine "to be drunk from the bottle as the peasants do," Grant said, and several kinds of cheeses and crackers, grapes and apples, a small soft loaf of bread and two carrot cookies. "The cookies double as our vegetable," he said with a twinkle in his eye.

They spread the picnic on a checked flannel blanket, and Grant gave a simple blessing of thanks to God for the beautiful day and the bounteous meal. Jan felt a completeness she had never felt before. He offered her the bottle of wine first while he cut the cheeses. They ate ravenously for a few minutes. When they were ready for the fruit, they lay back and relaxed.

"So, from what would a handsome, young, virile man such as yourself have to run?" Jan asked, plucking a stem of grapes and handing them to Grant.

"I'm ahead of you on this wine, so you drink some and I'll talk," he said.

"I went to undergraduate school at Appalachian State in Boone," he began. Jan nodded. "My father accused me of majoring in outdoor camping, but I graduated with a BA in history and pre-law. My father is a lawyer, a judge now with the Superior Court of Georgia, and I was raised to follow in his footsteps. I don't remember consciously choosing law, but it was always understood in our family that I would be a lawyer like my father."

"Are you an only child?" Jan asked.

"No, but I'm the only son. I have two sisters – I'm in the middle. They were expected to grow up and marry the right man, preferably a lawyer. We had the so-called 'perfect' American family – lived in Atlanta. Father was with one of the best law firms; we belonged to the 'right' church; my sisters and I went to the 'right' private schools; and we took a two-week vacation to the beach every year. I'm sure you can relate," he added.

"Sounds like an ideal childhood," Jan commented

"If it had been real, perhaps, but it wasn't. My dad was

demanding and a strict disciplinarian. He grew up during the Depression as a poor farm boy, and society and his place in it meant a great deal to him. He expected perfection in all of us, even in Mother." He took a breath.

"But from what you've told me in the past, your mother seems so natural, so real and unconcerned with societal pressures," Jan said.

"Oh, she is. But she still tried to be what Father wanted her to be. We all tried to be what Father wanted us to be. Only we believed in what we did – church, respect, nice manners and all that. Father, on the other hand, did it all for show. Everything he did, going to church, the way he dressed, even where we went on vacations, was to impress, to gain clients. None of it was from the heart.

"And as often happens to the man living a life with no convictions, no inner values, he began to take on a secret life. Mistresses, gambling trips to Las Vegas, daytime drinking – you know, all the fanfare that follows the modern successful politician or businessman. His family was not aware of these details. We only knew that he was home late each evening and seldom on weekends. My mother rarely went with him unless it was a social affair connected to a client or politics. It all came to a head two years after I graduated from college.

"I had put off going to law school by telling Father I needed a break from studying and wanted to work with my hands for a few years while I was still young. He didn't agree, but Mom convinced him I would do better in law school if I waited. Anything less than top of the class would have been unacceptable to Father, so he agreed.

"I had a small house about a mile down from that first creek we crossed. It was just a cabin, really; heated with wood, but with electricity and running water. I worked the three summer months as a tour guide for river rafters. In the other nine months, I worked as a forester of sorts for the state. I also kept a record of local flora and fauna for Appalachian State. I had always wanted to be a botanist and had taken a few courses in college, but I learned most of what I know on the job and from reading. The pay was low, even for three jobs, but I was outdoors all the time. I loved my work.

"There were plenty of idealistic young people around. Artists, woodworkers, crafters and free thinkers are attracted to these mountains. We had a regular beer drinking group at the local bar in Sylva. After nine months I met a young woman who moved there.

She was three years older than me; I was twenty-three. Her name was Sylvia. I used to kid her that she moved to Sylva because it was so like her name. She'd grown up on a burley tobacco farm near Franklin, Tennessee; hers had been a poor but good-hearted family. She wanted a different life for herself, so she earned an associate degree as a legal secretary. Her first job was with a law firm in Waynesville. But she liked to keep her private life and work life separate, so she lived in Sylva.

"I knew this was the woman for me. She was a legal secretary, and I was going to law school, eventually. She was beautiful. Quite urban and sophisticated, or so I thought, for such a rural background. I learned later that she worked hard for that image. She liked the outdoors enough that I looked past many things. She would hike, raft, do all the outdoor leisure activities I enjoyed ... *properly* dressed of course.

"At first she hung out with a couple of other young men, too, but soon we were seeing each other exclusively. She was always asking me about my family, my father especially. She wanted to know about his judgeship and his political aspirations. I thought she wanted to know more about me through my family; I thought one day she would be my wife. So, naturally, I took her home to meet my family. My younger sister disliked her instantly, and she didn't pretend otherwise. My older sister liked her style. My mother disliked her strongly; she didn't trust her, but she was kind enough to keep quiet.

"But my father fell in love with her. Sylvia knew all the right things to say. She never passed up a chance to touch him, maybe on the arm, maybe on the shoulder, confidentially. I didn't see this at first. Suddenly, Father wanted to come visit me when he had business in the area. He didn't bring Mom, and he wouldn't stay with me. He stayed in a lodge in Waynesville. For a few months there, he was having a lot of business in my area. Every time he came, Sylvia and I would go out to dinner with him a night, maybe two. Then Sylvia started being more and more busy. A heavy case at work, she would say, or too tired, she would say. Then Father's trips stopped, but he was still telling Mom he had business in the area. Sylvia started going off whole weekends at a time. First, she had to visit family; then, a sick aunt, a lonely grandmother. I'd offer to go with her, but she would say no, it was better for her to go alone.

"It was Mom who told me that Sylvia and Father were seeing each other. She drove up unexpectedly on a Monday. She was waiting in my cabin when I came in; it was the first of November. I knew something was wrong as soon as I saw her.

"*Your father and I are getting divorced,* she said. She didn't cry. I hugged her, and she asked me to sit down and listen. She had a lot to say to me. She told me that she had known for years that my father had mistresses, that he had a life separate from her. She had never said anything because he provided for us so well financially. She said that as she grew older and spiritual matters became more important to her, she worried that she was raising us in a hypocritical life. Our father lived a lie and she did not love him. She said she was sorry for her part in this false life, but to be truthful, she probably wouldn't have changed anything if she hadn't seen Father with his new mistress. I tried to tell her that surely there was no difference between one mistress and another. If she wanted to start an independent life of her own, she should because Father was never worthy of her. A mistress shouldn't make the difference.

"*His mistress is Sylvia,* she said. At first I didn't think I'd heard her correctly. Then little bits and pieces began to fit together. I wanted to kill my father. I felt like such a fool – to her, to my father. I cried. I threw dishes, broke lamps. My mother sat silently and let me vent my anger.

"*Neither one of them is worth this or worthy of us,* she finally said. *Let them have each other, for they deserve one another. I told your father yesterday I wanted a divorce and he said he was relieved. He said he had fallen in love with someone else. I asked him why after all these years of mistresses he hadn't asked for a divorce. He said he never loved any of them, but he loves Sylvia. I asked him about you. He said that you're young, you'll get over it,* she said."

Grant paused. He was not sad, but reflective. He reached for the bottle of wine and took a few swallows. "I think I need to catch up with you now," he grinned.

Jan smiled and waited for him to continue.

"Anyway, Sylvia moved to Waynesville and continued her job there until Mom and Father were divorced. Then she and Father married. She's made the perfect politician's-younger-second-wife. I, in the meantime, stayed here for another year and a half and took to roaming the woods more than ever. That's when I found this place, and I've found it has given me great solace since then for all sorts of other minor life crises. Now that I don't live here, my visits are fewer and further between. I like to think a broken-spirited Indian made the first path here and that it has been a place of refuge for others since," Grant said, handing a cookie to Jan.

"Now you see that we all have our hidden hurts and sins," he said.

"But you didn't sin. Your father and Sylvia sinned against you, not the other way around," Jan said.

"Oh, no. I sinned. I hated all women, except my mother and younger sister. I went out with women, lots of women, for one reason only – to take them to bed and make them want me so I could leave them behind for someone else. I took my hurt and turned it into pain for other innocent people who really cared about me. I abused God's gift of sex."

He paused, reflecting. Jan watched him remember. After a moment, he sighed and went on.

"Right after Sylvia and Father married, I came up here for three days. It was cold, just before Christmas, and I realized that I didn't even enjoy sex any more, so why was I doing that to those women? I knew then that if I were to get on with my life, I would have to forgive my father and forgive Sylvia. My mother had begun a new life of her own. She had a business, friends, an active social life. They hadn't hurt her. My father had set her free, in a sense. Sylvia was not the woman for me, and I would have found that out in time. The problem was within me."

He offered a small, sad smile.

"I did forgive them by the time I came off the mountain. I still don't care for the type of people they are, but I care for them as family. We write at Christmas and I see them every few years. Then, I had to forgive myself. I had hurt a lot of women. I had never known I was capable of that, but I was, I am. I contacted each of those women and told her I was sorry and why; told her that she was a good person and that I hoped she could forgive me. I packed up my belongings, went to Mom's for Christmas, and told her I was enrolling in seminary at University of the South in Sewanee, Tennessee. And here I am now."

"So, how did you decide to become a minister?" Jan asked.

"Actually, I had secretly wanted to join the ministry since I was a teen acolyte. I was very close to my minister during my teen years. I could never tell my father, of course. Father Lambert and I discussed every theological question I could think to ask. I see the ministry as not much different than law. I use the Bible much as I would use law books if I were a lawyer. I counsel on points of spiritual law rather than human-made law. Now you know all there is to know about me," Grant laughed.

"Weren't there ever any more women in your life?"

"No."

"Not even one you liked more than anyone else?"

"No," Grant turned serious, "until I met you."

"But I'm married, and I could be going to jail," Jan said lightly.

"Now, I didn't say I was going to try to get you into bed or ask you to marry me. I just said I like you more than anyone else," he grinned.

Jan turned red. "I like you, too," she replied sheepishly.

"Yes, I know," he said.

"You know, being a sinner and knowing sin are two different things." Jan leaned back on her elbows and watched a hawk soar. "I mean, we are raised knowing we are sinners, but it wasn't until I was raped that I knew sin. I think I can finally see that act as a whole now, as sinful nature, without feeling guilty about it. But I feel no guilt for killing a man, and that's why I need forgiveness."

Grant made no comment, but reached in his pocket and took out something he held gently and rubbed with his fingers.

"The cross stands for forgiveness, but forgiveness is a work of the soul – an inner experience. The first thing required of us is the recognition of the depths of our own guilt." Grant turned to Jan who sat up and leaned against a rock.

"Jan, up to this point you've been unable to see this Punk as a fellow human; you see him only as an evil that you conquered. But you will begin to see him differently, in time. And when you do, you'll feel the depths of your sin, and you'll ask for forgiveness, and it will be given to you. God will work with you concerning justice. Don't punish one chosen of God – that's you, my friend – and waste a precious life that could produce so much good because you dared to defend yourself against one chosen by the source of evil. God alone has the right to judge."

"Chosen of God," Jan scoffed. "Don't you see that the rape, the killing, they are only two sins? I'm filled with sin to the brim!" she shouted. She began pacing the narrow meadow. "Don't you see, it is through this horrible nightmare that was thrust upon me that I can just now see how awful a person I am? I have lived my life as a lie; I have not been myself to my friends, to my family; I do not love the man I am married to ...." Jan stopped in mid-sentence, realizing what she was confessing to Grant.

Grant smiled. "I know that. I've known that since the first time I met David. You made a mistake and married the wrong person for the wrong reasons. That is no sin. The sin has been denying your true self as God made you. I know because I have committed the same sin. But now you are beginning to seek out the truth of yourself."

Grant stood and stepped closer to Jan. "I want to give you something." He opened his hand to show what he had taken from his pocket. It was a pearl. The largest, most beautiful and most perfectly shaped pearl Jan had ever seen.

"Why, you should have that on a chain, or in a box. You'll lose it that way," she exclaimed.

"No, I won't, and neither will you," he said pushing the pearl toward her.

"I can't. I don't deserve it," she said taking a step back.

"Deserving has nothing to do with it," Grant insisted. "A pearl is made when a piece of grit enters the wound in an oyster shell. It is the only gem produced by a living process. Without the wound, there would be no pearl. It's only through times of trial and tribulation that our spirits are forced to form something beautiful out of something ugly or painful. Like the pearl," he said as he held the pearl steadily before her.

"If I'm the pearl, then Punk is the pearl maker. I cannot afford him that honor," Jan argued.

"No, Jan. The material necessary to make the pearl is called *nacre* – the mother-of-pearl lining inside the oyster shell. You are the oyster; its meat is your soul. Punk is only the invading grit – the irritant; but God is the *pearl maker*, for He provides that soothing mother-of-pearl, the spiritual protection for each of our souls. Isolating that which tries to hurt us. Wrapping the hurt in soothing layers. Protecting us from its harm."

Jan slowly held out her hand. Without taking his eyes off hers, Grant placed the pearl in her palm and closed her fingers around it.

PART THREE

Chapter One

Jan was not surprised when the grand jury returned a true bill of murder. Her life was following a predestined path and she seemed to know each step before it came.

Her family was shocked; her lawyer and psychiatrist vowed to work harder for her defense, and newspapers around the nation editorialized on the state of the nation's judicial system. But Jan was unaffected by the outrage. She had to play the drama to the end, whatever that might be.

Jan was introspective during the rest of the wait in Brevard. May and Meemaw thought the overhanging decision of the Grand Jury was the cause of her mood. John was not there to see it. He had to fly to Kingsford and didn't return until Friday when the Grand Jury announced its decision.

Dr. Carey had warned John that this could happen. He in turn soothed May's concerns – she called him several times a day – with Dr. Carey's projections of Jan's behavior.

Grant had had to go to Atlanta for a diocesan meeting, but he also returned on Friday. He alone was not worried about Jan's self-absorption. She had to experience every level of her human nature to discern the real from the delusion. She must reach the base of herself before she would be able to surface through the layers whole, a human pearl.

Jan did not have a clear picture of her present state of mind. She only knew that the pearl Grant had given her had a profound affect on her inner peace. Unlike anything David had ever given her, even her engagement ring, the pearl was more than a gift of love from Grant; it was a spiritual symbol of her soul. She was quiet on the outside, but inside Jan was moving at breakneck speed on the path from a material existence to a soulful one.

When May called Dr. Carey the second day of Jan's withdrawal, he warned her not to try to draw her daughter out. So Jan, thankfully, was left alone. Those last days in Brevard, May and Meemaw drove Jan through the mountains for hours, not bothering her, but chatting quietly in the front seat, pointing out views and shops. They saw a good deal of Western North Carolina, they stopped and browsed in antique stores, but they never took their attention from Jan. The concerned wrinkle across the brow became ingrained in the otherwise well-preserved face of her mother.

Emotions on Friday were hidden by the mundane necessities of packing. John and Grant had their roles as attorney and minister. There was breakfast and lunch to be arranged. Checking out proved difficult, as the press had rediscovered their lodgings. The car had to be gassed, and then there was the silent trip home.

The phone rang off the hook upon their return. Julia Ann and Peterson called, friends called, Uncle Ralph called and David ... but Jan would talk to no one.

How could she tell David she no longer loved him? That she had been false in her relationship with him since the beginning because she had not known herself? How could she not have seen her life more clearly before now? She had had strong inclinations to follow her heart, but she had ignored them to do what everyone expected of her. She did what society expected. Hell, she had never liked bridge! The game was too competitive, and most of the women were so hateful in their gossip that Jan felt guilty hearing what they said about others. Yet, Jan had done many things to win these women's approval.

No, she couldn't talk to David just now.

David sensed the change. Truth seeped through the cracks of his own self-illusion. He avoided calling Jan as much as she avoided calling him. More than once, May expressed to Jan her concern that this should be a time to reach out to her husband. Lamar was secretly angry with David for not phoning Jan more, not coming to see her. That was no way for a husband to act. But her father also saw Jan pushing David out, so he kept quiet.

David actually heard the grand jury's verdict over the six o'clock news. Jan was traveling toward Kingsford and Lamar had not been able to reach him at his office. All week, David could think of nothing but the outcome of the grand jury's decision. If she were declared innocent, then there would be no real reason for Jan to stay in Kingsford. David honestly didn't know if he wanted her to come back or not. He didn't think he could be there for her – not here at their home anymore than when she was five hundred miles away.

David had been seeing Lucy Meadows, Jan's teaching friend. He was accustomed to Lucy's attentions and her need for him. They had spent the last few weeks sneaking around in and out of town. At first David thought his feelings for Lucy were sexual and emotional relief. He was truly grateful for her being there for him. Now, he was beginning to see that he and Lucy were much better suited as a couple than he and Jan had ever been.

Lucy encouraged David to listen to his father and consider moving back to Atlanta. Jan had said that David would lose his freedom working for his father. But this was freedom? Living in a dumpy little town where the agricultural market determined whether or not he had friends? Where there was no cultural entertainment? Where he had begun a life with Jan that now had crumbled before his eyes?

If Jan had known of David and Lucy's relationship, she would have been relieved. She knew that Lucy was David's social escort and that she cooked him an occasional meal. She secretly hoped that they would get together when she was out of the picture. She thought they were much more suited for each other, after all.

A week after the grand jury hearing, David told Jan that Lucy came once a week to clean and cook for him. "That's some nice friend you have there," he said. "I hope you let her know how much you appreciate her."

Jan refrained from saying that the favor was for David. "You're right. She has been so nice about writing me and telling me what's going on at school. I'll have to drop her a note. If you see her, tell her how much I appreciate what she's doing for you."

"For us," David corrected her.

"Yes, of course, for us," she said.

"I thought knowing that I'm taken care of would ease your mind. I know you have enough worries facing a trial. Did you know that I had to hear it on the news to find out? You could have called me."

"I'm sorry, David. I really am. Only I haven't felt like talking to anyone. I just need to think, to readjust," she tried to explain.

"Not even to Father Tyler?" He emphasized *Father*.

"Look, David, I have to go. There's quite a lot that's not the same about us. Please, let's try to understand it instead of taking it personally," she said. "I'm truly happy that Lucy is helping out. I do worry about you; only I'm not in a position to do anything about it. Just try to use this experience as a time for self-renewal and understanding. I'll try to call you soon. Goodbye, David."

"'Bye, Jan." David was annoyed.

"So, did you tell her?" Lucy asked David that night at the Back Door. "What'd she say? Did she sound jealous?"

"She said she was very appreciative that you are taking care of me, because she can't right now. She said you have been a good friend and have even written her news about school." David leaned closer. "You know, Lucy, that really is nice of you to write her."

"We were friends before, and I just feel terrible for what happened to her," Lucy said. "What else did she say?"

"Oh, the usual psychological bullshit," he said irritated. "She did say one thing, though, that kind of made sense. She said there's a lot not the same about us and we should try to understand it instead of taking it personally."

"Do you think she knows about me?" Lucy asked.

David looked at her a moment. "No. I think she's too busy with that so-called minister to notice."

"David!" Lucy admonished. "He's a minister. This is definitely a time that Jan needs a minister, and what safer man for her to be around? Besides, even if she did have a thing with the minister, which I know she wouldn't, wouldn't that make it easier for us?"

David smiled. "You're right. Let's not talk about it anymore, okay? You want another beer?"

Chapter Two

"Come on, Jan, spit it out. You haven't really talked to me since before you went to Brevard." Dr. Carey was worried about Jan. It was possible that having to relive the experience at the cabin and then be ruled guilty had thrown her deeper within. Jan was functioning in the world; she was working for her father; she talked of yard work. She just didn't have much to say.

Jan looked up and gave him a half smile.

Dr. Carey stood up and moved to the chair next to Jan. "Maybe you're trying to tell me to diagnose you as post traumatic stress syndrome so that you can plead insanity, is that it? Have I misjudged and pushed you too far?" Dr. Carey's concern showed in his face.

"No, of course not, Dr. Carey. I'm not insane, I assure you. I've just had a great deal to think about, and I'm not through sorting it all out yet," she said.

"Perhaps thinking aloud will help. You can think aloud to me and I won't offer an opinion. That's what I'm here for, Jan," Dr. Carey said earnestly.

"I don't know if I can put it into words," Jan said with the hint of a beginning. She stood and walked to the bookcase, as she often did when she was pondering, and ran her right index finger along the titles.

"It seems to me," she began without looking at him, "that twelve representatives of a community, twelve normal, across-the-board men and women, would not all agree that there was a possibility of guilt on my part unless there was. Maybe I'm missing something here. I mean I can understand how one politically motivated man like Frank Woods might find guilt," she continued as she reached the end of the bookcase and turned to retrace her steps, "but twelve randomly picked people. I know right now that if I had to do it again I would kill that man." She looked at Dr. Carey. "Maybe that's the point. Maybe my disregard for him as a human *is* my guilt."

"Jan, we've been over this. Self-protection has nothing to do with guilt," Dr. Carey said.

"You promised no opinions," Jan smirked at him. "I didn't say my killing him was my guilt; it's my not respecting him as a fellow being created by God." She paused and looked to see if he was going to respond.

Dr. Carey smiled and kept his mouth shut.

"Do you remember 'The Rime of the Ancient Mariner' by Coleridge? I teach this poem in class, and this tale has intrigued me for years. The ancient mariner and his crew are swept by fierce storms toward the South Pole. They encounter drifts of ice in heavy fog and fear they will wreck. But an albatross comes flying through the fog. They feed it their strange food, and the seabird leads them through the fog and between the maze of shifting ice islands out to open, clear waters. The escape is followed by a good south wind and the albatross becomes their friend, coming when called to eat or just to play. Every evening at nine, whether it be misty or cloudy, the albatross perches on the mast at vespers, a word that could mean just evening or an evening worship service. I don't know what Coleridge meant for the word to mean, but I like to think that the crew held a vespers service at nine. But then, would these shallow men worship? I never have decided." Jan looked up, realizing that she was rambling.

Dr. Carey sat patiently, listening, waiting for her to continue.

"Anyway, the ancient mariner kills the albatross. At first it seems that he killed the bird for no reason. Coleridge never gives the mariner a reason, but the men do. First, they curse the mariner for killing the bird of good luck. They say the bird made the breeze blow. Then, they change their story when the sun rises high in a clear sky and they say the mariner was right to kill the bird, for it brought the fog and mist. So now, they're guilty too, you see. They base their praise or accusations on irrelevant weather changes. The mariner never tries to justify why he killed the albatross, by the way.

"The trip continued with good winds and clear skies. The destination I don't remember, but they end up at the equator. The ship is becalmed; heat and stillness become unbearable. The men are dying without water. They feel a demon spirit nearby, ready to take them in death. They blame all their problems now on the mariner, and they hang the dead albatross around his neck. Gross. I would not wear Punk around my neck." She smiled.

"The men would have blamed their present plight on the albatross if the mariner hadn't already killed it. They see a ship, and the mariner realizes it's the death ship; his two hundred crewmen die with a curse for the mariner in each man's eye. So, the mariner is left there alone; he can't die; he tries to pray and can't; and he hates that he and the slimy sea creatures are alive while these men lie dead. Then one night the moon causes the water snakes to look shiny white with elfish light and they are so beautiful, these happy living things, compared to the dead men at his feet, that he unconsciously blesses them. At that moment, he is able to pray ... and albatross falls from his neck."

Jan gazed evenly at Dr. Carey. "This trial is the albatross around my neck," she said with certainty. "It won't fall away until I can bless the slimy things – Punk. The mariner says that his kind saint took pity on him and helped him to bless the water snakes, though he wasn't aware of it.

"So, where's my saint?" she asked.

"You said the ancient mariner couldn't pray before he blessed these snakes. Can you pray? I know you spend a great deal of time in your church's chapel, but have you been able to pray?" Dr. Carey asked.

"Yes and no. I mean, I talk to God all the time, not just in the chapel, but I don't know if you'd call it praying. I ask a lot of questions. I rant and I rave. I ask for a window of truth into this mess, but I remain confused. I feel I'm on the right track, but I'm going forward blindly, in the fog and mist, if you will." Jan stopped pacing and took her seat next to Dr. Carey.

"My time is literally about up. I have no answers; only questions," she said.

"Ah, but Jan, these are questions which will lead you to yourself. The rest will fall into place," he said.

"You know, Dr. Carey, I'm afraid of the next step. I don't know what I thought before the grand jury hearing, but now the reality of going to prison scares me. I envision being cornered in a cell by a guard just like Punk," Jan said quietly.

Dr. Carey hugged her. "Jan, this is the self-protective reaction of fear, and that same self-protective instinct will carry you through this trial." Dr. Carey held her by both shoulders and looked into her eyes.

"You killed that man in self defense. Whatever spiritual battle you've been thrown into, the law says that killing in self-defense is justifiable. This trial is not part of your spiritual battle, and you're going to have to take an interest in it on the physical level if you are going to win," he said. Dr. Carey abruptly dropped his arms and moved to the chair on the other side of his desk.

"I am not saying this to you only as your psychiatrist," Dr. Carey said. "I am saying this as someone very concerned about your immediate and ongoing future. On a psychological level, the spiritual battle, as you see it, is the process of going through all the built-up layers and coming to the core of yourself. This is necessary, and you have many layers to go through. In the meantime, a trial which will determine your future is happening on the outside, and unless you want your fears realized, you better come out here and fight this. Don't just let this happen to you."

Jan looked at her hands for a long moment before responding. "You're right. I know you're right. But I fought back before I was raped. I fought with all I had, and still I was raped. What if I fight and still go to prison? I don't think I could bear that," she pleaded.

"Jan, this is not the same. I see your point, but these are not deranged, sick individuals. They are normal people …."

The phone buzzed. Dr. Carey hesitated before picking it up. "Yes," he said roughly. "Five minutes? Thanks for telling me." He hung up.

Jan jumped up. "Let me guess. We're five minutes into your next patient's time. I tried to tell you." She smiled at him. "I'm going to try to get involved in my defense," she said earnestly.

"That's all I ask," he said as he opened the rear office door for her.

It's just the end of January and the trial won't be until late March, Jan thought to herself on the drive back to Kingsford. *Perhaps Dr. Carey's right. Perhaps I need to force myself outside for a while. I could get more involved; take an art course, explore Atlanta's cultural side.*

Jan couldn't muster any enthusiasm for either of these ideas. The drive home was dreary. There had been almost two full weeks of cold, damp, cloudy weather, full days of drizzle as fine as a mist and measuring still less than half-an-inch accumulation. The weather report offered no hope for a break, and another cloud system and cold front were headed to the Southeast. Jan unconsciously rubbed the pearl between her thumb and forefinger.

Instead of going directly to her father's office to work, Jan drove to St. Peter's and parked near the chapel. Grant's car wasn't there and there was no indication of life. She was glad to be alone.

Inside, she sat in her customary pew on the right side. From this angle, she had a better view of the wooden sculpture of Mother Mary. Mary looked like a young, shy, beautiful girl, yet there was something strong in her face. Jan loved this statue best and felt such peace when she watched it for a while. The cross on the altar also drew her gaze. It was a large sterling silver replica of the wooden cross on which Jesus died. The shiny silver somehow gave the cross strength that transcended the blood shed there.

Today, her gaze fell longest on the sculpture she liked least – the dark, wooden sculpture of Jesus from the waist up as he hung on the cross. The crown of thorns, the nails, the pained expansion of the rib cage were all so realistic that Jan felt uncomfortable looking. Jesus' chin was almost to His chest, but His eyes were raised upward. Below, an inscription was carved: *I look unto these hills from whence comes my strength.*

Jan wondered if Jesus said this before he was able to ask God to forgive the people who crucified Him because they didn't know what they were doing. Or did he look up after He forgave the crowd and the two thieves dying with him. If He said it before asking for forgiveness for their sins, perhaps God gave Him the ability to forgive. Perhaps God could give her the same ability to forgive and bless. She waited quietly, waiting to forgive and bless Punk. Nothing happened. Her feelings had not changed.

"So, what do you want me to do?" she addressed the cross on the altar. "Do you want me to ask You to make me forgive that man? To make me bless that less-than-human bum?"

Jan looked at the Mother Mary sculpture, so calm, so accepting, yet so intense. She dropped to her knees on the kneeling bench. "Lord," she began, looking at the cross. She looked back at Mother Mary. "Lord," she said again. This time she raised her eyes above. *I look unto …* Nothing. She looked back at the Mother Mary, at the cross, at Jesus. Then she began to laugh. She laughed out loud. She laughed until her sides hurt. And then she stopped. "You know, you're probably just a bunch of icons anyway," she addressed them. "I doubt you can go beyond those clouds up there any more than I can." She stood. "I know

I can't get beyond those clouds, so maybe there's nothing beyond them to get to," she said in a loud, angry voice.

She raised first her eyes then her entire face to the ceiling. "How can I find strength if I can't find the hills to look unto?" she shouted. "Are you listening to me, God? Where are you?" Her shoulders shook and she hung her head and cried.

"He's listening. He's listening," she heard at the same time she felt warm, strong arms around her shoulders. She turned into Grant and cried herself out.

Jan looked up at Grant. "This isn't the first time you've caught me in here like this," she sniffed.

"But this is the first time I've been able to hold you and give you physical comfort," he said gently. He sat her down and took both of her hands in one of his and raised her face to his with the other hand. "God is listening. Don't give up this spiritual battle. Peace will come when you least expect it."

"How did you know I was having a spiritual battle?" Jan asked, reaching into her pocket for a Kleenex.

"I'm a minister. It's my job to know," Grant said kindly.

Jan found herself wary. "You mean you would know that about anybody on the street or anyone you knew?" she asked.

"I'd have to get to know them first. But I've been aware of the spirits fighting within you since we met. It's like I've always known you," he said. "I don't know if my mission is to help you in the battle or if it's more. But you're not alone. Not in the spiritual or the physical realm."

"I'm just so tired. I'm weary of dealing with such heavy thoughts. I don't seem to be getting through," she said as she gazed at the cross.

"You are. Hang in there. Even Jesus had to wait three long days before He rose again," Grant said.

"Say," Jan said, changing the mood, "How long have you been in here? How did you know I was here?" she asked.

Grant stepped back and Jan could see the pain in his face. "Arnie Lochman was killed last night. Shot in the back by a guy who thought he was Arnie's older brother. The older brother is into drugs, and I think he is dealing on a top level." He paused.

"Oh, Grant, I'm so sorry," Jan said as she stood and reached her hand to touch his arm.

"I took the after-school crowd to Arnie's parents' house this afternoon. Then I took them out to the national forest campground, and we talked about Arnie, about death, about their hopes for a better future," he continued sadly.

Jan left her hand on his arm and her eyes on his eyes.

"Anyway, then I took them each home. When I walked in my office the phone was ringing. It was your father. He said he had expected you back around lunch time after your appointment with Dr. Carey. I didn't see your car here because I came in on the other side, but I figured the first place to check was the chapel," Grant smiled.

"When is the funeral? Where will it be?" Jan asked.

"The mother is a staunch member of the Bethel Redeemed Church of the Brethren, and she wants the funeral there, but she wants me to be part of the ceremony. Day after tomorrow." Grant sat on the pew with his elbows on his knees and wiped the corners of his eyes.

"What about the older brother? He must feel awful," Jan commented.

"He hasn't been seen since," Grant stated bitterly.

Jan sat beside Grant. "Life's not fair. He was taken in his innocence," Jan said of the thirteen-year-old.

"You know," Grant began, watching the floor in front of his feet, "I do not believe that God causes such tragedy as Arnie, as you. But God can help us through. Arnie is in heaven in his innocence. That's a blessing. He could just as easily turned out like his older brother. He could have continued the life of poverty and crime that has been part of his family for at least two generations. He could have turned out like Punk, who probably had a similar background, and gone to the next life with no shred of goodness left.

"But you, Jan," Grant turned his head to look into her eyes, "you had your innocence stolen from you. God is not going to leave you after that. There's just something more you're supposed to know, to understand. Only you will know what that is when it comes to you."

Jan looked puzzled for a moment. "Please don't say that Punk could have been like Arnie at his age," she said in alarm. "Please don't tell me that Punk was a victim."

"Jan? I didn't mean to upset you. What he was or wasn't before your encounter with him is of no consequence. What you met was a truly evil being," Grant tried to reassure her.

"But I would have never killed someone like Arnie, even if ..."

Jan tried to say.

"Of course not, Jan. Why is this upsetting you so? Is it because Arnie is dead?" he asked, concerned.

"Yes. No. I don't know." Jan would say no more.

After a while Grant said, "I promised your father I'd call him if I found you. Do you want me to? What do you want to do?"

Jan looked toward the stained glass windows. "It's dark outside," she said. "What time is it? How long have I been here?"

"It's about six-thirty. I would guess you have been here all afternoon. Why don't we call your father and let him know you're all right, and then we'll go out to dinner somewhere," Grant suggested. "Would you like to do that?"

Jan slowly smiled. "Yes. I would. Thank you." She shook her head as if to erase something from her mind.

Chapter Three

District Attorney Frank Woods had a noticeable spring in his gait Friday morning, March 10, as he headed into his office. He could relax now, though the Ferguson girl's trial was only a month away. He had just been handed a link that would assure a guilty sentence.

Woods realized early on that if he were going to convince a jury that the young teacher should be convicted of killing a fellow human, he would have to work on the victim's image. The man had been in prison, twice; he was a hoodlum, and a low class hoodlum at that. What could produce more empathy than a mother or a sister?

In no time, Woods hired a private investigator to dig into Punk's background. The investigator was a retired sheriff's deputy who had grown up in those remote mountains and knew most everyone there. Lortimer Dell, the investigator, said that area was farther back in the woods than any of his family had ever settled. According to Lortimer, those people were "kinda crazy acting, bad to fight, known to be right clannish, even in who they marry." But he was never one to turn down a challenge, so he set out to find out more about Artemis Delmer "Punk" McQuirk.

Lortimer knew that first he was going to have to spend time with them and become accepted by these folks before they were going to tell him any of their business. So he packed his duffle, kissed his wife and mother-in-law, and set out for the backwoods. He had left February 1, and Woods had not heard a word from him since – until last night.

Lortimer had showed up on Woods' doorstep, stinking a bit, but looking okay. He had his bag with him. He said it had taken him longer than he figured to get in with those folks. He had told them he was running away for a bit to hide out and rest.

"Some of the older ones could relate to that," he said with a grin. "So I bunked in with an old widower and got to know some about the folks and their ways a little at a time. Then I couldn't just rush on back, once I got the information, you know, or they would've been mighty suspicious. They're not half bad, you know?"

"Okay, okay," Woods said impatiently. "Get to the main point at hand here. What'd you find out?"

When Lortimer had first rung the doorbell about seven p.m., he had interrupted Woods in a game of Scrabble with Willa Lander. Woods and Willa were an accepted item in and around Brevard, though they liked to think that nobody knew about their relationship.

Sometimes Willa brought home what she called courthouse work, which was officially not allowed to leave the courthouse. Sheriff Lander had known this, but he said nothing. What Willa brought home were copies of every county transaction the McQuirks ever made, which weren't many. There were several families living together on Artemis McQuirk's homeplace, and from what Willa could determine his father and two, maybe three, brothers lived in one house.

The McQuirks hadn't paid income taxes in years, for they made no visible income. Willa had heard that the family were moonshiners since way back before prohibition and that they always paid their property taxes, only they did so every two years instead of annually. One of the brothers always brought the property tax in cash directly to the courthouse. It had been rumored that a middle brother, possibly Artemis' father, had been killed during an active feud almost thirty years ago.

There were no records of any of them registering to vote or owning a vehicle, and no wedding licenses were on file. Death certificates were all that could be found. There were few birth certificates, for many of the women in the family birthed their babies at home the best they could. A few of the children and some babies had died, but only one of the brothers had died in adulthood. Willa had no idea how Artemis fit in.

Social Services had taken note of the family and had paid a visit within the past five years. The report stated that three girls under sixteen were pregnant and that while most of the children attended school periodically before they were sixteen, two had never attended school and no one had ever finished. The visit had been frightening to the social worker, so the matter was turned over to the sheriff's department.

Sheriff Lander knew from experience that it was best to leave some people to themselves, after all they had been left to themselves for generations. But after the incident with Jan, Lander was starting to think that maybe it would be best to find all the children of those backwoods families and offer them a choice to live a different life.

By March 8, when Lortimer showed up at Woods' house, Willa had lost fifteen pounds, and though she was still overweight, she had a figure offset by her beautiful long hair. Lortimer had known Willa since she was born, but he had never seen her look so attractive. He'd heard the scuttlebutt that "she and this Woods fella were hanging around together," but he had never seen them together until now.

"Why, Miss Willa, howdy-do ma'am. Didn't expect to find you here," Lortimer said, trying not to offend her. "If you don't mind my saying so, you look right nice."

"Willa, why don't you go to the kitchen and make us some coffee?" Woods ordered.

Willa wasn't the least offended because she knew that Lortimer would talk more openly without her in the room. She also knew that Frank would tell her everything anyway. He always did.

"Sit down, Lortimer," Woods offered stiffly. "Now, tell me anything you know that will make this man appear more human."

"Well, sir, like I said, it took me a while to be considered one of them," He hurried on as Woods waved his hand impatiently. "This Artemis, or Punk as they call him, was the oldest son of the middle McQuirk brother. This middle brother – that's what they call the brothers, Elder, Middle and Junior – married a girl from over the county line. Well, her family, the McIvers, didn't like her marrying into the McQuirks. But nothing ever came of it, and Middle and this girl (Zucci, she's called) moved in with the rest of the clan. They had that boy, Punk, when she was fifteen, and then a girl, who died when Zucci was sixteen. Middle was shot at his baby daughter's funeral – ambushed. No one saw who did the shooting, but everyone's sure it was the McIvers.

"Anyway, Punk was about a year and a half then. The mother stayed with the McQuirks. She figured the McIvers would kill her if she went back. At first she didn't get along with the McQuirks' other wives. People say she was sleeping with their husbands on the sly. Not having a regular daddy to tend to him, Punk grew up wild. Then Punk's mother married Elder's eldest son, Elder Jr., who was twenty. Punk's mother was about nineteen by then. Once she weren't no threat to their husbands, the other wives got to liking her."

Frank Woods just listened intently.

"By this time, Punk was unmanageable, even for a McQuirk," Lortimer went on. "His mother's husband, who was also his first cousin, took to beating him regularly and locked him in the barn when he didn't want to hear his screaming. Punk was always running away, and the McQuirks, two generations of them, would go to fetch him back for another beating. Then Elder Jr. and Punk's mamma had a bunch of more kids, five I think. When he was fourteen, Punk was caught raping his eight-year-old half-sister, and he was thrown out of the house. He was a loner from then on, living just out of reach of the McQuirk area, but still back in the remotest regions of the county.

"The old widow man I lived with told me that over the years, several women hikers had been raped, and he just knew it was Punk. Said he never could keep his pecker in his pants," Lortimer grinned.

"Never mind with that," Woods said abruptly. "Give me evidence that the man is human. He had a mother. Did she talk about him?" the D.A. pushed.

"Some. I asked her how she felt about the law persecuting the girl that killed her boy. She got all teary-eyed, you know, said it was a terrible thing what her boy did to that girl, but that he didn't take her life so that girl shouldn't of taken his," Lortimer continued.

"Does she plan to come to the trial? What does she know about it? If we could get her to come to the trial, that would be fantastic. Just think, the mother crying over the loss of her son. Go on," he goaded.

"She didn't say nothing about coming to the trial. Said she found he was dead from a sheriff's deputy who came and got Elder to identify the body. All the rest they've heard from this person or that; hardly none of them read newspapers, you know. She did say it was sad to think of her firstborn dying before her."

"Did she say she was close to him? Did he do stuff for her? You know, help out?" Woods asked.

"She said the last time she had seen her oldest boy had been the spring before. Said he came to a family reunion held once every ten years. Said it sure was good to see him and all, but when he started being rough with the young girls, she remembered why he'd had to leave." Lortimer paused.

Woods was no longer listening.

"Look, Lortimer, do you think you can take me up there to see this mother for myself? Saturday maybe? If I can word things right, well, she might just get indignant enough to be a character witness for her boy. You obviously didn't ask the right questions. You've got to lead their thoughts. So, can you get me to her place on Saturday?" Woods asked eagerly.

"I reckon I could. I'd have to come up with some story about how I happened to be telling you all this. I mean, these people trusted me, and I don't want them thinking otherwise or else I might pay a mighty big price," Lortimer said cautiously.

Woods paid Lortimer and sent him home with plans to meet at the café at six o'clock Saturday morning.

Willa came in with coffee just as Lortimer was leaving. "Why, he left before he had his coffee," she said coyly. She had purposely taken her time because she didn't want him hanging around. He smelled bad.

"He wanted to go home," Woods answered. "Did you hear what he said?" he asked Willa.

"Yes, most of it," Willa said.

"We'll get the mother to come for the trial. We'll put her up in a motel, feed her well, pay for everything. I don't care if I have to pay for it out of my own pocket, that woman must be a prosecuting witness at the Ferguson trial," he said.

Saturday came, and Lortimer and Woods walked into the McQuirk commune about nine a.m., just in time for a mid-morning break from chores. Lortimer introduced Woods as a man who could bring the girl who killed their kin to justice.

"You know, when I got back to Brevard, after having such a wonderful rest up here with you folks, I thought there must be something I can do to repay you for your kindness. So, I'd been reading in the paper about this prosecutor, Mr. Frank Woods here, and figured, you know, here's a man might just be able to help you folks at least see that justice is done for your boy," Lortimer rambled on.

He went on to say some more about Frank Woods' reputation and how he was out for the underdog and all, and that they could see how government and justice can really work for them. The two brothers, in their sixties now, the wives, the cousins, the children and children of children weren't listening. A wary people, they could read folks with a look. When Lortimer finished his long-winded introduction, silence ensued for a full three minutes.

Then Elder spoke. "Zucci," he directed to Punk's mother, who was married to his eldest son, "You wanta see justice done for your boy?" he asked without taking his eyes from the intruder.

Zucci crossed her arms and thought hard. "Yes, Elder, I do. I figger, even though my boy harmed that girl, she didn't have to take his very life."

"Ella, you care anything about justice for the daddy of your unborn baby there?" Elder said to a young girl who was no more than fourteen, his granddaughter. She stood in the back of the crowd, eight months pregnant with Punk's child. He had done more than been rough with her last spring.

Ella spit on the ground. "I'm glad that girl kilt him."

"I didn't ask you how you felt, girl. I asked you if you care anything about justice for the daddy of your young-un," Elder said sternly.

Ella glared at the ground just in front of her toe; her feet were covered with socks pulled over layers of wrapped newspaper. "I want justice for his baby. I want this baby born in a regular hospital, and I want help bringing it up far away from here," she glared at her grandfather. She hated him as much as she hated Punk, for Elder had been molesting her since she was nine. Punk just happened to get her when she reached puberty.

Ella's rebellious remark gave Woods an idea. Because the father of that unborn child was wrongfully killed, the girl could sue the Ferguson girl's family for birthing care and child support. What a notch in his belt – a rich family sued for the upbringing of a poverty-stricken child.

"Why, you poor child," Woods said patronizingly. "Justice can be done for you. I can guarantee you a hospital birth and a place where you'll be taken care of until the time of delivery," he said.

"What about after the baby comes?" Ella asked.

"You'll both be taken care of," he answered.

"I might not want to keep this baby," Ella said, looking defiantly at her grandfather.

"I can take care of that, too," Woods assured her.

"Mr. Woods, seems Zucci wants to see that justice is done that you're talking about. And you go on and take Ella with you now and do whatever you want with her, but she's never to come back here," Elder said. Then he turned and went back into the woods to finish cutting firewood.

The group dispersed and only Zucci remained in the common yard, waiting for the justice man to tell her what to do. Woods told her that he would send for her on Sunday, March 25, the day before the trial began, and put her up at the Comfort Inn at the edge of town. Zucci tried not to show her excitement.

"Now, I need to ask you a few questions for the record, if you don't mind," Woods said.

Zucci nodded her head.

"Tell me, Mrs. McQuirk," Zucci liked being addressed with such respect, "what was your son's connection with the kidnapping ring that brought the Ferguson woman and her two students to this area? Had he done work for them before?" he asked.

"Wellsir, mister, I'll tell you, it's like this: I don't know if Punk done work for those men before, but poor folk are always looking for a way to make a dime and, knowing that, city folks oftentimes use us to do their dirty work. Punk probably didn't know what those men were up to; he just did what he was told, for the money," she said.

"So, am I right in saying that you believe Punk was not involved with the criminal goings on of those men, but just did a job he was paid for?" Woods asked carefully.

"Why, yessir, I b'lieve that. 'Course, anybody in these parts knows that you get Punk around some booze and a young girl, and there's no telling what he'll do. But these men ain't from around here and they didn't know that. Still, that's no reason for my boy to be dead, is it? It seems to me like he's taking blame for what those men did; he ain't got no business with kidnapping teachers and whatnot," she said defiantly.

"Mrs. McQuirk," Woods began patronizingly, "surely you know that because your son accompanied these men when they first kidnapped the teacher and her students, and then guarded them, he was an accessory to the crime."

"He may be an accessory there, like you said, but he didn't think it up or nothing, and yet he's the one dead from it, not those men who started it. If they'd left my Punk alone, he'd be alive today," she argued.

"Now, Mrs. McQuirk, those men didn't kill your son. Mrs.

Ferguson, the schoolteacher, killed him," Woods said.

"Same difference. My boy's dead from a schoolteacher kidnapped by someone else. I want justice for that," she forced her face into sadness.

Unlike Elder Sr. who wanted no part of these doings, Zucci's husband, Elder Jr., had told her that they could maybe get rich off this girl that killed her oldest boy. They could make some easy money if Zucci played her cards right and made Punk look better than they knew he was.

"I understand you want justice done, Mrs. McQuirk. I want to make sure that you know that by agreeing to come into Brevard for the trial, I may put you on the witness stand and ask these same questions in front of a courtroom full of people. In addition, the defense attorney will ask you questions, maybe some I haven't asked you, and you must answer truthfully. To lie on the witness stand in a judicial court in this country is a serious offence. Do you understand what I'm saying?" he asked harshly.

Zucci nodded her head.

"You may be staying at the Comfort Inn for several days, maybe even a week, do you understand that?" he asked.

Zucci nodded her head again, forcing herself not to smile.

As Woods finished making arrangements with Zucci, Ella came out with a shawl tied in a bundle and a wearing tattered cloth coat. She said nothing, but followed Woods and Lortimer down the mountain to their car. She never looked back. By Saturday night, Ella had her own room in a home-for-unwed-mothers provided by the Presbyterian Church. Woods had made reservations at the Comfort Inn for Zucci's stay, and he and Willa spent an exciting late dinner in Hendersonville discussing this new turn of events.

"There's always the press," Willa said slyly, sipping on her third glass of wine. The two never had more than two glasses of wine, but this was a special occasion, so they had ordered a whole bottle.

"Of course," Woods said matching her sip. "Doesn't that fresh-faced reporter with the Brevard paper go to your church? You could mention that something new has turned up for the prosecution and that Punk's family wants to see justice done. We don't want to look like we're throwing information to them. Let this young reporter do what he wants and then we'll wait for the big papers to pick it up. Act like we were trying to keep it a secret," he continued. "Only, let's keep Ella out of it. No one need know about her; if she were to tell how she got pregnant, it could turn sentiment toward the Ferguson girl."

Willa nodded.

"We'll wait until we get a conviction before we bring Ella forward," he said. "In the meantime, we'll let the unwed mother's home and Social Services take care of her."

Chapter Four

Finley Holbert, local cub reporter for the *Transylvania News Journal*, jumped on the chance to scoop the journalistic world with new aspects of the Ferguson trial. Every Sunday, Finley would find Willa after church and ask if anything was new with her. If there was any news that would make Frank Woods look good, Willa would tell, as if in confidence, all she knew.

This Sunday, Willa tarried behind her parents, waiting for Finley to catch up with her. To his usual "anything new?" she took his arm and whispered secretly.

"No one else knows this, Finley, but our district attorney has found a new link in his case against Mrs. Ferguson," she whispered excitedly.

"Why, what is it, Miss Lander?" he asked

"Well, I shouldn't be telling you this, so you'll have to contact Mr. Woods yourself, but I will tell you that the murdered man's family wants to see justice done," she said importantly. "You know, Finley, you ought to keep this one for yourself," she suggested.

Finley called Woods before Willa could get to his house with the report after her usual Sunday family dinner.

Woods was careful not to mention Ella, but he played up the grieving mother for her oldest son and said that the mother, Zucci McQuirk, would be available as a character witness during the trial.

"But, sir, I would like to interview her now. I can't wait until the trial," he pleaded.

"I can't take you to her, but I can let it slip the name of someone who knows how to find her. The rest is up to you," Woods said.

Finley found Lortimer before the end of Sunday lunch and begged him to escort the reporter to the McQuirk homeplace.

"Well, boy, I don't rightly know," Lortimer said, wiping his mouth with his napkin. "Why don't you set here a minute, have a piece of my wife's apple pie and let me make a phone call?"

Lortimer went into the next room, carefully closing the kitchen door behind him, and dialed Woods number. "This'll cost you, Woods," he said without identifying himself.

"Oh, all right. I'll give you another fifty dollars for this one day's work," Woods said.

"A hundred and fifty," Lortimer countered.

Before press time Monday, Finley would have a story about the new character witness for the prosecution and a personal interview with the grieving mother, who didn't act all that grieved, in his opinion.

So, for the third time Lortimer made his way up to the McQuirk place, with Finley excitedly asking him all he knew and swearing that anything he said would be off the record.

There was nothing in Finley's background to prepare him for the McQuirk family. He had never seen such people in his life. There was an odor completely unknown to him. The men were sitting around a fire burning in an old barrel; they were whittling, fixing a gun, or just staring. The women were occupied with dishes or children. Children darted here and there, squealing, biting, kicking and pinching each other. One little boy, he couldn't have been more than two years old, was curled up asleep at the foot of the fire barrel.

The men stared for several minutes before Elder Sr. spoke up. "You been comin' up here a little too reg'lar," he said meanly.

"Yes, sir, I mean no harm," Lortimer started talking fast. "Only, Mr. Woods wanted me to bring this newspaper boy along to interview Miz Zucci, if you don't mind, of course, so that the public will know the true story and justice can be done," he stammered.

"I mind," Elder said gruffly, giving Finley his most ominous look. "But it's none of my affair, and it shouldn't be yorn. Zucci, come out here. This newspaper boy wants to see you." Elder continued whittling until Zucci came out of one of the side cabins.

She walked over to Elder, holding a quilt around her to keep warm.

"This here boy wants to talk about justice for Punk to put in the newspaper. How you feel about that, Zucci?" he asked, not looking up.

Zucci's hands went to her hair and she began smoothing it into place and straightening her skirt. "Why, I reckon it'd be okay," she said smiling tentatively at Finley.

Elder looked harshly at Finley. "You stay right here and ask what you're going to ask." He gave Finley a crooked smile.

"Yes, sir," Finley answered, trying to ignore the fear knotted in his stomach. "Uh, Mrs. McQuirk, could you please tell me a little about your son and his involvement with the kidnapping ring that brought Mrs. Ferguson and two of her students to this county?" he asked.

"Now, boy, you listen up and listen good. Don't you go dragging the McQuirks into no big crime mob. We mind our own business and expect others to do the same," Elder threatened.

"Yes, sir. I understand, sir," Finley answered nervously. "I was trying to establish why Punk was in the cabin with Mrs. Ferguson and her students. I didn't say he kidnapped them."

Zucci looked defiantly at Elder. The newspaperman was here to interview her, Punk's mother, not Elder.

"That mob used my boy to do their dirty work. They knew he needed money, and they used him to guard that teacher and those boys. But my boy had no part in that mob, and he didn't kidnap nobody," Zucci said.

"Yes, ma'am," Finley said. "So, your son happened to be there as a side job, is that right ma'am?" Finley asked.

Zucci nodded. "That's right."

"Do you think Mrs. Ferguson was justified in killing your son for raping her?" he asked.

"Now, I'm not saying what my boy did weren't wrong, but that don't make it right for that schoolteacher to take his life. She still has hers, don't she? Her bad time's over, but I have to live without my oldest child for the rest of my life," she said dramatically. "My poor boy had to grow up without a pa, his pa being shot by the McIvers and all when Punk was just a hip-rider. Then, whenever I married his cousin here," she paused to point to her husband who was standing guard behind her, "they like to never got along, what with me having so many more young'uns and all. Whatever else he was mixed up in, he was just doing this job for money. Anybody around here'll tell you Punk couldn't keep his pecker in his pants, but that's no reason to shoot him, to kill him. He ain't never killed no one I know of," she continued.

"And how do you know that schoolteacher didn't egg him on, try to rub up to him to escape?" she added. "I hear tell that my Punk threatened to shoot those boys, but how you know he wasn't just bluffing to get them back inside so he would get paid for his job? Why didn't they just tie him up or wound him? They had no call to go and kill my boy, no call!" Zucci couldn't finish because she was crying loudly, wiping her face on her sleeve.

Her husband stood behind her smiling approval. Elder Sr. never changed his expression.

Finley was writing fast and furiously on his yellow legal pad. "Did your son ever give you money? What I mean to ask is, does his death cause a hardship on you and your family?" he asked.

"Why he was always bringing us birds and squirrels and raccoons when he'd shot more'n he could eat," Zucci said. She didn't mention Ella or the incident long ago with her daughter, Punk's half-sister. "We'll miss that extra food, for sure."

"Did he live here with the family?

"No. He lived off by hisself – other side th' ridge there." Zucci pointed to the left of the McQuirk camp. "Seems he was destined to live his adult life alone."

"Did he have a wife and children?" Finley asked.

Elder snickered.

"No, never took no wife," Zucci answered, throwing Elder a look.

Finley didn't ask again about children. It never occurred to him that the man would have children if he didn't have a wife. And the McQuirks weren't going to give away any free information.

"Don't you think you got enough there, boy?" Elder said sternly. "You got anything else to say, Zucci?" he asked her with a warning look.

She looked down at the ground. "No. That's all, I guess."

"Now, you get on out of here, newspaper boy, and don't come back and don't you tell nobody where we are, or you'll regret it," Elder said gruffly to Finley. "And you, mister," he said to Lortimer, "you ever come into these parts again, you might not be going out."

It was after dark by the time Finley and Lortimer returned to Brevard. Finley didn't care if he had to stay up all night, this breaking news article would be in tomorrow's paper.

McQuirk's Death Causes Hardship on Mother, he typed first. No. *Prosecution Finds New Evidence in Ferguson Case.* No. *Slain Man's*

Mother to Testify. No. The mother was not really testifying; she wasn't a witness. She was just a character witness for her son. *Slain Man's Mother To Be Character Witness.* No. Whose mother wouldn't support her child?

Slain Man's Mother Seeks Justice.

"There, that says it all," Finley said to himself. "Now to make this man sound human somehow, like the DA's approach to the case."

The DA had confided in Finley off the record, and he was grateful.

"Why don't you just say the district attorney of Transylvania County has discovered a new angle which will come out in the trial against Mrs. Ferguson, an angle that he believes will prove that Mrs. Ferguson was not justified in killing her attacker," Woods had said. "You can also say that the district attorney has located the bereaved mother of the deceased," he said.

When Finley first saw the young teacher, he felt sorry for her. Now, with Woods' help he was able to see that there are two sides to every story and that justice must be carried out for all people. His story would prove this.

SLAIN MAN'S MOTHER SEEKS JUSTICE
By Finley Holbert

A new turn of events has surfaced in the upcoming March 26 trial of Mrs. Jan Ferguson for the murder of Artemis Delmer McQuirk, according to Transylvania County District Attorney Frank Woods.

Transylvania's DA has located the bereaved mother of the deceased who will attend the trial as a character witness for her son.

McQuirk's mother, Zucci McQuirk, told the *Transylvania News Journal* yesterday, "I aim to see justice done for my oldest boy. I know what he done to that school teacher was wrong, but there was no call for her to take his life," Mrs. McQuirk said. "She's over what she went through, but she's alive. He ain't got no second chance," she said.

Mrs. Ferguson has been charged with the November 10, 2005, shooting death of McQuirk. Mrs. Ferguson and two of her students, Caleb Johnson and Murray Simpson, were kidnapped by a professional organization for ransom and then allegedly left in the care of McQuirk. The ransom was never picked up.

McQuirk apparently raped Mrs. Ferguson before she could escape. Mrs. Ferguson allegedly shot McQuirk as she and her students were later escaping from the cabin in which they had been held captive.

The *Transylvania News Journal* is not at liberty to disclose the location of the McQuirk homeplace, but McQuirk's background is one of poverty and violence. He was fatherless as a baby after his father was killed in a family feud in a neighboring county, Mrs. McQuirk said. Mrs. McQuirk later married her son's first cousin; however, by her own account, the new husband and the boy never got along. McQuirk left home to live alone when he was still a teen.

Mrs. McQuirk denied that her son had anything to do with the international kidnapping ring, which allegedly was responsible for bringing Mrs. Ferguson and her two young students to Transylvania County from Riverdale, S.C. McQuirk was reportedly only a "hired hand" in the operation, his mother said.

Mrs. McQuirk said she plans to be on hand at the March 26 trial in Brevard.

District Attorney Woods said he expects family and friends of McQuirk to attend the trial.

Finley had originally included a paragraph about McQuirk's mother saying she admitted her son had a problem "keeping is pecker in his pants." After running the article by Woods prior to publication, Finley also omitted a paragraph stating that the DA planned to prove that the shooting was revenge for the rape rather than self-defense.

"Boy, you ought to know by now that to include my prosecuting strategy will get us slapped with a change of venue and throw me out of the picture," Woods said patronizingly to Finley. "And I don't think the public needs to know that this man's mama admits he had a problem controlling his pecker, do you?"

"Yes, sir, you're right. I don't know what I was thinking. I'm sure glad you were up late to look this over," Finley groveled.

"The rest of the story is real good. You've done a fine job, Mr.

Holbert," Woods said.

Finley glowed with pride.

The news wires picked up Finley's story, but not from the *Transylvania News*. Virgil Noland read Finley's story the following day and was on his way to Brevard before his editor could ask why the Asheville paper didn't have the same information.

It was Virgil's story that the news wires picked up two days after Finley's original story was printed. Virgil was at Frank Woods' office door in record time, with Finley's article clasped in one hand.

"Why didn't all the press know this?" Virgil demanded after bursting into the DA's office unannounced.

"I beg your pardon, young man," Frank admonished. "We are having a work meeting. If you have specific questions regarding specific cases, you may wait outside of my office until we have completed the business at hand here," he dismissed Virgil.

Virgil was mad, so he found his way to the basement for a Coke to calm down. It was obvious that Woods was using Finley Holbert and leaking news purposely to make himself look good. Virgil was not a game player. He reported what was what, not what was wanted.

Virgil had seen that young teacher. She was very attractive and young. His heart went out to her for what she must have endured at the hands of that scum ... and in front of her students. He could remember his high school math teacher. She was right out of college and there wasn't a boy in the school who didn't have a crush on her.

Virgil had been around enough to know what some of those backwoods families were like. They lived in makeshift houses, lived hand-to-mouth. The men were mean and big. He knew Woods was trying to make McQuirk look better than he was. Jan Ferguson was clearly the victim in this horribly violent case, not that man. Virgil had seen the effect of society's clamor since the sixties and seventies for the rights of the criminal. The result gave the rights of criminals precedent over the rights of victims. The wounded was first the criminal's victim and then the judicial system's.

What could he do to prove Woods was out for recognition? He knew there had to be a leak somewhere, and the rumor mill at the courthouse pointed to the sheriff's daughter, Willa Lander.

Thirty minutes later Woods summoned Virgil into his office. He knew better than to alienate Western North Carolina's most prestigious newspaper.

"Now, you know, Virgil, I am always available to the press, but certain information I am not at liberty to reveal," he said.

Virgil thought to himself, *Yeah, but you reveal through your girlfriend what you want known.*

"I assume you are here concerning the Ferguson case," Woods continued. "Please, ask anything you want, and I'll answer what I can." Woods led Virgil to a chair in front of his desk; then he sat in his own imposing chair.

"Thank you, sir. Mr. Woods, is it true that you plan to put Artemis McQuirk's mother on the witness stand?"

"Just as a character witness. After all, I'm sure you know that a person's spouse or parents may not testify," Woods answered.

"I see. Does creating a better image for McQuirk by bringing forth his mother prove that Mrs. Ferguson, at the moment she pulled the trigger, did not kill McQuirk out of self-defense?" Virgil braved.

Woods was flustered for a moment. "Artemis Delmer McQuirk was lying flat on his back, facing away from Mrs. Ferguson, when she pulled the trigger. Now, you tell me how that can be self-defense. No matter what his reputation, Artemis Delmer McQuirk is a human being who deserves the same justice as anyone else," he said strongly.

"What about justice for Mrs. Ferguson?" Virgil asked.

"Mrs. Ferguson should have left justice up to the courts instead of taking the law into her own hands," Woods replied.

"Do you honestly think that Jan Ferguson or those two students would be alive today if she had not 'taken the law into her own hands,' as you say?" Virgil pushed.

"Sir, the courts are not concerned with what could have happened. They are concerned with what did happen. Now, I have a very busy schedule. Do you have any more brief questions?" Woods said brusquely.

"Just one, sir. You say that Finley Holbert called you and asked specific questions. How did he know what to ask? Do you suspect a leak in the courthouse employees? I mean, I'm sure you have no deliberate intention to have the press know such delicate matters," Virgil said.

"Sir, I resent your insinuations. I do not feel it is my job to run to the press every time I have new information about every case. However, I have nothing to hide in any case. I don't try to sneak surprise information in. I let the judge and jury know from the start my reasons for supporting such a case on behalf of the state. Now, if you'll excuse me." Woods stood up.

"One more question, sir. Did McQuirk's mother come forward voluntarily, or did you go round her up?" Virgil jumped in headfirst.

"I will have you know that the district attorney has more important things to do than 'round up' witnesses. Now, if you'll excuse me, I'm a very busy man. Good day, Mr. Noland." Woods opened the door and ushered Virgil out.

Virgil knew exactly what Frank Woods was up to, and he wasn't about to let him take a step up the political chain on top of Jan Ferguson. The thing to do now was to get in touch with Mrs. Ferguson's attorney.

"Mr. Larsen, this is Virgil Noland with the *Asheville Citizen*," Virgil began.

"I'm sorry, Mr. Noland, but I make no public comments concerning my clients," John said.

"I understand, sir. Only hear me out. There was an article in today's *Transylvania News* stating that the district attorney had found McQuirk's mother and plans to bring her in as a character witness during the trial. He is making a real campaign to show McQuirk as a decent person. I suspect that Woods is playing for a political position and is trying to accomplish something dramatic toward this end."

"I'm aware of that," John cut in.

"I would like to see justice done for your client, Mrs. Ferguson. You don't have to give me comments, just give me a lead. Where can I go to find some dirt on this guy? Is there any dirt to find?" Virgil insisted.

John paused, considering the effect of giving a reporter leads to McQuirk's past records. He knew that the man's character had nothing to do with the moment he was killed. The public already sees Jan as justified, but it's not the general public he has to sway. It wouldn't hurt the jurors to know that the man had raped before.

"Check with Sheriff Lander for files of McQuirk as a suspect. He'll probably let you see it. He wants Jan cleared as much as I do," John said. "And you might check with Social Services. They may not tell you anything, though. As far as my client or my approach to her defense, I have no comment," John ended.

"Thank you, Mr. Larsen," Virgil shouted. "I owe you one," he said as he hung up.

"Yes!" Virgil yelled out loud from the corner of the post office lobby where he was using his cell phone. He glanced at his watch and hurriedly dialed a South Carolina number. He phoned Riverdale lawyer Bryson McNeil, who was representing Caleb Johnson and Murray Simpson. "Mr. McNeil, this is Virgil Noland with the *Asheville Citizen*."

"That's up near Brevard, isn't it?" McNeil asked. "What can I do for you?" Unlike John, Bryson McNeil was glad to share his client's stance with the news media.

"Tell me, sir, are you aware that the district attorney in Transylvania County is going to to use Artemis McQuirk's mother as a character witness?" Virgil began.

"Why, no. But that shouldn't bother our case. My clients feel that the shooting was strictly self-defense and they are thankful to Mrs. Ferguson, their former teacher, for their lives. I don't believe that producing a grieving mother will change that," he answered.

"Oh, no, sir. I agree. Only, if the case is so clearly self-defense, why does the state feel like it has such a strong case?" Virgil asked.

"I wouldn't know, other than the technical fact that the man was shot while he was lying down and facing away from Mrs. Ferguson. Of course, I'm sure you've already gathered this information from the coroner's report," McNeil said.

Virgil slapped himself on the back of the head. Of course, why hadn't he thought of the coroner's report? The report given to the press simply said that the man died from several gunshot wounds to the head.

"Thank you, sir. Thank you for your time," Virgil said quickly and hung up.

By press time, Virgil had successfully received the detailed copies of not only the coroner's report, but the sheriff's report and a few old suspect warrants and quotes from Sheriff Lander on Artemis McQuirk.

With his immediate editor hanging over his shoulder, Virgil fleshed out the story begun by Finley Holbert. By late evening, the wires had picked it up and had it in morning editions across the nation. The sudden hoopla over the article was Virgil's only saving grace from his very angry editor for missing the story in the first place.

Chapter Five

Murray found Caleb in the school gym shooting baskets.

"Caleb," Murray called over the echo of the bounce. "I thought you were going to ride with me over to Bryson McNeil's this afternoon? What's up?"

Caleb shot another basket before turning around.

It was a Wednesday, March 15. Caleb was always up early, and he brought the paper into the kitchen to read the sports section during breakfast. He rarely even glanced at the front page, and he never read it.

This morning, however, Caleb had popped the rubber band off the paper, unrolled it and stared at his, Murray's and Mrs. Ferguson's pictures splashed across the front.

MCQUIRK'S MOTHER SEEKS JUSTICE AT FERGUSON TRIAL, the headline read.

A quote was inset near the start of the article: "*I know what my son did to that girl was wrong, but she has healed from her wounds. My oldest boy won't have that chance; he's dead,*" said McQuirk's mother, Zucci McQuirk.

Caleb could read no more. He felt nauseated. To think that that man, that scab, would have a mother ... and a mother who was taking up for him! Caleb could not contain the rage welling up his torso and into his fists and throat. He threw the screen door open and went out to the wood pile and picked up the heaviest axe neatly stacked in the shed he and his father and brother had built. He picked up the largest section of log and placed it on the chopping stump. It was six fifteen a.m. and by the time his father came into the kitchen at six forty-five, Caleb had split almost a half a cord of wood.

What in the world? Bud Johnson wondered, as he watched his son tirelessly bring the axe clean through each log. He turned to start the coffee and saw the paper thrown to the floor. When he picked it up, he understood what was wrong with his son, and his heart hurt for him.

Bud decided to leave Caleb alone for a while, even if he were late to school. On Sundays, Bud always made the family a large breakfast. Though it was the middle of the week, he began pulling out sausage, eggs and pancake makings. Caleb had come through the door at seven, just as the sausage was ready and the first egg had been thrown into the pan.

"Dad? What're you doing?" Caleb asked. "It's not Sunday."

"I know. I just thought I'd fix you a little breakfast, that's all. You must be mighty hungry after splitting all that wood. Thanks," Bud said.

Caleb saw the paper opened on the table and he knew his father also had seen the article, and that all the world had, too. Instead of going to school that day after breakfast, he went directly to the gym. And that's where Murray had found him.

"Man, I can't stand this," Caleb said. "How can they make that pig look human? He deserved to die, man. He deserved to die for what he did to her, for what he did to us. He was going to kill us! You know as well as I do that we would be dead right now if not for her!" he yelled into the rafters. He grabbed the basketball and threw it as hard as he could to the opposite end of the court behind Murray.

"I saw it, too," Murray said. Murray's father had seen the article first. He awakened Murray and sat on the side of his bed while his son read through it.

"I'm here for you, son," Jim Simpson said.

"Thanks, Dad." Murray read beyond the headline and the opening quote.

Virgil Noland's story underplayed the mother and played up the violent and threatening past of Artemis McQuirk. The *Charlotte Observer*, where both boys read the Associated Press version of Virgil's story, pointed to the controversy and drama of the mother seeking justice for a wayward son slain after committing an act of violence. Murray saw the sympathy for Jan farther down in the story. The Charlotte article quoted the *Asheville Citizen-Times* version by Virgil Noland. He wrote of documented records, of complaints filed against McQuirk for assault, and of the suspected rape of two female hikers several years ago.

The AP story sensationalized the human-interest side of Punk: his mother's grief over her oldest child, and the family's loss of extra meat from McQuirk's hunting. The heart of the story, however, revealed a mean and vicious man who had never been part of society, and who was the product of a father who had met a violent death when his son was just a toddler. A social worker revealed that, as an adolescent, McQuirk had molested his half-sister. She also revealed that McQuirk recently had boasted of fathering a child by his niece.

Jan was characterized as the victim. Murray and Caleb were called "the brave students whose lives she had saved." The reporter had not called the boys for this testimony but had called their attorney.

Murray felt a twinge of humiliation, but he also saw that these facts printed for the world to see made Jan appear the victim of both a violent crime and now the judicial system. He could and would suffer humiliation or anything else to save her from prison. He hadn't been able to save her then, but he would do all in his power to save her now.

Caleb reacted differently. His anger turned to disgrace when he realized the whole world knew, could read between the lines, that he, Caleb Johnson, had been unable to save Jan and that she had to save him. Did they know that he had heard, had experienced, had mourned with her and wept like a baby?

"It doesn't matter what other people think of us, Caleb," Murray said. "Those people don't know us. Our families and friends who love us know the true story. What matters most right now is Jan. Don't you see? It's a chance to redeem ourselves," Murray picked up a loose basketball. "If you let this article, or any other article about the trial, about us or about Jan bother you, then you are playing into Frank Woods' hands. You'll lose the conviction you've shown these last four months. Her suffering will have been in vain," he pleaded.

Caleb looked at his friend. "You're right, man. We'll make it right for Jan."

So, they got to work.

"I want you boys to get over to the courthouse and find all recent cases of self-defense claims in murder trials," their attorney said when they walked in his office. "And I'm sorry about the article, boys," McNeil said. "It just means we have to work even harder."

Chapter Six

MOTHER OF SLAIN RAPIST SEEKS JUSTICE FOR HIS DEATH

Brevard, N.C. — The mother of a man slain by the woman he raped is seeking justice in the death of her oldest son.

"I know what he done to her is bad, real bad, but she still has her life. He won't get no chance to change now, to be better," said Mrs. Zucci McQuirk, mother of Artemis Delmer McQuirk who was shot and killed Nov. 10, 2005, by Janet Jameson Ferguson shortly after he had raped her.

Ferguson, 26, a high school English teacher at a small private academy in the agricultural community of Riverdale, S.C., will be tried next week for murder in this seat of Transylvania County in Western North Carolina.

Ferguson and two of her students, 17-year-olds Murray Simpson and Caleb Johnson, both of Riverdale, were kidnapped Nov. 9 by what is believed to be an organized kidnapping ring that sought ransom from Ferguson's wealthy Georgia family.

Mrs. McQuirk claims that her son was not part of the kidnapping ring, but only a poor, uneducated man manipulated by others.

"That girl's family's got money, and she can get all the help she needs. My boy's never had nothing; he was just trying to make some money to live on. He can't get no help now," Mrs. McQuirk told a Brevard reporter.

Transylvania County District Attorney Frank

Woods said he plans to put Mrs. McQuirk on the witness stand during the trial to establish that McQuirk had a turbulent childhood and had experienced violence since an early age.

"All men are entitled to justice under the law. The state does not deny that Mrs. Ferguson was raped, but we do not believe that murder is a justified punishment. It is my job to see that the average citizen does not take the law into her own hands," Woods said from his Brevard office.

However, Ferguson's attorney, John Larsen of Kingsford, Ga., said his client acted in self-defense to protect not only herself but also her two students. Larsen said that he could not reveal the details of the defense he plans for Mrs. Ferguson.

Ferguson and her two students escaped from their mountain cabin prison in remote Pisgah National Forest after she shot and killed McQuirk. No trace has been found of the kidnapping ring members, according to FBI sources. The organization allegedly left the teacher and her students in McQuirk's charge while attempting to obtain ransom from their families.

The ransom money was never collected.

Ferguson is the granddaughter of Georgia real estate magnate Ralph Calhoun.

Jan read the AP story in the local *Kingsford Herald* during her lunch break. Since the middle of the previous week, she had been going into Lamar's office only in the mornings, choosing to spend the afternoons working in her garden. The weather had turned warmer, and the last five days had been sunny and inviting. Jan wanted to have her fingers in the dirt, to feel the sun on her back and to hear the birds returning from their winter sojourn. She wanted to leave humankind behind and throw herself into the comforting arms of Mother Nature.

Only Grant had been able to enter into her sanctuary. Jan quit going to church and refused to go out anywhere in town other than her father's office. She had not gone to Thursday night dinner at the Jamesons' for two weeks. Her parents were worried. May called Dr. Carey after each of Jan's sessions. She called Rev. Tyler in his office, trying to do something, anything to help. She was doubly frustrated when both Dr. Carey and Rev. Tyler told her to give her daughter space.

Grant was not surprised when Jan quit coming to church, quit coming by his office, quit accepting dinner offers. He left her alone at first, but over the weekend he arrived in gardening clothes and worked silently beside her. He came for most of the day Saturday, all Sunday afternoon and Monday an hour before dark. He worked without talking and understood when she offered no dinner invitation. He left when it was too dark to work.

Jan rarely read the bolder headlines of the newspaper. Rape, murder, child abuse, and all the other daily subjects of violence depressed her. But that Wednesday, she felt compelled to read the AP story in its entirety three times. She had never considered the fact that Punk had a mother. She had never even believed he had a childhood. Now she was compelled to find out more about him and the life she had taken.

Forgetting that Grant was due over later that afternoon to help plant a row of potatoes and English peas, Jan drove to the Kingsford Library. She found the same AP wire story in most of the papers there. She also found an editorial concerning her upcoming trial in the *Atlanta Constitution*. She took her pearl from her pocket and held it tightly as she read.

PENDULUM OF JUSTICE SWINGS AGAINST THE WEALTHY

Editorial comment on a criminal trial before it has begun is not usual procedure for the *Atlanta Constitution*; however, we believe that a murder charge should never have been brought against South Carolina teacher Jan Ferguson. Next week, Mrs. Ferguson will go on trial in the Superior Court of Transylvania County in western North Carolina for the murder of the man who raped her. Media attention has played up Mrs. Ferguson's wealthy upbringing as the granddaughter of Georgia real estate magnate Ralph Calhoun. She is also the niece of state congressman Ralph Calhoun, Jr. In fact, it is her family connections that prompted her kidnapping by organized corporate kidnappers.

According to today's front page AP wire story, Mrs. Ferguson's family's wealth has been contrasted with the poverty and less fortunate childhood of the man who raped her. This man allegedly was not a formal part of the kidnap ring, but he aided in kidnapping Mrs. Ferguson and two of her high school students. The mother of the rapist, Artemis Delmer McQuirk, has said that the crime of rape does not deserve death and that Mrs. Ferguson will have a chance to heal from her wounds. Mrs. McQuirk also implies that her son's poverty-stricken and violent life has somehow contributed to his own acts of violence, and that Mrs. Ferguson will "get over it" because of her family's wealth.

Did we not learn anything from Patty Hearst's imprisonment? Have we not learned from the past few decades that the victim's rights have been lost in our concern for the cause of a criminal's act of violence?

It is regrettable, pitiable even, that Mr. McQuirk had such a violent, poverty-stricken childhood; however, does that fact excuse him for his act of violence against Mrs. Ferguson? Is the fact of Mrs. Ferguson's family background, her family's wealth and social position really what is on trial here? It is certainly the cause for so much media attention.

Mr. McQuirk's unfortunate upbringing has nothing to do with Mrs. Ferguson. Mrs. Ferguson's family background has nothing to do with a young woman kidnapped and raped who would stand up to protect not only herself but also her two young charges who, by mere fate, were with her.

We dare say that Mr. McQuirk's mother is wrong when she says that Mrs. Ferguson's wounds will heal. She may never be able to retrieve what she has lost: her damaged trust in the world and in humankind. Her wounds are perhaps as permanent, in their own way, as Mr. McQuirk's death.

Jan felt as if she were reading about someone else. The *Mrs. Ferguson* portrayed in the editorial sounded like a spoiled, pampered daughter of wealth. Her upbringing wasn't like that at all. She worked for a living; scrimped to pay bills and afford her few extras; cleaned, cooked and all the rest required of a working spouse. Her mother was social, as were Julia Ann and her grandmother, but Jan wasn't; her father wasn't.

How could anyone paint such a picture of her, of her family, without meeting them?

Jan agreed with the editorial. Punk was portrayed as a victim of his environment, when the truth was he was a mean man. Jan remembered the lecherous, slovenly man in the dream she'd had before Punk came to get her. He, too, demanded and took, giving nothing back.

The editorial pinpointed her pain. The rape, the shooting, would be an indelible mark that would be with her *always*. Even if she were forgiven, even if she could forgive herself, she would never forget. It was not just a chapter in her life.

The other news publications at the library carried the AP story. Jan wanted to know the source.

She left the library and drove to the oldest section of town where there now was a liquor store, a second-hand furniture store, an empty storefront and a magazine and tobacco stand. She scanned the newspapers along the top two rows. On the end of the second row was a publication out of Western North Carolina, the *Asheville Citizen-Times*, which had a front-page story on her upcoming trial. She pulled the paper out of the stand and began to read.

"You got to pay before you read, Miss," said an older black man behind the counter.

"Oh, of course. How much?" Jan asked flustered.

"Fifty cents. Says it right on the upper right corner there," he said.

"Sorry. I wasn't paying attention." Jan fished in her purse for fifty cents and could only find a dollar bill. "Keep the change," she said as she carried the paper back to her car.

The man behind the counter thought it odd that the young lady would read the paper in her car instead of driving to a more private place.

FERGUSON TRIAL MAY BRING OUT RAPIST'S PAST RECORD
By Virgil Noland
Staff Writer

Jan Ferguson is not the only woman Artemis Delmer McQuirk has been accused of raping, and past complaints against this man for incest, rape and attempted rape are on file in the Transylvania County

Sheriff's Department.

Ferguson will be tried next week for murder in the shooting death of McQuirk who helped kidnap the 26-year-old high school English teacher, along with two of her students. McQuirk later raped her.

Though Transylvania County Sheriff Melvin Lander was reluctant to hand over files, he said he could not withhold public information. He pointed out that complaints are not the same as charges and that McQuirk was never formally charged with rape in the previous case.

Files on Artemis Delmer McQuirk include a 1997 warrant for his arrest on suspicion of the rape of two female hikers in Pisgah National Forest, the same forest where the three recent captives were held. However, McQuirk was never found and, therefore, never brought in for questioning.

The Department of Social Services has on file complaints of incestual rape against McQuirk around 1990. Details of those complaints are not public record.

Files show that social workers refused to visit the McQuirk family after 1990 when several men of the family physically threatened one social worker.

District Attorney Frank Woods told a local Brevard reporter that he would bring McQuirk's mother to the trial to testify to his violent and impoverished family background. However, Woods told the *Asheville Citizen-Times* that McQuirk's past records should not be part of the trial.

Woods implied that too much pre-trial publicity could force the court to have Mrs. Ferguson tried in another district.

The defendant's attorney usually requests a change of venue. Ferguson's attorney, John Larsen of Kingsford, Ga., said he has no plans to ask that the trial be moved. Larsen would not comment on other aspects of the defense.

Ferguson and two of her students, Caleb Johnson and Murray Simpson, both 17 at the time, were kidnapped from their private school in rural Riverdale, S.C., Nov. 9, 2005, by what has been described by authorities as a corporate kidnapping ring.

The kidnappers were reportedly seeking ransom from Ferguson's Kingsford, Ga., real-estate-magnate grandfather and contractor father, as well as from the boys' families. Brevard FBI agent Harry Leamon reported that the ransom money was never retrieved.

FBI files on the kidnappers picture a nation-wide corporate operation which is well organized and run by knowledgeable businessmen. Past FBI records on the operation show that kidnapped targets are always returned unharmed.

Leamon said that he suspects McQuirk was used by the ring-leaders to guard Ferguson and the students. He said, "The ring members probably returned to the cabin after seeking ransom and then called off the operation when they found McQuirk dead."

Jury selection for the Ferguson trial is expected to begin Thursday, March 23, according to the court docket.

Knowing that Punk had a past record of sexual assault made Jan feel better. At least she wasn't the only one to attract such scum. Her thoughts were running into each other. "He was human, with a mother, a pitiful childhood. He was trash, rotten, no hope." She couldn't straighten these images out.

Jan placed the newspaper beside her on the car seat and, holding her pearl as she drove, headed to her farm sanctuary.

Virgil Noland had done his homework, and Frank Woods was furious. He felt temporarily relieved that the AP wire service had picked up Finley Holbert's story first instead of Noland's article. This *Citizen-Times* article could make him look very bad. Most papers would print no more for fear of being accused of affecting the outcome of the trial. Other pertinent details these papers would save for the trial.

Noland's story made Woods look as if he were deliberately leaking information. The DA couldn't be responsible for what others told reporters, he justified. He had to play his cards right. He still had his trump – the raped cousin pregnant with McQuirk's orphaned child. He would have to take extra precautions to assure that no one found out about her. She seemed too much of a simpleton to take advantage of the situation. If anything, the girl seemed grateful to Woods.

When Finley first read Noland's article, he knew that he had been out-reported. He had been heady when the wires had picked up his story. This was a first. He even called his mother to tell her. She was proud, but she couldn't relate to the importance of the story.

After Finley read Holbert's story and then the *Atlanta Constitution* editorial, his bubble burst. Woods had used him to manipulate public emotion. It was clear as day, and Finley was disgusted with himself for not having recognized this before. He had helped to further this image of the poverty-stricken, violent man versus the wealthy, spoiled socialite. Finley had seen Jan Ferguson; he had looked closely and carefully into her face. She was no socialite. She was just a young woman working for a living like anyone else.

What to do? He could do nothing and accept the fact that he was a mediocre reporter; or he could turn himself around and go after even more detail than Virgil Noland. He would show Frank Woods that he wouldn't be used. He picked up the phone on his desk and dialed.

"Mr. Woods, please. Finley Holbert calling .... Mr. Woods, this is Finley Holbert with the *Transylvania County News*. Sir, could you tell me about Artemis Delmer McQuirk's past records on file in the sheriff's office? Is it true that he has been accused of violent sexual crimes before? What does Mr. McQuirk's mother have to do with this trial?"

Silence.

"Mr. Woods? Are you there? I notice in the Asheville paper that you were reluctant to talk with their reporter, but since that's not the case with me, I thought you wouldn't mind answering a few more questions," Finley said defiantly.

"Mr. Holbert, I appreciate your interest in this case. However, I'm afraid the information you seek is not something I, as district attorney, can reveal. I think it best you put this story to rest until the trial, young man," Woods said condescendingly.

"But, Mr. Woods, you were so anxious for me to know about Zucci McQuirk. Why the sudden change?"

"Young man, I do not know who originally told you that story, but I merely answered questions that you asked. You obviously heard that from someone else," Woods answered defensively.

"Yes, as a matter of fact, I heard it from your girlfriend, Willa Lander, who couldn't wait to tell me the news after church. Tell me, are there other twists to this trial that you need me to reveal for you? I know you won't answer, but I'm telling you, whatever it is, I'll find it," Finley said, winding into a frenzy.

"Excuse me, Mr. Holbert, but my time is quite valuable. If you have no further silly accusations or empty threats to make, I'll hang up now." Woods slammed down the phone.

Finley left for the sheriff's office.

"What you want, boy?" Sheriff Lander asked Finley when he saw him. Sheriff Lander had been furious when he'd read Finley's article and the follow-up wire stories. He knew what Frank Woods was up to, and he knew exactly who first told Finley about Zucci McQuirk – his own daughter, Willa.

Lander wasn't mad at Finley. He knew he was just out of college, just getting his feet wet and didn't know any better. If Woods planned to play dirty with the press, Lander figured he could play, too. He would do anything in his power, short of breaking the law, to protect that young teacher from Frank Woods and a judicial system gone awry.

"Sheriff Lander, were those complaint files you showed to Virgil Noland public information? Why haven't I been allowed to look at them before?" Finley asked.

"You never asked before, that's why," Sheriff Lander answered.

"Are complaint warrants public record if no charge is filed?" Finley asked.

"Well, it depends, son. We save only the ones that guarantee to repeat such behavior. If we'd ever caught that man, he would have been charged. I wouldn't be surprised if there are more young women out there he has terrorized. That man was a menace, had been for years, and it don't make no sense for some district attorney trying to charge that poor girl with murder after what he done to her," Sheriff Lander spouted.

"I agree," Finley said, and Sheriff Lander looked at him funny.

"I see now that Woods was just using me. The real story came from Virgil Noland in the *Asheville Citizen*," Finley said. "Now I want to do everything I can to stop Woods and help that teacher."

The sheriff smiled slowly. "Yeah, that Woods is a slick one, all right. I seen through him the minute he stepped foot in Transylvania County, and I didn't like what I saw. You know, boy, Virgil didn't go to the Department of Social Services and look up those records; he only took the complaint filed here by Social Services. You might want to take a look at theirs. I bet you'd find some real interesting facts there. But getting those records might be hard. Those women over there are big and they're tough." He laughed. "I know you can handle them, though."

"Thanks, sir. Could I look at your files while I'm here? I want to see everything for myself," Finley asked.

"Sure, son. Just follow me."

Chapter Seven

Grant became frantic when by dark he still could not locate Jan. Her mother and father had called him more than once. When she didn't answer her phone, he drove out to the farmhouse anyway. Her car was not there. He drove back to the church and checked the chapel. No Jan. Where could she be? He was sure she had read the newspaper article. Who would she turn to if not to him?

May and Lamar also rode out to the farm. They left a note saying to please call. Even David tried to call her after reading the story. They had no choice but to go to bed and worry, praying she would show up the next day. No one wanted to keep her from being alone, but the worry was reminiscent of the kidnapping.

Thursday Jan did not show up for her 9 a.m. appointment with Dr. Carey. At first he thought she was running late, though she had never done so before. Fifteen minutes into her appointment he called John Larsen.

"I'm quite concerned John. Jan has never even been late for an appointment, much less missed one," Dr. Carey said.

"The entire family is concerned," John confessed. "We figured she went on to Atlanta last night and would show up at your office today. Now I don't know what to think. Her parents have alerted the sheriff here and the highway patrol. I guess all we can do is wait."

Grant wasn't about to wait. He had kept vigil over the chapel most of the night, and before the sun rose, he drove back out to the farmhouse. This time her car was there. Her parents' note was still on the door. If she were sleeping, he didn't want to disturb her, but he wanted to make sure she was all right. He went to the windows of her bedroom, but the curtains were drawn. He could see into the small den, but she wasn't there. He tried the front door; it was unlocked.

Inside he found her purse. Her bed had not been slept in. Where could she have gone? He checked every room, every closet for a clue. He noticed that the flashlight that usually sat on the counter next to the front door was gone.

Grant walked to the old barn, a distance down the road. She had told him once that she found solitude in barns. There was not a sign of her. He was frantic. Had he read her wrong? Had she done something drastic? Had that article thrown her over the edge?

As he walked back to the farmhouse, he glanced toward the knoll where he had walked with Jan and her family at Thanksgiving. It was worth a try.

Grant saw no sign of Jan through the first section of woods before the gate they had closed that Thanksgiving Day. But he saw that the gate was opened just enough for someone to slip through. He walked ever so quietly. The deeper he walked through the carefully planted pine thicket, the more alert his sight and hearing became. A twig snapped and he turned in time to see a doe flee out of sight. A camouflaged toad leapt silently out of his way.

He could smell the promise of spring. He felt peaceful, despite his worry over Jan, as if he were not alone. He followed the trail to the end of the property, and still there was no Jan. The peace he felt prevailed.

While retracing his steps, something caught Grant's eye. Not a movement, not a sound, not a smell, just something he couldn't explain. He looked to his right and a good hundred yards into the pine thicket he could see a bundle that looked like nothing that belonged here. His heart pounded with the fear of what he might find, but just as quickly, it calmed and he made his way silently toward the bundle.

Jan was propped against the trunk of one of the larger pines, wrapped in a blanket with her knees drawn to her chest and her cupped hands resting on her knees. As Grant drew closer, he saw that she was sleeping, her face peaceful, and the pearl held gently inside her cupped hands.

He was overcome with relief and a love he had not known before.

Not wanting to disturb her, Grant slowly lowered himself to the ground beside her and watched her face as she slept. Gone was the worry that had become ingrained in her face in the past few months.

Gone was the slight downturn at the corners of her mouth. She looked so peaceful he had to look twice to make sure she was breathing. Grant could no longer deny the urge to hold her, to protect her, to enfold her into himself. He carefully placed his arm around her and pulled her head to his shoulder. He dropped into a deep and peaceful sleep.

It was nine a.m. before either Jan or Grant awoke. Perhaps it was the doe who came close to check out the sleeping humans that woke them. Or perhaps it was the trill of the cardinal in the tree next to them. Jan and Grant opened their eyes simultaneously, feeling refreshed. At first they were only aware of the beautiful morning, the pureness of the nature surrounding them and the comfort of human love.

It was Grant who first remembered why they were there and he hugged her to him tightly. "I was so worried about you, Jan," he said softly. "I was afraid that God had taken away the companionship He had brought to me."

"Worried? I'm sorry. I didn't mean to cause anyone worry. I just needed to come here for a while. What time is it?" she asked.

"It's Thursday morning, and judging by the sun, I would call it about nine o'clock," he said, reluctant to release her to the present.

Jan sat up straight with a jerk. "I have an appointment with Dr. Carey at nine this morning. He must be worried, too." she said.

"You can call him and your parents and everyone else who have been on pins-and-needles about you when we get back to your house," Grant said gently. "First you need to finish your purpose for being here."

Puzzled, Jan looked at him. "You know my purpose here?"

"Same intention you had in your escape in Pisgah. The time with nature allowed you to separate and find your strengths. You have had this time to understand and accept," he said, looking deep into her eyes.

"You do know," she said, and she leaned quietly back against his shoulder. "You've known all along, haven't you?" she asked.

He squeezed her shoulder. "Makes no difference whether I've known or not. It has to be God's time."

They sat in silence for a few minutes.

"Do you believe humans are all born equal and it's our life's circumstances that turn us toward good or evil or emptiness?" Jan asked.

"What do you believe?" he asked her.

"I think that a violent and unloving childhood creates an adult who has no respect for himself or others, and therefore, no conscience towards others. I also believe we are born with our personalities and are prone toward good or evil. Or perhaps we're all empty to start with and our good or our evil is another spirit inhabiting our emptiness. Do you think we have control over which spirit comes to live there? Do I have the right to snuff out the life of another human for the actions of the evil spirit within him?" she pondered aloud.

Grant didn't answer, but let her continue.

"No. I don't." She paused. "But I do have the right to protect myself from evil. I've known that all along. The question has not been my right to self-protection, but whether or not my motive was revenge. Could I have shot that man if I had seen him as a boy, a small boy neglected and beaten and subjected to witnessing human decadence? No, I couldn't," she answered herself.

Jan turned to face Grant. "I did have that split second before I pulled the trigger. I've known all along I had that split second of conscience, but I haven't until now been able to remember it as it was."

Grant nodded but remained silent.

"There was no trace of that boy in his face. I know it now. I remember that split second now," Jan said earnestly. "What I first heard before turning to see him with Caleb and Murray was that laugh – that wicked, venomous laugh. *I've been waiting for a chance to do something with you snot-noses*, he said. When I turned, I could see his finger tightening on the trigger. He was going to kill them in a matter of seconds, and I had to do something." Jan sounded desperate.

"I picked up a rock and, without thinking, threw it clearly to a spot I had picked out on the side of his head. When he fell, he could have thrown that gun in any direction, but it landed right at my feet. Don't you see? The gun was flung there for a purpose.

"But still I hesitated as I aimed. I remember looking down the barrel and stopping. I stopped because what I saw was pure malevolence. He would have killed the boys, and he would have raped me again before killing me. I knew that there was only one way to stop him. I knew this, but still I hesitated. What made me pull the trigger finally was his laugh – that vile, vicious laugh.

"Don't you see? He was taunting me. It was like he wanted to be released from his own evil. For so long I've been afraid that he sucked me into his evil, making me his equal for his murder. But now I know that maybe I helped that little boy he once was. He would have raped and killed again and again, and the little boy needed out; he needed to be free of the evil spirit that had taken him over."

Jan paused. She gazed at the pearl she still clasped in her hand. "But why would some oysters turn grit into pearls and others have their meat infected with decay? Isn't it the same with us? Aren't we born with our natures if God knows beforehand what road we will travel, what choices we will make? Why do I deserve to be the pearl any more than that little boy who, instead, turned into a depraved man? I feel so sorry for that boy that Punk was." Jan buried her head in Grant's shoulder and cried for the first time not for herself, but for the man she had killed.

Grant let her cry. When she calmed he said, "Now you understand grace, my darling. For it is only by grace, not by merit, that any of us can be saved. The same grace that has turned your soul into a pearl threw that gun at your feet to save you."

The two sat in peace before returning to the days and weeks ahead.

Dr. Carey usually refused all calls during a session, but he welcomed the interruption this morning.

"Dr. Carey?" Jan said.

"Are you all right? I've been so worried," he blurted without trying to shield the phone call from his patient.

"Yes, I'm fine. I'm so sorry I missed our appointment this morning. It wasn't intentional. I'll tell you about it Monday when I come," she said.

"Don't you want to make up this morning's appointment? Don't you think you need to see me more than once before you go to Brevard?"

Jan laughed. "I'm fine, really. Right now I have a self-defense case to help my attorney prepare," she said.

Dr. Carey couldn't believe his ears. Whatever happened to her since yesterday had finally opened her core. "Hallelujah!" he shouted, startling his patient.

While all of Kingsford had been searching for Jan, Finley Holbert had paid a call to the Social Services office in Brevard.

"Excuse me, miss," he said to the receptionist. "I would like to see the files you have on the McQuirk family that live in the far north area of Transylvania County."

The older receptionist looked at him over her glasses. "And just what is your interest in this family, young man?" she asked.

Finley had to think quickly. He knew that if he told her he was with the local newspaper he would be denied. "I, we, I have a cousin who is marrying into that family and she has a child. I want to make sure that she and her child are safe there," he said, making up the answer as he went along.

"And what makes you think they wouldn't be?" the matronly Transylvania native asked.

"Well, we, I've heard rumors that the family she's marrying into has been known to be rough. I searched around online but couldn't come up with anything on the guy. I thought maybe if I had physical proof, I could talk her out of it," he answered.

"Young man, all of our records are by law confidential. I cannot authorize you to look at anything but this front desk," she said.

"Then, I'd like to see your supervisor, please," Finley insisted.

"She won't tell you any different," the receptionist replied.

"Who won't tell you any different?" asked another woman much nicer than the receptionist.

"Ma'am, I am concerned about my cousin marrying into the McQuirk family who live on the outer northern edges of Transylvania County," Finley jumped in before the receptionist could say anything. "It is imperative that I see the supervisor here so that I can find out whether my cousin and her little girl will be safe in that family. I plan to warn her if she won't be. I've heard terrible rumors about that family."

"I am the supervisor," the woman said warily. The interest in the McQuirk family was rising since that man had been killed. The district attorney had been in, the sheriff, the attorney for the woman who shot him, and now this. "As a rule, our records are confidential. You understand the rights of the individual," she said.

Finley wasn't about to give up. "Look, ma'am, I know you have a job to do. I know the rights of the individual are most important, but I am desperately concerned about the welfare of my cousin, who is like a sister to me, and her young daughter. Could you at least check the files and advise me how to advise her?" he asked.

The supervisor hesitated. "Come with me. I can't show you the files, but I guess I can look in them for you and at least tell you whether or not you have need for concern for your cousin and her child," she said. The supervisor knew what those files said. She knew that she shouldn't even be taking this young man with her to look them up, but she had been the social worker assigned to that family years ago, who had been threatened herself. She had seen the incest, the desperate children, the pregnant young girls, and now the poor latest victim who thankfully was housed safely in a local and discreet home for unwed mothers. She had not been able to prevent those tragedies, but she was at least not going to let another one occur.

So, Finley followed the supervisor to the back of the Social Services building to the records room where only employees were allowed. As the supervisor opened drawers and pulled out files, he paid close attention to where she went in the outlay of the room. He would have to find a way to come back at night and see those files.

Then he spotted his way in. On the back wall of the record room was the only window in the room. It was high but situated just above a four-drawer filing cabinet. The window was slightly cracked open for ventilation.

Finley glanced away just before the supervisor looked up from the files she was holding. "Young man, I don't know your name, and I don't want to know you ... or your cousin's name. But I would urge her to find another husband ... and definitely another step-father for her child. I don't know which of the McQuirks she plans to marry, and I don't want to know. I could lose my job for this," she said as she quickly closed the folder and placed it back.

"Thank you. You could have saved a life," Finley said gratefully, shaking her hand.

A week later, at one a.m. on Monday, Finley stood on the roof of his truck's cab and forced the already opened window up. He hoisted himself over the sill and quietly stepped onto the top of the filing cabinet. He jumped to the floor before pulling the flashlight from his pocket. When his eyes adjusted to the dark, he could see the door to the outer offices and could remember where the McQuirk files were stored.

He hit the jackpot. Not only did the files contain reports of the dead McQuirk's rape of his half-sister, but also of an aunt ten years after that and, most recently, a cousin who was now eight months pregnant after having been raped by him. The cousin had recently left the McQuirk homeplace and was now living in a home right outside Brevard in preparation for the birth of her bastard child.

Now Finley knew the trump up Wood's sleeve. Woods was going to try and use this poor young girl, who was only fourteen according to the report, as a sympathy card for McQuirk's unborn child.

Finley left, careful to leave the window at the exact angle as when he entered. The dilemma now was what to do with the information. He couldn't print it, but he could go find the cousin, Ella, and he could make sure that the information was given to the accused teacher's attorney.

Finley was up by five the next morning He typed all the pertinent information he had accumulated just hours before, placed it in a large envelope, and carried it to Leonard Snelling's office, where he slipped it under the door.

Chapter Eight

Jan Ferguson and John Larsen entered the packed courtroom from the door left of the judge's bench at 8:57 a.m. on Monday, March 27, 2006. They sat at the defendant's table just before Judge Nathanial Vernon Abrams entered from his chambers. Murray and Caleb and Bryson McNeil were already seated in chairs provided just to the left of the defendant's table.

Woods was seated at the district attorney's table, shuffling papers in an attempt to look busy. Willa was positioned strategically behind on the first row of the courtroom's public seating.

Next to Willa sat Zucci McQuirk. She was dressed in pink chiffon – "the purtiest dress I ever seen," she had said proudly when Willa took her shopping at Frank's direction. Willa personally thought the dress looked more like the mother of the bride than the mother of the deceased, but Frank insisted on Zucci picking out anything she wanted at the discount clothing store on the edge of town.

Twelve jurors and two alternates had been chosen over a two-day period, Thursday and Friday.

The general public, polled randomly by the press, was overwhelmingly in favor of Jan and disgusted that the American legal system would even consider an attempt at prosecution. There were, however, a few die-hard, by-the-book legalists in the same vein as Frank Woods who believed that not to prosecute Jan would be a mockery of the judicial system.

The twelve jurors and two alternates who were chosen said they hadn't paid much attention to the papers and that they had no pre-conceived opinions about the defendant's guilt or innocence. There were two college graduates among the jury, and most of the others had a high school diploma. Six women and six men made up the jury with one male and one female alternate.

In order of their seating in the jury box, the jurors included: a waitress from the Brevard Fish Camp; a burley tobacco farmer; a day-care center director; the employee of a local exterminating company; a retired textile mill worker; a teacher from the local technical college; a housekeeper for a local wealthy family; a service station owner; the Motel Six manager; a housewife with no children; a secretary for the local Citgo Oil jobber; and a cashier at the Piggy Wiggly grocery. The alternates were a high school civics teacher and a used car salesman.

The waitress looked at Jan with pity. The Brevard Fish Camp employees had talked of nothing else except the Ferguson case since Jan and the boys found their way there. Thelma Johnson was a bit overweight, overly made-up, middle aged and motherly. She was dressed in her Sunday finest; proud to be a woman in a position to stand up for the rights of another woman. Thelma also liked that she would be the center of attention at the fish camp for months to come.

The tobacco farmer never looked at Jan. Marcus Burns only looked at whichever attorney asked him questions and he answered in monosyllables.

Bertha Mavis looked matronly and stern. She ran her day care center with a strict hand for both the children and their parents. Miss Mavis believed that each person was responsible for whatever happened in life. She had little sympathy for crying children, much less a wronged adult. She would see that the law was upheld as it was written, for that's what laws and rules were for. Break or bend one and you might as well break them all, Miss Mavis often said.

LuAnn Lytle's appearance didn't fit her occupation. She was petite and feminine and she dressed daintily. She was a bug snuffer for her husband's exterminating company. She talked softly when asked questions, and Jan could not read her face when the young woman glanced at her.

The only black male was Ernie Craighill, the textile mill retiree whose proud face fit his proud name. His face showed the prejudices he had suffered and survived. His eyes were kind.

The teacher from the local technical college was tall and lean with round, wire-rim glasses. He had a receding hairline followed by thin, frizzy wisps of hair. Hank Whiteside taught mechanical math, and he tended to view life in similar formulas. He would carefully weigh evidence from both sides in any given situation before making a final judgment. Unexplained events in his life were catalogued until they could fit into an equation with an answer. Mr. Whiteside was agnostic, because he could find no formula for God or things of the spirit. He was considered a liberal only because he had no emotional prejudices.

Mattie Mae Nichols could have been forty or she could have been sixty. She had no wrinkles on her beautifully chiseled, bronze face. She was tall and majestic. Jan believed she was a descendant of African royalty.

Buck Pittman did not reveal to either attorney that he had serviced the defendant's mother's car when she was in town for the grand jury hearing. Buck Pittman didn't let on much. He figured whatever he did and for whomever he did it was nobody's business, not even the courts. He was just as uncommunicative to his wife and children as he was to his clients. Jan could read nothing from his face.

Fred Priddy was the only apparent northern transplant. He and his wife had moved to Transylvania County ten years earlier to manage the Motel Six near Highway 64. The wrinkles on his face said to Jan that he had frowned most of his life. He was a sour person, but he was particularly irritable when he was chosen to be on this jury. Priddy had tried to get out of jury duty claiming that he couldn't leave his work, but the judge pointed out that his wife was there to take over. The man didn't want to admit to the courtroom full of people that he would pay dearly with verbal abuse from his wife about the extra work she had to take on while he sat all day in a jury box.

Violet Tucker was neat in her appearance, her gait and her mannerisms. She was a housewife married to a lab technician at the local hospital. Mrs. Tucker was in her late thirties, but she carried her pocket book draped neatly over her forearm as an old lady would do. When she sat, she folded her hands in her lap, her purse still connected to her elbow but resting on the seat.

Mary Robinson was secretary for the Citgo Oil jobber, where she had kept that business under control since she finished high school, she proudly told the prosecutor. She had a slight lisp and carried herself like a middle-aged spinster. She had lived with and worked for her father since her mother had died fifteen years earlier.

The youngest juror was a strikingly beautiful black girl who was a cashier at the Piggly Wiggly. "LaDonna Oakes, single, cashier," she answered proudly to John Larsen's inquiries. Jan noticed her poise and confidence. She was the only juror to look at Jan for any length of time. LaDonna studied her intently.

The two alternates were understandably not happy to have to sit through the trial in its entirety without being full-fledged jurors. Only one alternate showed an interest in the case as it unfolded. Janice Crum was particularly empathetic. She had taught high school civics for twenty years and she could see herself as that young teacher when she was first married and before she had her children. The devotion to their teacher of those two students who were kidnapped with her was a statement in itself, Mrs. Crum thought.

The second alternate was Larry Griffin, a used car salesman. He had no feelings about the trial one way or the other. His only concern was that he had to leave his business in the hands of his underlings for at least a week, if not longer. This trial was an inconvenience to him and he wanted it over with as quickly as possible.

Jan was not prepared for the crowd in the courtroom. People were pressed against the walls. Television, newspaper and magazine reporters were seated with law enforcement officers in the grand jury box to her left. Directly behind her in the front row opposite of Willa sat the parents of Jan, Caleb and Murray. Behind them sat Papa Ralph, Meemaw, Dr. Carey, Rev. Tyler and David. David had arrived in Brevard unexpectedly the night before.

Jan felt lightheaded.

"All rise," the bailiff announced as Judge Abrams entered the courtroom. "Be seated," he said as the judge settled on his bench.

"Your honor," the clerk of court began in the hushed courtroom. "The state of North Carolina, Transylvania County, charges Janet Leigh Jameson Ferguson with murder in the second degree of Artemis Delmer McQuirk on November 10, 2005.

Judge Abrams then read the usual charges to the jury, stating that the members were to determine the defendant's guilt or innocence. If they were to find guilt, they should find the defendant guilty beyond a reasonable doubt. The jurors were directed to take into consideration only the testimony given in this courtroom during the trial, and not any hearsay, media accounts or other sources of information pertaining to the case. Judge Abrams then thanked the jurors for their time serving on the jury and he extolled the importance of citizens taking part in the judicial process of the United States.

Then, in an unusual personal statement pertaining to the case at hand, Judge Abrams said, "Ladies and gentlemen of the jury, Mrs. Ferguson, members of the court and welcomed visitors, we are gathered here today to see that justice is truly executed and that the American judicial system protects the innocent and punishes the guilty."

He then turned to the prosecutor and said sternly, "Mr. Woods, I trust that you are fully prepared to try and prove the lack of innocence on the part of Mrs. Ferguson." The judge glanced at Jan.

"Yes, sir, I am," Woods answered with false confidence as he rose.

"Sir, please begin by telling this jury why you believe Mrs. Ferguson is guilty of murder in the second degree," he directed.

The reporters were furiously writing down Judge Abram's unprecedented challenge to the state solicitor. The press artists were sketching away, trying to capture Woods' expression as he received the challenge, a stubborn force of courage and self-importance as the DA put his papers in order before rising to address the jurors.

"Ladies and gentlemen of the jury," Woods began as he held the lapel of his suit coat with his right hand and held his pen aloft in the left. He paused to glance at Willa and Zucci, who was instructed to do nothing but sit on the front row and look sad at the loss of her son. The Bible from her hotel room that she brought and clutched in her lap was Zucci's idea.

"Ladies and gentlemen," Woods said again as he paced importantly to and fro.

"You've already said that, Mr. Solicitor," the judge reprimanded. "Now, get on with your address, and let's get this trial over with."

Woods cleared his throat nervously and redirected his attention to the jurors. "I intend to prove that the defendant," he pointed to Jan with his pen, "Janet Jameson Ferguson, willfully and maliciously shot and killed Artemis Delmer McQuirk. I do not ask you to judge why she shot Mr. McQuirk, for his crime is another matter. I ask you to consider Mrs. Ferguson's deed in the light of the security of our judicial system.

"Just as we cannot support vigilantes who take the law into their own hands, we cannot support a judicial system that allows citizens to break the laws which protect them." Woods paused for effect and glanced at Judge Abrams. He was met with such an obvious glare of disapproval that he became flustered and ended his opening earlier than he had planned.

"I – that is, the State intends to prove that Mrs. Ferguson was not in immediate danger and that she had a choice. The State contends that Janet Ferguson chose to shoot Artemis Delmer McQuirk, that she has stated that she chose to shoot him, and that revenge was Mrs. Ferguson's motive," he concluded haughtily.

Papa Ralph grunted disgustedly behind Jan, mirroring Judge Abrams' face. Judge Abrams had tried his best to avoid bringing this young woman to trial. The two students' testimony in his chambers was proof that this was a case of self-defense. But when Jan continued to insist that she had had a choice, a split-second choice, he had no recourse but to allow Woods to bring his charges before the court and a panel of jurors.

"Mr. Larsen," Judge Abrams said, "you may now make your opening remarks to the jury."

"Ladies and gentlemen of the jury," John said, directing his remarks only to the people who would decide the outcome of this trial. "I will not deny the statements my client has made that she believed she had a choice not to shoot and kill Artemis Delmer McQuirk, the man who helped kidnap her and later raped her. I mean to prove to you, in the course of this trial, that her statements made to the authorities in fact point to an innocent and honest woman who values human life so deeply that had this man been pointing a gun directly in her face when she shot him, she would have made the same statements.

"Not even the violent and humiliating act of rape, which she suffered in the audible presence of the students she sought to protect, could rid her from such an honorable feeling of responsibility for another man's life. If only we all could be such morally conscious humans, such responsible citizens, as Janet Jameson Ferguson – for then we would truly live in a peaceful society." Here John turned to Judge Abrams. "Your Honor, may the jury be the judge of my client's innocence."

Woods had not expected this tactic. He expected Jan's attorney to play up self-defense, possibly even to declare temporary insanity. Revenge would be harder to prove against such a picture of moral strength.

Woods called as his first witness Sheriff Melvin Lander. "Sheriff Lander, did you find the defendant and two young men at the Brevard Fish Camp on the morning of November 11?" Woods held his pen between the palms of his hands and rotated it while pacing. Each time he addressed the witness, he bent from the waist and placed his hands behind his back. Willa had coached him endlessly in these "acting techniques." The effect would have been comical if the occasion weren't so solemn.

"Yes, sir, I did," the sheriff replied.

"Did you take a statement from Mrs. Ferguson at that time saying that she had, in fact, been kidnapped by a group of men and left in the custody of Artemis Delmer McQuirk, whom she knew as Punk?" he continued.

"Yes, I did," the sheriff answered.

"And did Mrs. Ferguson further state that she and the two young men, her students, had, in fact, escaped from their jailer, but were again confronted by this man before they could get away?" Woods paused. "Did she state that she was ahead of the boys and when she turned around, she saw Artemis Delmer McQuirk holding a gun on her students, so she picked up a rock and threw it at Mr. McQuirk, knocking him to the ground and causing him to toss the gun at her feet?"

"Yes, sir," the sheriff answered again, wondering why Woods didn't just let him tell his story.

"In her statement, did Mrs. Ferguson say that she picked up the gun while McQuirk was lying harmlessly on the ground on his back facing away from her and shot him in the head?" he hurried through triumphantly.

"Objection," John shouted as he jumped up. "The district attorney is putting words into the witness' mouth that were not part of my client's statements."

"Objection sustained." Judge Abrams said. "Go ahead, Sheriff Lander."

"You have to understand that all of this happened in a very short time; yet under stress, it probably seemed like a slow motion action to Mrs. Ferguson," Sheriff Lander tried to explain.

"I didn't ask you about the time element, sir. I asked about the action itself," Woods said pointing the pen at the sheriff. "Would you kindly tell the jury the make of the gun Mrs. Ferguson picked up and used to shoot Mr. McQuirk while he was lying on the ground?"

"It was an old Marlin .30-30," the sheriff answered. "Lever action."

"And unlike a shotgun which would spread its blast over a wide area, wouldn't Mrs. Ferguson have had to aim the gun in order to shoot the man in the head as she did?" Woods asked.

"Objection," John called. "The DA has no right to conjecture the manner in which Mrs. Ferguson shot her attacker."

"Your Honor, the point is valid. Aiming to shoot a man and shooting wildly are clearly different intents," Woods whined.

"Objection overruled," Judge Abrams said.

"Well, as I see it, Mr. Woods, the human head is a lot bigger area than a bullseye on a target or even a bottle on a fence, so a shot just about anywhere in the head area would kill a man," the sheriff retorted.

"But couldn't she just as well have aimed for, say," Woods paused again and held the pen to his lower lip for a pensive effect, "the leg or the arm or anywhere that would have rendered him helpless, yet not dead?"

"As you said, sir, the head was closest to her and the rest of his body was pointed away," the sheriff said. "You have to consider the time. She didn't have a whole lot of time to figure things out, you know," the sheriff said.

"Even regardless of time, couldn't she just as easily have aimed elsewhere?" Woods continued pressing.

"I don't rightly know," the sheriff answered. "I wasn't there, and I've never been in the same situation, so I don't think I'm qualified to answer."

"But surely, Sheriff Lander, in your line of work, you could surmise."

"Objection, Your Honor. A court of law is not a place for conjecture," John said jumping from his seat.

"How right you are, Mr. Larsen. Objection sustained. Now, Mr. Woods, I will have to remind you that this is a court of law," he admonished Woods. "Kindly stick to the facts and get on with your questioning."

"Your Honor," Woods said indignantly, "I would like to offer as evidence this statement made by Mrs. Ferguson to Sheriff Lander that she knowingly shot the man she calls Punk in the head as if he had been a snake. Do you remember that statement Sheriff Lander?"

The sheriff met his gaze. "I do. But I also know something about snakes. You better kill one while you got the chance or it's going to strike you."

"Nevertheless, we are not discussing a snake here, but a human being," Woods replied. "Your witness," he said to John.

"Sheriff Lander, would you please describe Mrs. Ferguson's mental and physical state when you first found her and her two students, Caleb Johnson and Murray Simpson, at the Brevard Fish Camp?" John asked calmly.

"Well, I believe she was in shock," the sheriff started.

"Objection!" Woods shouted. "The sheriff is not an expert on such conditions."

"Objection overruled," Judge Abrams frowned.

Sheriff Lander began again. "That poor girl had been through a lot, you know. She hadn't eaten in a while, and she had just finished a ten-mile trek through Pisgah National Forest at night, and it had got right chilly that night, too. She appeared to have been beaten. She had a black eye and a bruise on her left cheek, and she had been, well, you know ... " the sheriff hesitated.

"Raped, you were going to say sheriff?" John filled in.

"Yes." He said.

"How did you know that Mrs. Ferguson had been raped?" John asked.

"As soon as I came into the fish camp, Murray, one of her students, came and identified them and told me what had happened up at that cabin," he answered.

"And you secured immediate medical attention for her, didn't you?" John asked.

"Yes, sir. I took her to Dr. Sam Morris. He sees all our prisoners, and I thought it best to take her there instead of to the emergency room where news of this sort is more likely to get out," the sheriff explained.

John smiled. "Prior to taking her to Dr. Morris, however, you did talk with her, and you say she was in shock. What makes you believe that?" John asked.

"Objection," Woods shouted. "The sheriff is not a medical expert."

"Yes, but he saw her condition when it was most heightened, and the jury needs to see what the sheriff saw," John clarified.

"Objection overruled. Now, please, Mr. Woods, let the witness get on with his testimony."

"The poor girl would talk to me calmly one minute and start weeping the next and then be calm again and then cry, back and forth, you know," he recounted.

Jan sat unmoved through this first part of her trial. She didn't blink when the sheriff described her physical condition that morning, or when John said the word *rape* aloud. She felt as if that person the sheriff was describing wasn't her, but a strange woman she didn't know. It was as if she were hearing this story for the first time. She felt such empathy for that poor girl that she could have cried for her. Then she heard sniffing behind her and she knew she had to be composed for her mother.

"I understand," John said to the sheriff. "And as the head law enforcement officer in Transylvania County, you, I'm sure, contacted all the right authorities as well as Mrs. Ferguson's family and the families of the boys? And as the head law enforcement officer of the county, did you have any intention of arresting Mrs. Ferguson for murder in the death of Artemis Delmer McQuirk?" John asked.

"No, sir," the sheriff said emphatically. "As I saw it, that girl shot that man in self defense and to protect her students. If it had been up to me, we wouldn't be having this trial here today," the sheriff said, looking at Woods.

"Thank you, Sheriff Lander. That will be all," John said as he returned to his place beside Jan.

"We have time for one more witness before we break for lunch," Judge Abrams announced.

"The state calls Dr. Sam Morris to the witness stand," Woods stated.

While Dr. Morris was sworn in, Papa Ralph leaned over to May and Meemaw and whispered that he was going to slip out to reserve a place for them all to eat in a private room at the local country club.

Jan knew that her grandfather could not stomach hearing the physical details of her tragedy. She also knew how much courage it took for her father and for David to stay. Her mother and grandmother would stay because they were women and they must.

Frank Woods questioned his next witness. "Dr. Morris, did you examine the defendant Janet Ferguson on the afternoon of November 11 in your office?" he asked.

"Yes, sir, I did," the doctor answered. Dr. Morris had silently prayed since that afternoon last fall that no one would know of the confession that Jan had made in his examining room. To sit on the witness stand now meant that he could be asked at anytime what she said to him in her exact words.

"And would you describe her mental state at the time," Woods asked.

"I would say that Mrs. Ferguson was in a state of shock when she arrived at my office," the doctor answered.

"You say your office? Why wasn't Mrs. Ferguson taken to the emergency room if she was in such bad shape?" Woods barked.

"Sheriff Lander called and requested that I see Mrs. Ferguson privately to avoid the questioning and attention that she would receive in the emergency room," Dr. Morris explained. "My office is well-equipped and more discreet for such a situation as Mrs. Ferguson had been through. As I was saying, Mrs. Ferguson was in a state of shock. She appeared to be feeling no emotions from her ordeal ...." The doctor was interrupted before he could finish.

"I am not interested in Mrs. Ferguson's emotions, Dr. Morris, I am interested in her physical state. You are, after all, a physician and not a psychiatrist, are you not?" Woods berated.

"Physically, Mrs. Ferguson was severely cut in several places and bruised over much of her body," he answered.

"Could not many of those cuts and bruises come from climbing out of a window and traipsing through the woods all night?" Woods asked, as if her escape with the boys had been an adventure instead of running for their lives.

"No, sir, they couldn't," Dr. Morris challenged Woods. "Mrs. Ferguson had a bruised right cheek where she had been hit by a person much larger than herself; she had several contusions on the lower back of her head and upper neck where she had been slammed against something ... "

Again Dr. Morris was interrupted.

"But those bruises could just as easily come from a fall in the forest or ..."

It was Woods' turn to be interrupted.

"Mr. Woods!" the judge shouted. "Please allow your witness to finish answering the questions that you have posed." The judge regained his composure before turning to the witness. "Please continue, Dr. Morris."

"Mrs. Ferguson also had severe contusions on the upper part of the inside of both thighs and the portion of her skin between the vulva and anus was torn. That, sir, could not have come from a fall in the forest," Dr. Morris said defiantly.

Woods was flustered a moment by the graphic description the doctor gave. He continued. "Have you, since the alleged rape, had a chance to examine Mrs. Ferguson?"

"Yes. I gave her a complete physical exam when she was here for the grand jury in January," the doctor said. "I have also been in touch with her family doctor in Kingsford."

"Were there any lasting physical effects of the alleged rape?" Woods asked.

"Why does he keep saying *alleged?*" Jan leaned over to whisper to John. Woods' manner was so maddening that Jan became irritable.

John patted her hand. "Don't let him get to you. He's a small man in the big picture of things, honey."

"The bruises have healed, but there is scar tissue where she was torn that can be bothersome at times and even painful."

"But she is basically physically whole, as if nothing happened, is that correct doctor?" Woods pressed on.

Jan knew where Woods was headed. How could anyone equate physical healing with mental and emotional healing? She clenched her fists in her lap and glared at Woods. She should feel sorry for such a man with no soul. Pitying him calmed her, and she unclenched her fists.

Dr. Morris explained from a medical viewpoint the mental and emotional trauma that rape causes, but Woods wasn't interested.

"Thank you. So, as medical doctor you have testified under oath that in the four and a half months since the alleged rape, Mrs. Ferguson has healed physically. And yet, Artemis Delmer McQuirk will not have the chance to heal, will he? No further questions. Your witness," he said to John.

"Dr. Morris, have you given medical attention to rape victims before?" John asked.

"Yes, sir. In my business, we see the best and worst of life," he answered.

"In comparison to these other rape cases, could you rate the severity of Mrs. Ferguson's physical condition when you first saw her?" John asked.

"Objection," Woods yelled. "Other rape cases are not on trial here. Mrs. Ferguson's rape is not even on trial."

"Overruled, but note Mr. Woods' objection," the judge said. He nodded to the witness to continue.

Woods sat down and pouted with his arms crossed.

"I have seen more battered women, about the face and torso, but I have never seen such a serious tear between the vulva and anus," he answered.

"Have the other rape cases you have tended suffered mental and emotional anguish beyond the healing of their physical wounds?" John asked carefully.

"Yes. Though I am a medical doctor, not a psychiatrist." Dr. Morris looked at Woods. "I have referred these patients for mental and emotional counseling."

"Thank you, sir." John turned to the bench. "As Dr. Morris has already graphically described, the physical effects of the brutal sexual attack Mrs. Ferguson endured, I have no further questions." John returned to his seat.

"We will adjourn for lunch. Court will reconvene at 2:30 sharp," Judge Abrams said as he brought the gavel down hard on the bench.

Chapter Nine

Frank quickly gathered up his papers and headed out the chamber door on the other side of the jurors' box. The jurors had been dismissed first, led by the bailiff to the jury room where lunch was provided.

Willa left by the back door with all the other spectators. She knew that Frank was not pleased with his opening remarks, but she would not go to him now. They would not be seen together at all during the trial, they had decided, but she would go to him tonight, bring him take-out and rub his shoulders.

Woods unwrapped the sandwich Willa had prepared for his lunch. "Damn that judge," he thought. "Abrams just doesn't like me." At least he had Zucci as a constant reminder to the jury that McQuirk had been human. He planned to save that little pregnant cousin until the last day when he gave his closing arguments. She would sit forlornly on the front row beside Zucci, and jurors would empathize with a young woman carrying an unborn baby who would have no father.

The DA met with Ella several times at her shelter home. Frank made Ella believe that he had saved her from an unbearable life with the McQuirks. All he asked in return was that she not tell anyone how she came to be pregnant, and that she show up in court the last day of the trial and look lost and scared.

No problem, the girl replied, pointing out that she had lived those feelings her whole life. Ella was not aware that she could have stayed in that home and had help starting out with her new baby without Frank Woods. Not knowing about Social Services, Ella couldn't help but be thankful to Frank Woods for saving her from her miserable life.

John Larsen found Ella thanks to Finley Holbert. John assured Finley he had done the right thing coming to him instead of revealing the girl's existence through the media.

"Woods is using her and you probably have saved Ella as well as Jan Ferguson," John told Finley over a dinner he bought him.

John first visited Ella on Thursday, the first day of the jury selection. At first she was reluctant to talk. She didn't want to give up all that the district attorney had promised her, she told John more than once. Finally John was able, with the help of the couple who ran the home, to explain that all of these promises were hers just for the asking. Any young woman in her situation is eligible for such help.

"That's what Social Services are all about," John said.

"You mean I don't have to go sit in that courtroom and act like I would love for that nasty beast to be alive with me and this baby?" she asked.

"You don't have to go to court unless you want to, and you don't have to hide the truth," John assured her.

What a little sneak that Woods is, John fumed to himself. *Taking advantage of ignorance is the worst kind of injustice.*

Ella offered to take the stand and tell how she became pregnant.

"That isn't necessary," John said. "You might not be accepted because you were not a witness to the shooting. Go to the courtroom and sit with Zucci the last day of the trial, just like Mr. Woods arranged, and if a chance arises, I'll call you to the stand."

This was the first time Ella had a chance to stand up for herself. She was raised in a family where the men own the women and the children; they were property with no rights, not even those of one's own body. Punk had been raised the same way. Ella vowed her child would not grow up the way she did.

When the first recess had been called, Sheriff Lander had come to Jan's side. She was to stay in temporary custody during the trial. He had lunch brought in from the local diner for himself and Jan in his office.

"You won't eat any finer food anywhere," the sheriff said proudly as he placed dishes and flatware around a worktable he had cleared.

Sheriff Lander had other business to attend to after he hurriedly ate his meal. He offered his apologies for having to leave her alone for a while. "Now, Barney Lister is right outside here if you need anything.

You know where the facilities are. This won't take long. You're welcome to lie down on that cot over there. My wife put fresh coverings on it just this morning." He paused and patted her hand before he put on his hat and strode from the office.

Jan felt like she had on her wedding day. Though she was the center of attention, she was sequestered into a small room and left alone while everyone ran to and fro making last minute preparations.

Since her arrival in Brevard last Wednesday, the sheriff had kept a deputy at the hotel with her rather than making her stay in the small county jail. She took her morning and evening meals with her family in the hotel room with a deputy outside the door. Woods protested that Jan was receiving special treatment, but the sheriff obtained court permission from the judge to allow her to stay under guard in her hotel room. Judge Abrams knew he couldn't hold the DA off forever, however, and he ordered Jan to accompany the sheriff during trial breaks.

Jan was thankful for a change of scenery. If she'd had to sit through another meal staring at that mauve and gray hotel art, she thought she would scream. Her mother's hovering, her father's nervous growling, her grandfather's bursts of indignant rage were getting to her. She found the sheriff's prattle consoling.

Jan's incarceration at the Brevard Inn brought home the real possibility that she could be going to jail. In her spiritual battle, Jan had not considered the reality of jail. Seeing the deputies bring in prisoners, hearing law enforcement talk, brought that potential home. She felt trapped in a vacuum of time with two possible futures at the end of this new ordeal. The twelve jurors sequestered elsewhere had control over which path that would be.

Her thoughts were interrupted by a knock on the door.

"Jan? It's me. David. May I come in?" he asked as he opened the door. "The deputy said it was all right."

"Why, David. Didn't you go to lunch with the others?" Jan asked.

"No. I told them I had some business calls to make. I do have calls. My supervisor understood about me coming, though it's not a good time right now. Of course, there hasn't been a good time to get away this whole year," he said making conversation.

Jan nodded. She had too much on her mind to worry about soothing David.

"I hope you don't mind my coming. I couldn't stay away, you know," he smiled at her.

"Thank you," she said. "I know this hasn't been easy on you. I'm sure you're confused about how I could abandon you, abandon our marriage like this," she said.

"I was at first, but I understand now. You know, I hate to admit it, but you're the most at ease with yourself I've ever known you to be. For that, I'm happy for you," he said.

She smiled. "I hope Lucy is still ... helping you out," she said. "You know, the two of you have a lot more in common than we ever did." She hadn't meant to say this, but the words came naturally, and they fit the time.

Jan saw a fleeting look of *How did you know?* cross David's face and realized for certain that David and Lucy had already found each other. "She's a really good person, David."

"She said she may try to get off at the end of the week if the trial is still going on," David answered. "She really loves you as a friend, Jan. She wants to be here for you, too."

"I hope you feel free without feeling hurt," Jan ventured. She had pushed her plate aside for lack of an appetite. "I know I've been terribly unfair."

"Not really. I heard the testimony in there. What you went through would change anyone. I finally know what you mean when you say each person has to be true to himself first. I'm seriously considering working at my father's bank in Atlanta when I wrap things up in Riverdale," he said. "I don't think you'd be happy there, yet I think it's the place for me now," he added.

Jan reached over and grabbed both of David's hands. "You're a good man, David. You deserve the best of what you want out of life. I was unfair to marry you before I really knew myself. For that, I'm sorry. Eventually the lie I lived would have come out anyway. Can you forgive me?"

David reached over and hugged her tightly. He felt sad, but he also was relieved. "Of course, I forgive you. If you forgive me for being such a selfish chump."

Jan smiled and nodded.

"You know," David said more seriously. "When this first happened, when I first realized you were missing, I felt responsible somehow for not protecting you."

"David," Jan interrupted.

"No, please hear me out," David said, looking her in the eyes. "When your mother called and I realized it was your family receiving ransom notes, that I wasn't considered a significant financial source, I felt even more ineffectual. It's not easy coming to grips with one's own insecurities, jealousies and all those other natural male chauvinist tendencies," he laughed.

They hugged again and the finality of their relationship was solemnized with tears and forgiveness.

Lamar had left the lunch group early. He wanted to see Jan. He arrived just as David was leaving. Her father's presence quieted Jan as it had when she was a child. She finished off a large bowl of banana pudding.

"It's time, Mrs. Ferguson," a deputy said, sticking his head in the door just as John Larsen arrived.

"I know I can't tell you to break a leg like I used to when you were small, but I want you to know we are all praying for you and we love you," Lamar said. "Keep your chin up, and go out there with a positive outlook like a winner," he said, hugging her to discourage the tears that threatened to spill over.

Jan took a deep breath before looking at John. "I'm ready. Let's get this over with," she said.

When Jan reentered the courtroom, she found her family situated in their seats. May nodded her head and smiled; Meemaw kissed her hand and blew it Jan's way; Papa Ralph winked; Lamar gave her an okay sign; and David gave her thumbs up. Where was Grant? He wasn't in the seat he had occupied that morning. She looked around the courtroom, but he wasn't there.

Just before she turned to sit, Jan heard a commotion in the back of the courtroom. There were Julia Ann, six months pregnant, and Peterson walking down the middle aisle toward the rest of the family.

Jan reached nervously in her pocket to clutch the pearl that had become her solace.

Chapter Ten

The afternoon session and the next two days were spent hearing from Coroner Buddy Lee and the FBI agents. Woods knew that the only leg he had to stand on was the fact that Punk had been shot while he was lying on his back, facing away from Jan when she shot.

The DA had Buddy Lee tell the jurors over and over again the position of the body, the evidence proving Jan was behind and above him when she shot him. He reiterated that the defendant had verified the position of the body to the coroner.

Judge Abrams finally cut Woods off. "We all know from this man's witness the position of the body when shot. If you have anything else you want with this witness, ask it now, or sit down and let's get on with this trial."

John didn't make Coroner Lee repeat any of his previous testimony. His questions dealt with the condition of the body and results from the autopsy. "Had this man been drinking?"

"Yes."

"What was his blood alcohol level?"

"Point-two-three."

"Isn't that more than twice the legal limit?"

"Yes, sir, it is."

"Did you find any old wounds on his body?" John asked.

"Objection. What do old wounds have to do with the fatal wound administered by the defendant?" Frank yelled.

"Your Honor, I am leading to signs of the violent life he lived. I believe if you allow the witness to answer this question, my point will be proven," John said patiently.

Judge Abrams paused before answering. "Proceed, counselor.

Objection overruled, but please note it in the record," Judge Abrams directed to the court recorder.

"Yes," Buddy Lee answered. "There was one old bullet wound in his left side, and several serious knife scars, one diagonally across his chest, one on his upper right thigh and one under his chin."

John asked this question because Ella told him she had stabbed McQuirk in the upper thigh with a kitchen paring knife. She said she wouldn't be surprised if a lot of others hadn't tried to kill him before and they just weren't strong enough, like her.

Woods grilled the FBI agents – Ken Thompson, Harold Lee and Harry Leamon – on the same points he had covered with the coroner. What was the position of the body? What did Mrs. Ferguson say to you?

Judge Abrams held back the urge to stop the DA, letting him run his course.

"Does your investigation not prove that the deceased was merely a pawn of the kidnappers, that he had no forethought to kidnapping and raping this young woman, that he was just caught up in the moment in which he found himself?"

"Objection," John said. "Leading the witness."

"Sustained. Mr. Woods, please don't lead the witness," Judge Abrams directed.

The FBI agents answered alike. Yes, McQuirk accompanied the two kidnappers to the school to abduct Mrs. Ferguson and her students. Yes, McQuirk had worked for this outfit before.

The jurors listened intently to each witness. Each, at some time during these hours, turned to watch Jan, trying to read her face.

Mattie Mae Nichols, the housekeeper, and alternate Janice Crum were watching Jan first thing Thursday morning when John called Murray Simpson to the stand. They saw a teacher proud of her student. They saw the close look pass between them.

John was counting on Murray to go first. He was saving Caleb's emotion for last. John expected Murray to give a more unemotional and detailed account of their escape and recapture by Punk.

"Mr. Simpson, I would like for you to recount for the jury as clearly as possible the events that brought you to become a prisoner of the deceased Mr. McQuirk in a cabin in Pisgah National Forest," John began as soon as Murray was sworn in.

Murray retold the story of their kidnapping from the school, of their first meeting with Punk when he had burst into their classroom with one of the other men, of their arrival at the cabin, and of being locked in the bedroom just before the two other men left.

"Up to this point, did you at any time feel personally threatened?" John asked Murray.

"Well, sir, I didn't know what to expect, but the two men who kidnapped us were very polite and assured us that we would experience nothing more than inconvenience until our parents could pay the ransom they were asking."

"Did this man you know as Punk in any way threaten you personally with bodily harm?" John continued.

"Not at first," Murray answered. "But I could tell by the way he was eyeing Mrs. Ferguson that he intended to harm her."

"Objection!" Woods yelled, jumping to his feet. "Objection. The witness can't know what was in the mind of the deceased," he said indignantly.

"Sustained," Judge Abrams answered. He turned to Murray. "Young man, try to tell the same story with only what you saw happen with your eyes and what you heard said with your ears," he instructed.

Frank sat down triumphantly as if he had just scored a point.

"What do you mean, intended to harm her?" John probed Murray.

"I *saw* him" Murray emphasized, "looking her up and down and stuff ... like she didn't have any clothes on or anything. He was real obvious."

John nodded for him to continue.

"While we were eating, we could hear the other two men talking about Punk getting into some trouble with a girl they had kidnapped before because he had been drinking. They said they had made sure that Punk had nothing to drink. They said they searched the cabin thoroughly before they brought us there. Then the two men left, and we played cards for a while," Murray said.

"Yes. Keep going," John encouraged.

"We played cards for a while, and Mrs. Ferguson was getting nervous because we could hear a lot of banging around in the next room. We tried to keep her mind off of him. Then he came in with a gun and ... "

"What kind of gun?" John interrupted.

"An old deer rifle. I believe it was a Marlin. Like one of those old Winchester styles," Murray said. "He told us he would kill us if we didn't do what he said. I believed him. I tried to tell him that those other two guys would kill *him* if he harmed us, but he just laughed. He had a really wicked laugh. We could tell he'd been drinking. A lot."

"How could you tell?" John asked before Woods could object.

"We could smell liquor really strong, and he had this, you know, drunken grin on his face. Plus, we could see a half-empty whiskey bottle on the table in the room behind him." Murray looked at the district attorney. "George Dickel. He told me to tie Caleb up with some rope he gave me. I tried to tie Caleb real loose, but Punk came over and tightened the rope. He hit Caleb with the butt of the rifle and kicked him when he fell over. He was yelling and cussing, saying all the things he'd like to do to hurt us. Then he grabbed Jan, uh, Mrs. Ferguson. He grabbed her around the neck with one hand and motioned me with the gun into the bathroom. I opened the door and he hit me with the butt of the rifle, and when I fell in he locked the bathroom door from the outside. I could hear her screaming and then he slammed the door to the bedroom and locked it." Murray hesitated.

"What could you hear from inside the bathroom once the door was closed, Murray?" John asked quietly.

"I could hear Caleb, yelling and thrashing around on the bedroom floor, struggling with the ropes. All I could hear from the other room past him was muffled bumping and her screaming and Punk yelling," Murray said.

"Could you tell the jurors about how long you were in the bathroom and what you did while you were in there?" John pressed.

"I don't know how long I was there. I felt so helpless, and I tried to get out the window, but it was one of those that have little glass slats and a handle that turns to make them slit open. I tried to knock the door down with my shoulder. I tried talking to Caleb, but it was like he couldn't hear me. I could hear him groaning."

"How long were you locked in that bathroom?" John asked again.

"It seemed like forever." Murray was visibly shaken.

"Let's move on to when you escaped," John said. "Please tell the jury in your own words how you and Caleb and Mrs. Ferguson were able to escape ... and what happened."

"After a while, Punk unlocked the door and dragged Mrs. Ferguson in by her hair and threw her into the room. When Mrs.

Ferguson could stand, she unlocked the bathroom door and helped me untie Caleb. She was so upset. We tried to make her feel better, but there wasn't much we could do. She was bleeding a lot, around her skirt and all. Then she locked herself in the bathroom. She was in there a long time, taking a bath or something is what we thought. It was Mrs. Ferguson who found a way out. She figured out how to get those glass slats out of the window using a razor for a screwdriver." Murray's admiration for his former teacher was evident. "She came out and told us what she was doing, and we all got the rest of the panes out so we could fit through."

"Weren't you afraid Punk would hear you?" John asked.

"Sure we were! We listened at the door. He was drinking again. We could hear the bottle going up and down. Then his breathing became snoring, and once we heard the bottle drop to the floor, we knew he must have passed out. We knew this was our only chance to escape before ... " he hesitated.

"Before what?" John urged.

"Before he came after Mrs. Ferguson again," Murray answered. "Jan went through the window first and went ahead to scout the way down the mountain, while Caleb and I were climbing through the window. I'm the biggest and I had a harder time getting out, so Caleb stayed and helped me. That's when Punk showed up. I had just brought my last leg down from the sill when I heard a gun cock behind me. We were caught and there was no way out."

"Do you believe you were in immediate danger?" John asked.

"Well, yeah! He asked where Mrs. Ferguson was and said he meant to have her again before he finished us all off," Murray related.

"You said that Punk said he planned to finish you all off," John said.

"He did. And he started laughing and told us to get back in the cabin. About that time something hit him in the head and he fell backwards, flinging his rifle into the woods behind him. I looked where the gun went, thinking I better get it before he did, and then I saw Jan, Mrs. Ferguson. The gun landed right at her feet and she picked it up and before Punk could get up again, she shot him in the head. His head was back and he was looking at her, laughing that awful laugh." Murray looked at Jan.

"Your witness," John said to Woods.

Woods was nervous about the outcome of this trial. He

concentrated again on the position of the body when shot.

"You said before that Mr. McQuirk was lying defenselessly on the ground, where Mrs. Ferguson had forced him with a projectile missile, when she shot him?" Woods asked

Murray looked at John, who nodded for him to answer. "Well, yes, but he was getting up," Murray said.

"But he wasn't up. In fact he was no immediate threat to Mrs. Ferguson or yourself or Mr. Johnson, now was he?" the district attorney wheedled.

Murray was angry and met the challenge. "He was no immediate threat if you consider ten seconds not to be immediate, because I can remember thinking that in about ten seconds he would be up and have shot us and taken Mrs. Ferguson and then killed her, too! I knew we were doomed, but Mrs. Ferguson saved us; she saved me and Caleb and herself from death, from murder," Murray raised his voice.

"And, young man, since you could not be in Mr. McQuirk's mind at the time, just how did you know this?" Woods asked.

"Because the men who brought us there had already discussed getting rid of Punk – I *heard* them – so when they found out what he did to Jan and that he had been drinking, they would have killed him for sure. He knew this; he had nothing to lose." Murray ran through his words to make sure he covered all the *whys* that to him should have been as clear as the stupidity of the DA.

Judge Abrams smiled.

"You cannot take as fact a conversation you overheard between two men who had just kidnapped you. I dare say you were also under stress at the time you heard it," Woods challenged.

Murray was exasperated. Judge Abrams came to his rescue.

"Mr. Woods, Mr. Simpson was there and is trying his best to let the jury know exactly what he heard and said and saw so that they can make a fair decision. It is you who is trying to sway this jury and I don't appreciate it in my courtroom," the judge said sternly. "Now, if you have no further questions, please allow Mr. Larsen to call his next witness.

"I call Caleb Johnson," John said.

Caleb's knees were shaking and his lip quivered as he took the oath of truth.

"Caleb, I want you to take a deep breath and relax," John coached. "To the best of your ability, tell us what happened in the cabin and what happened as you were escaping," John said.

"I, uh ... " Caleb looked nervously around the courtroom. Jan smiled encouragingly at him and nodded for him to continue. "I, uh, it was pretty much like Murray said," he stammered.

"Yes, but the jurors would like to hear it in your own words," John said.

"Punk's the one who drove my truck. See, when they first came into our classroom, it was Punk and the shorter of those other two guys. They tied us up and put us in the van. Punk took my car and the other man drove the van through a hole cut out of the back fence. Later, I don't know how much time it was, you know, but later we stopped and picked up the other man in a suit. I think he had driven Mrs. Ferguson's car to where the cops found it. Anyway, we didn't see that Punk man again until we got to the cabin about sun-up the next morning.

"The men put us in the bedroom. They told us that if we stayed quiet and didn't stir up Punk, we'd be safe. Told us they'd be back that night sometime. Then we heard them talking about Punk when they sent him out to get some wood. They said after that last incident maybe they ought not use him any more after this time, and maybe he ought to go on a *trip*." Caleb took a breath.

"What last incident?" John asked.

"They didn't say. I know what I thought they meant, but they didn't say," he ventured.

John nodded for him to continue.

"They left, and we played cards, and later Punk brought us some lunch. Then he comes back in there – just barges in with this gun. Next thing I know, I'm tied up. He hits me with the butt of the rifle and then kicks me in the side out of meanness, and he drags Mrs. Ferguson by her hair into the next room. I could hear Murray hollering through the bathroom door.

"He was dragging Mrs. Ferguson around by her hair and she was screaming. I tried! I tried to get loose!" Caleb looked down at his hands and swallowed hard. "I tried to get out. I, uh, I just couldn't. The ropes were too tight. I could hear her screaming and cussing." He looked at John. "I never thought Mrs., uh, Jan, uh, would cuss like that ... but she was mostly screaming. I could hear her trying to run ... bumping into things, throwing things, and him yelling all the time, yelling nasty things, dirty things. I tried to get loose. I just couldn't."

Caleb took a deep breath and gathered his wits. He may have failed Jan once, but he was going to come through for her now. He pushed bravely on in the hushed courtroom.

"When he was through, he just flung her back into the room, like she was a ragdoll or something. She was crying, sobbing, and I couldn't stop her. I told her I was sorry; I tried to get her to hear me." Caleb looked at Jan and found her encouraging gaze. "Then she untied me and let Murray out of the bathroom. Like Murray said, Mrs. Ferguson is the one who found a way out. When Murray got stuck, I panicked. When he got free, I felt so relieved, only to turn around and see that gun pointed at us. We hadn't even heard Punk. I knew I was going to die in the next few minutes.

"He laughed at us – real wicked. He said he was glad he had an excuse to kill us. He called us something, some name, I can't remember what. Then something hit him and he fell down. That's the first time I saw Mrs. Ferguson. She had the gun pointed right between his eyes and he was looking up at her, upside down like, and he laughed at her. That's when she shot him." Caleb was through. He sat waiting.

"Your witness," John said to Woods.

Woods stood slowly and changed to a milder approach. "So, Mr. Johnson, why do you think Mr. McQuirk laughed?" he asked.

"Who knows? A dare? A threat? Meanness? That was one mean man," Caleb replied.

"Did he attempt to get up, to raise up even on his elbow?" Woods asked.

"No, sir; he just cocked his head back so he could see Mrs. Ferguson. At first I thought I heard him say something, but then he let out that laugh. I know he would have killed us and raped her again and then killed her, too," Caleb answered with the conviction of his youth.

Frank decided that if he still had a chance of prevailing, he'd better stop right there before he allowed the only two eye-witnesses to this crime to dig too deep a hole for him to get out of. "That's all."

"Court is adjourned until nine a.m. tomorrow at which time we will begin final arguments from the attorneys," Judge Abrams said wearily, ending the day with a stroke of his gavel.

Chapter Eleven

John gently brushed Jan's forehead with his lips. "I'll meet you back at the hotel later. I have something I have to do."

Sheriff Lander and his deputies quickly surrounded Jan and ushered her through the back door. The judge had issued an injunction to keep reporters from hanging around the back of the courthouse and from gathering on the inn property. Jan had to endure shouted questions as she entered the safety of the patrol car, and again from the car to the inn entrance.

She was overly tired. Her mother had called the inn ahead and ordered a hot bath drawn for Jan. For once, Jan appreciated her mother's caring. The family left her alone to unwind before someone brought her dinner. She could only have one visitor at a time. May and Lamar took turns, unless John had business to discuss with her. It was the hour or so to unwind that Jan cherished most.

Today, as Sheriff Lander escorted Jan through the inn lobby, Jan caught movement out of the corner of her right eye. Before the sheriff could stop her, a young woman, no more than a teenager and at least eight months pregnant, ran in front of Jan.

"Please, Mrs. Ferguson. Please, I must speak to you."

Sheriff Lander stood between the girl and Jan. "Look here, young lady," but before he could say more he recognized the young girl from the McQuirk family, a cousin, that had been moved into town to the unwed mother's home. He stepped aside.

Ella dipped her head in thanks and continued. "Mrs. Ferguson, you don't know me, but I, uh, I'm Ella McQuirk. I know you're upset and all, but I have to talk with you, to ask you something real important," the girl pleaded.

Jan looked at Sheriff Lander who nodded approval. "Okay, I guess we can go to my room."

The three walked silently to Jan's room; the door was guarded by a deputy on either side. The sheriff nodded for the guards to let them in. He entered with the two young women and had the guards shut the door.

"What I have to say, what I have to ask, concerns only her," Ella said sullenly.

"Okay." The sheriff hesitated. "Mrs. Ferguson, I'll be right outside this door if you need me." He stepped out, pulling the door closed behind him.

"Sit down, please." Jan motioned to one of the room's two chairs; she took the other. A round table sat between them stacked with books and magazines May had brought trying to divert her daughter's attention.

Ella looked at Jan, then down at her clasped hands and then back at Jan. "I want to know if he hurt you, you know, not like a bruise or scratch or something, but like really hurt you in your soul?"

Neither of the women took their eyes off the other as Jan answered, "Yes."

"Did he fill you with terror and empty his ugly evilness into you?"

"Yes."

Ella leaned over the table with her small, underdeveloped hands on the edge. "Do you think this baby is evil?"

Jan thought a moment, keeping her eyes on Ella. "No. Babies are made the same way, whether it's by an evil act, like you and I both experienced, or by love. I believe the child's spirit enters the baby when he takes his first breath of life and he is separated from God. It's not so much how the baby is conceived, but what environment he is born into – evil, hatred, insecurity, violence ... or love, security and goodness." She paused and finally looked away. "That's what I believe anyway."

"Then I believe it, too, and I can raise this baby different than I was raised," she said with youthful defiance.

"Yes, you can. And with education, you can provide a lot more, too," Jan said.

"You know that lawyer of yours? He told me that I was entitled to those things, you know, money every month for food and rent, a cheap place to live, and education. But Mr. Woods only promised me all that if I told how forlorn I was without this baby having a daddy," Ella spoke out bravely.

Jan nodded.

"Mr. Larsen said he would be asking me questions, too, even though I'm called by that other man's side. So, it doesn't matter what I tell that district attorney man, I can tell your lawyer the truth, and still get all that stuff," she said.

"The truth is what you should tell no matter who tells you what. Sometimes the truth is all we have in life. If we didn't believe that truth would win out, that poetic justice rules the universe, there would be no hope at all."

Ella looked at the young teacher. "I guess that's sorta like *what goes around, comes around*," she said.

Jan laughed. "*And the truth will set you free*," they said simultaneously, and then chuckled together.

Ella became serious. "You know, I'd help you any way I could even if I weren't getting nothing for it. Not many people made me feel the way you and me felt. We got a bond, you know?"

"I am proud to have a bond with you, Ella, and I know you can make a real life for yourself and this baby. You seem like a good person, Ella, and don't you ever forget that," Jan said as she leaned over to hug her.

The sheriff knocked. "Your mamma's here with your supper, Mrs. Ferguson," he said officially. "Is your visitor through?"

"Visitor? What visitor?" The two young women could hear Jan's mother bustling about outside the door.

"Well, I better be going. They don't be knowing I'm gone, so I gotta get back," Ella said as she rose to leave.

"Thank you, Ella," Jan said sincerely.

"For what?"

"For helping me see the truth and for sharing your hurt with me. It's better knowing someone else feels like I do and can understand," Jan answered.

Ella thought a minute. "I already knew you 'cause of reading all about you in the papers. But you didn't know about me. Now you do, so we can share it." She held out her hand.

"Well, hello. And who it this?" May demanded in her most polite way.

"Mother, this is Ella McQuirk, a friend of mine," Jan

announced.

Ella beamed.

May stared noticeably at Ella's belly.

"Thank you for coming," Jan said, escorting Ella out of the room. "Sheriff Lander, could one of your deputies take her home?"

Sheriff Lander sent along the youngest deputy and asked him to "escort the young lady home and see that she doesn't get into any trouble with her house parents or that DA."

By now, Jan's bath water was cold. "Come eat this before it gets cold, too," May called from the bathroom where she was letting out the cold so that she could add hot.

Jan smiled when she re-entered the room and saw the tomato soup sitting on the little table ("made fresh in their kitchen," May yelled from the bathroom) and a grilled cheese sandwich. There was also a basket of saltine crackers and pats of real butter in a dish of ice. "I told them to make it with cheddar, not American," May yelled about the sandwich. A large glass of ice water with a wedge of lemon sat next to a large Wendy's cup.

Jan opened the lid and smelled the whiskey just as her mother came out of the bathroom drying her hands on a towel.

"I poured you an extra large double. I just put it in a cup from lunch so that they wouldn't ask, in case the answer would be *no*," May rattled on, keeping busy.

May finally sat in the other chair across the table as Jan ate her dinner.

When the children were sick or feeling low, May had served them tomato soup, grilled cheese sandwich and crackers with butter. Once they were adults, whiskey was also a healer of all ills. Jan truly appreciated both the food and the spirits, for she felt deliciously tired, not tense and wakeful as she had been most of her nights here.

Meeting Ella had boosted her spirits. Ella had been brutally raped by Punk also, and now that young girl was thrown into motherhood. Yet, because of Jan's traumatic experience, Ella had found her way out of that violent family with a chance to improve herself. What would have happened if Jan had not been raped by the same man and then killed their mutual ogre? Would Ella have ever had a chance to escape? In some small way, the trial was worth it for no other reason than to bring Ella to a safer life. The situation had also forced Jan away from Riverdale long enough to look at her life and her marriage honestly and to see that it was wrong. If not for these lengthy legal procedures, she'd not have stayed in Kingsford or spent time with Grant or moved to the farm. Jan smiled.

But what if she were found guilty? The thought came in the middle of the second half of her grilled cheese. She shuddered. Then she reached for her bourbon and water and drank deeply.

"Thank you, Mother," she said. "This drink is just what I needed. I think I'll read some tonight and turn in early."

"Don't you want to finish that other half of your sandwich?" May asked.

"No, you can take the tray. Just leave the saltines and butter, in case I get the nibbles," she said. She put the crackers and butter and her drink on the bedside table. When she turned around, May was standing with the tray in her hands, staring quizzically at her daughter.

"There's something different about you this evening," her mother said. "You seem more relaxed. Maybe I mean more relieved. No. Well, I can't think of the word, but you seem different. But it's a good different, so I'm not going to worry." She walked toward her leaning forward for a kiss. "Good night, darling, and sleep tight," she said. "Call me if you need me, even if it's just because you can't sleep. I'll probably be awake anyway. I'm not sleeping so well these days. 'Night, sweetheart."

Chapter Twelve

Chad Carey sat straight up in bed. "Of course," he said into the night. "That's it. Punk did threaten her! He said something that threatened her so deeply that she wiped out the threat, not the man."

"What is it, Chad?" his wife asked sleepily. "Is it something that can wait until morning?"

"Go back to sleep, honey." Dr. Carey went downstairs to his study. Both those boys mentioned that Punk mumbled something. He must have said something so menacing that Jan reacted to his words as if they were actions. She did shoot in self-defense. The boys wouldn't have heard it because the man's mouth was aimed at Jan.

The closing arguments were to begin tomorrow. He would have to get John to postpone the closing arguments somehow. It was four a.m. and Dr. Carey had much work to do before his eight a.m. flight to Asheville. He'd have to drive a rental on to Brevard from there.

Dr. Carey couldn't locate John Larsen, so he called Lamar Jameson, the most level-headed in Jan's family. "Do not let closing arguments begin until John meets with me. I should be there before lunch."

Lamar gave John the message before he entered the courtroom. John couldn't understand why Dr. Carey would want to delay the trial more. He had no more time to consider Dr. Carey's strange request, however, because Ella came to him from the corridor of the courthouse.

"Mr. Larson," she spoke quietly while grabbing on to his arm. "I need to speak to you." Ella paused and looked around suspiciously. "In private."

John led her into an office used by defense attorneys. "Yes, Ella?"

"Can I talk for you, I mean for her, instead of for him, the DA?" she asked.

"Why, what do you mean, Ella?"

"Last night I went to see Mrs. Ferguson." Ella paused to register the surprise on the attorney's face. "And, when I got back, that other lawyer, the DA, had been to see me and was real mad 'cause I wasn't there. He didn't know where I'd gone, nobody knew. I told them I had supper with an aunt that lives in town and that I'd caught a ride in with one of the other girls," she explained. "The DA called about an hour after I got back and said I shouldn't have gone off like that and I better watch my step if I want to be of help to him and get my Social Services. Tell me again – he can't take my Social Services away, can he?"

"No, Ella. You are entitled to the Social Services regardless of your being one of the prosecutor's witnesses. All you have to do if you are called to the stand is answer his questions truthfully and answer my questions truthfully. I get to question all of his witnesses, too," he explained. "When did the DA say you were needed in court?"

"He said two this afternoon. He's sending a deputy 'round to get me about twenty 'til, or so."

"You better go back now before he sees you. How are you getting back to your place?" he asked.

"Same way as I got here – on foot."

John picked up the phone provided in the tiny office and called his college friend's wife and asked her to pick up Ella and take her home. The woman was glad to help in any small way.

When John entered the courtroom at nine a.m., Woods greeted him with a Southern smile of victory, so sure he was of his surprise introduction of Ella and his closing arguments.

"Good morning, Your Honor!" he jumped eagerly from his chair and shouted before Judge Abrams was fully settled at his bench. "Your Honor, I have a new request to place before the bench," he said walking quickly toward the judge's bench.

"Yes, Mr. Woods, what is it?" the Judge asked warily.

"Sir, I request that Jan Ferguson be moved from her special privileged location to the local jail for reasons of security, cost, and public concern, considering the seriousness of the charges against her in this court of law," he said importantly.

"What public concern would that be, Mr. Woods?" Judge Abrams asked.

"I have had numerous phone calls of concern that Mrs. Ferguson is receiving special treatment at the taxpayers' expense," he said knowingly.

"And how many phone calls is numerous exactly? Twenty?"

"No, sir."

"Ten? Five?" Judge Abrams continued calmly.

"Well, no, sir."

"Then what is the number of phone calls you have received concerning the custody of the defendant in this trial?" the judge demanded harshly.

"Two, but two reputable citizens," he pushed stubbornly ahead.

"Name them," Judge Abrams insisted.

"Our own clerk of court," Woods said confidentially as he leaned forward toward the bench.

The clerk of court glared at Woods for betraying his confidence. Though the clerk had at first questioned the validity and cost of the defendant staying at the Brevard Inn, he had since found out that the teacher's family was paying not only for the accommodations, but for three twelve-hour shifts of bodyguards so that the deputies could rotate the regular number of officers on duty. But Willa had not waited long enough before running to Woods with the information after clerk Billy Ray Pace mistakenly asked his questions aloud to one of the assistant clerks while Willa was in the room. She had neglected to listen for the answers.

Judge Abrams purposely kept his gaze from the clerk, and without acknowledging Woods' first reference, asked for a second.

"The *Asheville Citizen*'s state reporter," the DA answered.

Abrams slammed his gavel on the bench, startling Woods and everyone else in the courtroom. "You would talk with a member of the news media about such a sensitive case?"

"But, sir, I didn't reveal anything sensitive about this case. I only listened to his questions and told him that I could not comment. One of his questions was about the seemingly special treatment of this defendant and the cost of special lodging and law enforcement coverage… "

He was interrupted by the judge. "And, worse, you would take the advice of a newspaper reporter?" Judge Abrams tried to hold temper. "Mr. Woods," he said more calmly, "your request is denied. And let the record show that the defendant's family is bearing all costs for her accomodations. Now, please, sir, will you get on with it and call your first witness of the day?" And he brought the gavel down.

The morning was taken up by endless maternal grief on the part of Zucci who was called to the stand by the freshly chastised district attorney. Woods emphasized the mother's loss of food from her family because of the death of her eldest child. John Larsen, however, had Zucci tell the court just how much meat Punk actually provided during a year.

"'Bout twice a year," Zucci answered proudly.

When court was adjourned for lunch at eleven-thirty a.m., John found Dr. Chad Carey.

"John!" Carey called out as he pushed his way through the crowd to catch John.

"It's too risky," John shook his head. He and the doctor ordered room service in Carey's hotel room. "What if she insists to the jury that she shot the man on purpose? What if she tells them she has no more regrets for shooting that man than if he'd been a snake?" John worried. "Besides, I'm not sure I'm convinced Punk said anything to her before she shot him or if he just laughed. The boys both emphasized the laugh. They didn't hear anything. Even if he said something to her, there are no witnesses."

"But I'm convinced he did. I wouldn't put Jan in jeopardy any more than you would," Dr. Carey pleaded. "Every time I asked her if he said anything after he had fallen to the ground, she looked at her hands. She wouldn't answer yes or no, she just talked about that laugh. Both Murray and Caleb said on the stand they thought Punk mumbled something." Dr. Carey knew he was right. He would stake his professional reputation on it.

"All right, Chad, but only if Jan agrees," John gave in. He wolfed down the last half of his sandwich. "I'll go talk with her now. Do you think you ought to come along?"

"No. I think it would be best that she not suspect we're trying to get something out of her subconscious," Dr. Carey said.

The Rev. Grant Tyler knocked on the sheriff's office door just as Jan and John finished talking. The guarding deputy allowed him to visit before the afternoon session began.

"Hello. I thought I would just stick my head in. And hello to you, John. Are you preparing for the afternoon's closing arguments?" Grant asked.

John looked at Jan. "I'm going to take the stand this afternoon," Jan told Grant.

"How could you let her do that?" Grant looked to John.

John didn't answer.

"I have wanted all along to take the witness stand," Jan said defending her stance. "I am not afraid of anything Frank Woods can say to me or ask me," she declared.

Grant could see the pearl rolling between her thumb and first finger of her right hand. "Let's pray before you go," he said.

Grant and Jan knelt where they were and John bowed his head in his seat. "Dear heavenly God, look down on your servant Jan Jameson Ferguson. Give her courage and wisdom to face out the end of her ordeal. Protect her from her enemies, and fill her with the peace that passes all understanding. Amen."

Grant hugged Jan and shook John's hand. They left the small office together, Grant to go to his seat in the courtroom audience and Jan to her seat at the defendant's table.

"All rise," the clerk of court said, announcing the judge's entrance.

"Please, be seated," the judge nodded. "Now, counselors, are we ready to hear our final witness?" he asked.

Ella was on the front row next to Zucci, but before Woods could introduce her as his last witness, John Larsen stood up. "Your Honor, I would request the court to hear one more defense witness."

Woods' head snapped around so fast he cured the crick he had developed over the past few nights of poor sleep.

"Your Honor, the defendant, Jan Jameson Ferguson, would like to take the stand," John said loudly in the hushed courtroom.

The reporters' pens were flying.

Judge Abrams looked at Jan. "Young lady, are you sure you want to do this?" He knew too well that if Woods could get her to say that she chose to shoot McQuirk for what he did to her, the jury would have little choice in its verdict. He wondered why John Larsen would take such a risk.

"Yes, sir. I want to take the stand," Jan said.

Judge Abrams nodded and the clerk of court rose. "The defense calls Janet Jameson Ferguson to the witness stand," he called out loudly.

Jan looked at no one. She gave no sign that she was the least bit nervous.

"Mrs. Ferguson," John began professionally after she was sworn in. "Jan," he said gently. "Please tell the court in your own words about the events that led up to the shooting of Artemis Delmer McQuirk, the man you know as Punk," he stated.

Jan took a deep breath. She looked at her family. Her mother made no effort to wipe the tears flowing freely from her eyes. Her father and grandfather sat stoically. David looked as if he would cry. Jan knew they didn't want to hear this; but she knew they had to for her sake if not for their own. Only Grant smiled encouragingly. He nodded slightly, and Jan turned then to the jurors whom she addressed throughout her story.

She spoke clearly but quietly. Jan told how she felt when she was snatched out of her life. She told her fears throughout that long night and the following day. She described in detail the violent battle that raged in the cabin. She told her every bruise, every bump, every word exchanged. She told of hearing herself scream as the man forced himself into her.

Jan didn't pause between the act of the rape and the story of escape. She pushed on. "I took careful aim, because I knew that if I missed, he would kill the boys right then and rape me again before killing me, too. But the stone found its mark, and he fell to the ground, tossing the gun behind him as he fell.

"I saw the gun and picked it up. He was on his back, facing away from me, but his head was tilted back toward me; his lips were moving. I heard ...." Jan was lost in thought.

"What did you hear, Jan?" John pushed. "What did you hear?"

Jan came out of her reverie. "What?" She refocused on John. "I heard him laugh, and I aimed the gun between his eyes. He was still laughing. I squeezed the trigger, but he wasn't still, so I shot again and again." Jan painted a picture that the jurors could see as clearly as she did.

"Did Punk say anything at all to you before he laughed?" John tried again.

Dr. Carey recognized the blank look on Jan's face. "Dear God, save us," he prayed.

"No," Jan said.

"When you escaped, did you have any thought of killing Mr. McQuirk? Did you plan to kill him ahead of time?" John asked.

"No. I took the only opportunity offered to escape," Jan said.

John looked briefly at Dr. Carey who shrugged his shoulder slightly. "That will be all. Your witness," he said to Woods.

What had he done? John berated himself for allowing Jan to go on the stand.

"Now, Mrs. Ferguson, let's go back to the moment of the shooting. Do you have any experience with rifles?" Woods began.

"Yes, I took riflery at camp," Jan answered.

"How many years did you take riflery at camp, Mrs. Ferguson?"

"Five."

"Were you good at riflery at camp, Mrs. Ferguson?"

"Yes. I reached the highest level of marksmanship."

"When you, an expert marksman by your testimony, aimed that rifle at Artemis Delmer McQuirk, you meant for him to die, didn't you Mrs. Ferguson?" the prosecutor hissed.

"I aimed to stop him," Jan answered evenly.

"But you could have stopped him just as well if you had wounded him, say, in the thigh, the arm, anywhere but between the eyes, Mrs. Ferguson," Woods said.

The prosecutor never gave the witness a chance to answer. "His body wasn't facing you, now was it? His body was facing away from you; he was helpless on his back; and you had only his head to aim at, now isn't that true, Mrs. Ferguson?"

The words themselves were not bad, but the voice that delivered them was so grating, so threatening, so demeaning. Like Punk's.

"I aimed where I could to stop him," Jan repeated.

"But a graze could have stopped him just as well. After all, you are an expert marksman, are you not?"

He was taunting her. Judge Abrams looked at John to see if he wasn't going to object, but the defense attorney sat quietly watching.

"Could you not have had the boys tie him up? Couldn't you have run and kept the gun to protect yourself? Did you have to kill him, to shoot him not once, but a second and third time? What could he have possibly done to you if you had the gun and he was flat on his back?" Frank shouted accusingly at Jan. He didn't expect her to answer.

"He said, *It's you or me, girlie!*" Jan yelled back. "He said ...." her voice caught. "He glared back at me when he fell to the ground. He looked me straight in the eyes and said, so quiet, so mean, with that nasty leer, the fetid drool on the corners of his lips, *It's you or me, girlie.* Then he laughed. And I knew," her voice caught again, "I knew he was right. If I didn't shoot him now, he would kill me – and he would kill Murray and Caleb. If I let him get up, I wouldn't be able to stop him from that. He laughed, that demeaning, demonic laugh, as if he knew I wouldn't shoot him. He didn't think I would do it; he didn't think I had the guts to save myself. He thought I wouldn't act on my own will."

Jan looked at the jurors. "But I did. I knew that he was right. It was him ... or me and the boys." Jan said no more.

Woods had no more questions. He knew he had just lost his last card. There was no sense in putting Ella on the stand now. "That's all, Your Honor," he said with as much composure as he could muster, and he turned to sit.

Jan was still looking at the jurors when Judge Abrams repeated, "You may step down now, Mrs. Ferguson."

There wasn't a dry eye in the courtroom. Jan nodded thanks to the judge and returned to her seat.

John, Grant and Dr. Carey clasped their hands in thanks simultaneously.

The questioning had lasted less than twenty minutes. It was only 2:25 when Judge Abrams looked at his watch. "Are there any more witnesses for the defense?" he asked the defending attorney.

John looked at Ella before answering. "No, Your Honor," he said.

"Then we'll take a twenty-minute recess before the attorneys present their closing arguments to the jury." Judge Abrams quickly left the bench.

Frank Woods wanted time to get his thoughts together. He gathered his notes, trying to hide the panic he felt. He didn't even give Willa a glance as he stomped out of the courtroom.

Jan did not look at her family, not even at Grant. She walked quickly out of the back of the courtroom with John. She needed a Coke, water, anything.

"Good going, girl," John said as he gave her a hug.

Jan was crying from relief. "I could never remember that before. I could only remember his face, but I could see his lips moving." Jan hugged John. "I really did kill him in self-defense," she said in stunned amazement.

"Honey, everyone has known all along that you killed that man in self-defense," he said, puzzled.

"I didn't."

John brought her a cold Coke from the machine in the hall. "The trial isn't over. If you're really shaken up, I know Judge Abrams would postpone closing arguments until tomorrow. But it is to our advantage to go ahead with them now."

"No. I want this over as soon as possible," she answered.

"Good. You still have fifteen minutes to compose yourself."

The jurors had their own facilities and drink machine in their room. "Well, I'm glad that's over and after today we can get back to our normal lives," ventured juror Mary Robinson.

Mr. Priddy looked at her askance. "As they say in the opera, 'It ain't over 'til the fat lady sings' ... or in the courtroom, 'It ain't over 'til the DA whines,'" he said.

Woods had had his closing arguments prepared for days now, but this outburst of clear self-defense threw everything off. He had a lot of scrambling to do before the end of this twenty minutes.

"Your Honor, ladies and gentlemen of the jury," Woods began after court was reconvened. "I have maintained throughout this trial that the defendant," he turned to nod in Jan's direction, "Janet Jameson Ferguson, was violently wronged by the deceased. However, I continue to contend that the deceased had just as much right to a trial for his crime as the defendant has for hers. Artemis Delmer McQuirk is dead and cannot take advantage of this right. Do you see any lasting scars of Mr. McQuirk's crime against Mrs. Ferguson? Does his crime against her warrant death?

"Why would Mrs. Ferguson say all along that she chose to kill Mr. McQuirk? You heard the witnesses. The sheriff, the deputies, and the doctor say that she claimed a choice. I ask you, does that sound like self-defense to you?" Woods had his hands in his suit pants pockets and he leaned dramatically toward the jury.

"Now, at the eleventh hour, so to speak, the defendant claims that Mr. McQuirk verbally threatened her as he lay physically helpless on his back on the ground with only his upside down face towards her. But Murray Simpson didn't hear this threat. Did Murray Simpson tell us on the witness that he had heard this threat? No. And Caleb Johnson didn't hear this threat. Did Caleb Johnson say he heard the threat? No."

"And why didn't Mrs. Ferguson tell Sheriff Landers of this threat? Why didn't she tell anyone of this verbal threat until she sits on the witness stand facing a murder charge? I'll tell you why; to save her neck. We have laws, ladies and gentlemen of the jury, laws that are meant to keep society from justice-of-the moment, from revenge. And we must uphold these laws at every turn, every threat, to ensure that our society will not revert to the lawless days of the Old West.

"Janet Jameson Ferguson," Woods paused here to look back dramatically at Jan, "is not a criminal who will go kill again, but in a fit of rage and understandable hysteria common to women wronged, she chose, as she told us in her own words, she chose to shoot between the eyes the man lying down, defenseless and already injured by her hand, not once, but two and three times. I ask you, ladies and gentlemen, if you can, beyond a shadow of doubt, call this self-defense?"

Woods paused, looked at the jurors in a sweeping gaze and bowed. "Thank you," he said as if he had received applause.

When he returned to his chair, Woods glimpsed Willa smiling proudly on the front row next to Zucci McQuirk. Zucci looked bored. The trial was not going the way she wanted. She would be back at her old life in too soon a time.

"Mmph," Mattie Mae Nichols let out as she sat with her arms crossed in disagreement.

Woods turned quickly and scanned the faces of the jurors to see who had been so disrespectful. But all the faces had the same expression of disgust.

"Why, this man ain't got the brains God gave a goose," Marcus Burns thought to himself.

While Frank's back was turned, Judge Abrams, looking down at his own hands, let slip a tiny smile of agreement with Mrs. Nichols. "Mr. Larsen, you may direct your closing arguments to the jury," the judge said before Woods was seated.

"I believe, ladies and gentlemen, that we have had on trial here much more than murder charges against Jan Ferguson. On trial this week was every victim's right to self-protection. Has our judicial system fallen into such technical pettiness that the victim becomes the accused?

"Murder charges against Janet Jameson Ferguson should have never been made and certainly should have never come to trial. But the charges were made; the defendant has been tried. Yet no jury could have been harder on Jan Ferguson than she has been on herself. What we have witnessed in addition to divine justice has been divine healing. You saw today a person so determined to do what is right and so devastated over taking another person's life that she could not free herself of the responsibility for that life.

"The sheriff said all along this was self-defense. The FBI agents involved in this case, her psychiatrist, they have all testified that this was clearly self-defense. The only reason this young woman has had to go through this public trial is that Jan Ferguson was already so traumatized, snatched out of life as she knew it – from a secure childhood to her secure adulthood as a teaching professional – and thrown into a horror you and I can only imagine, that she had to search for a way to rationalize that horror clearly. This young woman, in spite of all she had endured through no fault or action of her own – this young woman was still willing to take responsibility for the loss of another person's life.

"Psychologically speaking, her doctor would tell you that Mrs. Ferguson had blocked out the final fear when she pulled the trigger. With those words – *It's you or me, girlie* – Punk represented not some abstract fear of being raped, but the sure knowledge of what that meant, what it now felt like – knowing that she would die that way – that her students would die. And it took this experience today, of being badgered and degraded, verbally rather than physically, in a situation equally absurd and shameful, for something or someone to remove that barrier."

John looked at Woods who was slumped down in his chair with his arms crossed defiantly over his chest.

"What were we, the American system of justice, thinking when we allowed the victim to become the accused? How can we, a people who call ourselves *just*, sanction such a judicial system that takes away so obvious a right to self-defense?

"We mustn't. People like you twelve jurors can decide justly on right and wrong instead of technicalities; you can judge with your hearts in conjunction with your minds. Jurors, men and women of all ages, races and professions, you can put the *just* back in *justice*."

Chapter Thirteen

It was 4:30 when Judge Abrams sent the jurors back into the jury room. Woods approached the bench in one last effort to get the judge to postpone the juror's verdict until the following day, considering the late hour.

"I don't expect the jurors to take long," Judge Abrams answered.

At 4:45, the jurors filed back into their seats.

"Have you reached a verdict, Mr. Foreman?" the judge asked Buck Pittman.

"Yes, sir, we have. We find Janet Leigh Jameson Ferguson not guilty of second degree murder," he read.

Cheers went up throughout the courthouse. Reporters and deputies hugged each other. Strangers patted Jan's family members on the back.

"Order!" Judge Abrams quieted the crowd.

"Your Honor?" Buck Pittman asked.

"Yes, Mr. Foreman?"

"Would it be appropriate for the jury to apologize to Mrs. Ferguson for our county bringing her to trial in the first place?" he asked.

"Now that, I believe, is perfectly appropriate. Let me do it for you," Judge Abrams said in a much less stern manner. "Mrs. Ferguson, will you kindly approach the bench?"

Jan was calmer than the rest of the courtroom. The outcome of the trial had lost its threat to her when she remembered why she had shot Punk. No jail could be as harsh as her own self-judgment. She was truly free of Punk now, for she was free of the burden of his loss of life. She had truly and clearly had no choice, for he had already decided for her that one of them would have to die. *It's you or me.*

"Janet Jameson Ferguson," Judge Abrams looked into her eyes, "this court sincerely apologizes for wrongfully charging you, the victim, with a crime. And we apologize for making you suffer more than you already have."

Judge Abrams stood, walked down from his bench and stood humbly before Jan. "I want to shake your hand," he said and he grasped the hand she held out with both of his. "Court dismissed," he said to the rest of the courtroom as he led Jan out the back way with John, followed by her family, Grant, Murray, Caleb and Dr. Carey.

David, the Simpsons and the Johnsons remained behind. The boys' families didn't want to be in the way. David stayed because he didn't feel part of the family circle anymore. As he turned to leave the courthouse, he saw Lucy walking toward him. He hurried to meet her.

"Lucy, what are you doing here? Have you been here long? Have you heard?" He hugged her.

"I just couldn't stand it any longer. I told the school I was sick and had to go home, but I drove straight here. I had to be here for you, David, no matter which way the verdict went. I thought you'd have to wait over the weekend to find anything out, and I wasn't going to let you be alone."

The bailiff held off reporters who were frantically shouting questions. Woods, however, was an easy and willing target.

"Gentlemen, as you have witnessed today, this trial would have never taken place if the defendant had not thought herself to be guilty," Woods said importantly. He smoothed his lapels.

"It is a shame that the courts had to bear the cost of Mrs. Ferguson's psychological revelation," he began.

"Mr. Prosecutor," a newspaper reporter interrupted. "Do you find offense at the defense attorney's personal attack on you during his closing arguments for bringing this case to trial?"

Woods looked sharply at the reporter. "Those were not personal attacks on me. He was merely pointing out that our complex judicial system is sometimes too technical to *appear* strictly just to the untrained eye," he twisted the words around. "If today I had the same facts presented to me as were first presented to me in the Ferguson case, I would be forced to make the same charges based on the *facts* of the law. I am sworn to represent the state and to uphold its laws, and that is what I have done and what I will continue to do."

"Mr. Woods is it true, as you intimated in your closing statements, that you believe all women who have been raped confuse emotional hysteria with self-defense?" a woman reporter asked.

"I didn't say that," he said defensively. "If you are going to misconstrue my every word, then I have no comment." He and Willa disappeared in a huff behind his office door.

Finley Holbert did not write down the words of the district attorney. He considered the news media to be just as guilty as the courts for allowing victims to become the accused.

When the dust had settled, Jan found herself in her parents' suite at the inn, surrounded by her parents, her siblings, her grandparents, John, Dr. Carey and the boys. Lamar and Papa Ralph were fixing drinks, and everyone was talking at once.

Jan saw David making his way across the room toward her; behind him was Lucy Meadows. She smiled warmly at them both.

"Jan, I'm going to head on back to Riverdale now. I'm happy for you. And I'm proud of you," he said with a hint of regret. He hugged her awkwardly. "See who else is here?"

"Lucy," Jan greeted her with a hug meant for strangers.

"Jan, honey, I just couldn't stay away. I just had to come and be here for my best friend. Now that everything has turned out all right, I best be getting on back to Riverdale myself. I've got to take Mama shopping tomorrow and, well, you know how it is," Lucy rambled on.

"I know you'll be happy with David in Atlanta," Jan said directly.

"Why ... " Lucy said as she looked at David.

"She knows about us, Lucy, and she really is happy for us," David said quietly.

"Why, Jan, I really had no intention. I just wanted to help you, that's all, and since there was nothing I could do for you, I thought, well, I could at least take care of your husband and, well, one thing led to another. You've been gone such a long time, you know," she sputtered.

"It's all right, Lucy," Jan interrupted. "I wish you the best of life."

"David," May exclaimed. "I saw you in the courtroom. Why on earth didn't you sit with us?" May gave her son-in-law a polite peck on the cheek. "And who is this?" May extended her hand to Lucy. "I'm Jan's mother, May Jameson."

Lucy took her hand but did not look in May's eyes. "I'm Jan's friend from school, Lucy Meadows."

"Well, Lucy, it looks like you're David's friend, too," May said.

"Uh, well, I helped out around the house while Jan was gone," she stammered.

"David," Lamar entered the circle. "Good to see you here, son." Lamar shook David's hand. "And who might this be? I'm Jan's father, Lamar Jameson," he said as he reached to shake Lucy's hand.

Lucy looked pleadingly at David as she shook Lamar's hand.

"Dear, this is Jan's friend from the academy. She has been taking care of David while Jan was gone," May said pointedly.

"It looks like you're leaving," Lamar said to David, ignoring May's cynicism.

"Yes, sir, I'm going back to Riverdale. I've decided to move to Atlanta and work in my father's bank. I have a lot of loose ends to tie up before I can leave," David said meekly.

"You're leaving without Jan?" Lamar asked.

"Dad, it's all right. We've decided we're not meant for each other," Jan said calmly. "David suffered from what happened to me, but through it we discovered we are different people than we appeared to be on the outside." She looked warmly at David. "I wish him all the happiness in the world." Jan turned to her father. "I'm going back to Kingsford. I'm going home."

Lamar slowly sipped his beer and gazed intently at David. "Son, I don't know what to say. I thought you'd have tried harder, but I guess you two know what's what."

"Sir, Lamar, it wasn't all my idea," David began explaining.

"Daddy, we would have found out we weren't right for each other sooner or later. It's best to end it now before we had children," Jan said.

"Well, I wish you the best, I guess, David," Lamar said as he held out his hand. "Not much else I know to say."

Lucy tried to sneak out the door unnoticed, but Papa Ralph stepped between her and David. "What's this? David, you leaving so soon? Aren't you going to celebrate with your wife? Why, who's this?" he asked turning to Lucy.

"Daddy, you don't want to know," May said to her father. "David and Jan have decided to split. We've never had a divorce in our family," she complained.

"Mom, Uncle Ralph is divorced," Jan said.

"That's different, dear. His wife was impossible to live with."

"Couldn't stick it out, could you?" Papa Ralph directed at David.

"Papa Ralph, it's not David. It's me," Jan interrupted before her grandfather turned abusive. "We each married the wrong person, that's all. We would have found it out sooner or later. I'm coming back home to Kingsford."

Papa Ralph hugged Jan. "Well, at least there's some good news." He turned to David. "Goodbye," he said holding out his hand. "You too, little lady," he said in Lucy's general direction.

Papa Ralph turned his back on David and Lucy and they quietly left. David gave a quick glance to Jan before closing the door. She met his gaze and smiled. He smiled back.

"Jan," Murray said as he came up beside her. Caleb was close behind. "We have to go now. Our parents want to start back tonight." He paused awkwardly.

"Will we see you back in Riverdale?" Caleb asked. "I know you don't want to teach now, but we can get together."

Jan reached up and pulled them close to her in a hug. "You will always be my friends, no matter where I go or what you grow up to be," she whispered. She stood and wiped her eyes. "I'm not going back to Riverdale. David and I are divorcing and I'm moving back to Kingsford."

"Oh, man, that's awful. What happened?" Caleb asked

"Caleb, that's rude. If she wanted us to know she would have told us," Murray said.

"No. No, we're friends, and you have a right to know. We both married the wrong person. It took this ordeal to bring it to light. There are no hard feelings, we're just completely different people. Let this be a lesson to both of you to wait for the right person."

Jan paused and looked fondly from Murray to Caleb. She smiled. "There's e-mail, telephone and slow mail, so I expect to be informed of every part of your lives *from here on out*. Now go, before I start crying again." She patted them both on the back and led them to the door.

"Goodbye, boys! Thank you, Murray, Caleb. God bless you, boys!" rang out in the room.

Jan joined Dr. Carey, John and Peterson on the bed's edge.

"Well, Sis, you beat 'em fair and square," her brother said, putting an arm around her. "I'd say you got some mighty big balls, excuse my expression."

"I'm glad you're here," Jan chuckled, then turned her attention to her lawyer and psychiatrist. "I had a good team."

"You're not mad at us?" John asked.

"Mad? Why would I be mad? You *saved* me by putting me on the stand."

"But we put you on the stand to break you," Dr. Carey said quietly. "For that, I apologize. I knew there was something you hadn't remembered, but I staked your freedom on that knowledge. I guess we should thank the DA for being such a badgering asshole."

They laughed.

"I can help you find a competent psychiatrist in the Riverdale area. I still have connections," Dr. Carey broached.

"I won't be going back to Riverdale, so I suppose I'll continue with you, for a little while at least," Jan said.

"What about David?" Peterson asked.

"David and I decided to go our separate ways," she stated.

"Man, I missed all the signals. From where I sat at school, things seemed fine, according to Mama." Peterson gave Jan a hug. "I'm really sorry, Jan."

Meemaw asked Papa Ralph to refresh her drink, so Jan jumped up and asked for another also. They were staying another night and for once she wouldn't have deputies outside her door. The court order against the press, however, would remain until after they left.

The phone rang. "Yes? … Hello, dear. … Yes, she's right here," May said on picking up the phone. "Jan, dear, it's Uncle Ralph calling from Atlanta."

"Hello?" Jan answered.

"Jan, sweetheart, I've just heard the news," Uncle Ralph said from his end of the line. "I'm glad for you. We all knew you were innocent. Hope you understand my not coming up there and all, what with an election to run and state business to attend. But you were in my thoughts and prayers. We're real proud of you, hon. If there's ever anything I can do for you, let me know." Uncle Ralph oozed political distance.

"Thank you for that, Uncle Ralph. I appreciate all my family's support. It's what's gotten me through these months. Thanks for calling." And she placed the phone in its cradle.

Jan looked around. Everyone was excitedly discussing the trial and its outcome. But where was Grant? She hadn't seen him since May whisked her out of the courthouse and into their car. Jan moved toward Meemaw, who was sitting off by herself, just as Grant burst into the suite.

"Jan, Ella is having her baby! She wants you there! My car's out front. I'll take you to the hospital," Grant said.

"How do you know? Where've you been?" Jan asked.

"I went to the home to offer a prayer for the baby and for Ella. She went into labor while I was there! I promised I'd bring you to her," he rushed, grabbing her arm.

"I think we'll go too, dear," May said gathering her and Meemaw's purses.

"May ... " Lamar started.

"It's the least we can do for that poor girl, let her know someone cares. The only difference between her and Jan is that she got pregnant from that scum," May said in uncharacteristic compassion. "Julia Ann, you come with us. You might learn something," May said as she patted her daughter's pregnant belly."

Lamar had nothing to say to that. "Come on, Ralph. Looks like we're going to a birthing."

"Well, good luck to all of you," Dr. Carey said. "I've got a plane to Atlanta to catch." He hugged Jan, saying "I'll see you soon," and stepped briskly out of the room.

Jan and Grant were gone, too, by the time the parents, grandparents and siblings could organize themselves into Julia Ann's van.

Grant wasted no time on the road.

"Ella?" Jan leaned cautiously into the birthing room. "Ella, it's me, Jan. I came to be with you."

"Oh, thank God. I prayed with your minister man that you'd come. I know you have no reason to be concerned with me and this baby here, but I wanted you here to pray into its soul when it comes out," Ella said just before another contraction hit.

Jan ran to Ella's side and held her hand. A nurse came to the other side of the bed to breathe with Ella. "Mrs. Ferguson, you can do this with her. Breathe in slowly, breathe out. Breathe in slowly, breathe out."

Jan continued the breathing pattern and squeezed Ella's hand through the contraction.

"Two minutes apart," the nurse announced. "Looks like we're going to be having a baby real soon now."

Grant came to the bed with a bowl of water and a fresh linen cloth. He had on his collar.

"What are you doing?" Jan asked.

"I want to be baptized before this baby comes," Ella said weakly. "He started to do it at the home, but I commenced contractions before he could finish. I answered all the questions right, didn't I?" she asked of Grant.

"Yes, you did, Ella. Now lie back and I'll finish before your next contraction comes. We're going to jump to the end." He leaned over the bowl of water. "We thank you, Almighty God, for the gift of water. We thank you, God, for the water of Baptism. In joyful obedience to your Son, we bring into his fellowship those who come to him in faith, baptizing them in the name of the father, and of the Son, and of the Holy Spirit."

Grant touched the water. "Now sanctify this water, we pray you, by the power of your Holy Spirit, that those who here are cleansed from sin and born again may continue forever in the risen life of Jesus Christ our Savior. To Him, to You, and to the Holy Spirit, be all honor and glory, now and for ever. Amen."

Ella sat up and faced Grant. "Amen," she said loudly.

Grant dipped his finger into the holy water and made the sign of the cross three times while he continued. "I baptize you in the name of the Father, and of the Son, and of the Holy Spirit. Amen." Grant then place his hand on Ella's head. "You are sealed by the Holy Spirit in Baptism and marked as Christ's own forever. Amen."

Ella choked out another 'amen' as another contraction took hold. She lay back on the pillow and said through clenched teeth, "Now this baby will have a baptized mother ... and a clean start."

Once that contraction ended, Jan thought to ask, "Ella, have you thought what you're going to name your baby?"

"I always thought Pearl was the prettiest name ever was," Ella replied. Grant and Jan shot each other a startled look of disbelief mixed with awe at the perfect synchronicity, but they just smiled and said nothing.

Ella looked directly into Jan's eyes. "Janet Pearl. That'd be right nice." But the next wave of discomfort immediately overtook her.

Jan coached Ella through that contraction, which was followed immediately by another. "Should we go get the doctor? I think this baby is on the way," Jan said to the nurse.

The nurse moved to the foot of the bed to check Ella's dilation. "You got that right. The head's crowning. I'll be right back."

The doctor was there in another two minutes.

"Looks like we're ready for a new baby in here," she said jovially. "I'm Dr. McCormack."

"Aahh," cried Ella.

Dr. McCormack disappeared between Ella's legs. "Push real hard and he'll come right out," the doctor instructed.

With Jan breathing and holding Ella forward, it took only one push before a bloody, pink blob emerged in the doctor's hands. The nurse cut the umbilical cord while the doctor syringed the baby's nose and held him for a quick slap. The baby squalled with its first breath.

"Quick, bless the baby's spirit," Ella called in desperation to Grant.

The minister took the baby. "Bless this child and preserve," Grant paused and looked under the blanket, "his life; receive him and enable him to receive you, that through the Sacrament of Baptism he may become the child of God; through Jesus Christ our Lord." Grant made the sign of the cross on the babe's forehead with the holy water.

"It's a boy, Ella," Jan exclaimed.

The doctor took the infant from Grant and handed him to his mother. "Why don't you try and nurse him before we take him to the nursery to check him out," she said.

"That's my cue to leave," Grant said, raising his eyebrows as he gathered up the holy water and linen cloth.

"Jan, will you stay with me? I don't know what I'm doing," Ella said.

"Your baby will teach you," Dr. McCormack said. The doctor pulled down the shoulder of Ella's gown and laid the suckling baby on her breast. "You're doing just fine. I'll leave you alone now."

Jan stared in awe. She had never seen the beauty of a baby nursing. He was so small, so wrinkled, so utterly perfect. His little mouth latched onto the nipple before him and he sucked for all he was worth.

Ella also stared. An involuntary surge of milk streamed from her nipple, while undying love flowed from her to her child. "His name is John Jameson McQuirk," she announced. "*John* for Mr. Larsen. He's setting me up with counseling and Social Services, and he's my *pre bano* lawyer."

"*Pro bono?*" Jan laughed.

"Yeah, that's it. It means he's free. And *Jameson* for you and the wonderful family you were raised in. That name'll remind me of the family I want to give him, the family and love Punk never did know. Nor me, neither. And then, 'course, *McQuirk*, because that's what's in his blood.

"But I'm going to call him Jameson." Ella smiled at Jan.

Jameson had fallen asleep. The nurse reached over to take him. "You just start on the other side next time. You did real good, honey." She carried the baby out.

"You should get some rest now," Jan said pulling the sheets up over Ella's shoulders and lowering the bed.

"I am kinda tired," Ella responded. "Will I see you 'fore you leave?"

"I'll stop by in the morning before I leave town. The doctor's going to let you stay here an extra day to rest up and for parenting counseling. Jameson is a beautiful baby, Ella. I know he'll grow up to be a fine young man with you as his mother." Jan leaned over and kissed Ella's forehead as she shut her eyes.

Jan found her family at the nursery window.

"Peterson, you looked similar to that baby over there," May said to her son pointing to Jameson.

The nurse put the baby's name on the end of the bassinet: *John Jameson McQuirk.*

"Why, it's Ella's baby!" May exclaimed.

"Are they all that tiny?" Julia Ann asked in disbelief.

"Yes, dear, they are. Isn't he perfect?"

Lamar, Papa Ralph, John and Grant stood silently watching the baby from behind May. "John. See that, men? She named that baby after me," John said proudly.

"But she's calling him Jameson," Jan said from behind.

Meemaw was off by herself, staring at the baby from afar and crying quietly.

"Why, Meemaw, what's wrong?" Jan asked putting her arms around her grandmother.

"The birth of a child is always such a miracle. Birth is hope for the world that this child will be raised in love and security to erase the evil of his origins." Meemaw turned to Julia Ann. "We have our own family birth to look forward to. Life goes on, and each birth is a hope for something better, a new start."

"Lamar, what say we start a trust fund for this baby?" Papa Ralph asked his son-in-law. "I'll set up a meeting with the bank president for next week."

"I'm in," John echoed.

"I sure don't understand all this fuss over a baby from someone we don't even know," Peterson said.

The family laughed gently.

"Well, I'd say it's time to find some chow and turn in early for our trip home tomorrow," Lamar announced.

Grant walked over to Jan. He offered his hand, and she grasped it along with the pearl she held in her own.

"I'll bet I know a garden that's missed your touch. Let's get you rested and then get you home, Janet Jameson," he said.

"Yes, I'd like that. Home is exactly where I want to go."

Printed in the United States
65988LVS00002B/352-408